THE WEST
of the
IMAGINATION

Alfred Jacob Miller, *The Lost Greenhorn.* Courtesy The Warner Collection of Gulf States Paper Corporation, Tuscaloosa, Alabama.

THE WEST
of the
IMAGINATION

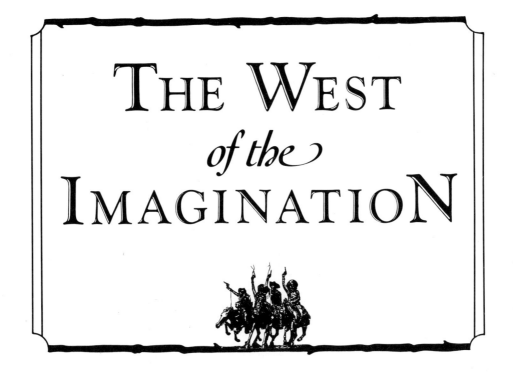

WILLIAM H. GOETZMANN

&

WILLIAM N. GOETZMANN

W·W·Norton & Company · New York · London

The text of this book is composed in Goudy Old Style, with
display type set in Goudy Handtool. Composition by Vail-Ballou Press, Inc.
Manufacturing by Balding & Mansell Ltd.
Book design by Antonina Krass
Printed in Great Britain

First Edition

Library of Congress Cataloging-in-Publication Data

Goetzmann, William H.
The West of the imagination.

1. West (U.S.) in art.   2. Arts, American.
3. Arts, Modern—19th century—United States.   4. Arts,
Modern—20th century—United States.   I. Goetzmann,
William N.   II. Title.
NX653.W47G6   1986   700′.978   86-8487
ISBN 0-393-02370-2

W. W. Norton & Company, Inc., 500 Fifth Avenue, New York, N.Y. 10110
W. W. Norton & Company Ltd., 37 Great Russell Street, London WC1B 3NU

1 2 3 4 5 6 7 8 9 0

To Mewes and Mariko
and
"The family"

CONTENTS

INTRODUCTION

This is a book about the West of the imagination—a country and a saga peopled by characters who, because they have a special place in our collective national consciousness, are as alive today as they were a hundred years ago. Tracing the stories and analyzing the works of the artists and photographers and other image-makers who portrayed the West, we hope to point up the elemental power of their visions, their magic, and the ways in which they contributed to what might be called "the tale of the American tribe." For the visual image-makers have contributed as much as the writers to the fundamental myth of the American experience—the story of the peopling of a vast new continent by emigrants from the old European world who were forever moving West. To a surprising degree, the men and women who were engaged in this movement West over the North American Continent, were conscious of their place in history. They knew somehow that they were part of one of the largest mass migrations in history. So those that could write or remember—from the mountain men in the vanguard, to the builders of railroads and towns and cities—kept a record, a memory of their experiences which has become the shared inheritance of the American people. The artists, and a bit later, the photographers, were also part of this process of history-making, and as they nostalgically looked backward upon the whole experience they, too, like the writers and the storytellers, became America's premier mythmakers. And the more we look at the way in which these artists pictured the Western experience and brought it to life in all its variety, the more we become aware that there is not just one history of the West. We realize that history, or myth, is in the eye of the beholder. In this book we hope to show you some of the best of the works of the beholders. It is a rich, varied, and fascinating series of glimpses into the heart of an American experience that makes our culture and some of our heroes unique in the world.

In addition, it is our aim to call attention to the fact that, though it is the iconographic bearer of history and the magic of myth, the art of the American West is also a vital part of the corpus of American art. For far too long it has been ignored or accorded second-class status by an art world intent upon evaluating our art by the standards of European critical clichés, or else as a prelude to an imagined world dominance by the New York School of Abstract Expressionists. For the most part, the art of the American West is not abstract, but representational, because it is conveying a great deal of information about an unknown land and a host of critical experiences. It is telling a monumental story and its creators, although as widely varying in their styles as their stories, had little time or audience for the artistic narcissism that so pervades much of the art world of the waning years of the twentieth century. Rather, it has reached outward to its viewers around the world, expressing as clearly as possible the beliefs and values of American and Native American cultures, as well as the epic experiences inherent in peopling a continent. Perhaps there is no better time than now, when the exhaustion of modernism is so apparent, to take stock of this rich visual inheritance from the West that has been so influential on our behavior, but so neglected by a European-oriented world of professional art connoisseurs.

But in the minds of Americans, where did this "West" exist? Did it begin at the Cumberland Gap made famous by the first American hero, Daniel Boone? Was it Kentucky, that land of tall bluegrass and the spilled blood of generations of red men and white—a land which moved one ecstatic backwoods preacher to declare, "Oh my dear honies, heaven is a Kentucky of a place,"[1] just as white treaty negotiators wrested the last of it away from a powerful Cherokee Chief, Dragging Canoe? No. Well, then, was it the forested Ohio country of Tecumseh and his brother the Prophet who foretold earthquakes?

Or was the real West to be found away up north beyond the reaches of "the English Lakes?" Actually, as Americans came to conceive of it, the West was none of these places. They were instead considered "frontiers," a unique American use of the old European reference to national borders. In these cases, Americans referred to a continuously westward moving belt of settlement wherein the pioneer confronted and conquered the wilderness and the Indian. It was the land of Cooper's Leatherstocking.

The West that came to dominate the minds of our artist visionaries was the vast land beyond the Mississippi that Napoleon sold to President Jefferson as "Louisiana." There is a possibly apocryphal story that fits the situation faced by the early Western artists perfectly. When Napoleon's foreign minister, the great Tallyrand, asked the diminutive First Consul to explain to him just what he should tell the Americans they were buying, Napoleon replied, "If an obscurity [concerning Louisiana] did not already exist, it would be perhaps good policy to put one there." Tallyrand accordingly suggested that the new American purchasers were free "to construe it in their own way."[2] Thus the West was born a cryptogram in the minds of Americans. Louisiana immediately became that great mystery: the West. To a large extent, in the early nineteenth century, it seemed as if the moral, if not physical, future of the United States of America hinged upon what the West had to offer. To Jeffersonians it was a potential Eden. To the opposing Federalists it was a chimera towards which "we rushed," declared the New Englander Fisher Ames, "like a Comet into infinite space."

In 1803 the West was indeed something of a chimera. It was a mass of shallow rivers flowing down from some unknown mountain source, down and down across an endless plain that border men described as "a great prairie ocean." One of those rivers, called by the Indians the Missouri, was known to extend at least two thousand miles up north and west across the prairies and into some mountains only vaguely and variously described as "the Stoney Mountains," or, as mountains of pure crystal that might run north and south, or perhaps east and west across the continent. Far up that river Missouri in 1738 a family of French fur traders, the Vérèndryes, discovered a village of "Welsh Indians," the Mandans, descended, thought the Vérèndryes, from Prince Madoc, who, according to the English historian Richard Hakluyt, had sailed west over the sea in the year 1170. Other eighteenth-century explorers, notably Jonathan Carver, looking for the fabled Strait of Anian or Northwest Passage, declared that beyond the vast prairie wasteland was a mass of towering mountains in the heart of which bubbled a vast reservoir of lakes and fountains that flowed east to the Mississippi, south to the Rio Grande, and west to the Pacific Ocean.[3] By 1792 an American skipper sailing the Pacific, Robert Gray, had discovered one of those rivers which he named after his ship, the *Columbia.* A few years later, the river's mouth and interior course for over 100 miles were mapped by an English fleet under Captain George Vancouver, and it seemed apparent, at least to Jefferson, that there was some direct portage across the Stoney Mountains from the Missouri to the Columbia and thence to the Pacific.

What the Spaniards knew about the West was a well-kept secret. Coronado had begun the entrada with his expedition of 1540 and his captains had found Zuñi, then the sky-high Indian apartment houses along the Rio Grande, but they failed to find the fabled city of Quivira or the incredibly rich Seven Cities of Cibola. By 1776 the Spaniards had penetrated the heart of the Rocky Mountains and had reached Utah Lake. They had crossed the plains of Texas and they had crossed over Oklahoma and Kansas to the French outpost at St. Louis. They had also established a string of missions along the coast of California and in 1776, the very year that Padres Dominguez and Escalante gazed down upon lonely, barren Utah Lake, Don Gaspar de Portola and his men traversed what one poetic soldier called "the pastures of heaven" and began to plan a mission and presidio at San Francisco Bay. To the Spaniard, the West was "the Rim of Christendom," and the vast plains and the Rockies guarded them from unwelcome intruders and European rivals.

Beyond the above, little was known of the West when President Jefferson made it an American mystery.[4] A few traders, following the route of the Vérèndryes down from Canada, had reached the Mandan villages on the Missouri, near present-day Bismarck, North Dakota. And some French and Scottish explorers were known to have mapped the river upward from St. Louis to those fabled villages. They had also come back with tales of powerful riverine Indian villages and stories of hair-raising scrapes with painted savages who rode horses like the wind blowing across the dangerous prairies. Some men said the West was a vast desert. Others, citing herds of buffalo that rumbled and thundered on without end across the prairie, and antelope to be had on every hand, described the West as a paradise of flocks and herds. No one knew just who inhabited its mountain fastnesses, or even just where these mountains lay— except the Spaniards, who were not telling. Thus, in 1803, all that Jefferson, who had an extensive collection of books and maps describing Louisiana, knew for sure about the West beyond the Missouri, was that the Canadian fur trader, Alexander MacKenzie, had crossed the continent far to the north and, after a difficult march, reached the Pacific. A continental crossing was thus feasible. Jefferson also knew that the American sea captain, Robert Gray, had discovered a great river flowing from the interior into the Pacific Ocean at latitude 40° 31′ N. Thus a relatively easy passage across Louisiana via the Missouri and Gray's river (the Columbia) was a distinct possibility. In purchasing Louisiana, the United States might not only have gained a vast, rich interior land mass, but also control of the long sought passage to India. Otherwise, the West was what you made it—or how you looked at it. Jefferson was determined to demystify it and exploit it in the name of science and the United States of America. He selected his studious secretary, Meriwether Lewis, for the task, and sent him to Philadelphia to sit at the feet of the new nation's leading savants. It was no secret that Jefferson was engaged in an intellectual, yet political, debate with the great Comte de Buffon, Europe's leading naturalist, over the nature of the New World.[5] Buffon, seconded by the impudent Voltaire, had declared America a land of miasmal swamps but lately risen from the sea, whose creatures were small and inferior, and whose savages, lacking facial hair, were also distinctly lacking in "amative powers," and would soon be extinct. Jefferson believed the opposite, of course, and he hoped, too, that Lewis would find and capture, if not that creature, the Megalonix that had left a giant claw at Big Bone Lick in Kentucky, then a live mastodon of the sort whose bones had lately been raised and put together in a miracle of reconstruction by the Philadelphia artist-naturalist Charles Willson Peale. It was appropriate that Jefferson linked Peale and his friends, the naturalists of Philadelphia, to the West and the debate over the merits of the New World because they served two purposes. They were naturalists of good repute in European centers of learning, and at the same time many of them, like Peale and his extensive family, were artists who could vividly and accurately portray what they discovered. They would be the vehicle that de-mystified the West, and Meriwether Lewis would be their instrument of demystification. Thus, the art of the American West was born out of a representational and exacting scientific tradition. It would not always adhere to these scientific standards, but it would always be an art of information—or misinformation that took on the characteristics of myth.

PREFACE AND ACKNOWLEDGMENTS

The conception and creation of *The West of the Imagination,* both book and television series, have had an interesting history. As a cultural historian, as well as a Western historian, I was interested in devising a course that would merge my two interests, and hopefully capture the attention of my students. Gradually the concept emerged as I considered how much enjoyment I had derived over the past decade spent in such great museums of Western art as the Amon Carter Museum in Fort Worth, Texas, the Joslyn Art Museum in Omaha, Nebraska, and the Buffalo Bill Historical Center in Cody, Wyoming. I had even taught courses involving Western art at the Center for Western Studies, which I helped to found, in the Buffalo Bill Historical Center. It soon became clear to me that in telling or teaching the story of the so-called "real West" we were all leaving out an important dimension of that reality: the West as people imagined it, that was part of reality, too. The key to telling this story was, of course, all around me in museums, libraries, and in private collections. I would tell the exciting story of the American West through the stories and works of its image-makers. No one had ever made a sweeping survey of the visual images of the West that included paintings, drawings, cartoons, photographs and films. The prospect was both breathtaking and exciting. I knew that such a daring experiment would appeal especially to students at The University of Texas, a state that figured so prominently in the history of the West.

Then began a series of even more breathtaking events. A friend at the Dallas public television station, KERA, phoned and asked if I had any ideas for a major PBS series. By that time of course I did, and when I outlined the concept of *The West of the Imagination* to her, she promised to make me a star—right then and there. Little did I suspect how much work and personal "adventure" were to be involved in the project.

We raised the funding for the television series through the incredible generosity of the Nelda and H. J. Lutcher Stark Foundation and that of Mrs. Nelda Stark, herself an authority on the Taos and Santa Fe painters. By that time I was deep in the process of teaching the course, while at the same time conducting the massive research that the series and this book required. I had written the shooting scripts so that the project was well underway in the hands of Pantechnicon Productions, and was facing a deadline for this and two other books at the same time, as well as the pleasing prospect of teaching another full-time schedule, when a second surprise overtook me, in the form of a "myocardial infarction," a silly but chilling phrase which meant heart attack. Given this situation, what was I to do? The book, not to mention the final television scripting, loomed before me like gigantic chasms into which I was slated to drop immediately and forever.

Just then my family came to my rescue in ways that no impersonal foundation or "think tank" could. My wife, Mewes, kept my spirits up and the seat of my pants on the chair researching and writing, sometimes in a central room in the house with dogs and visitors coming and going while the faint sound of TV talk filled in with background noise. But most of all, my son Will, who had been director of the Museum of Western Art in Denver, flew down to help me write this book. His knowledge of Western art, gleaned over a relatively short time, nearly matched his knowledge of "the great traditions" of American and European art. In addition, he is a film maker who, at the time, was writing scripts for programs on Augustus Saint Gaudens and Thomas Eakins. Like the cavalry in the old West, Will came to my rescue and we worked on this book together. It became his work as much as mine. Working with one's children (however grown up they are) is often very difficult, but I found this collaboration one of the high points of my life. Day by day, when I was able to write, we climbed the mountain, "roped together like mountaineers," as the late Walter P. Webb would have it, in search of high adventure.

The book grew. So did my "family." Graduate students pitched in to help. Who can forget their names: Melissa Totten, chief researcher and scalawag, Lawrence Walker, Cheri Diesler, Emily Cutrer. Dr. Linda Vance also became part of the team, which was presided over by my matchless secretary, Sarah Shelby. Then, from far and near others became part of my family. My wife Mewes actually liked helping with the research, while my younger son Stephen learned a great deal about digesting books and articles. Others joined the "family" with their many, often unusual kindnesses. Book dealer Dorothy Sloan bought a Republic of Texas two-dollar bill so that we could photograph it for inclusion in the book. Bill Reese, the prince of Western Americana dealers, made available to me Cullum's lectures at Catlin's Indian Gallery in London, and showed Will Frederic Remington's revealing notes on color. Lois Flury, the leading dealer in Edward S. Curtis materials, sent pictures from Seattle. Dealer Gerald Peters of Santa Fe made his whole collection available to us. Griff Carnes, director of the Cowboy Artists of America Museum at Kerrville, Texas, introduced me to many Western artists and placed his magnificent facilities at our disposal. Marshall Kuydendal, Mary Margaret Albright, Becky Reese, assistant director of the University of Texas Art Collections, and Francine Carraro of the American Studies Program, contributed in important ways; not the least was their continuing interest.

Maud Lipscomb provided expert photography and expert humor. Professor Ricardo Romo was my guide in matters of Hispanic murals and art. Sheila Jenkins, Mick White and Kay Sloan were excellent advisors and researchers at one stage of the project as were Ann Graham and Terry McKay. In Philadelphia, an old friend, Victoria Lilley, was our congenial guide. Linda Goldstein of the Museum of Western Art was continuously helpful. Patricia Geeson of the National Museum of American Art was an especially helpful friend, as was Nancy Anderson of the same institution, who has now become a leading authority on Albert Bierstadt and George Catlin. She is a masterful researcher and good friend, as is Joan Stauffer of Tulsa, Oklahoma, a lady better known as Nancy Russell.

Then, too, in countless ways the members of the series advisory committee, all good friends, provided invaluable help in the writing of the book as well as critiquing the series episodes. First we should mention the late Marlou Quintana of the Taos Pueblo and Santa Fe who provided immense help to the project. We hope she is resting now serenely on the shores of the Sacred Blue Lake, high up in the Taos Mountains. In addition to Marlou the following have also been godparents to this book: Jim Ballinger of the Phoenix Art Museum, Elizabeth Cunningham of the Anschutz Collection, Dr. Brian Dippie, University of Victoria, British Columbia. No one knows more about Custer and Charley Russell than Brian, a former student of mine. Add to this list Peter Hassrick of the Buffalo Bill Historical Center, where parts of the series were filmed, Dr. Gerhard Hoffmann of Wurzburg, Germany, the authority on contemporary native American art, Bill Howze and Ron Tyler at the Amon Carter Museum, Fred Myers of the Gilcrease Museum, a mecca for researchers in Western history and art, Dr. Joseph Porter, historian at the Joslyn Art Museum and recent author of a stunning biography of Captain John Gregory Bourke who was "on the border with Crook." Two final names conclude this roll call. Bill Truettner of the National Collection of American Art provided help time and time again. He is the very model of a modern art historian, as well as a gracious gentleman. And last but certainly not least, I need to mention Dr. Barbara Novak of Barnard and Columbia Universities. She provided encouragement and she has been a colleague in Georgia O'Keeffe's words, from "Far Away Nearby."

With the help of these amazing friends, including Pat Perini of KERA, Donn Rogosin of KLRU, and Pat Russell of Pantechnicon Productions, William N. Goetzmann and I completed this book, which at first paralleled the television series, then became its chief research resource, and finally transcended the series in scope. It is not the series voice-over word for word. It is not a "cousin" to the series. It is the "environment" for the series, a landscape that we have traversed in the shadows of the works of other scholars, "delectable mountains" who came before us in search of that elusive phenomenon, the West of all our collective imaginations, the national family's "Tale of the Tribe."

William N. Goetzmann   William H. Goetzmann
New Haven, Connecticut   Austin, Texas

Part One

THE ROMANTIC HORIZON

CHAPTER 1

THE VIEW FROM PEALE'S MUSEUM

The West of the imagination began its existence not only among fur traders in the frontier town of St. Louis who dreamed of riches in beaver pelts for the taking away off in the Shining Mountains beyond the wide Missouri, but also in staid Philadelphia, on the Schuylkill. Certainly we know that on a spring day in 1794, a strange procession marched its way through the streets of that city. Led by an energetic man of middle age, a procession of boys carried a curious burden out of a house on Lombard Street and into the chambers of Philosophical Hall, which stood hard by famed Independence Hall, where the nation was born. But on that day in 1794, here came the lads, carrying a stuffed and mounted buffalo, a panther, a deer, a wild turkey, a "tyger catt" and a literal profusion of specimens from the animal kingdom of North America and from other exotic places as well.[1] The gentleman leading them like a Pied Piper, with a keen sense of theatre, was Charles Willson Peale, who styled himself an artist-naturalist. He was the sole owner and proprietor of America's first respectable museum, and at this moment it was being recognized as such by being accorded quarters in Philosophical Hall, in the very heart, if not mind, of the new nation.

Charles Willson Peale, *The Artist in His Museum,* (1822). The Pennsylvania Academy of Fine Arts, Joseph and Sarah Harrison Collection.

Eventually, Peale took over most of the second floor of Independence Hall itself, occupying what was called "The Long Room." As an old man he could look back on those days with a good deal of pride. In fact, he did. In 1822, at the advanced age of 81, he painted perhaps the most famous self-portrait in American history, *The Artist in His Museum.* Some would ask, "What was an artist doing with a *museum?*" Artists had studios, but not Peale. He derived his inspiration from all of nature, which he tried very hard to get into his famous museum. See him there in his self-portrait, standing right in the middle of the picture, light reflecting off his bald head, while, like a god—or at least a magician—he grandly pulled back the velvet, tasselated curtain of ignorance, to reveal his miniature world of natural history. There he is, bidding you step past a giant pre-historic molar and a half-stuffed American wild turkey; take note of the giant femur leaning against the table that held his simple artist's colors, and step right into the whole world of nature organized as it should be—according to the Great Chain of Being. Listen to his lecture while looking at the cases of stuffed and pickled specimens of nature, and the strange creature that towered majestically over all: the marvelous mastodon.

Peale would start his lecture, "Let us now contemplate that infinite variety of animals, each formed in such fantastical, yet most proper, shape, each supporting its peculiar rank to keep the necessary balance that maintain millions of beings in life. . . ."[2] But did his mind wander to that wonderful year, that *annus mirabilis,* when, aided by his whole family, he had dug up the great mastodon from out of a manure bog in a place called Newburgh, in the State of New York?

He had felt like God that day in 1801, and he painted a picture of the scene. It was a whole new kind of history painting, one not of generals dying on a battlefield, or statesmen signing a treaty, but of Peale himself, like the Supreme Clockmaker, supervising the exhumation of the mastodon. There he was with his friend, Dr. Caspar Wistar, holding a drawing of the behemoth's mighty femur, while at the same time directing the operation of a clocklike apparatus of wheels and buckets, designed by him to carry the water away from the excavation site. He put all his family and friends in the picture in a great, excited crowd in pursuit of the knowledge which, like Shakespeare's Prospero, he was just then revealing to them. But just to show he was not too prideful, he added a storm cloud looming above as evidence of someone mightier, even, than he.

Charles Willson Peale, *Exhumation of the Mastodon,* (1806–1808). The Peale Museum, Baltimore.

By the end of the year, however, with the aid of Dr. Wistar and his own talented sons, all of whom he had named after painters, Peale had reconstructed and assembled the mastodon. The creature dwarfed even an elephant. It was 18 feet long and about 10 feet to its belly. When he opened his new mastodon room to the curious in December of 1801, he advertized it as "The Great Incognitum," and his black assistant Moses Williams, wearing an Indian feathered headdress, like a Wild West performer, rode a white horse through the streets of Philadelphia. He was preceded by a trumpeter proclaiming the creature "The Largest of *terrestrial* beings, the ninth wonder of the world!!!— buried since Noah's flood."[3] The museum ticket itself was something the English mystic artist-romantic William Blake would have been proud of. It featured a crudely drawn alligator, a pelican, a wolf, two monkeys, a songbird, and a toucan, all basking under a heavenly light out of which beamed like a beacon, *The Book of Nature.* Peale and his colleagues in the Philadelphia naturalist circle may have subscribed to all the Enlightenment tenets of Newton and Locke. They may well have seen the world as a gigantic clocklike machine for just a time, like the wheels and buckets in Peale's mastodon painting. But as he collected and attempted to classify the 200 quadrupeds, 1,600 birds, 400 insects, and 11 cases of minerals,[4] Peale had to have become aware of the visual quality and the abundance of nature. Add to this his capacity for wonder at it all, his showmanship, his delight in presiding over such a collection, such a never-ending drama of creation, and you have a true romantic at heart. There was no way that Enlightenment abstractions could stand against the actual experience of nature. Perhaps it was because of that romantic spirit, as well as the knowledge available, that President Jefferson, certainly a dreamer and a kindred spirit, sent his secretary, Meriwether Lewis, to sit at the feet of these Philadelphia savants to prepare for his great expedition across the North American continent.

Too bad Lewis arrived after the great banquet of 1802 that was held right under the belly of the mastodon to celebrate the departure of Rembrandt Peale for Europe with a second skeleton of the great beast. Since his days in Paris, of course, Jefferson had been engaged in debate with the great French naturalist, Buffon, and his naughty allies, the Abbe de Pauw and the witty Voltaire over the value of the New World. Unlike Franklin, Jefferson took this debate seriously, and wrote his only book about it. The book carried the no-nonsense title, *Notes on the State of Virginia.*

Meanwhile, when Rembrandt arrived in Europe with "The Great Incognitum," the matter would be settled instantly, and perhaps they could derive a bit of profit by selling the beast to some European curiosity-seeker. For though they pretended not to be so, most educated Europeans were as curious about America as they were about the South Seas. The whole continent was a "great incognitum." Thus, in toast after toast at the banquet under the belly of the creature, punctuated by tunes from Isaac Hawkins's ingenious Patented Portable Piano, the guests likened the great beast to America, the wonder of the Creator, and to the natural laws that governed it in the path of righteousness, in contrast to wicked Europe. No matter that the banquetees got a little tipsy and switched to double-entendre toasts honoring the boney-bonny ladies of Philadelphia, it was still a marvelous occasion, one that Lewis, or for that matter, Jefferson himself, who was President of the Philosophical Society as well as of the United States, would have enjoyed.

Instead, Lewis got instructions from the savants.[5] They drew up lists that included all manner of questions about Indians and divorce, Indians and melancholy, Indians and suicide, Indians and sex, and a hundred other topics in natural history. Andrew Ellicott, cartographer to the United States, showed Lewis how to make maps as precise as a physiognotrace outlined a face. Robert Patterson instructed him in the use of scientific instruments, and how to determine longitude by lunar calculations. (When he made his great map of the West, it was clear that Lewis had flunked this part of the course.) Caspar Wistar instructed him in medicine and anatomy, Albert Gallatin in hypothetical geography and Indians, Peale and Benjamin Smith Barton in natural history and the art of collecting and preserving specimens. Out of all this, Jefferson compiled a master list of instructions for Lewis, who had added his old friend, William Clark, to the expedition. Jefferson's list covered everything imaginable, from mineralogy to volcanoes to Indian trade relations, and since he believed that no creature could be extinct, that the Western Indians were telling the truth when they said they had seen them, Jefferson was undoubtedly confident that they would sight mastodons as well. But, alas, the one thing Jefferson, even with Peale's help, did not think to include, was the requirement that an artist be taken along on the expedition, if only to paint a *live* mastodon. Except for their numerous maps and marginal sketches in their journals, the Great Captains did nothing to picture the West. The lack of an artist on Lewis and Clark's epic journey, the complete non-visualization of the wonders and sights that they saw, only underscores the extremely important role that artists were to play in the future.

It is quite possible, however, that aside from the talented Peales, Philadelphia and, indeed, the country, in 1803, did not have an artist up to the monumental task of rendering the vast western spaces, and the strange native inhabitants. It would have taken a master of landscape painting, a painter with a scientific eye for landforms, an accomplished animal painter, and a penetrating, energetic portraitist, who was not afraid of Indians, to do justice to the sights seen on their journey. There were no such Renaissance masters in America at the time.

Nor were there later in 1819, when Major Stephen H. Long set off from the Missouri River west across the vast prairie, headed for the front range of the Rocky Mountains.[6] Long's expedition was originally part of General Henry Rice Atkinson's military force sent up the Missouri River to intimidate the hostile Aikara and to establish a post at the junction of the Yellowstone River and the Missouri. It became known as "the Yellowstone Expedition," though the whole military force never got past present-day Council Bluffs, where it went into a winter encampment that was soon ravaged by disease that killed the commander and nearly half the men.

The whole operation, as far as Major Long was concerned, had started off in modern scientific fashion. The soldiers started up-river in six modern steamboats. Long and the scientific contingent rode aboard one of the major's own design, the *Western Engineer*. It's bow was shaped like a dragon's head, and smoke and fire from the engine poured forth from its mouth, designed to intimidate any hostile Indians. One observer grasped the mix of military, scientific and technological expertise that the whole operation represented. He wrote,

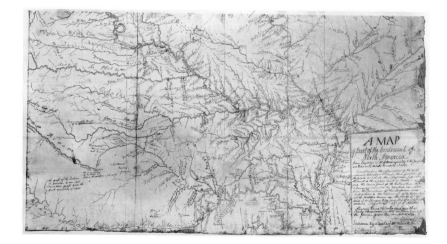

Lewis and Clark Map of 1809, Manuscript, Yale Western Americana Collection.

Titian Peale, *Steamboat Western Engineer*, (1819). American Philosophical Society, Philadelphia.

See those vessels, with the agency of steam advancing against the powerful currents of the Mississippi and the Missouri! Their course is marked by volumes of smoke and fire which the civilized man observes with admiration and the savage with astonishment. Botanists, mineralogists, chemists, artisans, cultivators, scholars, soldiers; the love of peace, the capacity for war: the philosophical apparatus and military supplies; telescopes and cannon, garden seeds and gunpowder; the arts of civil life and the force to defend them—all are seen aboard. The banner of freedom which waves over the whole proclaims the character and protective power of the United States.[7]

The designation was an apt one, as one can grasp from Titian Peale's sketch of the boat near Council Bluffs. Major Long, in addition to designing his own steamboat and assembling the materials with which to build it, had also put together a contingent of naturalists, largely from Philadelphia, some military engineers from West Point, and two artists. Chief among the scientists was Thomas Say, who had been one of the founders of the Philadelphia Academy of Natural Sciences. Long's instructions had been drawn up by the American Philosophical Society. And his two artists were Philadelphians. First, there was Samuel Seymour, an English-born engraver and viewpainter, who had been working for the Philadelphia engraver, William Birch, whose picture of Independence Hall was one of the earliest. Then, Long also added nineteen-year-old Titian Peale, the youngest son of Charles Willson Peale. Young Peale was to be the artist-naturalist who drew accurate pictures of the animal specimens secured on the expedition, as well as renditions of the flocks and herds of wild game observed en route. Thus, the Long expedition had a direct connection with the major scientific institutions of Philadelphia, the nation's intellectual capital.

When the Yellowstone Expedition stalled at the Council Bluffs in the winter of 1819, the scientific contingent went into winter encampment there and collected specimens that were sent back to Peale's Museum. Peale also made numerous gouache drawings, such as an interesting view of the sun setting on the Missouri River. Long, himself, went east to Washington and received new orders. He and his men were commanded to strike out across the great prairie, noting its fitness for settlement, and to keep moving west until they reached the Rocky Mountains. Then they were to turn south and march along the Front Range until they reached the Red River, considered the southern boundary of Louisiana. They were to mark this boundary as they traveled eastward back toward the Mississippi. This Long and his men proceeded to do, though in the end they failed to located the Red River, confusing it with the Canadian, much to their chagrin.

With a new naturalist, Dr. Edwin James, added to their number, they struck out in 1820 across the prairie along the Platte River, and via its south fork, approached the mountains. Neither Samuel Seymour nor Titian Peale were in any way prepared for the vast western spaces they encountered. The scientific men considered the prairie country, especially the high plains, a "Great Desert."[8] While Peale made numerous drawings of animals they encountered, wolves, badgers, buffalo, and even the ubiquitous prairie dogs, Seymour had little to sketch until, On July 3, 1820, they reached a spot near Bijou's Creek, near present-day Greeley, Colorado.[9] There he rendered perhaps his most important work, *View of the Rocky Mountains on the Platte 50 Miles from their Base.* The Rockies had first appeared to members of the expedition looking like a small cloud on the horizon. It was not until they reached the spot where Seymour painted his view that they fully realized they were gazing upon the great mountain wall. Seymour's view with a shortened title, *Distant View of the Rocky Mountains,* appeared as a hand-colored aquatint frontispiece to Edwin James's and Major Long's report of the expedition. Thus, it was the first eyewitness pictorial representation of the West to be placed before the American public.

At first glance Seymour's view seems conventional and unprepossessing. But upon closer inspection, it must be noted that he *did* capture the sense of awesome space, and the vast level plain. One does have that "as far as the eye can see" feeling as one stands beside the Indians in the foreground and takes a sweeping gaze across the plains. An endless string of tiny buffalo stretching off to an infinity on the right side of the picture as they cross the Platte from out of nowhere, reinforces this impression. And the mountains, though obviously

Mink and Ermine.   Muskrats.

Bison "Bulls".   Fox—Tree Trunk.

Titian Peale, *Four Drawings of Animals,* American Philosophical Society, Philadelphia.

very high, are an indistinct miragelike element in the far distance. Moreover, Seymour put a number of iconographic images in his picture: solemn Indians, fossil bones in the foreground, suggesting the antiquity of the ravages of the great Noachian flood, and the ubiquitous buffalo, which came to symbolize the plains for virtually every succeeding artist. Though a small work, Seymour's *Distant View of the Rocky Mountains* was in every way an epic picture.

As the expedition approached the mountain wall, his drawings became more exact, as Patricia Trenton and Peter Hassrick have pointed out in *The Rocky Mountains in American Art.* His watercolor, *View of the Chasm through which the Platte Issues from the Rocky Mountains,* is especially accurate, as is his *View Near the Base of the Rocky Mountains,* depicting, as tiny figures, the members of the expedition. One of his most dramatic pictures was his pen-and-ink watercolor wash drawing, *View of James Peak in the Rain,* actually the first view of Pike's Peak. It is conventionally framed by trees in the foreground, and a

Samuel Seymour, *Distant View of the Rocky Mountains,* (1823), frontispiece to expedition report. Humanities Research Center, The University of Texas at Austin.

figure is inserted to give a sense of scale, but the focus, this time, is indeed upon the mountain range and the storm (one that actually took place as he was making the picture), which adds a romantic touch to the whole scene. Very subtly in this picture, which also has considerable vegetation, Seymour is pointing out that the whole country is *not a desert,* as Zebulon Pike earlier, and James and Long in 1823, were to report. The James Peak picture showing rain was not included in the published edition of Major Long's report.

Assessing the value, both aesthetically and culturally, of Seymour's first views of the great West is an interesting task. His work seems spare, contrived and even clumsy to us today. But he was an artist in the topographical tradition that began to be in vogue in the mid-eighteenth century when exploring expeditions circled the globe, and continued through the mid-nineteenth century. The duty of the topographical artist was to render landforms as exactly as possible, to make of his works something like elevations in a picto-map. Barbara M. Stafford, in her recent book, *Voyage Into Substance,* regards them as visual recorders of the matter-of-fact.[10] This was clearly their mission, but as Seymour's renditions indicate, the artist's feelings of awe or wonder at the moment of viewing inevitably allowed his emotions to give form and character to the pictures. Trenton and Hassrick observe that, in the vicinity of Elephant Rock, Seymour allowed "his imagination a free rein . . . suggesting massive walls, pillars, and arches of a ruined edifice. . . ." They add, "there is an air of fantasy and antiquity about this view. . . ."[11] None of the topographical artists was really able to be objective. They brought associations and impressions to their art. Seymour's work clearly illustrates that all of them included some interpretations of this sort in their field drawings and paintings. Like the scientist, the scientific artist interpreted, even as he made his careful observations. During the period, topographical art made the aesthetic journey from Scottish Associationism to German Romanticism.

In all, Seymour made over 150 pictures on the Long expedition. Only eight of them ever appeared in either the American or English editions of the report.[12] Most of the rest of them, with the exception of the picture of *James Peak in the Rain,* have disappeared, and with them what might have been a first comprehensive view of the plains and Rockies.

On the other hand, because of the existence of his father's museum, which received the specimens from the Long Expedition, and the interest of the Philadelphia naturalists, over a hundred of Peale's animal and bird drawings have survived. Taken together, they attest to the abundance of life on the Great Plains—something Peale tried on several occasions to indicate by making oil paintings of great herds of animals, using Seymour's landscapes as the backdrop. Young Peale's drawings were exact, and so admired as scientific art that he became one of the artists on Lt. Charles Wilkes's "Great United States Exploring Expedition," that, between 1838 and 1842, sailed the South Seas and the waters of the Northwest Coast, as well as charting the ice-bound shores of the Antarctic Continent for the first time. Titian Peale's was an heroic and adventurous life.[13] But as he lived on into the 1870s, those first visions of the Far West seemed to haunt him more than anything else he had seen, and he painted them over and over again. In each rendition, science gave way more and more to art. One work in particular became a basic iconic

Samuel Seymour, *James Peak in the Rain,* (1820). Museum of Fine Arts, Boston, M. and M. Karolik Collection.

Titian Peale, *Indian Hunting Buffalo,* (1823). William H. Goetzmann collection.

image in the visual vocabulary of the West. This was a simple, almost clumsy rendition of an Indian on horseback, shooting a buffalo with his bow and arrow. The image, made into a lithograph by Thomas Doughty for the *Cabinet of Natural History and American Rural Sports,* probably was the most widely distributed view of the Far West in the decade of the 1830s.

CHAPTER 2

GEORGE CATLIN: SAVING THE
MEMORY OF A VANISHING RACE

Since the mid-eighteenth century, with the great voyages of Cap-tain Cook, science and art inevitably went together, and Charles Willson Peale saw nothing incongruous about displaying his portraits of famous men along with cases of stuffed birds and animals in his Philadelphia museum. In fact, from the beginning anthropology was an important aspect of Peale's Museum. It displayed not only the Indian paraphernalia brought back from the plains and the Rockies by Titian Peale, but also the Indian artifacts brought back by Lewis and Clark, including Lewis's buckskin hunting costume, decorated by dozens of ermine and white weasel skins.

This aspect of Peale's Museum was not lost on another citizen of Philadelphia, George Catlin.[1] Born in 1796 and raised on a farm near Wilkes Barre, Pennsylvania, trained for the law at Tapping Reeves's famous law school at Litchfield, Connecticut, where he was a classmate of John C. Calhoun and the Mayan explorer, John Lloyd Stephens, Catlin thwarted his family's plans for him and became a painter. He received most of his training informally in Philadelphia from 1824 onward at the Pennsylvania Academy and in the studios of John Neagle and Thomas Sully. Catlin's ambition was to be a history painter in the mode of the great Benjamin West, whose *Death on a Pale Horse*, an immense and powerful canvas painted in 1817, had only recently arrived in Philadelphia. Instead, Catlin earned his living by painting portraits, mostly miniatures that people carried around like keepsakes. At this he became very proficient. His miniature of Sam Houston is perhaps the best portrait of the Texan hero ever rendered.

But Catlin's experience in Philadelphia encompassed more than painting portraits to stay alive. He mingled with the artists, even became a member of the Pennsylvania Academy, but he was also caught up in the heady atmosphere of science that so dominated the city. He could not have missed a visit to Peale's Museum, nor, it appears, did he overlook the Indian artifacts from the Far West. More than the mastodon, more than the hundreds of stuffed birds and other natural curiosities, the Indian artifacts represented to Catlin a romantic horizon of the unknown. The climate of opinion, since the great voyages to the South Seas in the latter part of the eighteenth century, had become one that equated primitive peoples with nature and nature's laws, thus making them, in their grand simplicity, the people closest to God. Nature itself had become holy, and primitive man nature's nobleman. Endless numbers of Europeans rang the changes on this theme. Rousseau, Crèvecoeur, Chateaubriand, and Delacroix, the great French Romantics, were prominent spokesmen for the noble qualities of life in unspoiled nature. James Boswell and Joseph Wright of Derby in England were only two of many who built up out of John Locke's nature philosophy a similar cult in that country. In America, James Fenimore Cooper immortalized the theme in his Leatherstocking series featuring Natty Bumppo, or Leatherstocking, as a kind of allegorical nature god who, in company with the Indians, roamed early America from the forests and glimmerglass lakes east of the Mississippi to the vast western prairies. Cooper was one of Catlin's favorite authors, and he outlined the plots of each of the Leatherstocking novels with some care before undertaking his own writing venture, especially his *Letters and Notes on the Manners, Customs and Conditions of the North American Indians*, a two-volume work that he published in England in 1841. In fact, the tone of this, Catlin's most important work, is everywhere redolent of Cooper at his romantic and didactic best. In a very real sense, George Catlin became the Leatherstocking of American art, as he roamed the entire western hemisphere from Tierra del Fuego to Alaska, painting its native inhabitants. The American West to him was special, however. He called it, "The great and almost boundless garden spot of the earth, over whose green enamelled fields, as . . . free as the ocean's wave, Nature's

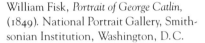

William Fisk, *Portrait of George Catlin,* (1849). National Portrait Gallery, Smithsonian Institution, Washington, D.C.

proudest, noblest men have pranced on their wild horses, and extended, through a series of ages, their long arms in orisons of praise to the Great Spirit in the sun, for the freedom and happiness of their existence."[2]

Though these themes of romantic science and art had begun to dominate his imagination, it was in fact a visit to Peale's Museum that galvanized Catlin into the actions that formed his "Leatherstocking" career. In 1826, just outside the Museum, Catlin saw a delegation of Indian chieftans who had come to Philadelphia en route to Washington for a visit to "The Great Father." He admired them instantly, and all of the strains of his imagination came suddenly into focus. "In silent and stoic dignity," he later wrote, "these lords of the forest strutted about the city for a few days, wrapped in their painted robes, with their brows plumed with the quills of the war eagle, attracting the gaze of all who beheld them." Inspired by this imposing panorama, Catlin remembered that then and there he decided that his contribution to scientific knowledge would be "the production of a literal and graphic delineation of the living manners, customs, and character of an interesting race of people who are rapidly passing away from the face of the earth—lending a hand to a dying nation, who have no historians or biographers of their own to portray with fidelity their native looks and history. . . ."[3]

Thus, at about the same time that John James Audubon took his study—some say his obsession—of exotic birds out of the confines of the museum into the open fields and woods, George Catlin in Philadelphia resolved to do the same for the Indian before, like the passenger pigeon and the great auk, he

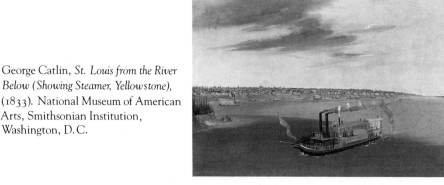

George Catlin, *St. Louis from the River Below (Showing Steamer, Yellowstone)*, (1833). National Museum of American Arts, Smithsonian Institution, Washington, D.C.

vanished from the earth. But, unlike Audubon, who did not hesitate to slaughter thousands of birds in his scientific quest, Catlin became the champion of the Indian and native peoples everywhere.

It was not until 1830 that Catlin was able to put his plan into effect, although in New York in 1826 he did a portrait of the famous Iroquois Chief, Red Jacket, overlooking Niagara Falls. In 1830, however, armed with letters from government officials like Commissioner of Indian Affairs Thomas L. McKenney, he made his way to St. Louis. It was appropriate that Catlin received support from McKenney, because McKenney had commissioned another artist, Charles Bird King, to paint the lordly chiefs as they came to Washington. In fact, McKenney's office, the walls lined with Indian portraits, was the first "Indian Gallery" in America, and, together with Peale's Museum, may have been the inspiration for Catlin's later creation of his more famous gallery.[4]

Once in St. Louis, Catlin was befriended by Governor William Clark, who took him to meetings with the Indians in and around St. Louis. Catlin later claimed that they traveled together as far as the famous Prairie du Chien pow-wow also recorded by a young Swiss painter then in St. Louis, Peter Rindisbacher. But, for the most part, Catlin painted portraits of Governor Clark and other St. Louis notables to secure funds for a 2,000 mile trip up the mysterious Missouri, then the high road of adventure for fur trappers and mountain men who followed in the wake of Lewis and Clark.

In 1832 he took passage on the American Fur Company's steamboat, *Yellowstone*, the first steamboat to ascend the Missouri River up past the Council Bluffs, to Fort Union at the junction of the Missouri and the Yellowstone rivers in present-day Montana. This was the first voyage of the *Yellowstone* up the Missouri, and Catlin shared the adventure with a delegation of chiefs returning from Washington, all still decked out in their finery, but with some differences. Many of them had replaced their own native costumes with the borrowed plumage of civilization.

On the way upriver, Catlin painted the Missouri in a series of surreal panoramas. On numerous occasions he got off the steamboat and painted the river views directly, some years before "plein air" painting become fashionable in Europe. To Catlin, the green enameled hills that stretched away in vistas of thirty miles or more, or the great bends and curves of the ribbonlike river offered "soul-melting" beauty and even a glimpse of the Creator. He also captured the Creator's handiwork from the point of view of the geologist.

> By the action of water, or other power, the country seems to have been graded away . . . the sides . . . conical bluffs (which are composed of strata of different-colored clays), are continually washing down by the effect of the rains and melting of the frost and the superincumbent masses of pumice and basalt are crumbling off, and falling down to their bases; and from thence, in vast quantities, by the force of gorges of water . . . carried into the river. . . .[5]

Catlin's sharp eye had caught the uniformitarian process of erosion at a time when most people still believed that such things as the conical hills were the product of the Noachian Deluge described in the Bible. Geological insights aside, Catlin's river scenes were hardly great art, but instead represented a strange kind of surrealistic vision of beauty. His views of the western landscape along the Missouri were the first widely distributed visions of the West. It is no wonder that the imaginations of people on the eastern seaboard and in Europe were moved to consider the West, not as the desert Major Long had described, but as a kind of enameled, brilliantly colored Eden, peopled with noble warriors who harkened back to the days of ancient Greece, or the pastoral visions of the *Aeneid*.

On the way upriver, Catlin also painted the "noble savages." At Fort Pierre, he made portraits of the Sioux, most notably the chief Ha-won-je-tah, "The One Horn," and Tchou-Du, "Tobacco," of the Oglalas. Catlin's characteristic method of painting in oils was to hurriedly line out the contours of the body, and then to spend more time on the facial features, so as to make each Indian an individual. Even then, he usually completed his portraits in a studio back in the East, but only after he had made careful notations as to the costumes, hair styles, body paint and weapons or totems carried by each of his subjects, for Catlin had come to realize that his mission was more that of the ethnographer than the artist. If he got his subjects down on canvas honestly and correctly, beauty would take care of itself. And if the paintings were not nec-

George Catlin, *Big Bend on the Upper Missouri, 1900 Miles Above St. Louis,* (1832). National Museum of American Art, Smithsonian Institution, Washington, D.C., Gift of Mrs. Joseph Harrison, Jr.

George Catlin, *Stu-Mick-O-Sucks, Buffalo Bull's Backfat, Head Chief, Blood Tribe,* (1832). National Collection of American Art, Smithsonian Institution, Washington, D.C., Gift of Mrs. Joseph Harrison, Jr.

George Catlin, *Pigeon's Egg Head (The Light), Wi-Jun-Jon, Assiniboine (Going to and Returning from Washington, D.C.),* (1837–38). National Museum of American Art, Smithsonian Institution, Washington, D.C., Gift of Mrs. Joseph Harrison, Jr.

George Catlin, *Medicine Man, Performing His Mysteries Over a Dying Man,* (1832). National Museum of American Art, Smithsonian Institution, Washington, D.C., Gift of Mrs. Joseph Harrison, Jr.

George Catlin, *Mint, A Pretty Girl,* (1832). National Museum of American Art, Smithsonian Institution, Washington, D.C., Gift of Mrs. Joseph Harrison, Jr.

essarily beautiful, then the novelty of them had its compensations. Only in the case of Mah-to-to-pah, "Four Bears," Chief of the Mandans, did Catlin admit to subordinating the details of costume to the demands of heroic portraiture.[6]

Two thousand miles up the winding Missouri, the *Yellowstone* and Catlin reached Fort Union, the headquarters of the American Fur Company on the upper river. Here Catlin stayed for over a month, his easel set up in the fort, painting dozens of prominent Indian dignitaries, who crowded in to have their portraits painted. Catlin's outdoor studio became, in fact, "a neutral ground," where mortal enemies, such as the Assiniboin and the Blackfeet, laid aside their hostilities as they awaited their turn to have their likenesses duplicated and preserved on canvas. They were usually pleased with the results. Buffalo Bull's Backfat, war chief of the Blackfeet, Catlin caught in one of his truly masterful portraits, while he could not resist making a statement about Pigeon's Egg Head or The Light, who, after his return from Washington in full dress uniform, became so arrogant that he was murdered by his fellow tribesmen.[7] The women, too, Catlin painted in spectacular fashion, as with the woman called "Mint," and he so pleased a Blackfoot medicine man with his portrait of him in full bear-skin regalia that the medicine man presented Catlin with his entire costume, thus beginning a collection of Indian artifacts that would help make Catlin famous.

While at Fort Union, and as he made his way downriver in a canoe with two French voyageurs, Catlin painted genre scenes of the Indians racing across the plains in great buffalo hunts. In one scene he even caught the bravest of the warriors jumping from the backs of the buffalos across the herd. Catlin painted so many buffalo hunts that he came to know the anatomy of the buffalo better than that of horses, who looked like something on a carousel, or even humans. The dying buffalo was his specialty—a wounded behemoth spurting blood while slowly sinking to the earth. This Catlin painted from the life, using as a model a buffalo he had mortally wounded, but who refused to die immediately while Catlin goaded him into different poses so that he could paint him. Like Peale's *Indian Hunting Buffalo*, Catlin's views of the buffalo hunt became basic iconographic images for all who came after him down to the present-day Western artists.

Less imitated, but equally vivid, were Catlin's wonderful paintings of immense prairie fires, with billowing black clouds and frightened animals fleeing like a scene out of Cooper's novel *The Prairie*. Catlin also painted antelope hunts in which the victims were attracted by a piece of cloth, or buffalo hunts where men in wolf skins stalked the herds. He was, in short, recording the everyday pursuits of the wild red men, as well as their blood-curdling dances and ceremonies.

Assisted by one James Kipp from Fort Clark, Catlin became the only artist to record the mysterious Mandan O-Kee-Pa, or torture, ceremony.[8] This secret ceremony went on for days with the women first being threatened by O-ke-hee-de (the evil spirit), a creature painted all black with white dots, who carried a huge artificial penis or "wand." When the women fled the village, men, clad in buffalo heads and skins, appeared, and the O-ke-hee-de tried to fertilize them, but was driven off by the infuriated women of the tribe who returned to throw yellow dust on him and literally break his "wand" so that he went howling away across the prairie. The ceremony climaxed with the young men submitting to being hung by wooden or bone skewers stuck through their pectoral or back muscles and made to stare directly into the sun. When they were let down they walked around dragging buffalo skulls from the incisions they were hung by until they dropped from exhaustion and loss of blood. The whole ceremony concluded with a grand race through the village.

When Catlin first described this ceremony in *Letters and Notes,* he was accused of fabrication. Years later, "in the interest of science," he published a very detailed account of the ceremony in a volume entitled *O-Kee-Pa,* that was not for general circulation, and contained a "folium reservatum" that was explicit about the sexual aspects of the ceremony. Catlin's book was also heavily freighted with testimonials, from lowly fur traders to the great German geographer, Alexander von Humboldt, attesting to the veracity of his account. The most important of these testimonials were, of course, those of Kipp and Prince Maximilian of Wied Neuwied, who spent the winter of 1833–4 living among the Mandans.[9] Catlin, however, was the only eyewitness recorder of this ceremony, because by 1837 most of the Mandans were wiped out in a smallpox epidemic, and the vitality went out of the tribe. Until the end of his days, however, Catlin believed that in witnessing the torture ceremony he was witnessing something out of the dark past of ancient Britain, because, taking the Mandan myth of their origins—the story of a great flood and a birchbark ark, or "Great Canoe"—at face value, he believed the Mandans to be the descendants of Prince Madoc of Wales, whom, Richard Hakluyt had said, sailed to America in the year 1170.

By the end of his journey up the Missouri in 1832, Catlin had painted over

George Catlin, *Buffalo Hunt (A Surround)*, (1844). Buffalo Bill Historical Center, Cody, Wyoming.

150 pictures, all the while being constantly on the move. Some of these he left with his friend and guide, Major Benjamin O'Fallon, in St. Louis, while others he displayed in exhibitions in 1833 in Cincinnati, Louisville, and Pittsburgh on his way back East.

In 1835 Catlin ventured out across the southern plains with a troop of dragoons commanded by Colonel Henry Leavenworth. This journey into the unknown lands of the hostile Comanches, in extreme southwestern Oklahoma, proved to be a near disaster. Cholera broke out among the troops, and Leavenworth died, leaving Colonel Henry M. Dodge in command, the dragoons reached their destination in the remote Wichita Mountains, where they were greeted by clouds of Comanches and Kiowa. By this time Catlin had fallen ill and taught his assistant, Joe Chadwick, to paint, so as to record these tribes in the event of his death. But Catlin survived and returned to Fort Gibson in the Arkansas Territory, where he lay ill for weeks. Meanwhile, many of the remaining dragoons daily succumbed to the epidemic, which seems not to have touched the Comanches, despite the carelessness of the soldiers.

When he recovered, Catlin mounted his favorite horse, Charlie, and alone rode over one thousand miles across the prairies of Arkansas, Oklahoma, and Missouri, to St. Louis.

In 1839 Catlin abruptly left a showing of his paintings in Buffalo to race out across the Great Lakes and the prairies of Minnesota to the secret Pipestone Quarry of the Sioux on the wavelike Coteau des Missouri, near the Minnesota-Dakota border. Other white men had seen this sacred ground before him, but Catlin painted it, and in bringing back samples of the pipe-making material which came to be called "Catlinite," received the glory of discovering the "long hidden" Indian quarry.

When he wasn't painting Indians in the West, Catlin painted Indians in the East. Most notably, he hurried to Fort Moultrie, near Charleston, South Carolina, to paint the noble Osceola, the captured chief of the warlike Seminoles of Florida. Then, while in Florida, he joined with John Howard Payne, author of the song, "Home Sweet Home," in protesting the treatment of the Indians of Georgia by the military authorities who were engaged in putting

George Catlin, *Dying Buffalo, Shot With an Arrow,* (1832–33). National Museum of American Art, Smithsonian Institution, Washington, D.C., Gift of Mrs. Joseph Harrison, Jr.

the civilized tribes on the "trail of tears" to Oklahoma. Payne was arrested by the soldiers, but Catlin made his way to Washington, where he confronted President Jackson directly, but to no avail.[10]

By 1840 Catlin could proudly write:

> I have visited forty-eight tribes, the greater part of which I found speaking different languages, and containing in all 400,000 souls. I have brought home safe, and in good order, 310 portraits in oil, all painted in their native dress, and in their own wigwams; and also 200 other paintings in oil containing views of their villages—their wigwams—their games and religious ceremonies—their dances—their ball plays—their buffalo hunting and other amusements (containing in all over 3000 full length figures); and the landscapes of the country they live in, as well as a very extensive and curious collection of their costumes and all their other manufactures, from the size of a wigwam down to the size of a quill or a rattle.[11]

All of these treasures Catlin attempted to sell to the United States Government; indeed, for the rest of his life Catlin pursued that goal, only to meet with frustration. Failing this, in 1839 Catlin put together the first traveling Wild West Show. It was called "Catlin's Indian Gallery," because its mainstay was the many pictures that Catlin had painted, but it also included numerous Indian artifacts, a Crow tepee, people—including Catlin's nephew—dressed up and painted as Indians doing the war dance, and lectures by George Catlin himself. Despairing of federal patronage, Catlin took his Indian Gallery to London where, on February 1, 1840 it opened at Egyptian Hall in Picadilly. There it was a great success. The exhibits were grouped into (1) Portraits, (2) Landscapes, (3) Sporting Scenes, (4) Manners, (5) Amusements and Customs (including four views of the O-Kee-Pa ceremony) and (6) Indian Curiosities and Manufactures.[12] At times Catlin was able to hire visiting groups of Ojibway or Ioway Indians to dance in his gallery, but if none was available, whites and relatives had to make do. That was enough. Queen Victoria and the Prince Consort came to visit the gallery, followed by most of the titled gentry and "scientific men" of England.

Though he was clearly interested in the Indians' welfare, from the very beginning Catlin was a showman. He held demonstrations of bow and arrow shooting at Lord's Cricket Ground. He invariably featured Indian dances, complete with drumbeat and war cries that sometimes frightened children. He discoursed on scalping and the use of the tomahawk, and he demonstrated the joys of the Catlinite peace pipe. He even traced down such common sayings as "a feather in your cap" to their Indian origin (in this case the slaying of an enemy). Perhaps most effective of all, Catlin played on moral and religious sentiment when he lectured, which, during the era of Methodism and abolitionism in England was particularly meaningful. In some cases he pointed out parallels between the Bible and Indian customs or sayings. And in virtually every lecture he expounded on three themes: (1) The rapaciousness of the American frontiersmen, (2) the evils of "poison-water" or whiskey, and (3) the amenability of the Indian to Christianity. One lecture, delivered by his English friend and assistant John Cullum, even ended with an Indian poem:

> He who is our mantle of comfort
> The Giver of life ancient on high
> He is the Creator of the heavens
> And the ever burning stars;
> God is mighty in the heavens
> And whirls the stars around the sky
> We call on him in his dwelling place
> That he may be our mighty leader
> For he alone is a sure defence
> He alone is a trusty shield
> He alone is our bush of refuge.[13]

During the five years that Catlin maintained his Indian Gallery in England it had its ups and downs financially. Ultimately he exhausted his audience in London and was forced to take the Gallery on a tour of the major cities of England, Ireland and Scotland. In 1845, by now slightly crazed with a show-business mentality, he seized upon the arrival of some Ioway Indians to take his Gallery to Paris, where he first occupied the Salle Valentino, and then, at the behest of the King Louis Phillippe, whom he entertained with his Ioways at St. Cloud, he moved to a large space in the Louvre. In Paris he painted numerous Indian portraits for the King, and a long series of works on the adventures of LaSalle in America. When the King and his family fled Paris during the Revolution of 1848, Catlin was left unpaid. In the meantime, his wife and only son had died of typhus.

By 1850 Catlin was back in London, at No. 6 Waterloo Place, Pall Mall, and by 1851 he was imprisoned for debt. The immediate cause for his imprisonment was the collapse of a Texas colonization scheme in which Catlin was the middleman. But from the time he first landed in England in 1840, Catlin

George Catlin, *Rainmaking Among the Mandans*, (1837–39). National Museum of American Art, Smithsonian Institution, Washington, D.C., Gift of Mrs. Joseph Harrison, Jr.

George Catlin, *O-Ke-Hee-Dee Held in Check by the Medicine Pipe*, from *O-Kee-Pa*, British Museum.

had been living on borrowed money, mortgaged paintings, and sales of pencil or wash drawn "souvenir albums," which were tracings or copies of the illustrations in his major book *Letters and Notes on the Manners, Customs and Conditions of the North American Indians* (1841), or from the expensive portfolio of lithograph prints which he had produced entitled *American Indian Portfolio*. One of his great patrons and "friends" during all this time was Sir Thomas Phillipps, one of the largest book collectors in England, to whom he sold numerous beautiful watercolor renditions of his Indian portraits, and at least one hand-drawn "souvenir album." A typical letter from Phillips to Catlin during the latter's period of greatest distress is as follows:

> My Dear Sir:
>
> I am extremely sorry to hear of yr bad success but I always thought it was a wild goose chase. I am in the greatest distress for money and your 100 pounds would be most serviceable if you wd repay it to me soon. But if I were to take it out in paintings how many would you do for me to discharge it?
>
> Believe me, yr. very truly
> T. Phillips

George Catlin, *Torture Scene in the Medicine Lodge,* National Museum of American Art, Smithsonian Institution, Gift of Mrs. Joseph Harrison, Jr.

To which Catlin replies, "I received your very friendly letter on my return from Plymouth. . . ."[14] Eventually Catlin's whole collection was purchased, not by the bargain-hunting Sir Thomas Phillipps, but by an American loco-motive manufacturer, Joseph Harrison, who shipped the paintings home, had them stored in his boiler factory, and forgot about them. Only upon his death were they discovered by his heirs and donated, ironically enough in view of all Catlin's earlier efforts, to the Smithsonian Institution.

During his most distressing years, 1851 and 1852, Catlin had continued to hope that the government would purchase his Gallery Collection. Earlier however, in 1846, he had abruptly refused to supply the illustrations for Henry Rowe Schoolcraft's six-volume compendium, *Historical and Statistical Information Respecting the History, Condition and Prospects of the Indian Tribes of the United States.* Angered at being thus rejected, Schoolcraft lobbied hard in Congress in 1852 for the rejection of Catlin's Collection. The bill to purchase it had failed by one vote. This left Catlin crushed, and indeed penniless, because he had borrowed heavily against the Collection.[15] Only Joseph Har-rison saved him from disaster. As it was he was reduced to dingy lodgings in the Hotel des Etrangers on the Rue Trouchet. The only news the family received of him in the year 1853 was via Anson Dart, who had sought him out in vain in Paris. According to Catlin's sister, Eliza Dart, all that her father-in-law could learn was "that he left Paris a year ago, in miserable health. . . ." She continued, "Pa thinks he is not living—he was in the last stages of consump-tion—discouraged and disheartened—poor dear brother George."[16]

Even as Anson Dart was searching Paris for him in 1853, Catlin was neither dead nor dying. Full of zest, he was heading for South America to hunt for gold.[17] As Catlin himself described it, in a later despondent state of mind, "I was easily led at that time, by the information got by a friend of mine, a reader in the Bibliothèque Imperiale of Paris, from an ancient Spanish work, relative to gold miners some 300 years since, in the Tumucamache (or Crystal) Mountains in the northern part of Brazil." Catlin added that Indians had massacred the miners, leaving the gold there all these years for the taking. He remembered "nuggets of gold of all sizes appeared in my dreams . . ."[18] He obtained a British passport and, traveling incognito, sailed for Havana and then to South America, heading for the Crystal Mountains of Brazil. Accom-panied by an Englishman named Smyth, who had a revolver pistol and rifle, he made his way to Guiana, and thence to the Amazon, and finally to the Tumucamache Mountains, which he found to be "a series of mountains of paleozoic rocks," and the trail to the lost mine blocked by an impenetrable wall of thorn bushes. At that point the gold fever deserted Catlin and he turned to painting the many Indian tribes he encountered in South America. In this he was accompanied only by a black servant, named Caesar Bolla, whose broad back often provided an easel for Catlin's paperboard sketches.

In all, Catlin made three voyages to South and Central America. The first of these, beginning with the futile search for a lost gold mine, was the most extensive. He and Caesar not only crossed over from Venezuela to Guiana and then northeastern Brazil, they also steamed up and down the Amazon, hunted ostriches on the Pampas, and crossed over the Andes to Peru. From Lima they steamed to Panama, San Diego and San Francisco, then took a sailing vessel to the mouth of the Columbia, Nootka Sound, Queen Charlotte's Island, to the Aleutians and Kamchatka in Siberia. They returned to visit the interior of the American Northwest, from Walla Walla to Fort Hall on the old Oregon Trail in Idaho. Along the way, Catlin made dozens of sketches of those Indians beyond the Rockies that he had not previously seen. His return trip took him from San Diego across the Southwest and down the Rio Grande to Matamoros, Mexico. From there he sailed to Sisal on the north coast of Yucatán, and painted the Mayas, while visiting the ruins at Uxmal. Upon his return to Paris, he went to Berlin "to see my old friend the Baron de Humboldt, then in his eighty-seventh year, who presented me to the king and queen at 'San Souci' [sic] and gave me a letter of introduction to Baron Bonpland in Santana in Uruguay, to which place I was prepared to start in a few days."[19]

It is arguable that, aside from a temporary lapse into gold fever begotten out of disappointment and despair, Catlin was always a romantic Humboldtean scientist.[20] By the time he had left on his first trip up the Missouri River, the great Humboldt had visited Jefferson in Washington, the savants in Philadelphia, and published his epic work *Voyage to the Equinoctual Regions*, as well as his treatise on New Spain. Catlin's exploring design, his search for completeness and yet exoticism in ethnographic description, is directly in the Hum-

Les Indiens a Paris, (1845). Lithograph advertising music composed in honor of Catlin's Indian Troupe. Archives of American Art, Smithsonian Institution, Washington, D.C.

George Catlin, *Comanche Warriors, with White Flag, Receiving the Dragoons*, (1934–35). National Museum of American Art, Smithsonian Institution, Washington, D.C., Gift of Mrs. Joseph Harrison, Jr.

George Catlin *Ostrich Chase, Buenos Aires*, (1856). National Gallery of Art, Washington, D.C.

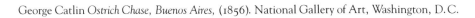

George Catlin, A Fight with Peccaries, Rio Trombutas. *The author and a Caribbe Indian coming to the rescue of Smyth, who is regular "treed," and his powder expended,* (1856–57). National Gallery of Art, Washington, D.C.

boldtean tradition. And when he tramped through jungles and over mountains in South America, through rain forests and over deserts in Western North America, Catlin was completing his own ethnographic version of Humboldt's *Cosmos.*

This he very nearly did, though as a result of his South American trips he became permanently deaf, but with a clanging, screeching sound that corresponded to his pulse forever reverberating in his head.[21] By 1857 the indomitable Catlin had made sketches of most of the Indians of South America, many of them replete with humor and anecdote as they chronicled his many adventures with Smyth (who was once treed by an army of wild peccaries) and Caesar Bolla (who was frightened out of his wits by leopards, crocodiles and an anteater). These sketches were done in pen and ink, then color was washed in. They became the basis for what Catlin was to call his "cartoon" collection.

From 1860 onward he settled in modest second-floor quarters near the Brussels railroad station and began to re-draw from memory all the paintings that he had lost when he lost his Indian Gallery. In addition, he published *Life*

Amongst the Indians: A Book for Youths (1857) and *Last Rambles Amongst the Indians of the Rocky Mountains and the Andes* (1867), in addition to *O-Kee-Pa*, published in 1867, at von Humboldt's instigation.

When his brother Francis visited him in 1868–9, he found Catlin stone deaf with pet mice as his only companions, but nonetheless happy, working furiously on his cartoon collection. He knew he was racing against time and he still had confidence that this new collection would find a permanent home at the Smithsonian in Washington; after all, it was the most complete visual ethnographic investigation ever undertaken! For Catlin, the "West of the Imagination" had broadened out to cover the whole western hemisphere, not just the American West of the Louisiana Purchase.

In 1870 Catlin returned to America, and his old friend Joseph Henry provided him with quarters in the Smithsonian, where he could complete his work. In fact, Henry gave him his own Rose Window quarters, and moved his office elsewhere. Beyond this, hopeful that Congress would finally purchase Catlin's collection, Henry ordered an exhibition of Catlin's work hung along the entire second-floor gallery in 1871, and in his *Annual Report* he urged Congress to purchase all 1200 of the works that the indomitable Catlin had re-created. It failed to do so, and by December of 1872 George Catlin was dead. He died at his sister's home in Jersey City, New Jersey, and was buried beside his wife and son in Brooklyn's Greenwood Cemetery, there to be forgotten until the rise of Indian anthropology in the twentieth century. Catlin's whole life, through bitter and sweet, had been one long adventure in discovery over the romantic horizon. His adventures in science and art had not been self-centered, though at times he was so desperate they seemed to be. Instead, he believed, like Humboldt, that he was serving the world. And most specifically he saw his work as a way of championing the American Indian. In his very first work he perhaps said it best:

> I have viewed man in the innocent simplicity of nature, in the full enjoyment of the luxuries which God has bestowed upon him . . . happier than kings and princes can be, with his pipe and little ones about him . . . I have seen him shrinking from civilized approach, which came with all its vices, like the dead of night upon him . . . seen him gaze and then retreat like the frightened deer . . . I have seen him shrinking from the soil and haunts of his boyhood, bursting the strongest ties which bound him to the earth and its pleasures. I have seen him set fire to his wigwam and smooth over the graves of his fathers . . . clap his hands in silence over his mouth, and take the last look over his fair hunting

ground, and turn his face in sadness to the setting sun. All this I have seen performed in nature's silent dignity . . . and I have seen as often the approach of the bustling, busy, talking, elated and exultant white man with the first clip of the ploughshare, making sacrilegious trespass on the bones of the Dead . . . I have seen the grand and irresistible march of civilization . . . this splendid juggernaut rolling on and beheld its sweeping desolation. And I have held converse with the happy thousands, living as yet beyond its influence, who had not been crushed, nor have yet dreamed of its approach. I have stood among these unsophisticated people and contemplated with deepest regret the certain approach of this overwhelming system which will inevitably march on and prosper; reluctant tears shall have watered every rod of this fair land; and from the towering cliffs of the Rocky Mountains, the luckless savage will turn back his swollen eyes on the illimitable hunting-grounds from which he has fled; and there contemplate, like Caius Marius on the ruins of Carthage, their splendid desolation . . . all this is certain . . . and if he could rise from his grave and speak or would speak from the life some half century from this, they would proclaim my prophecy true and fulfilled.[22]

For George Catlin, science and art and the human imagination that encompassed them both were ultimately moral.

CHAPTER 3

THE VOGUE FOR GALLERIES
AND COMPENDIA: STANLEY,
KANE AND EASTMAN

Catlin's moral message failed to stem the tide of settlers moving West, but his Indian Gallery inspired other painters. One of these was a fellow countryman, John Mix Stanley, the son of a tavernkeeper in Canandaigua, New York, a town near Buffalo.[1] Stanley was introduced to painting early in life. At age fourteen he was apprenticed to a coachmaker in Naples, New York, where his task was decorating the sides of coaches and painting occasional signs.

In 1834, when he was twenty, he moved to Detroit, where he studied art with James Bowman, one of the foremost art teachers of his day. Stanley soon became Bowman's partner, and they painted portraits on commission all the way from Baltimore to Chicago, traveling the highways and byways in search of business. On one of these trips, probably in 1837, to Baltimore, Stanley saw Catlin's Indian Gallery. It changed his life. He determined to create his own gallery of American aborigines. In 1842 he took on a business partner, Summer Dickinson, and headed for Fort Gibson, near present-day Muskogee, Oklahoma, with the intention of painting the civilized tribes that had been moved there from Georgia. He arrived in time to paint the Grand Council of Tribes assembled by the Cherokee chief, John Ross, in 1843. In the same year

John Mix Stanley, *Tehuacana Creek Indian Council.* Courtesy Susan and Pierce Butler.

he accompanied Indian Agent Pierce Butler to two other Indian conferences, one near present-day Waco, Texas, that involved the United States, the Texan government, and the Indian tribes on the Oklahoma-Texas border. There he painted the famous Delaware Indian, Jim Connors, who was slated to be the guide to the Lewis and Clark Expedition but declined, possibly losing the chance for immortality gained by Sacajawea. He also painted Ko-rak-koo-kiss, a Tonoccono warrior, who was attempting to steal horses from Fort Ben Milam. According to Stanley, Ko-rak-koo-kiss, caught in the act, was shot twice and received two sabre wounds on his arms, but miraculously escaped with his life.[2]

Stanley's painting reveals that at this stage of his career he was still a novice. Both horse and Indian look as if they were flying through the air pasted on a backdrop of the Texas landscape, while the horse is a typical carousel horse, and his Indian rider is several sizes too big for him. The best one can say for this work is that it is a spirited painting. Stanley went on to another conference with the Comanches along the Red River near present-day Lawton, Oklahoma, making him the first artist after Catlin to paint that fierce tribe.

In 1846 the important phase of Stanley's career began. He became the artist on Colonel Stephen Watts Kearny's Army of the West as it conquered New Mexico and marched across the Southwest to San Diego. On this epic march, Stanley painted landscape scenes in stunningly beautiful fashion, though on one notable occasion—at the junction of the Gila and Colorado Rivers—he embellished the scene by including giant cacti and numerous other specimens of exotic vegetation that were characteristic of the vast Southwest, all in the one picture. He topped the colorful extravaganza off with a romantic view of a noble stag (not native to the country) come down to the water to drink from its limpid pool. Clearly Stanley's role on the Kearny expedition was that of scientific illustrator, but in pursuing what he thought of as science, Stanley created not a real but a highly fanciful and romantic "typical" landscape. It was the sort of thing that could have been done in Peale's Museum, but which did not enhance the reputation of an on-the-spot viewpainter.

But Stanley persisted in his work. He traveled up the West Coast to the Oregon Country. There he painted perhaps his best work, a view of Oregon City. Then he ventured into the interior to visit the missions and fur trade outposts, just as an Indian war erupted. Stanley narrowly escaped with his life as he was about to enter Wailaptu on November 29, 1847, when a Cayuse Indian warned him that Marcus Whitman, Narcissa Whitman and all the inhabitants of the Mission were in the process of being massacred. Gathering up a band of survivors streaming out of the mission in panic, Stanley headed for Walla Walla, and ultimately Fort Vancouver. From there he sailed to Hawaii and then to Boston and New York. In November of 1850 he exhibited 135 paintings at a New York showing, which he called "Stanley's North American Indian Gallery."

Like Catlin, Stanley spent the rest of his life trying to persuade the United States Government to purchase his Gallery. He even loaned the majority of his works to the Smithsonian, where they were hung in a specially constructed wing. On the night of January 24, 1865, a fire destroyed the wing and with it much of Stanley's life work. A sizeable number of the remainder of Stanley's paintings was destroyed in two subsequent fires, one at P. T. Barnum's Museum, and another at Stanley's studio in Buffalo. Thus, in the end, Stanley was much less fortunate than the long-suffering Catlin, most of whose work at least survived. By a curious coincidence, both men died in 1872.

Judging from the few works of Stanley's that have survived, one would have to say that his vision of the West was decidedly uneven. His work on government expeditions, which was extensive, consisted of romanticized viewpaintings. Some of these, such as *Assiniboin Hunting Buffalo,* he worked up from field sketches into elaborate oil paintings. Much of his other work was done strictly in his studio at Buffalo, such as *Gambling For the Buck,* and *Young Chief Uncas.* Both pictures are colorful but highly posed works. The latter, for example, pictures an uncomfortable young boy dressed in full war-bonnet and other regalia (not plausible) posing as young Uncas, Cooper's Last Mohican.

The vogue for Indian galleries sparked by Catlin did not confine itself to Americans. Paul Kane, born in Ireland and raised in York (early Toronto), Ontario studied with Thomas Drury, Canada's most prominent art teacher.[3] Then he, too, drifted south to Detroit and worked with James Bowman. Having acquired a proficiency at painting portraits, Kane steamed down the Mississippi to New Orleans and then to Mobile, Alabama, where he made enough money to finance study in Europe. He sailed out of New Orleans to Marseilles, then to Genoa, and finally to Rome, where he copied the Old Masters, along with all of the other students. By 1841 he was in London and there saw Catlin's Gallery. He became friends with Catlin and, struck by his initial success, headed back to North America to create his own Canadian version of Catlin's Indian Gallery. This required two sketching treks west across Canada under the auspices of the Hudson's Bay Company, whose posts he painted along the way. By 1846 he was at Fort Vancouver, and in 1847, the year of the Cayuse Indian uprising and Stanley's visit to the same country, Kane had just preceded the American and was making his way back to the east.

Unlike Catlin and Stanley, Kane did not meet with total failure to sell his collection, perhaps because he did not expect as much from his government. In 1848 he exhibited his Western paintings in Toronto in a show entitled "Kane's Indian Gallery." He also, like Catlin, wrote a book about his adventures, *Wanderings of an Artist amongst the Indians of North America from Canada to Vancouver's Island and Oregon Through the Hudson's Bay Company's Territory and Back Again* (1859). Kane's Gallery collection was purchased by one George W. Allan, and eventually ended up in the Royal Ontario Museum. His studio collection, which consisted of a large number of spectacular works, was eventually purchased by H. J. Lutcher Stark and is one of the jewels of the Stark Museum in Orange, Texas.

Kane's view of the West was much closer to that of Catlin. He went to great pains to portray authentically the Indians of the Pacific Northwest and their exotic artifacts. He painted their huge carved war canoes, their templelike dwelling places, and, most of all, their hideous transformation masks. Though

John Mix Stanley, *Gambling for the Buck*, (1867). Stark Museum of Art, Orange, Texas.

John Mix Stanley, *Chain of Spires Along the Gila River*, (1855). Phoenix Art Museum.

Paul Kane, *Medicine Mask Dance,* Courtesy of the Royal Ontario Museum, Toronto.

Paul Kane, *Mount St. Helens with Smoke Cone.* Stark Museum of Art, Orange, Texas.

his portraiture left something to be desired, Kane's ethnology was excellent. His landscapes were also striking, especially his views of Hudson's Bay posts like Norway House, and his views of Mount St. Helens in eruption in 1847. His daylight scene showed Mount St. Helens spewing a mushroom cloud, while in his night scene it resembled a Fourth of July fireworks fountain going full blast. One would have to term Paul Kane's work definitely romantic, if not exotic. Moreover, it seems clear that in his western work, except for an ersatz picture of Indians chasing a buffalo, which he based on an Italian print showing two youths chasing a bull, Kane really forgot or abandoned most of his European training.[4] His paintings have a rough authenticity about them.

From a consideration of the "Indian Gallery" painters, Catlin, Stanley, and Kane, it is apparent that ethnology and scientific illustration far outweighed aesthetic considerations, though clearly aesthetics were not ignored. These explorer artists, often the first to venture into dangerous and unknown territory, were concerned with conveying impressions of what they saw. Theirs was an art of information. It was hardly objective nor was it solely ethnographic annotation. Indeed, so amazed by what they saw were these artists that they became instant romantics. So exotic were the sights that they had seen that only a "gallery" or show featuring their entire work, and in Stanley's

Captain Seth Eastman, *Indians Playing Ball.* Stark Museum of Art, Orange, Texas.

case a moving panorama, would do these sights justice. For them art was the-atre. But like Peale's Museum, it was a theatre of scientific information in which "truth was stranger than fiction." And among the three Indian Gallery artists, only Catlin had a mission to save the vanishing American. All three seemed to take his disappearance for granted with Stanley actually participat-ing in the process of "civilizing" the West in the year of Manifest Destiny.

If one considers the Indian Gallery painters together with the work of Cap-tain Seth Eastman, a drawing teacher at West Point who subsequently began serious study of the Indians of the Mississippi Valley while serving at Fort Snelling in Minnesota, the concept of early Western art as an "art of infor-mation" becomes all the more apparent.[5] Eastman and his wife, Mary, made a serious study of Indian customs, religion and folklore. Mrs. Eastman's *Dakota: Life and Legends of the Sioux* formed the basis of Longfellow's famous poem *Hiawatha*. Captain Eastman was selected as the principal illustrator for Henry Rowe Schoolcraft's definitive study of the Indian, a position rejected by Catlin. As such, Eastman did not paint vivid scenes of war, massacres, or even buffalo hunts. Indeed, he eschewed most of the dramatic conventions established by Catlin and somewhat uniquely concentrated on the everyday life of the North American aborigines. He was the sociologist of Indian life at his best in works like *Indians Playing Ball in Winter,* or in pictures of Indian women performing daily tasks. Indeed, the life of the Indian family was one focus of his work, while depicting Indian legends was another. In so doing Captain Eastman created a panorama of Indian life in the Mississippi Valley that was often visually colorful, but artistically sentimental, rather than high romanticism. The "message" in his works was not that of the "vanishing Indian," but rather that of the virtually domesticated Indian with whom the white man could live side by side, if only through conscientious study there was mutual understand-ing. His work and that of Schoolcraft, who really disliked the un-Christian red man, glossed over the "juggernaut" qualities in the march of white civili-zation by portraying the Indian as picturesque curiosities, or, in some cases, just like "the folks next door."

But some years before the heydey of the Indian Galleries and Schoolcraft's massive pseudo-scientific compendium with its sentimental message, there would be other artists who also visited the West and came away with spectacular visions of what they saw. One of these was a young Swiss artist, who accom-panied a German prince. The other was a fastidious Baltimorean who went to the mountains with a Scottish Lord and a caravan of hard-bitten mountain men.

CHAPTER 4

EUROPEAN SCIENCE
AND THE NOBLE SAVAGE

*On the Fourth of July, 1852, the German Prince Alexander Phi-*lipp Maximilian of Wied Neuwied, accompanied by his hunter, David Drei-doppel and the Swiss viewpainter Karl Bodmer, stepped ashore at the port of Boston in the United States of America.[1] They found themselves in a relatively populous place in the midst of a celebration of the national Independence Day. Strains of an unfamiliar tune, "Yankee Doodle," filled the air, though not unpleasantly. The Prince remarked with some surprise that the "motley assemblage" of Americans produced "no impropriety of conduct or unseemly noise." In fact, as he traveled incognito down the East Coast, the Prince found America entirely too civilized. Like most Europeans, he was looking for a savage America, the vast dark and bloody ground of forests and savannahs inhabited by Daniel Boone and Leatherstocking, who were popular in Europe. In Philadelphia, in fact, he did not even see an Indian in Peale's Museum as had George Catlin.

Then, on a tour of bookstores and printing establishments, the Prince became even more exasperated. Only the former Superintendent of Indian Affairs, Thomas L. McKenney. was engaged in portraying the red man for posterity.

Karl Bodmer, *Cave-In-Rock View on the Ohio.* Joslyn Art Museum, The InterNorth Art Foundation, Omaha.

Karl Bodmer, *View of Mauch Chunk, Pennsylvania with Railroad,* (August–September 1832). Joslyn Art Museum, The InterNorth Art Foundation, Omaha.

Not one of the famous Philadelphia Naturalist Circle even appeared to be studying these mysterious first inhabitants of the North American forests. It was a far cry from his earlier experiences in Brazil where everyone seemed fascinated by the natives and the jungles. But this being the case, Prince Maximilian tarried as briefly as possible on the Eastern Seaboard and instead headed west across Pennsylvania to investigate what the French writer, Chateaubriand, had called "the mysteries of the Ohio."

The Prince was a serious explorer and student of the unknown. His role model was the great Prussian explorer and polymath, Alexander von Humboldt, who had explored the Amazon and the Orinoco, and who had climbed the highest mountain in the world, Chimborazo, and lived to write about it in classic treatises like *Voyage to the Equinoctual Regions of the New World* and *Vues des Cordillieres.* Maximilian had met Humboldt in Paris while serving with the Prussian Army that had helped to defeat Napoleon. It was Humboldt who encouraged him to undertake his first exploring expedition to Brazil. He wasn't difficult to persuade because, like Humboldt, he had studied with Johann Frederick Blumenbach at Gottingen, and Blumenbach, with his interest in all aspects of nature, instilled in his students a sense of the romance of exploration and discovery in the remote, as yet unknown portions of the globe. He was especially interested in the types and varieties of mankind whom he presumed had spread over the globe from the Garden of Eden. His student, Prince Maximilian, had just now undertaken the task of investigating the North American Indian. He intended to make a close study of this savage species and to document his appearance and his environment as precisely as possible. To that end, he had brought along twenty-three-year-old Karl Bodmer, whom his publisher, Jacob Holscher, had recommended.

Bodmer was inexperienced in drawing animals and the human figure. At least his work up to the date Maximilian employed him gave no evidence that he had done much more than sketch postcardlike scenes of castles along the Rhine and Moselle Valleys that were published in a book of aquatints made by his brother Rudolph. Yet Karl Bodmer had studied long and hard with his uncle, Jacob Meier, an accomplished Zurich engraver, and he had acquired incredible skill at rendering animals, the human figure, landscape, natural history specimens, and anything else the Prince could think of for him to do. Along with America itself, Bodmer was one of the surprises of the Prince's 1832 expedition. Bodmer's incredibly beautiful watercolors rendered on the journey across Pennsylvania and the Ohio country, down the Mississippi and far up the Missouri constitute the best of all the views of the early American frontier. As an artist he far surpassed the French writer Alexis de Tocqueville, who was tramping about America at approximately the same time.

Bodmer is best known for his incredibly accurate and haunting pictures of the Indians who lived along the Missouri River. But before turning to a discussion of this aspect of his work, it is important to note that Bodmer also painted surprisingly important frontier scenes from the time he left former King of Spain, Joseph Bonaparte's sumptuous villa in Bordentown to the time he reached St. Louis. Like the Prince, he expected to tramp through a wilderness or float down the Ohio past the very epitome of desolation. Instead, he saw and painted Pittsburgh, already an industrial city in the backcountry of America. He rendered the large coal tipple at Mauch Chunk, Pennsylvania, as a kind of machine in the garden of America. He painted George Rapp's utopian colony and David Dale Owen's elaborate utopia at New Harmony, Indiana, where the Prince spent the winter. He sketched the tangled forests of the Wabash River, but he also painted the dog-run cabins of farms that were spread out across the fertile prairies of Indiana and Illinois, reaching out from county seats with pretentious courthouses and clusters of small cabins just waiting for the population to catch up, as the tide of settlers indicated it surely would.

And on the Ohio and the mighty Mississippi, Bodmer was dazzled by the steamboat culture that was to so fascinate Mark Twain a whole generation later. He painted, and even drew crude plans of steamboats with names like *The Napoleon*, *The Delphine*, the *Homer* and the *Lionesse*. In the case of the latter, which he saw loaded with some 1,500 bales of cotton, he was persuaded, perhaps by some gents whom he met while painting the raw river town of New Mexico, Missouri, that the heavily freighted vessel could carry some 1,200 more 400-pound bales. On a winter trip downriver to New Orleans, Bodmer made some of his best paintings of the river culture in the heartland of the American frontier, from the steamboats (which he could not see in Europe) to the keelboats, the rafts, and even the top-hatted gamblers who inhabited the river towns. Because his other work was so spectacular, this aspect of Bodmer's America is often overlooked, but all this activity that he observed must have had a profound effect on him. Instead of a dark and savage wilderness, he recorded a rapidly growing frontier civilization. Perhaps this is the reason he never returned to paint America. Like Catlin, he knew that the "juggernaut" of civilization was rapidly passing over it; that in a few years the forests of Barbizon outside of Paris, where he chose to live out his life, would present more unspoiled wilderness than rapidly developing America. Certainly

Karl Bodmer, *View of the Stone Walls,* (August 1833). Joslyn Art Museum, The InterNorth Art Foundation, Omaha.

Karl Bodmer, *Mih-Tutta-Hang-Kusch, Mandan Village,* (Winter 1833–34). Joslyn Art Museum, The InterNorth Art Foundation, Omaha.

Karl Bodmer, *First Chain of the Rocky Mountains Above Fort McKenzie,* (September 1833). Joslyn Art Museum, The InterNorth Art Foundation, Omaha.

nothing he saw once he and the Prince reached bustling St. Louis would change this impression. But he had not yet ventured up the long reach of the Missouri into the exotic country of the Indians who called themselves "people of the first man."

At St. Louis, Bodmer and the Prince were befriended by territorial Governor William Clark, who had led the famous American expedition across the continent at the beginning of the century. They were also befriended by Indian Agent Benjamin O'Fallon, who showed them a large collection of George Catlin's paintings of the Indians upriver. Bodmer's work was directed to the same anthropological end, but his would be very different from Catlin's paintings. The young Swiss, trained as an engraver, brought a great deal more precision and draughtsmanship to his work, especially since he knew that the Prince intended to reproduce his watercolors in an aquatint atlas. But because his technique differed markedly from that of Catlin, this did not mean that Bodmer approached his subject without emotion and artistic intuition. Like

Prince Maximilian (and for that matter Catlin) he saw the Indians as exotic creatures who had stepped out of the dawn of time and were somehow living in grand and lordly dignity just in advance of the tide of frontier civilization. He could not know it, but many of the Indians he was to paint in 1833–4 would perish hideously in a smallpox epidemic brought by the white river traders in 1837. The lordly, beautiful people and cultures that he was to observe and paint on his trip upriver with the Prince would never be the same again. Bodmer could not know this for sure, but he must have sensed it, for he poured all his talents and emotions into precise but incredibly mysterious and romantic renditions of the red men and women he encountered along the Missouri. His was indeed an observation along a romantic horizon. It should be difficult for anyone with a sensitivity to artistic nuance to miss the powerful romantic emotions that lie behind Bodmer's haunting portraits of individual Indians, his capturing of wild and savage ceremonies and his stunning renditions of the upper Missouri landscape.

On April 10, 1833, Bodmer, the Prince and Dreidoppel set out upriver aboard the American Fur Company steamer *Yellowstone*. When they departed from St. Louis in the face of a gorgeous blood-red sunset it seemed like they had signed on for a pleasure cruise. But the blood-red sunset heralded a storm that buffeted their steamboat for days, caught them up repeatedly on river snags, and finally knocked over one of the two smokestacks. Still they steamed on upriver. At Bellevue Post, near present-day Omaha, Bodmer painted his first two plains Indians in situ: Omahas, a father and son. They also witnessed, by the light of the moon, their first Indian dance performed by what the Prince called "a grotesque band . . . uttering their wild cry, together with the loud call of the night raven. . . ." It reminded the Prince at last of savage Brazil.

Farther upriver, at Sioux Agency, they met the proud Dakotas, and Bodmer painted one of his most famous portraits, of Wahktageli, "The Big Soldier." The Prince was amazed that this warrior posed patiently all day for Bodmer. He was even more amazed when The Big Soldier gave him his entire costume. At Fort Pierre they saw even greater numbers of the mighty Sioux or Dakota, and then farther upriver at Fort Clark they met their enemies, the Mandans, the Hidatsa and their relatives the Crow, who had journeyed far to the east to support their kin against encroachment by the Dakota. Bodmer, already dazzled by the Dakota, then concluded that the Crow surpassed them all in dignity and beauty of form.

Eventually, Bodmer and the Prince reached the American Fur Company's main headquarters at Fort Union far up the Missouri at its junction with the

Yellowstone. This was as far upriver as Catlin had traveled. But Maximilian wished to push on, so they boarded a keelboat equipped with a sail and left Fort Union on July 4, 1833. They had been in America exactly one year, and now they were about to experience a West that transcended anything their imaginations could conjure up. They penetrated the badlands, or Mauvais Terres, beyond the great bend of the Missouri, where strange, castlelike rock formations looked down upon them and the scale of the vast landscape dwarfed anything they had known in Europe. Bodmer painted these panoramic views whenever he could, and his skill in this genre far surpassed that of Catlin. One only has to compare their respective views of Fort Union to determine this. Where Catlin's landscapes were strange, impressionistic diagrams, Bodmer, in a very professional manner, made exquisite use of line, color and light. His landscapes, such as his view of *The White Castles* above the Missouri, the *The Stone Walls* or *The Great Gate* which he made on August 6, 1833, *The View from the Hills above Fort Mackenzie,* painted in stages because of fears of Indian attacks, and his wintery scene, *View of the Mandan Village Mih-Tutta-Hang-Kusch near Fort Clark,* done in 46 degrees below zero weather, are all masterpieces of landscape art. The latter, especially with its sense of the dirty gray leaden sky, the snow-covered terrain, and the line of Indian women and starving dogs struggling wearily across the ice-covered river, gave a vivid sense of the Missouri as it wound through the bleak Dakota prairies. Such scenes add a whole new dimension to our imagination of the West. But then so too, did Bodmer's Indian portraits.

When the Prince's party, struggling up the Missouri River, reached Fort McKenzie near the mouth of the Marias River, they found themselves not only nearly 3,000 miles up the world's longest river, but also in the country of the fierce Blackfoot Indians. They were in the very heart of that savage America that the Prince expected to study. They even became eyewitnesses to a bloody Indian battle. On the morning of August 28, 1833, they looked out from the fort and saw a horde of Assiniboin warriors attacking the twenty or so Blackfoot lodges that surrounded the fort. The attackers slashed open the tepees and killed men, women and children alike while the air was filled with screams and wild cries. Soon Blackfoot reinforcements arrived and drove the attackers off. The Prince even helped, as he fired his rifle from the parapet of the fort. The wounded and dying were dragged inside the enclosure and attended to while the first assault gradually died down. The skirmish between the two tribes lasted for a week, however, and the country around the fort was never safe, which made Bodmer's landscape paintings an all the more daring enter-

Karl Bodmer, *Pioch-Kiaiu, Piegan Blackfeet Man (Distant Bear),* (August 1833). Joslyn Art Museum, The InterNorth Art Foundation, Omaha.

Karl Bodmer, *Iron Shirt, Mehkskehme-Sukahs, Piegan Blackfeet Chief,* (August 1833). Joslyn Art Museum, The InterNorth Art Foundation, Omaha.

Karl Bodmer, *Wahktagheli (Gallant Warrior), Yankton Sioux Chief,* (May 1833). Joslyn Art Museum, The InterNorth Art Foundation, Omaha.

Karl Bodmer, *Mato-Tope, (Four Bears), Chief of the Mandans (Formal Dress),* (April 1834). Joslyn Art Museum, The InterNorth Art Foundation, Omaha.

Karl Bodmer, *Pehriska-Ruhpa, (Two Ravens), Hidatsa Man,* (March 1834). Joslyn Art Museum, The InterNorth Art Foundation, Omaha.

Karl Bodmer, *Fort McKenzie, August 28th, 1833.* Joslyn Art Museum, The InterNorth Art Foundation, Omaha.

prise. In a sumptuous *Atlas* of maps and aquatint engravings too, Bodmer executed a stirring rendition of the Assiniboin attack. It was the only eyewitness painting of an Indian battle. But this work had to be composed from memory and sketches made from behind the safety of the fort's walls because in the finished picture the point of view is in the midst of the battle, a place where Bodmer most definitely did not position himself.

After the battle, a number of Blackfeet attributed their survival to Bodmer's having painted their likenesses in what could be considered some of his most striking work. Though he was painting ethnological types, Bodmer also tried to capture the essence of his subjects as human beings. He caught Distant Bear, a Piegan Medicine man or shaman, as the seer, his eyes gazing off into an infinity that others could never see. Iron Shirt, a war chief, on the other hand, he painted staring straight out at the viewer through fierce red-rimmed eyes set in a blackened face. In each portrait Bodmer's sense of color was striking, and this made his exact rendering of the detail of the Indian costumes all the more dramatic. He knew he was painting a kind of hieroglyphic language when he painted the Indian dress, so he included everything exactly, such as the single bear claw, the white weasel, and the colored feathers hanging from Iron Shirt's matted hair, as well as his otter-collared buckskin hunting shirt with porcupine quill designs and clam shell buttons. On one tall, mysterious, pipe-smoking Piegan warrior the images Bodmer rendered on his white tanned elk hide robe distinguished the warrior as the tribe's master horse thief. In the *Atlas,* Bodmer cleverly placed him near a hard-riding Sioux warrior as if to say, "I'll get that horse sooner or later."

As autumn set in, the Prince finished his detailed researches of the Blackfeet and the exploring party set off downstream to winter at Fort Clark among the Mandans. Fort Clark was a cold, ramshackle post where one could easily freeze to death on the Dakota prairies, but the Prince wanted to test the current theory mentioned earlier that the Mandans were really Welsh descendants of Prince Madoc who had reputedly sailed west over the sea to America in 1170. This legend had persisted among European scholars for about a century, since the French explorers, the Vérèndryes, first laid eyes on the Mandans in 1738 and returned claiming to have seen blond, blue-eyed Indians. Even after he lived among them for part of a summer, George Catlin believed this legend, and it nearly destroyed the credibility of everything else he wrote about the Indians.

So the Prince, Dreidoppel and Bodmer spent the severe winter of 1833–4 in a drafty, freezing, hastily built cabin at Fort Clark on a peninsula sticking out into the Missouri River. The fort was between the Mandan and Hidatsa summer villages, but the Indians moved for the winter into special dirt mound huts built among the trees in the ravines and bottom lands away from the windswept plains. In seeking such refuge in ravines and bottom lands, they imitated the buffalo, their life source.

Day after day, despite the cold which froze the Prince's ink and Bodmer's paints, the two men studied the exotic river tribes. Bodmer painted Mato-Tope, chief of the Mandans, who had also posed for Catlin, in both his stripped-down war costume and his ceremonial finery. He painted the giant, seven-foot tall Mandan warrior, Flying Eagle in all his elaborate finery, including his bear claw necklace, elaborate leggings, and wolf tail moccasins, which signified that he had killed an enemy in battle. But perhaps Bodmer's best portrait was that of the Hidatsa Dog Dancer, Perishka Ruhpa. This chief appeared in mid-dance, gorgeously plumed in a fanlike headdress, clutching a bow and arrow in one hand and a rattle in the other. Some have called it the greatest Indian portrait ever made.

Bodmer's first rendering of this dancing military leader did not fully include his lower limbs, but only the suggestion of his wild dance. It was his most effective version of Perishka Ruhpa because it left the rhythm of the dance to the viewer's imagination. In a later crayon version of the picture, Bodmer filled in the whole portrait and did so as well in the aquatint *Atlas*. Both of the latter pictures, being too literal, underscore the power of the mind's eye and the imagination. Watercolor, just then coming into vogue as the artistic medium of the Romantic Age, allowed for white spaces and unfinished sketches as part of the technique. Bodmer often made full use of watercolor in just this way to leave the imagination full play while yet appearing to get every detail of an Indian costume into his pictures. If one only looks at the *Atlas*, one misses this subtle Kantean touch and sees only the finished literal scene rounded out in a Paris studio. Often the lightness, the mystery and the imagination are gone, however beautiful the aquatints.

As for mystery, Bodmer missed the sacred O-Kee-Pa ceremony that Catlin had witnessed, but he did execute incredible scenes of the Buffalo Dance of the Mandans and the Scalp Dance of the Minnetarees or Hidatsa. In the former, he grouped the wildly dancing Buffalo-headed warriors in a classical pyramidal composition to suggest the sacredness of the dance. But despite the classical composition, the wild scene represents the very epitome of the savage America he and the Prince had come to see. As one looks at the gyrating dancers, one can almost hear the drums, the howls, the shrieks and the men-

Karl Bodmer, *Piegan Black-feet Man*, (1833). Joslyn Art Museum, The Inter-North Art Foundation, Omaha.

acing chants as the warriors attempt to "dance back the buffalo." And in the case of the Minnetaree Scalp Dance, depicting the women holding the scalps on the end of long bending rods that take the place of penises, one notes that for fallen enemies there is no dignity in death in the land of savagery. There is solemnity and celebration, but without one's scalp there is no dignity for the deceased. All in all, Bodmer and Maximilian had penetrated to the very heart of Mandan and plains Indian life. Thanks largely to the wide distribution of Catlin's, as well as Bodmer's pictures of plains Indians through the medium of lithographs and aquatints, and pirated books featuring them, the public's view of the American Indian became almost invariably that of the mounted plains Indian. They began a stereotype that was of course reinforced many times over by later painters, especially those who illustrated the Custer battle. But from the beginning, after the work of Catlin and Bodmer, the eastern woodlands Indian without the horse—the kind that had stalked Daniel Boone— became iconographically obscured.

By the time spring came to the northern plains and Fort Clark, Bodmer, and particularly the Prince, had had enough of the land of savagery. The Indians were not the reason for their departure, but the crude habits of the white traders truly did them in. The Prince wrote on March 11, 1834, just before they left to head downriver and back to civilization,

We are tired of life in this dirty fort to the highest degree. Our daily routine is conducted in such a filthy manner that it nauseates one. Since our Negro cook Alfred suffers from a severe rheumatic disease, we now have a filthy attendant and cook named Boileau . . . who sets down among us and handles the cups and plates with his disgusting fists after cleaning his nose according to the manner of our peasants. This is also the manner of the clerk of the fort, Kipp, who, along with his wife and child scatters these items about and then cleans his fingers on the first object that comes to hand. The little boy has a gap in his trousers, both in front and in back, so that he may relieve himself quickly and without formality on the floor of the room, which happens frequently during meals.[2]

None of this appeared in Bodmer's Paris Exhibition of his work in 1836, the first large exhibition of paintings of the American Indian ever shown in Continental Europe. Nor did the fur traders' crudeness or the crudeness of frontier life of any kind appear in the 82 aquatint illustrations in the *Atlas* to Maximilian's account of his journey. Rather, Bodmer and the Prince presented European and American viewers with stunningly beautiful renditions of America's noble savages.

Karl Bodmer, *Bison Dance of the Mandan Indians.* Joslyn Art Museum, The InterNorth Art Foundation, Omaha.

CHAPTER   **5**

THE MOUNTAIN MAN:
A FAIR LIKENESS

"There is in truth . . . a great deal of humbug about Mr. George Catlin," wrote Alfred Jacob Miller to his brother from London in February of 1842.[1] Miller had been to see Catlin's Indian Gallery and had read his way through Catlin's *Letters and Notes . . . On the North American Indians.* As a consequence he added, "He has published a book containing extraordinary stories and luckily for him there are but few persons who travelled over the same ground." Who was this Miller and who was he to question the heroic labors and veracity of George Catlin?

Alfred Jacob Miller was the only man to paint the mountain men or fur trappers from the life, deep in the heart of the Rocky Mountains. Originally from Baltimore, from whence he sailed to Europe where he studied to be an artist at the Ecole des Beaux-Arts, Miller, in 1837 had just opened a studio at 123 Chartres Street in New Orleans, when a dignified, ramrod-straight man accompanied by what looked like an Indian in buckskins, strode into his salon.[2] This was Captain William Drummond Stewart of Murthley Castle in Perthshire, Scotland, and with him was Antoine Clement, a first-class mountain man. Captain Stewart, a decorated veteran of Waterloo, had come to America in 1833 because of two unfortunate incidents; he had quarreled bitterly with his older brother John, Lord of Grandtully and Murthley Castle, and he had been forced to marry a servant girl whose ankles he had admired just before impregnating her. It is not clear whether there was any connection between the marriage and Sir William's quarrel with his brother. At any rate, in 1833 Stewart had first come to America and headed for the Far West to hunt with the mountain men, those "banditti of the Rockies," whom Washington Irving described so well. While in St. Louis Stewart had urged Prince Maximilian and Karl Bodmer to accompany his caravan across the plains and into real Indian country deep in the mountains. The Prince had been cautious, and Stewart had little time for science. It would interfere with his hunting, the wild chase over the prairies after buffalo that he so loved. So it was just as well that they went their separate ways. But Stewart noted Bodmer's presence. Some day he, too, would take along an artist to record *his* deeds and to illustrate the novels about Rocky Mountain life that he intended to write.

The time had come in 1837. Stewart's brother John lay ill in Paris, and if he died Stewart would be required to return to Murthley Castle permanently. There would be no more annual hunts in the Mountains of the Wind with the likes of his friends, the legendary trappers, Jim Bridger, Black Harris, and Tom "Broken Hand" Fitzpatrick. Therefore, after looking over Miller's paintings carefully, Stewart hired him to record what might well be his last fling in the Rockies.

Miller's mission, therefore, had nothing to do with science or ethnography. It was his romantic style, full of dry scumbled mist like W. M. C. Turner and the dashing, exotic figures of Eugene Delacroix's paintings that Stewart admired. If the Comte de Mornay could take Delacroix into the deserts of Algeria, he, Sir William Drummond Stewart, could take Miller into the Rockies. Miller, in turn, would produce visions of the West and its noble savages in the current European high romantic style combining Delacroix's dash and dynamism with Turner's glowing misty images. His role was to be an historian—a storyteller in pictures—a role Miller more than fulfilled, though not without grumbling.

In fact, Miller produced such exciting and authentic views of the wild, free life of the mountain men and Indians that even today, 150 years later, his paintings inspire contemporary mountain man rendezvous re-creations all over the West, and even in Europe. Dusting off cherished black powder replicas of Hawkin rifles and dressed in buckskin costumes taken directly from Miller's paintings, rendezvous groups today celebrate the Rocky Mountain trapper's

Alfred Jacob Miller, *Louis—Rocky Mountain Trapper.* Courtesy of the Buffalo Bill Historical Center, Cody, Wyoming.

rituals on the same ground that the events took place more than a century ago. Contemporary rendezvous are inspired by published accounts of the mountain men themselves, by the hundreds of volumes written by historians of the West, but most of all by Miller's unforgettable images. They helped to create, in the fur trapper, the Far West's first authentic hero, and to visualize in detail the very beginnings of the Anglo myth of the West. Miller portrayed the first chapter of "the tale of our tribe."

It was not a vision of war and the clash of cultures. Rather, Miller portrayed the life of the mountain man and Indian as a kind of immortal pastoral adventure. To be sure, there was danger, as Sioux warriors threatened to attack their train as it crossed the plains along the Platte River. And tales told around campfires at sunrise and sunset related the hardships and dangers inherent in the trappers' life: the bone-chilling cold that crept over one while planting traps in Rocky Mountain streams in the dawn's early light, the loneliness, the dangers from Indians—Pawnee, Crow, and Blackfeet. Stewart, himself, had tales of danger to tell, and Miller faithfully recorded them. In one scene he substituted Stewart for another mountain man in their dashing escape from the fierce Blackfeet. In another he painted Stewart and Antoine confronted by what looked like all the Crow Indians in creation, with Stewart heroically unfazed.

Alfred Jacob Miller, *Setting Traps for Beaver*, (1837). Joslyn Art Museum, The InterNorth Art Foundation, Omaha.

Upon reaching the Sweetwater at the head of the Platte, they suddenly came upon what could have been a mirage. It was actually Fort Laramie, a huge stockaded trading post on what had become the Oregon Trail. Miller was the only artist ever to paint it, which he did over and over again in dramatic views of its exterior standing like a bastion on a plain covered with Indian tepees, and views of its interior crowded with life. Like nearly everything else Miller painted that summer of 1837, it was the best view of a fur trade fort ever executed. But then the cavalcade pushed on into buffalo country beyond the front range of the Rockies.

There began the buffalo chases, by both Indian and white man alike. This was the great sport of the plains, and the immense herds extended beyond the front range and the Sweetwater all the way to Independence Rock, the gateway to the South Pass below the Wind River Mountains and across the Continental Divide. First, there was the mad chase after, and sometimes into, the herd, the thunder of a thousand buffalo hoofs as the frightened beasts charged in all directions, dust, shots, whizzing arrows, shouts, yells, the ever-present danger of prairie dog holes and unseen declivities. Then there was the yell of triumph, the skinning of the buffalo, and later, the roasting of the delicious hump ribs. But let David L. Brown, who was along on the Stewart expedition of that year, tell it:

> We ascended to the summit of the rock [Independence Rock]. . . . As far as the eye could reach . . . the field of vision was literally covered and blackened over with multitudinous herds of buffaloes. I had heard or read of such things; but here was the reality, far exceeding in its naked truth the romantic exaggeration of the novelist. . . . It was a sight never to be forgotten. . . .
>
> In the space of a very few minutes every man who owned or thought he owned a good horse or mule was mounted upon his back determined to try his luck in a neck-or-nothing chase after those shaggy denisons of the western wilds. . . .
>
> On a pre-concerted signal being given by Capt. Stewart each man put spurs to his horse, and at utmost speed we dashed upon the traces of the already flying bisons. . . . I found myself in the centre of a living cataract almost blinded by the stream of sand and gravel thrown in my face from the hoofs of the terrified mass in their desperate and headlong flight. . . . As yet I had not fired a shot. . . . The gigantic animals . . . were literally pressing my horse on every side. . . . To have checked my horse at this time would in all probability to incur instant death, as the masses behind would certainly have trodden me, horse and all, into a jelly. I did that which was much safer. . . . I fired into an immense bull that pressed heavily against my right stirrup, and as the muzzle of my rifle touched its ribs, its report was immediately followed by the fall of the huge animal which rolled headlong on the ground.
>
> The effect of this shot was electrical. The herd which before had borne and pressed upon my horse to a very alarming degree, now divided and burst away on every side, as if a volcano had suddenly risen in their midst. . . . The enormous creature lay prostrate on the ground, with its head twisted partly under its bulk, its only visible eye white and glazed.[3]

Then from Independence Rock the route lay past the Devil's Gate, a narrow ravine through which the Sweetwater flowed and thence west to Notch Mountain, a day's ride far in the distance. It was Stewart's custom that he and all his men refrain from drinking water all the way across the great sage plain that formed the South Pass until they reached the Big Sandy at the far western base of the Wind River Mountains. Miller didn't much care for this kind of discipline on the trail, though by now Stewart had assigned him a man to tend his horse and pitch his tent, so that he could paint more pictures unimpeded by trivial duties.

As they approached "the Mountains of the Wind" it began to rain furiously, and when the rain stopped a squadron of roughly dressed men rode directly down on them, firing rifles and pistols with abandon. They weren't Indians, but mountain men come to welcome them to rendezvous. David Brown described it: "We came suddenly upon a long line of beautiful Indian tents ranging in regular order, and stretching away for at least two miles in perspectus and terminating in a wide and circular array of the same romantic and fairy-looking dwellings."[4] Miller immediately began to paint what became a series of paintings of the rendezvous, the most striking of which were two pictures, one showing Stewart's camp on a low rise with Jim Bridger in a suit of armor brought to him by Stewart, and the other a very large oil painting entitled *Cavalcade* that depicted a huge line of Snake Indians stretching off to the Bear Mountains in the distance, led by their chief on a prancing white horse, come to pay homage to the ever-generous Captain Stewart. The chief's white horse more than matched the white charger that Stewart always rode on his mountain hunt.

Miller found the rendezvous on Horse Creek close by the upper Green River a strange, riotous baccanal where drunkenness and letchery abounded, though he failed to avert his eyes at the sight of naked Indian nymphs bathing or swinging from trees. While painting these scenes, however, for morality's sake, he camped with the priggish missionary, William H. Gray. Actually, the rendezvous was like some trade fair of the Middle Ages where wagon loads of trinkets from "civilization" were swapped for beaver and other skins that would eventually find their way to London and far-off Leipzig in central Europe. At the same time contests of skill ranging from drinking bouts to horse races were held. Wagering and good fellowship between red men and white abounded on this once-a-year occasion.

Alfred Jacob Miller,
*Buffalo Hunting Near
Independence Rock*, (1837).
Walters Art Gallery,
Baltimore.

Alfred Jacob Miller, *Stewart and Antoine Confronted by Crow Indians*, (1858–60). Walters Art
Gallery, Baltimore.

Alfred Jacob Miller, *Stewart's Camp, Wind River Range, Western Wyoming*, (c. 1865). The Peale
Museum, Baltimore.

Alfred Jacob Miller, *Fort Laramie or Sublette's Fort (Near the Nebraska or Platte River.* Joslyn Art Museum, The InterNorth Art Foundation, Omaha.

Alfred Jacob Miller, *Trappers Saluting the Rocky Mountains.* Courtesy the Buffalo Bill Historical Center, Cody, Wyoming.

When the rendezvous was over Stewart took his party far up into the Wind River Mountains, which the explorer, Lieutenant John C. Fremont was to climb five years later. There they hunted bear, elk, catamount and moose on glacial lakes like Fremont Lake and New Fork Lake, which, according to Miller, were "as fresh and beautiful as if from the hands of the Creator." Miller painted scene after scene of these lakes at dawn and sunset, when the light made the colors most dramatic. Often criticized for their romantic, even impressionistic look, Miller's paintings of these mountains and lakes were never meant to be geologically accurate renditions. They were meant to evoke feelings of surpassing, almost unreal beauty—a feeling that comes over one today if he follows Stewart and Miller's trail ten thousand feet up into the Wind River Mountains and on to the unbelievably beautiful Green Lake, dominated by a huge flat-topped mountain that resembles God's mighty pulpit. When they reached Green Lake, Stewart and Miller had reached the source of the mighty Green River that flowed southward all the way through the Grand Canyon to the Gulf of California. It came as close to that mythical "grand reservoir of lakes and fountains" described by Jonathan Carver and Zebulon Pike as anything could be. In the hundreds of pictures Miller painted that year, he was painting a dream. And though he didn't know it, he was painting a way of life that was about to vanish forever. The Rocky Mountain fur trade had passed its zenith, and in painting the rendezvous of 1837, Miller produced what turned out to be historic views of its last great gathering. There would be other rendezvous as late as 1843 on the Popo Agie, at which even Captain Stewart would be in attendance, but nothing ever again matched the massive party staged by mountain men, Indians and Captain Stewart with his lavish supply

Alfred Jacob Miller, *Cavalcade*, (1858–1860). Walters Art Gallery, Baltimore.

of European delicacies and his "magic" Persian carpet there on the upper Green River in the year of the Great Spirit, 1837.

The following year, Stewart learned that his brother had died, and that he had to return to Scotland to become Lord of Murthley Castle. While in New Orleans for the winter to buy cotton, Stewart urged Miller to make haste in turning his field sketches into finished paintings. In that one year Miller painted eighteen large oils and nearly two hundred smaller watercolors,[5] working first in his New Orleans studio, and then back in Baltimore. In the spring of 1839 the eighteen large oils were displayed in an exhibition at New York's Apollo Gallery where they received rave reviews from the press. The critics especially liked the *Cavalcade*[6] when they saw it at Miller's studio. One critic called Miller's exhibition "the best exhibition of American painting ever presented to the public." These paintings were, of course, eastern America's first view of the Rocky Mountains, a view that was replete with all the charms that high romanticism and emotional energy could bring to them. If one only had Miller's views to depend upon, the great prairies and "the Mountains of the Wind" indeed looked *like* a "garden of the gods" at first creation. And in one view, Miller painted Stewart like a god perched high above the rendezvous, surrounded by admiring Indians. The Captain must have prized this view especially.

Soon the paintings were shipped to Murthley Castle, and Miller went with them to paint more scenes based on his sketches and notes. His original field sketches were bound in a great book that lay on a table in the main hall of the castle, and at his death were willed by Stewart to Mr. Power, his tutor and servant. They were eventually purchased by Mae Reed Porter, who rediscovered Miller's work almost one hundred years after his mountain adventure. Mrs. Porter had them made into glass slides, and lectured extensively on Miller and the mountain men. Eventually she produced an excellent biography of Stewart entitled *Scotsman in Buckskin,* while Bernard DeVoto exploited the paintings in his famous work, *Across the Wide Missouri.* Porter's collection was eventually sold to the Joslyn Art Museum, though it appears not to have included all the field sketches, some of which can be found in other museums today.

It appears to be clear that Miller all along maintained a full set of sketches for himself, because he spent the remainder of his life painting and re-painting the views he had originally made for Captain Stewart. One of his largest orders came from William T. Walters that today forms the basic collection at the

Alfred Jacob Miller, *Pipe of Peace at the Rendezvous*, (1837). Stark Museum of Art, Orange, Texas.

Walters Art Museum in Baltimore. He painted another set for Alexander Brown and still another set for William C. Wait. He also filled single orders for customers. Unlike Karl Bodmer he did not resent his excursion into the Far West, though it left him permanently impaired with rheumatism.

It is fitting to conclude this part of our story with the high romanticism of Alfred Jacob Miller. Though his Indians were just as real, having been painted from life, they projected somehow beyond the confines of ethnology to a human, almost droll quality, while in sketching the mountain men at work and play he preserved for succeeding generations a lost world of American history that without any exaggeration involved the romantic image of man in close contact with nature. In the mountain man, despite his negative comments on their drunken behavior at rendezvous, Miller created the Anglo "noble savage." He multiplied Daniel Boone and Leatherstocking many times over, and then placed nearly all his images in the time capsules of Murthley Castle, and the Walters, Brown, and Wait Collections, leaving them as a lost romantic horizon to be discovered by historians in the mid-twentieth century, just as indeed the whole corpus and legacy of Western art with all its magic and mythic associations has just, in recent years been rediscovered as the long-hidden, perhaps enduring mainstream of American Art.

Part Two

THE GOLDEN LAND

CHAPTER 6

DESTINY AND DEMOCRACY

*When they came down out of the redwoods it was evening. Over-*head a meteor shower flared in the night sky. When they heard the rumble of an earthquake, and thought it was waves crashing on the Pacific shores, they knew they were figures of destiny. "The idea of being within hearing of the *end* of the *Far West*," wrote one of their number, "inspired the heart of every member of our company with a patriotic feeling for his country's honor. . . ."[1]

The year was 1834. The writer was Zenas Leonard, and he was one of a band of tough mountain men who had made their way from the Rocky Mountains to California under the leadership of Joseph Rutherford Walker. In so doing, they had laid out most of the overland trail from the United States to California, along which thousands of white-topped wagons would roll in just a few years. Walker, Leonard and the band of sixty mountain men were basically common folk looking to escape poverty by trapping for beaver in the mountains. But in this instance they knew that they represented something more than this. The ringing phrase "Manifest Destiny" would not be coined by editor John L. O'Sullivan for another eleven years, but these common mountain men already knew its meaning. It had been ordained by the Almighty that the United States would be a continental nation that stretched from the

George Caleb Bingham, *Fur Traders Descending the Missouri,* (1845). Metropolitan Museum of Art, New York, Morris K. Jesup Fund, 1933.

George Caleb Bingham, *The Verdict of the People,* (1854–5). From the Art Collection of the Boatmen's National Bank of St. Louis, Missouri.

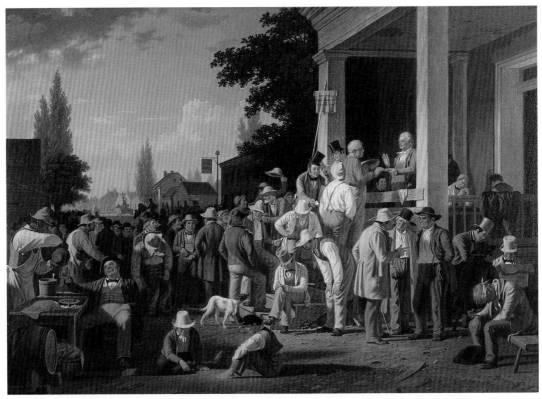

George Caleb Bingham, *The County Election (No. 2)*, (1851–2). From the Art Collection of the Boatmen's National Bank of St. Louis, Missouri.

Atlantic to the Pacific. Even the lowest member of Walker's band believed it, especially after the meteor shower and the earthquake had given them a sign. Leonard spoke for most Americans when he wrote:

> Much of this vast waste of territory belongs to the Republic of the United States. What a theme to contemplate its settlement and civilization. Will . . . her hardy freeborn population here plant their homes, build their towns and cities, and say here shall the arts and sciences of civilization take root and flourish?

The visionary Leonard must have contemplated this dream for a moment, then answered his own question unhesitatingly:

> Yes, here, even in this remote part of the Great West before many years will these hills and valleys be greeted with the enlivening sound of the workman's hammer and the merry whistle of the ploughboy.[2]

Thus Zenas Leonard saw not the gold that lay in California's mountains, but an agrarian vision that extended rural America all the way to the Pacific with the yeoman farmer in the vanguard. The kinds of people and institutions that Zenas Leonard foresaw populating the hills and valleys of California were, at that time, the plain yeomen families of the Middle Border along the Mississippi and the lower Missouri rivers. They formed the characteristic population, for example, of Missouri—the jumping off place for nearly all expeditions into the Far West.

A little over ten years after Leonard's return from the shores of the Pacific, a young self-taught Missouri painter, George Caleb Bingham, began a career in Arrow Rock, on the Missouri River near the center of the state, painting those "hardy freeborn citizens" who would lead the move westward bringing with them those republican and democratic institutions that Leonard so cherished.

In the 1840s and 1850s, at the high tide of what was being called, "the Era of Manifest Destiny," Bingham recorded for all time in a series of masterworks the "Middle Border" culture that went West in an endless stream of wagon trains. Bingham's portrait of this culture, in towns and villages like Arrow Rock and Franklin and Columbia, was in part the portrait of a Jeffersonian republican idyll. In a pastoral vein he painted the country folk fishing in the Missouri, shooting for a prize beef, canvassing for a vote, or standing puzzled in civil court. He also painted (ten years after Karl Bodmer) realistic pictures of river life on the Missouri and the Mississippi. And finally, he rendered masterful views of those institutions of democratic republicanism, so celebrated by Zenas Leonard in perhaps the best political paintings ever executed by an American. So effective are they that, even today, they are the fundamental iconographic images of western democratic institutions in action. It seems clear, however, that Bingham, who was directly engaged in Whig Party politics, realized that he was documenting a passing era with loving, sometimes sardonic precision.

His first widely known work was the portrait of the end of an era, *Fur Traders Descending the Missouri*, which he painted in 1845. It depicted an old French fur trapper and his half-breed son paddling a dugout canoe down the placid Missouri River. The trapper and his son look directly out of the picture into the eyes of the viewer. Their expressions are widely different, however; the trapper looks stern and suspicious, whereas the boy, a child of nature, is caught up in reverie, reflecting the dreamlike quality of the whole picture. At the bow of the boat a mysterious black animal sits chained to the canoe. It is a bear-cub, a wild creature who, like the half-breed boy, is heading for domestication. Behind them flows the river around a wooded island in a golden haze of memory on to that vast infinitude that was once the wild upper Missouri country. Much has been written about this painting, which is one of America's masterpieces, but the primary effect of it is that of nostalgia for a bygone era—one that even Sir William Drummond Stewart lived to mourn and Alfred Jacob Miller to commemorate for the rest of his life. Bingham's work, however, summed up the fur trade era in one unforgettable climactic image. The American Art Union, headquartered in New York, understood this, and distributed an engraved version of Bingham's picture by the thousands over the United States and in Europe.

Bingham had a sense for the climactic picture. Any one of his versions of flatboatmen—*The Jolly Flatboatman, Boatmen on the Missouri, Raftsmen Playing Cards,* or *Watching the Cargo by Night*—could stand for life on America's two great rivers, the Missouri and the Mississippi. Carefully built up out of pencil, brush and ink sketches of the individual figures, Bingham's pictures were usually pyramidal or conic in composition. In the early works, like *The Jolly Flatboatman,* Bingham's geometric composition was obvious. They were based in part on engravings of the Renaissance masters that he had seen in widely distributed artists instruction manuals like J. Burnet's *A Practical Treatise on Painting. In Three Parts. Consisting of Hints on Composition, Chiaroscuro, and Colouring. The Whole Illustrated by Examples from the Italian, Venetian, Flemish and Dutch Schools* (London, 1828).[3] All of these river pictures, however they were composed, depicted carefree men dancing a jig, playing cards, swapping tales or just drifting lazily down the mighty river. They were happy, moving, patriotic scenes of experiences that made you glad that Bingham had frozen them in time forever. These and Bingham's other genre scenes represented the way the Far West was supposed to look once the pioneer overlanders reached the promised lands in Oregon and California. They reflected happiness and contentment, but, as in the case of the dancing, jolly raftsmen, they also represented a sense of American energy.

Bingham's political paintings were especially important studies of Americana. *The County Election,* painted in 1851–2 was the first of these works. On a canvas approximately three feet high and four feet long, Bingham assembled over fifty figures that, as they flowed across the canvas, depicted democracy in action. Bingham's good friend Major James Sydney Rollins wrote of it that:

> It is pre-eminently a *National* painting, for it presents just such a scene, as you would meet with on the Aroostock in Maine, or in the City of New York, or on the Rio Grande in Texas on an election day. He has left nothing out, the courtier, the politician, the labourer, the sturdy farmer, the 'bully' at the poles [sic],

George Caleb Bingham, *The Jolly Flatboatmen,* (1846). National Gallery of Art.

George Caleb Bingham, *Stump Speaking,* (1853–4). From the Art Collection of the Boatmen's National Bank of St. Louis, Missouri.

the beer-seller, the *bruised* pugilist, and even the boys playing 'mumble the peg' are all distinctly recognized in the group. . . . The elective franchise is the very corner stone upon which rests our governmental superstructure and as illustrative of our fine institutions, the power and influence which the ballot box exerts over our happiness as a people. . . .[4]

This must have been the way Bingham's painting was perceived in its time, but, like his other political paintings, it also has a Hogarthian touch of satire about it. Clearly free whiskey is being passed out to the voters by the candidate, whom we learn from a "key" to the painting made by a contemporary resident of Arrow Rock, Dr. Oscar F. Potter, is Darwin Sappington, Bingham's arch rival in several elections.[5] Drunks abound in the picture with one of them even being dragged to vote in a semi-conscious state by a Sappington campaign worker. In the center of the picture money seems to be changing hands, or at least crossing a man's palm. The candidate, Sappington, egregiously tips his hat to a man, even as another campaign worker, in the shadows, offers the same man a substantial glass of whiskey. The pompous individual administering the oath to a voter is Governor M. M. Marmaduke, Sappington's brother-in-law. He is being assisted by another of the candidate's relatives, William Sappington, who is sharpening his quill pen just behind the pompous governor. Perhaps, as a measure of the authenticity of his "key" to the picture, Dr. Potter identified himself in the middle ground at the center of the picture, hands on knees observing a man sitting on the steps sketching. The seated sketcher is none other than George Caleb Bingham himself, in a high stove-pipe hat. He is positioned almost directly beneath Sappington in an ironic touch, since Bingham almost invariably lost his political contests with Sappington. Potter's "key" also indicates something of the way Bingham must have worked. Clearly drawing on his experience as a portrait painter, he sketched very rapidly, and his surviving sketches indicate that he invariably sketched individuals, then later put them together in a kind of collage composition that probably preceded the final careful composition of the picture. Potter's "key" also makes it clear that the place is indeed Arrow Rock (which remains much the same today) and the people in the picture are real people.

Major Rollins, in his unstinted praise for the democratic quality of the election process, seems to have missed something of Bingham's sly commentary on the process. But so have most commentators on the painting, from Bingham's time to the present. Indeed, the many buyers, all over the country, of John Sartain's engraving of the picture, also do not seem to have noticed the irony. "A Friend of Genius" in the *Weekly Missouri Statesman* for October 29, 1852, declared that the picture was "destined to become one of the most popular paintings ever produced on this continent," while the *Daily Louisville Times* for April 6, 1853, asserted that it was a painting "sufficient of itself to immortalize the man who achieved it." Displayed in a store window, even in a copied version, it attracted "throngs of people."[6] Bingham wrote Major Rollins, gleefully, "It was pronounced superior to anything of its kind which had yet been seen in America." And in this judgment he was undoubtedly right. Even the great William Sydney Mount, whose genre scenes of Long Island rural life Bingham seems to have on occasion taken for models, had not done anything approaching this in complexity. Bingham had created a monumental genre scene that surpassed even Hogarth's work in numbers of characters and complexity of arrangement, and yet at the same time the picture was more than genre: it was a true historical rendition, warts and all, of democracy in America; a visual exclamation point to Count Alexis de Tocqueville's recently published volumes on the same subject.

The combination of history and satire set down on canvas in a classically composed form, described in detail by critic E. Maurice Bloch, seems to characterize all three of Bingham's major election pictures. In *Stump Speaking* or *The County Canvass* of 1853–4, an orator identical to Sappington, dressed in a white coat, is delivering an address, while his brother-in-law, Colonel M. M. Marmaduke, sits like a fat-bellied alderman behind him, as does a self-portrayed Bingham busily scribbling notes for his own speech or rebuttal. The platform group itself is an irony, but Bingham, through skillful use of light and patterns of white, clearly indicates that Sappington is not at all interested in the country louts who come to hear him speak. They are either nodding or looking on with imbecile faces. The only important person in the audience is a rich man clad all in white who seems to be the county "padrone." He looks on attentively, but at the same time self-satisfied in the knowledge of his own political power. In the foreground stands a slouching man with a cane, dressed in a long, ill-fitting coat, who looks at the speaker incredulously, as if he had just wandered in from another country or planet and wondered what the palavering was all about.

In Bingham's final grand election picture—his most famous one—*Verdict of the People,* painted in 1854–5, the primary Hogarthian irony is presented right in the foreground of the picture. In the midst of a democratic celebration of "victory for the people" slumps a black man, a member of Missouri's mudsill

class of slaves, in the posture of the famous classical statue, *The Dying Gaul.*
He rests in the dirt, hanging his head, while directly over him flies the American flag. To the right, their backs turned to him, two boys are awaiting a slice
of melon. To the left his wife, a handkerchief around her head, trundles a
wheelbarrow with which to take him home. In the joy of election victory,
only she seems interested in him. When one remembers that in 1854–5, due
to the Kansas–Nebraska Act which cancelled all the other compromises, the
future of slavery was on everyone's mind, particularly its future in the West,
this painting becomes an incredibly powerful statement. Not only were the
new western states, Kansas and Nebraska, involved, but all the territory wrested
from Mexico as a result of the recent war. California, by this time filled with
immigrants and gold seekers, was divided into northern and southern camps
so violent that every day shootouts occurred. And when the child-singer Lotta
Crabtree waved tiny American flags in the "Southron" gold camps, she was
heckled from her makeshift stage.

Bingham's political paintings, in addition to being artistic masterpieces,
clearly showed that, as the pioneers moved westward with their political and
cultural institutions, they brought with them serious problems that threatened
to offset all the "promise" in the new "land of promise." And as the future of
the West became an object of struggle between North and South, the "land
of promise" became a "land of perplexity." But that is getting ahead of our
story—the lurid story of Manifest Destiny as seen through the eyes of countless
other artists and image-makers, or trumpeted by some of America's most gifted
prophets of glory. As for George Caleb Bingham, perennial Whig Party candidate for office and inveterate foe of Darwin Sappington and the pro-slavery
wing of the Democratic Party, it should be noted that this was not the first
time or the last time in American history that an artist used his brush and
colors in a political cause. Indeed, it is difficult to allude to any period in
American history when art was not in some sense political.

CHAPTER 7

SHATTERING THE
RIM OF CHRISTENDOM

The Missouri culture of the American Middle Border was in sharp contrast to the Hispanic settlements in Texas, New Mexico and California, where, in the 1830s and 40s, the clashes of Anglo with Hispanic cultures that denoted the true meaning of Manifest Destiny took place. Regrettably little in the way of contemporary artistic portrayals of the Hispanic cultures exists. Rather than paint contemporary scenes, the Spanish people devoted their principle talents to architecture: the design and building of the numerous missions, presidios and aquaducts that dotted their "rim of Christendom" from Texas to California. When they painted, the Spaniards portrayed religious scenes and pictures or painted wooden statues of the saints which they called "Santos." These decorated their churches and offered glory to God, whose help they sometimes desperately needed, especially in the harsh Southwest lands dominated by hard-riding Comanche, Apache, Kiowa, Navaho and Ute Indians.

Perhaps the most evocative images of the old Hispanic culture were those rendered by James Walker, in California, and Theodore Gentilz and Herman Lungkwitz, in Texas. The California that Joe Walker and Zenas Leonard saw in the 1830s had as its capital Monterey, which, along with San Diego, was

the major port on the west coast of North America. California had been settled by means of a string of missions up the coast, established by the Jesuit
father, Junipero Serra, with the aid of military commander, Don Gaspar de
Potola, in 1769–76. By the time American fur trappers began infiltrating into
California in the 1820s, the Jesuits had been ousted and replaced by the Franciscans, who "reduced" the thousands of California Indians to mission life.
With Captain Juan Bautista de Anza's overland expedition from his presidio
at Tubac, (near modern Tucson) Arizona in 1774, the missions became, in
effect, huge cattle ranches. These ranches were secularized in 1836 and became
vast spreads under the ownership of favored hidalgos. The Indians were then
further reduced to serfdom as they tended the vast herds of cattle and sheep.
As California became secularized, its ranchers turned outward towards the
Pacific. Soon a heavy trade in cattle hides developed between the rancheros
and ships of many nations, not the least of which were from the United States.
Eventually, a U.S. consul, Thomas Larkin, took up residence in Monterey,
where he was visited by the American military explorer and agent provaca-
teur, Lieutenant John C. Frémont, in 1844, and again in 1845.

One of the most famous impressions of old California was conveyed in Richard Henry Dana's book, *Two Years Before the Mast*. In 1834–6 he sailed in the
brig *Pilgrim* from Boston round the Horn to the coast of California, where
during the course of a year, he sailed up and down the coast, serving as a

James Walker, *Roping Wild Horses*, (1877). The Thomas Gilcrease Institute of American History
and Art, Tulsa.

common seaman in the hide trade. His description of California's delights was offset by his observations of the anarchic effects of Mexican rule:

> Ever since the independence of Mexico, the missions have been going down; until a law was passed, stripping them of all their possessions and confining the priests to their spiritual duties, at the same time declaring the Indians free and independent *Rancheros.* the change in the condition of the Indians was, as may be supposed, only nominal; they are virtually serfs, as much as they ever were . . . the great possessions of the missions are given over to be preyed upon by the harpies of civil power who are sent here in the capacity of *administradores* . . . and who usually end, in a few years, by making themselves fortunes and leaving their stewardships worse than they found them. . . . [T]he *administradores* are . . . men of desperate fortune—broken-down politicians and soldiers—whose only object is to retrieve their condition in as short a time as possible. . . . the venerable missions were going rapidly to decay.[1]

Nonetheless, Dana took part in the social life of early California.[2] He marvelled at its beautiful coastline, where he spotted his old Harvard professor, Thomas Nuttall, trousers rolled, standing in a tidal pool off San Diego collecting natural history specimens. Dana also went to fandangos and engaged in flirtations with comely senoritas. He risked his life smuggling hides down off the cliffs of Santa Barbara at night, and he enjoyed riding the Spanish horses across the great interior valleys of California, where the ranches seemed to stretch away to an infinity usually associated with Texas. Dana's view of California, published in his book in 1840, made it seem a kind of Eden loosely held by profligate, would-be Mexican aristocrats on the make. His book, *Two Years Before the Mast,* along with Lieutenant John C. Fremont's official report of his expedition of 1843–4, made California seem a pastoral paradise ripe for the taking.

But it was not until years later that anyone painted the visions of old, pre-conquest California that these men had seen. The artist was a young British-born adventurer, James Walker.[3] Trained in New York, he had found himself in Mexico City when war broke out with the United States. He was taken prisoner by the Mexicans, but escaped and made his way to General Scott's army marching inland from Vera Cruz. He served as Scott's interpreter and sketched Scott's battles on the road to the conquest of Mexico City. After the occupation, he remained in the Mexican capital until 1848. By 1850, he had set up a studio in New York City, and become, along with Carl Nebel, America's foremost military painter. He made many scenes of the Civil War. Then, in the early 1870s, he set up a studio in San Francisco and began the series of works on pre-conquest California for which he is most remembered. Walker eschewed painting the crumbling missions, for the most part, and concentrated on recording the life of the flamboyant vaqueros. In a sense, he was the first cowboy painter, with scenes like *Roping Wild Horses,* where the men in the sombreros and colorful suits demonstrated the use of the lasso. He also portrayed them roping and branding cattle in a corral, and even using their lassos to have sport with one of the ubiquitous California bears. In a period from about 1870 to 1889, when he died in Watsonville, California, Walker executed hundreds of works in this mode. So authentic looking were his romantic views that most people derive their picture of pre-conquest nineteenth-century California from them. Few realize that he was not there at that time, and that these are history paintings, rather than reportage.

And his emphasis on the busy, flamboyant world of the vaquero, rather than on moonlit missions and slumbering padres, does indeed catch something authentic about pre-conquest California culture. In Walker's paintings action is always apparent, and the vividly costumed vaqueros, whom he had actually seen in Mexico before 1846, stand out in unforgettable iconographic images. He re-created old California life for a later generation. His paintings became part of an Edenic myth of pre-conquest California subsequently advanced by publisher Charles Lummis, who arrived in Los Angeles in 1885. Walker's paintings and Lummis' writings revived an interest in the whole cultural horizon of the Spanish Southwest, from California to the Texas border. Walker foreshadowed a cult that would create still another "West of the imagination."

In Texas, perhaps the best recorder of Hispanic life was Theodore Gentilz, a Parisian coach painter who came to San Antonio in 1844 as a member of the Belgian Count de Castro's colony.[4] Gentilz painted the decaying missions, San Francisco de Espada, San Jose de Aguayo, San Juan Capistrano. But he also painted pictures of Comanches on the warpath, Lipan Apaches in their villages, the Count de Castro's surveyors at work and countless scenes of San Antonio life in fandangos, cantinas, church processions and horsemen racing through the streets. His one essay into history painting was indeed a vivid one. It portrayed the captured Texan survivors of a raid on Mier facing a firing squad. Each of the seventeen doomed men had drawn a black bean, which meant death, from a jar furnished by their Mexican captors. Gentilz called his painting, *Shooting of the Seventeen Decimated Texians at El Salado, Mexico.*

Later in the 1850s, a German artist, Herman Lungkwitz,[5] would paint the romantic landscape of central Texas—its limestone caves, domed Enchanted Rock, near the settlement of Fredericksburg, and tree-lined hidden rivers,

James Walker, *Roping a Wild Grizzly*, (1877). Denver Art Museum.

complete with exotic white herons—in extremely moving and professional fashion. But, looking at the work of all three artists—Walker, Gentilz and Lungkwitz—it is easy to extrapolate backwards several decades to the 1830s, and to see that the Hispanic West was a pastoral West in which, though the missions had lost their power, the rancheros and vaqueros still operated much as they had in the age of Cortez. To Americans, the Spanish Southwest and California was a bureaucratized culture of pseudo-aristocracy and stasis, far different from the raucous "Middle Border" vision to be found in Bingham's *The County Election.* Clearly, as Anglo-Americans saw it, democracy was something new. It harnessed the energies of *all* the people in some fashion and, in so doing, it attained such a velocity, so much social energy, that it was bound to prevail over Indian and Mexican alike. Something of this atti- tude was behind the Texas War for Independence of 1836, a war that might be called "the morning gun of Manifest Destiny."

Significantly, most of the artistic renditions of the Texas War for Indepen- dence came long after the fact, as did Walker's paintings of old California. Only Theodore Gentilz attempted a rendition of the seige of the Alamo, in 1844, but the result was a cold, analytical military engineer's view of the start of the battle. This is in contrast to the avalanche of versions of Custer's Last

Stand that followed closely upon the event. Why this is so is difficult to explain, because the Texan Revolution clearly inspired vast numbers of citizens of the United States, and not far from Texas, in New Orleans, was one of the young country's major art colonies. John James Audubon, James Jackson Jarvis, Paul Kane and Alfred Jacob Miller were all painting there in the years of expansion, as were many more artists of lesser stature.

At any rate, only two pictures of any real importance were painted of the life-and-death struggle at the Alamo, and both appeared after 1900. The most ambitious was by Henry McArdle, who was born in Belfast, Ireland, and came to the United States at age fourteen. His family settled in Baltimore, where he acquired art instruction at the Maryland Institute for the Promotion of the Mechanical Arts. It was either at the Maryland Institute or the result of serving as a cartographer and topographical engineer under General Robert E. Lee that McArdle developed his distinctive "picto-map" style of painting battle scenes. In an earlier painting, *The Settlement of Austin's Colony*, he painted in a normal way, so that we know he reserved the "picto-map" style for his battle pictures.

Dawn at the Alamo (1905) is a sprawling, luridly lit agglomeration of scenes of individual hand-to-hand combat. Only the battered walls of the Alamo itself give a framing or focus to the picture. The action spills from the left background, where the famous mission building stands, to the right foreground and middleground, where the badly drawn figures are larger. William B. Travis dominates the picture, as he stands atop a dead Mexican soldier on a parapet. He is dispatching one Mexican soldier, while behind him another Mexican soldier, his face contorted with sinister rage, prepares to bayonet Travis in the back. It is the act of a coward. It is also not factually correct, for Travis died of a bullet wound in the forehead.[6] Despite the fact that McArdle did research for the picture over a span of thirty years, taking care to get such things as guns, uniforms, swords and even flags correct, when it came to setting down the whole scene correctly he seems to have let his imagination run riot.

Examples of this abound in the painting. Just below Travis, who should have been dead, since he was killed early in the battle in the Alamo chapel,[7] McArdle depicts Davy Crockett, who was actually on the other side of the Alamo.[8] And in the left foreground of the picture, Major Robert Evans is shown in the process of trying to blow up the powder magazine, which actually is in the chapel bastion in the far left rear of the painting.[9] Evan's face, lit by dawn's lurid rays and the fire from his own torch, is that of an early Christian martyr, keynoting the cliché that all of the Alamo defenders were "martyrs to

Henry McArdle, *The Battle of San Jacinto*, (1895). State Capitol Building, Austin.

liberty." Clearly, in this painting McArdle was trying to create a "usable historic past" for Texas, though that had already been accomplished by the historians, Noah Smithwick, H. K. Yoakum, and the *Texas Almanac*, which began publication in 1857. McArdle was also trying to distill all of the events of the Alamo battle into one climactic moment, the moment just before its fall, when all its heroes were still alive to be represented in the picture.

In direct contrast to the "picto-map" style of McArdle, Robert Jenkins Onderdonk, a student of Walter Shirlaw and William Merritt Chase at the New York Art Student's League, painted a strong close-up view of Davy Crockett fighting off a horde of Mexican soldiers. His intention, he wrote to his patron, the historian–collector, James DeShields, was to portray "battle murder and

William Huddle, *The Surrender of Santa Anna*, (1886). The State Capitol Building, Austin.

sudden death!" He added that "the grouping and lines are all made with reference to showing the overwhelming rush of the Mexicans and the determined stand of the few Americans. . . ."[10] Onderdonk believed that Davy Crockett was killed "defending the gateway of the building in the front assault." Recent research, however, indicates that he was captured and executed by Santa Anna.[11]

In any case, Onderdonk's painting, *Fall of the Alamo* (1903), which was painted at the same time as McArdle's, has a much firmer sense of reality and composition. The figures are well-formed, especially that of Crockett clubbing a rifle on the right center of the composition. The precision of the figures may be due to the fact that Onderdonk photographed members of his family and other carefully chosen models posing in costume, and then worked from the photographs.[12] Possibly his only flaw in depicting the Texan line is to be found in the man just behind Crockett; he appears to be shooting his own leader in the back. Beyond this, Onderdonk painted a sophisticated and relatively powerful picture. He used light well to illuminate the Texas heroes and to place the Mexican attackers in the shade, while the rays of dawn project from the background. Proof of Onderdonk's accomplishment is the fact that his painting has become the standard iconographic cliché for depicting the fall of the Alamo. One only has to turn to the John Wayne motion picture version of the Alamo siege to see the impact of Onderdonk's painting. Unlike so many would-be early American history painters, Onderdonk essayed only this one venture into the genre. The rest of his life he devoted himself to painting landscapes and quaint semi-impressionistic pictures of San Antonio. In contrast to McArdle, he was more interested in art than history.[13]

McArdle's other work, *The Battle of San Jacinto* (1895) was still another "picto-map" view of sprawling battle. This painting seems to be entirely historical and analytically oriented, because there is little evidence of composition in it. McArdle did, however, provide a fascinating "key" to the scene, identifying Sam Houston, Deaf Smith, Thomas Jefferson Rusk, Colonel Edward Burleson, Santa Anna, Mexican officers, General Castrillion, Don Esteban Mora, Don Dion Cos, Antonio Trevino and Colonel Romero, vainly attempting to rally the surprised and panicked Mexican troops. The "key" identified, in all, 59 actual people involved in battle.[14]

Perhaps the most famous picture to emerge from this, the climactic battle of the Texan Revolution, was William Huddle's *The Surrender of Santa Anna* (1886). Huddle, a Virginian who had served with Nathan Bedford Forrest's Confederate cavalry in the Civil War, was, along with McArdle and Onderdonk, one of the founding members of the New York Art Student's League in

Henry McArdle, *Dawn at the Alamo*, (1876–83). State Capitol Building, Austin.

1875.[15] He had also studied art in Munich. Upon his return from Europe, Huddle decided to paint a view of Santa Anna's surrender, in honor of the fiftieth anniversary of Texas independence. His painting is justly famous, if only for the fact that it hangs in a prominent place in the Texas Capitol building. But Huddle did, indeed, bring some measure of professional compe-

Herman Lungkwitz, *(Guadalupe River) Landscape*, (1862). Houston Museum of Fine Arts, The Bayou Bend Collection, Gift of Miss Ima Hogg.

Robert Jenkins Onderdonk, *Fall of the Alamo,* (1903). Friends of the Governor's Mansion, Austin.

tence to his view of General Sam Houston, lying wounded under an oak tree, receiving the surrender of the humiliated Mexican dictator, clad in a private's uniform. Many of the prominent figures in the Revolution are portrayed in the picture, but all of them, including Sam Houston, are upstaged by Deaf Smith in the foreground, hand cupped to his ear in order to catch every word of the glorious proceedings. Smith must be easily the best-known deaf person in Texas history.

The picture did have a number of things to recommend it. For one thing, Huddle knew how to compose his picture so that it had a focus—on Santa Anna and Sam Houston—distorted slightly by Deaf Smith. His rendition of Dr. Ewing's medical box is almost *trompe l'oeil,* and the landscape setting (possibly painted by his friend, Herman Lungkwitz), is far better than that of McArdle.[16] The plain fact, however, is that the visualization of the Texan Revolution—one of the most dramatic events in Western and American history—was badly served by artists, most of whom painted long after the event and would not even have done so then except that they were prodded and supported by the indefatigable antiquarian historian, James DeShields. Thus, the entire visualization of the Texan Revolution, however much the artists claimed to have done research, was a product of the imagination.

CHAPTER 8

PICTURING
MANIFEST DESTINY

In 1822 Samuel F. B. Morse completed his first history painting.
It was an unusual work that featured no battles, no statesmen forging a treaty
or founding a nation. Instead, it was a painting entitled *The Old House of
Representatives.* Inspired by the tide of nationalism after the War of 1812 and
John Quincy Adams's successful negotiation of a transcontinental boundary
treaty with Spain in 1819 that gave the United States a window on the Pacific,
Morse's painting celebrates plain republican government. Educated first at
Andover and Yale, Morse then went to England to study with the great history
painter, Benjamin West. He returned to America in 1815 and earned his
living painting portraits until he went to Washington in 1821 to paint the
House of Representatives. The painting was actually composed of eighty-six
miniature portraits for which the various Congressmen, clerks, newsmen and
other officials sat. For example, on the far right of the picture is Joseph Gales,
the reporter for the Whig *National Intelligencer.* Morse wrote, "The time chosen is at candle lighting while the members are assembling for an evening
session. . . ." He added, "The primary design of the . . . picture . . . [is] to
exhibit to the public a faithful representation of the National Hall, with its
furniture and business during the session of Congress."[1]

But there is more to Morse's picture than this modest description. In a sense the clerk of the House is lighting the lamp of republican promise and illuminating the country's Manifest Destiny. Morse slyly makes this clear by portraying one of the painter Charles Bird King's Indians, Petalasharoo, peeking out of the gallery at the right. That very evening perhaps Congress will decide *his* destiny, and that of his people, as the nation turns to the West.

By the 1840s the old simple republican idyll had begun to be replaced by more obvious scenes of Manifest Destiny such as this garish painting by John Gast, variously titled *Westward Ho* and *American Progress.* It was made into a lithograph and distributed by the thousands. All the mid-century symbols of progress are evident in the picture. The Goddess of Liberty floats through the sky, carrying a book of laws and linking the continent with a telegraph wire. As she leads the march of "civilized" progress that George Catlin so feared, she is "tying the nation together" with a telegraph, invented by none other than the artist Samuel F. B. Morse who, like Charles Willson Peale, managed to combine the life of the artist with that of the man of science.

As the Indians, buffalo, and wild bears retreat before them with churlish backward glances, the sturdy pioneers move forward with the "sacred plow," the covered wagon, the stagecoach, and ultimately the railroad. In addition to an age of expansion, a new age of technology had also come into being with trains, steamboats, Concord coaches as rapid, even elegant means of transportation, and the ingenious telegraph that provided not only instantaneous communication, but an American System for mapping the continent through simultaneous signals tapped out more than fifty miles apart. Most of all, the telegraph was a boon to the news media. The Mexican War of 1846 was the first war in history to be reported by telegraph coming up from New Orleans. Richard Caton Woodville's painting *News From the Mexican War* (1848) conveys something of the excitement this advance in communications generated.[2] Remarkably enough, it was painted in Dusseldorf, where the young Baltimore student of Alfred Jacob Miller had gone to study. In fact, he had been in Germany three years when the painting was executed. But so good was his memory that he was able to paint genre scenes that were almost the equal of William Sidney Mount and George Caleb Bingham, though he was not able to sketch on the spot. One of his other paintings, *Waiting For the Stage* (1851), is also remarkable for its fidelity to Middle American rural life and, in addition, it shows the same fascination with American communications as *News From the Mexican War.* The three characters wait in a small-

Samuel F. B. Morse, *The Old House of Representatives,* (1822). The Corcoran Gallery of Art, Washington, D.C.

Samuel F. B. Morse, Detail of Indian in balcony in *Old House of Representatives.*

John Gast, *Westward Ho (American Progress)*, (1872). Library of Congress.

time stagecoach station while one of their number, sporting dark glasses, intently reads a newspaper, *The Spy*.

News about the events that constituted the war with Mexico was indeed critical news. On the one hand the American people were showered with bombast like that from expansionist Gilpin who in 1846 flatly declared:

> The *untransacted destiny* of the American people is to subdue the continent—to rush over this fast field to the Pacific Ocean—to animate the many hundred millions of its people, and to cheer them upward—to establish a new order in human affairs—to set free the enslaved—to change darkness into light.[3]

News From the Mexican War. Engraved by Alfred Jones after painting by Richard Caton Woodville, (1853). New York Historical Society.

On the other hand, the American people had to be concerned with President Polk's policy of "brinksmanship," in which, by moving General Zachary Taylor's army to the Rio Grande he courted war with Mexico (which indeed had already declared such a state to exist) and by challenging Britain over Oregon, he was challenging the most powerful nation on earth. The United States, despite its bellicose oratory, was not ready for one war, let alone two at the same time.

Polk, however, managed to secure an Oregon Boundary treaty by compromising at the 49th Parallel, which gave the United States the excellent harbors at Puget Sound. Then he was prepared to go to war with Mexico, ostensibly over American claims, but actually to secure New Mexico, California and the Southwest from Texas to the Pacific. On May 9, 1846, he called a meeting of his cabinet and proposed sending a war message to Congress. The meeting had adjourned with Polk, his cabinet (with the exception of Secretary of the Navy George Bancroft) behind him in supporting a declaration of war over American claims. That night, via the telegraph, Polk learned that Mexican cavalry had attacked Captain Thornton's command north of the Rio Grande, killing and wounding several, while taking the rest prisoners. Thus, the next day, reinforced by Mexican General Arista's boast, "I had the pleasure of being the first to start the war," Polk could announce to Congress that "war exists by the act of the Republic of Mexico."[4] Three days later, after some debate, he received Congress's support. By that time General Taylor had already won the battles of Palo Alto and Resaca de la Palma, and the war had created its first two American heroes: dashing Captain May at Resaca de la Palma, and "Old Rough and Ready" Taylor himself. This was enough for American newsmen and printmakers, who went to work making thousands of lurid chromolithograph prints of the new heroes as propaganda and devices for recruiting volunteers from that same Middle Border country where formerly peace and calm had prevailed.

The example of Captain May's exploits should suffice to illustrate the point. Three different firms produced lithographs of "Gallant Captain May."[5] F. and S. Palmer featured the charge of Captain May's dragoons at Palo Alto; Nathaniel Currier portrayed Captain May in the act of capturing Mexican General Vega twice. In one dashing picture May is seen as a beardless youth, hair flying behind him, leaping over a cannon to shove a pistol into the face of an indignant general. In a second lithograph May is still seen leaping the cannon, but this time he appears in full beard, seizing the sword-wielding arm of the Mexican general, who appears to be smiling. Sarony and Majors's lithograph shows Captain May, the spirited horse, the cannon, and an evil looking general with a common soldier cringing behind him. Clearly the artists for these mass-distributed lithographs of the first engagements of the Mexican War knew nothing about it. Some depicted mountains, and other jungles, whereas the engagements took place on a rolling coastal prairie. None of them agreed on May's appearance, and several of them disagreed as to which battle saw his remarkable feat. Justin Smith, still the foremost authority on the war, wrote of Captain May:

> May, very tall and straight, with long black hair and a black beard that reached to his waist, became a newspaper hero, and for reasons that are rather hard to understand, was promoted several times during the war; but he seems clearly to have been a cowardly sham. In this fight [Resaca de la Palma] he seized a cannon, but only the infantry prevented the enemy from re-capturing it. . . . He claimed the credit of making General Vega his prisoner, but the real captor was a bugler.[6]

Ron C. Tyler, the only person to make an extensive study of the Mexican War lithographs, concludes that all of the pictures were based not on eyewitnesses, but on newspaper descriptions coming out of New Orleans.[7] Some lithographs, like James Baille's *Soldier's Adieux*, were pure sentimental clichés. In this popular picture a sweet looking soldier in full dress uniform holds his high shako hat aloft while embracing his rather dull looking wife or sweetheart on the steps of an Andrew Jackson Downing Gothic cottage. His aide waits discreetly at the gate. Such pictures, showing stalwart young men striking heroic poses, must have been used widely as recruiting devices.

There were a number of eyewitnesses to the battles and movements of troops who made sketches. Captain Daniel C. Whiting, for example, published five reasonably accurate lithographs in *The Army Portfolio* in 1848, and Henry R. Robinson produced a print of the Battle of Buena Vista from a drawing by Major Amos B. Eaton, General Taylor's *aide-de-camp*. There were also a number of lithographs produced in Lieutenants Emory and Abert's reports of their campaign with General Stephen Watts Kearny in the conquest of New Mexico and the march to California. Abert in particular produced excellent views of Bent's Fort on the upper Arkansas River, and a panoramic scene of Santa Fe. The drawings for Lieutenant Emory's report were produced by John Mix Stanley. As lithographs they did not reproduce well, but Stanley turned what must have been field sketches into some astonishingly beautiful Southwestern landscapes in oil, which are now part of the collection at the Stark Museum in Orange, Texas.

The Mexican War produced the first war correspondents, the most famous being George Wilkins Kendall of the New Orleans *Picayune*. Kendall had been captured by Mexican troops on the ill-fated Texan Santa Fe Expedition of 1841. Ultimately he was released and had come to be part owner of the *Picayune*. Possibly it was his dispatches that stimulated the lithographers. He was with General Zachary Taylor at the capture of Monterrey, and later with Scott's Army that fought its way into Mexico City.

In addition to war correspondents, the War with Mexico also saw the production of an American occupation newspaper, *The American Star*, and the war was the first in history to be photographed. Though relatively few daguerreotypes of the war exist today, *The American Star* was full of advertisements by traveling daguerreotypists who urged the soldiers to "send a keepsake home to your wife or sweetheart." These Mexican War daguerreotypes are, very probably, the first photographs of the Far West.

Some of the most interesting eyewitness pictures of the Mexican War and parts of the far Southwest are the work of an amateur, Samuel E. Chamberlain, who served as a volunteer with various units of the U. S. Cavalry, attached to General Wool's army.[8] Sam Chamberlain left a classic manuscript diary of his adventures, *My Confessions: The Recollections of a Rogue,* profusely illustrated by his own hand. It appears that long after his wartime adventures were over, Chamberlain continued to embellish his diary and add to the numerous illustrations as he served as warden of the Wethersfield State Prison in Connecticut.

Samuel E. Chamberlain, *Mystery of the Desert,* from My Confessions: The Recollections of a Rogue (New York: Harper & Bros., 1956).

Carl Nebel, *Battle of Buena Vista*, (1847). Courtesy Amon Carter Museum, Fort Worth.

Chamberlain notes that as he was growing up in Boston he became a "muscular Christian" at Sheriden's Gymnasium, as well as a devotee of the novels of Walter Scott and James Fenimore Cooper. His excesses of gallantry on behalf of young women continually got him into trouble. Expelled from the

Samuel E. Chamberlain, *Buena Vista, February 28, 1847*, (1849). San Jacinto Battlefield Monument, La Porte, Texas.

Bowdoin Square Baptist Church for beating up the minister, Chamberlain, at age sixteen, found himself headed west to Alton, Illinois. On the way to the west he was smitten by the beautiful daughter of a recently deceased Senator from Arkansas. Any long term arrangement with her became impossible when he had to flee Alton, Illinois, due to his having laid out both his uncle and his cousin.

Eventually Chamberlain found himself in San Antonio, and enlisted in the First U. S. Dragoons under the command of Colonel William S. Harney. The First Dragoons were under General Wool's command, and Chamberlain records his participation in the street battle for Monterrey, the battle of Buena Vista, and the little mentioned continual skirmishes with Mexican guerrillas. All of these scenes of combat and his multifarious chivalric encounters with women he recorded in a series of charming folk paintings. But perhaps the most interesting of his works came after he deserted from the Army and rode through Sonora and Arizona with the Glanton band of outlaws. There he saw the Grand Canyon and painted scenes of fights with the Apaches and a burned-out wagon on the Mojave desert. Lugubrious folk art that they were, Sam Chamberlain's private collection of paintings that finally came to light in the twentieth century, were among the earliest American views of the Southwest, including Texas, North Mexico, Arizona, and California.

The Mexican War generated many forms of popular art, including illustrated sheet music like "Santa Anna's Wooden Leg." But it was really recorded as history by three principal artists: James Walker, Henry Walke, and Carl Nebel. All three men painted grand operatic history paintings of the war's

Currier and Ives, Unknown artist, *Capture of General La Vega by the Gallant Captain May* Courtesy Amon Carter Museum, Fort Worth.

Currier and Ives, *Battle of Resaca de la Palma, May 9th, 1846.* Courtesy Amon Carter Museum, Fort Worth.

battles. The works of Walke, who painted principally the naval engagements from the deck of the bomb-brig *Vesuvius,* commanded by Matthew Calbraith Perry, and Scott's campaign, and of Carl Nebel who painted all of the major battles in Mexico, were made into incredibly beautiful and expensive lithographs for wide distribution. James Walker painted the *Battle of Chapultepec* (the war's last battle) on a commission from the United States Government. Both Walker and Nebel had been in Mexico when the war started, consequently they knew it well. In fact, Nebel had already produced an exquisite set of lithographs of the then known archaeological sites in Mexico. His grand paintings of the Mexican War were all done from the United States' point of view. They appeared together with a text by George Wilkins Kendall, making up Nebel and Kendall's *Pictorial History of the Mexican War.* Nebel's illustrations were often made from on-the-spot sketches, though the *History* did not come out until 1850. This was due to the fact that both Nebel and Kendall wanted the illustrations to be of the finest quality. They secured lithographers and watercolorists in Paris, where Nebel apparently supervised the finishing of the pictures. The Paris correspondent for the New York *Herald* wrote that the set was "one of the most superb works of art ever achieved in Paris."[9] This was high praise in France where since Napoleon's campaigns, military art and military prints had been perhaps the most fashionable form of French art.

The war with Mexico had indeed turned the nation's eyes to the West. Scenes of battle, whether authentic or imagined, commanded attention, as did pictures of places like Bent's Fort, the fur trade bastion on the Arkansas. For virtually the first time the visual curiosity of Americans concerning the West was aroused, and this curiosity was heightened when, in the Treaty of Guadalupe Hidalgo ending the war, the United States acquired the remainder of its vast western territories, including California, often described as a land of promise. Thus, what were essentially wartime propaganda pictures and personal souvenirs, directly served the great national objective of Manifest Destiny. They glorified the "transacting" of William Gilpin's "untransacted destiny," but they also created a demand for more and more information about the Far West.

CHAPTER 9

THE GREAT RECONNAISSANCE

*A*s a result of the Mexican War, the United States gained a trans-
Mississippi empire which included New Mexico, Arizona, Utah, Nevada, parts
of Texas and California. Much of this was unknown country and, as a result
of public clamour for information about the newly acquired lands, during the
1840s and 1850s the United States Government sent numerous exploring
expeditions into the Far West. Taken together, they added up to a "great
reconnaissance" of the entire West. As dozens of profusely illustrated government publications came off the presses and were made available to the public,
for the first time Americans began to gain a comprehensive view of the geography of the Far West. Before this, as the historian, Bernard De Voto has
written, "Manifest Destiny was blindfolded."

Well, not quite. Even before the war with Mexico, a number of emigrant
parties began filing West over the South Pass, and then either via Fort Hall in
Idaho to Oregon or via the Humboldt River west of the Great Salt Lake to
California. The first important emigrant party to reach California was the
Bartleson–Bidwell Party, composed mostly of Missourians of the kind that
George Caleb Bingham was painting at the time.[1] In fact, one of its leaders,

John Bidwell, had just been robbed by a band of Missourians, and decided to head for the safer pastures of Mexican California to recoup his fortunes. These argonauts were guided part way by the same veteran mountain man who had guided Sir William Drummond Stewart, Tom "Broken Hand" Fitzpatrick. In 1843 two more parties were guided west to California by mountain men, one by J. B. Chiles, who had first made the trip with the Bartleson–Bidwell party, and the other by Joseph Rutherford Walker, with whom Zenas Leonard had been traveling in 1834 when he first had his vision, of California's American future. In 1844 the Stevens–Murphy party, composed of more "Middle Border" Missourians, crossed over into California via the Truckee Pass, near present-day Reno. Thus, there was already a push by Americans, invited or not, to invade Mexican territory or British territory in Oregon, as the case may be, and make them into American colonies. The "plain republicans" of Missouri, Arkansas, Tennessee, and other "Middle Border" states were almost inevitably fulfilling Zenas Leonard's prophecy, thus making Manifest Destiny seem a viable slogan.

These early emigrants were far too busy to make pictures of the country through which they passed. In fact, they were too busy and/or confused even to make maps. It was not until 1846 that T. H. Jefferson, a member of the ill-fated Donner Party, which had been stranded for the winter in the Sierras,

Preuss/Fremont, *Section of Emigrant Map.* Library of Congress.

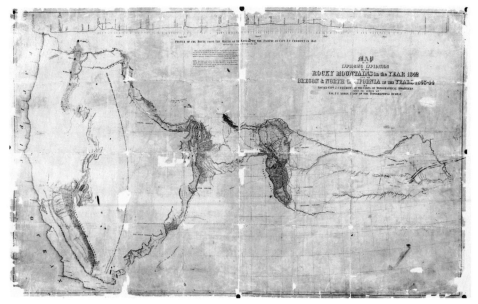

produced a viable emigrant guide map. By this time, the United States Government had turned its attention to the problem. In 1842, at the behest of
Senator Thomas Hart Benton of Missouri, the U. S. Army sent Benton's son-
in-law, the flamboyant Lieutenant John C. Frémont, to map the Oregon Trail
as far as the South Pass over the Continental Divide. Frémont carried out
these orders and more. He climbed what he thought was the highest peak in
the "Mountains of the Wind," or Wind River Range so beloved of William
Drummond Stewart, and raised a homemade eagle flag, declaring all the country around to be American territory. When his report was printed by Congress
and distributed in the thousands, Frémont's climb to the top of the Wind
River Mountains became a beacon and an inspiration to Americans contemplating the trek westward. It also made Frémont an instant American hero,
"the Pathfinder." Lieutenant Frémont became even more famous when, in
1843–4, he led a band of men all the way over the Oregon Trail, then south
along the mountain wall that stood before California, and finally over the
mountains and into California, which he described in glowing terms as a land
of promise. During 1843–4 Lieutenant Frémont "circumnavigated," or marched
around the whole West, and was responsible for making the first scientifically
derived map of the country, as well as the first accurate, detailed emigrant
map of the road to Oregon. These were actually drawn by Frémont's crusty
Prussian cartographer, Charles Preuss, who was constantly critical of Frémont,
but nonetheless served him well. These early maps were perhaps the most
useful pictures of the West that could be made at the time. In his 1843–4
report, however, Frémont also included some relatively crude drawings of the
country traversed, and of his assault on the towering Sierras in the winter.
The drawings, made either by Frémont himself or his cartographer, Preuss,
were scarcely informative, but they underscored the necessity for more and
better views of the country into which Americans, especially after the Mexican War, were certain to move.

The genre of art produced by the numerous military exploring expeditions
to the West in the 1840s and 1850s was a combination of romantic viewpaint-
ing and topographical renditions with pretensions to scientific accuracy. These
Western views of the Manifest Destiny era, because they were not art in the
grand or painterly manner, but, rather, sketches and watercolors, have been
largely overlooked by art historians. In fact only two books discuss the genre
in general.[2] The views were meant as scientific illustrations, and often appeared
in the government reports, along with detailed drawings of plants, animals,
fossils and Indians. They were done in much the same spirit that the Seymour

and Peale drawings on Major Stephen H. Long's expedition of 1819–20 were rendered. In fact, for much of the nineteenth century, in the United States there was a symbiotic relationship between science and art. These Western views of the middle period, designed to be made into lithographs, were only the most obvious examples of this relationship. For the most part the artists went out into the West with the idea of accurate documentation in mind, but so stunned were they by what they saw—ranging from rock formations to immense herds of buffalo—that they inevitably produced romanticized interpretations of the unknown territory.

It will not do here to discuss all of the thousands of views produced by the artists of "the Great Reconnaissance." Three examples should suffice. In the first instance, the year 1848 saw the three Kern brothers, Richard, Edward and Benjamin, from Philadelphia, heading West with John C. Frémont to search for a railroad route to the Pacific Ocean via the 35th parallel.[3] This particular expedition ended in disaster as Frémont and his mountain man guide, Old Bill Williams, led the exploring party into the impassable mountains of northern

Richard Kern, *Ruins of an Old Pueblo, Canyon de Chelly.* Library, Academy of Natural Sciences of Philadelphia.

Richard Kern, *Robidoux Pass, White Mountains, New Mexico, 1848.* Courtesy Amon Carter Museum, Fort Worth.

New Mexico in the middle of winter. A number of men died as the explorers tried to get down from the mountains. Some reports implied that, in starving condition, the men resorted to cannibalism. In the end, both Benjamin Kern and Old Bill Williams were killed by Ute Indians as they returned to reclaim baggage, including scientific specimens that the party had to leave behind. But during all the travail of the winter march, Richard Kern, who was also a member of the Academy of Natural Sciences of Philadelphia, bravely continued to sketch and paint in watercolors the rugged country in which he found himself. Most of the splendid watercolors were done on the pages of an artist's sketching book. All of the surviving views were highly romantic, despite the fact that Kern had previously spent a great deal of time at the Philadelphia Academy of Natural Sciences making the same kind of very exact drawings of animals and fossils, etc., as had Titian Peale. But, for example, *Robidoux's Pass, White Mountains, N. M.* (1848) exaggerates the gorgelike qualities of the pass which today is called Mosca Pass. Kern even managed to render a romantic winter landscape view, framed by trees and backed by a mountain in Claudian style, of the relief camp where he was ultimately rescued. He put himself and the others in the picture to the left as tiny, almost indistinct figures. Upon his return from this disastrous expedition Kern painted in watercolor what is

Richard Kern, *Taos Valley*, Courtesy the Amon Carter Museum, Fort Worth.

perhaps the first view of Taos Valley—the first, that is, in what came to be a very long line of artistic renditions of the scene, culminating in the Taos Society of Artists in the twentieth century, a group that also found the sparkling valley an irresistible subject for their brushes.

For a considerable time Richard and Edward Kern found themselves stranded in New Mexico, since Frémont went on to the West Coast, deserting them even before their rescue was completed. This proved to be a great opportunity for them, however, for in 1849 they accompanied Colonel John N. Washington's punitive expedition against the Navajos north and west of Santa Fe. They served under the direct orders of Lieutenant James H. Simpson, a humane and learned officer of the Corps of Topographical Engineers. On this expedition, the Kerns reached what one observer has called "The Luxor of America." In fact, they found two "Luxors" and one "Persepolis." Richard Kern was the first to paint the spectacular wonders of Canyon de Chelly. On September 8, 1849 he painted the ruins of an Anasazi cliff house tucked away beneath a massive overhanging cliff. It was a major iconic view of the mysterious vanished civilizations of the southwest and the scene was copied many times, most spectacularly by the photographer Timothy O'Sullivan in the late nineteenth century. Kern also visited the great Chaco Canyon in New Mexico, with its enormous apartment house pueblos. Chaco Canyon was the site of the largest pre-historic Indian civilization in North America, with the possible exception of Cahokia on the Mississippi opposite St. Louis.

The Kerns spent days inspecting and measuring the giant Anasazi structures. One of Richard Kern's drawings deserves especially to be remembered. It was a surprisingly accurate reconstruction of the Pueblo Penasca Blanco in Chaco Canyon as a semicircular, stepped-back apartment house, built around a ceremonial square.[4] The Kerns also came upon numerous other giant-sized, now silent and mysterious, structures. The Indians believed that they marked Montezuma's stopping place on his march southward into Mexico, but Kern recognized that here was evidence of a distinct, lost or vanished civilization, whose descendants might or might not be the pueblo dwellers along the Rio Grande. Given such wondrous and, at the same time, mysterious sites to inspect and paint, it is not surprising that Kern's artistic imagination ran to the romantic. The same impulse was striking viewpainters who went to Egypt, India, China and the South Seas at the same time.

And if Chaco Canyon and the Arizona Canyon de Chelly were not enough, the command marched south to Zuñi, the site of Coronado's "Seven Cities of Cibola." This complex was populated and hardly as mysterious, but El Morro, or Inscription Rock, nearby, upon which conquistadors and Indians alike had scratched their names, gave special significance to Zuñi. Kern and Simpson added their names to the desert ledger. On the way back to Santa Fe, Kern was fascinated by the sky-high city atop a mesa named Acoma. He painted this several times. But in addition, at the very start of the expedition at Jemez, Kern also was the first white man to descend into and paint or record the inside of a pueblo kiva. There would be possibly only three other white men in the nineteenth century to do this, Capt. John Gregory Bourke and Peter Moran at the Hopi Mesa Pueblo of Walpi, and Frank Hamilton Cushing at Zuni. Thus Kern's data, as well as his art, was of capital importance.

In 1851, while Edward Kern headed back to Philadelphia, Richard accompanied Captain Lorenzo Sitgreaves on a march across the Southwest via Zuñi, where he recorded the Indian Buffalo or Tablita Dance, the San Francisco Mountains below the Grand Canyon, the Mojave Villages near the junction of the Gila and Colorado Rivers, and the Mojave Desert on the way to San Diego. This expedition, constantly assaulted by warlike Indians, nonetheless also provided Kern with the opportunity to paint some spectacular views which, when made into lithographs, took on a curiously oriental look.

In 1853, while accompanying Lieutenant John Williams Gunnison on one

Heinrich B. Mollhausen, *The Grand Canyon of the Colorado,* (1861). Barker Texas History Center, The University of Texas, Austin.

of the reconnaissances for a railroad to the Pacific that year, Kern was murdered by Paiute Indians on the Sevier River near Utah Lake. His drawings survived, however, and were completed for the lithographer by John Mix Stanley, who was also on a railroad survey that year.

Indeed, 1853 was the climactic year of "the Great Reconnaissance." That year, under Secretary of War Jefferson Davis's orders, six exploring parties crossed the West in search of "the most practicable and economical route for a railroad to the Pacific Ocean."[5] There were seven surveys *across* the West: one along the 48th parallel, two (due to the death of Lieutenant Gunnison) on the 38th parallel, one on the 35th parallel, and two, one going west and one going east from California along the 32nd parallel, while two other expeditions marched north and south up and down the Pacific Coast. These railroad survey expeditions did not finally locate the transcontinental railroad route they were looking for, or at least one that would convince a very divided eve-of-the-Civil-War Congress. They did, however, provide a massive inventory of the West in thirteen large volumes.[6] Each area was mapped, and then these maps were combined into one climactic scientific map compiled by the overseer of all the surveys, Lieutenant Gouverneur Kemble Warren. Of all the maps that had begun to rapidly fill in the unknown vacant spaces in the West, Lieutenant Warren's was most complete. It was, after Lewis and Clark's map, the most important of all the western maps. But in addition to Warren's and other maps, the thirteen volumes were profusely illustrated with pictures of the flora, the fauna, the rock formations, fossils, Indians and landscapes. They represented a massive inventory of the West.

In addition to the scientific illustrators who drew the specimens brought back in Washington, twelve artists traveled in the field with the exploring parties, braving the dangers from Indians, as did Richard Kern, or the hardships of a hard land. Some of the artists were refugees from revolutions in Germany, but all of the survey artists' names are worth remembering, because theirs was one of the great epic adventures and contributions to knowledge of the nineteenth century in America, and they have yet to receive their due. They are Richard Kern, John Mix Stanley, F. W. von Egloffstein, Heinrich B. Mollhausen, Lieutenant Henry Tidball, Archibald Campbell, Charles Koppel, W. P. Blake, John Young, James G. Cooper, and Private Gustavus Sohon. The art historian, Barbara Novak, however, has aptly described what they were all about.

> In Europe, the tour de force generally received its scale from the artists' ambition, set resplendently within a major tradition. In America, it consisted in simply "getting there." The artist became the hero of his own journey—which replaced the heroic themes of mythology—by vanquishing physical obstacles enroute to a destination. For the ambition of the artistic enterprise was substituted the ambition of the artist's quest—itself a major nineteenth-century theme. In this displacement of the heroic from the work of art to the persona of the artist lay, perhaps, part of the attraction of unexplored territory for the American artist at mid-century.[7]

Most of the artists rendered view paintings that, though purporting to be scientific, were actually highly romanticized. Private Sohon seemed fixated on the Hellgate of the Snake River and painted it several times, once in winter

Private Gustavus Sohon, *Crossing the Hellgate,* (1854). Pacific Railroad Survey Reports. William H. Goetzmann Collection.

F. W. von Egloffstein, *Franklin Valley, Humboldt Mountains (The Great Reconnaissance)*, (1853).
Pacific Railroad Survey Reports, Vol XI. William H. Goetzmann Collection.

John Mix Stanley, *Oregon City on the Willamette River*, (ca. 1852). Courtesy Amon Carter
Museum of Western Art, Fort Worth.

and then in the summer, where one of his views resembled Gericault's *The Raft of the Medusa*. Campbell was especially effective in rendering the Southwestern deserts and the ancient marine terraces that would one day be marked as the sight of long vanished Lake Lahonton by the flamboyant geologist, Clarence King. The German, Mollhausen, painted the Southwest as if it were the surface of the moon, and all the Indians he portrayed as glum-faced— clearly sad that the white man was invading their territory. In a pique, his commanding officer, Lieutenant A. W. Whipple stated in his report that the only thing accurate about Mollhausen's drawings were the Navajo blankets. But then Lieutenant Whipple himself egregiously over-estimated the cost of a 35th parallel railroad route through faulty addition, and hence doomed the chances for the best compromise between North and South as to the western railroad route.

The work of two artists stood out. F. W. von Egloffstein painted immense and exacting panoramas illustrating the central railroad route. His drawings, with place names below the picture, were perhaps the only drawings that would have been helpful to railroad builders or site engineers. Yet these drawings, too, were highly romantic in content. One showed an Indian and his dog resting atop the Wasatch Mountains like some nature god sadly surveying all that he had once possessed.

The other significant artist is already familiar to us. He is John Mix Stanley, who was attempting to mount an Indian Gallery. Stanley traveled west on the 48th parallel route with the Washington Territorial Governor Isaac I. Stevens. In scenes like *Herd of Buffalos Near Lake Jessie, Panorama of the Rocky Mountains* (adapted from Sohon's splendid watercolor sketches), *Palouse Falls* and numerous other watercolor paintings, Stanley created spectacular views. Some of these watercolor field sketches he converted later into impressive oil paintings like *Scene on the Columbia River, Scouts Along the Teton River,* and a splendid rendition of *Oregon City on the Willamette River* as a prosperous and highly symbolic city set down in the wilderness. Taken together, Stanley's watercolors and oils, made as a result of his work on the Stevens survey, amount to an impressive body of work. Almost none of it, however, was of any real use to a would-be railroad builder. Like most of the other artists on the railroad surveys, Stanley painted scenes that conveyed atmosphere and a generalized idea of the country. And since the reconnaissance was made in the summer, he never portrayed the cold Dakota-Montana-Idaho winters. Only Sohon, in one of his Hellgate pictures, did that.

Mollhausen deserves special attention. He first came to America in 1849.

In 1851 he joined a countryman, Duke Paul of Wurttemberg, in a journey across the prairie to Fort Laramie. On the return trip, their wagon broke down, and the Duke left Mollhausen out on the wintry Kansas prairie alone with the wagon in the country of hostile Indians. Mollhausen bravely stood off the hostile Pawnee and a pack of hungry wolves with the small arsenal he had assembled, but the Duke never returned for him. Instead, he was rescued by some friendly Otoes.

As previously mentioned, Mollhausen served with Lieutenants Whipple and Joseph Christmas Ives on the 35th parallel railroad survey in 1853 with indifferent results. Then in 1857 Mollhausen and Egloffstein were selected by Lieutenant Ives to be the first explorers of the floor of the Grand Canyon. Egloffstein's vertical rendering of Black Canyon (now under Lake Mead) at first looks like a poor imitation of a print by Gustave Doré, as does his first view of *The Big Canyon*, but when compared with photos of the same spots they prove to be very accurate, though charged with romantic atmosphere.[8] To Mollhausen must go the honor of making the first real pictorial representation of the Grand Canyon. It is a moody scene with vultures and dead trees clinging to the banks above, but it does convey the vastness of the Canyon. Mollhausen later became famous back in Germany as he walked the streets of Potsdam, invariably clad in a mountain man's costume, and was referred to by his friends as "Der alte Trapper." When the American painter, Charles Deas, tried the same thing in St. Louis, he was put into an asylum for the rest of his life, which may say something about the difference between the Old World and the New. Of course, Mollhausen's circumstances were a bit different. He also wrote some forty novels in German about the American West, and in some circles was known as the German Fenimore Cooper. Thus, his hairy costume may have been regarded on the Kurfurstendam as a form of advertisement for himself.

By the time the Great Reconnaissance was completed, much of the data collected was beside the point for the average would-be western traveler. It was more important to the scientific world than to western argonauts. This was so because, hearing of the fertile Oregon Country, a host of farmers headed off along the Oregon Trail to the new land, to opportunities symbolized by Stanley's painting of *Oregon City on the Willamette*. After the discovery of gold at Sutter's Mill in 1848, another host of Forty Niners headed West by every possible route, including overcrowded ships around the Horn, or fever-ridden caravans crossing the Isthmus of Panama. Thus the historian, Daniel Boorstin is in part correct when he writes, "the West was settled before it was explored."[9]

10

OVERLAND TO AN EMPIRE:
DREAM, NIGHTMARE AND REALITY

It is difficult to tell just what first drove Americans to Oregon's promised lands in the 1840s. The Boston schoolmaster, Hall Jackson Kelley, had propagandized ceaselessly for an American occupation of Oregon since the joint occupation treaty with Britain in 1818. Missouri politicians like Lewis F. Linn and Thomas Hart Benton made the American occupation of the Far West the subject of most of their orations, some of which bordered on the preposterous. Benton, for example, rose in the U. S. Senate and figuratively "toppled" the "Great God Terminus" who barred the way to the promised land in the West. On top of that, he drew himself up on another day, still in the Senate and, pointing *West*, declared "There lies the East. There lies India," and he would have agreed with William Gilpin and Alexander von Humboldt that mass migration westward along an "isothermic zodiacal belt" was indeed America's "untransacted destiny." But Benton's speeches and those of Kelley and Gilpin were no more preposterous than the sight of the tall, straight Vermont missionary, Jason Lee, taking a poor, deformed Indian boy with a sloping forehead from town to town proclaiming that it was the citizens' Christian duty to bring the light of civilization to the Flathead Indians away out in

Fanny F. Palmer, *The Rocky Mountains. Emigrants Crossing the Plains*, (Currier and Ives Print), (1868). The Thomas Gilcrease Institute of American History and Art, Tulsa.

Oregon. Indeed, "the poor, benighted heathen" had asked for such help in *The Christian Advocate*. Who could turn down such a plea from people whose heads were barbarously and cruelly being flattened?

And so the white-topped wagons rolled, first in the 1830s, loaded with missionaries and guided by mountain men. Then in the 1840s plain citizens like Joel Walker and the Jesse Applegate party headed for Oregon, in the latter's case at the head of a cow column. They would settle the beautiful Willamette Valley, while the Stevens–Murphy and Bartleson–Bidwell parties

J. Goldsborough Bruff, *A view from the Summit of Independence Rock exhibiting the Sweet-water river and Mountains, and the Washington City Company corralled, at noon, July 26, 1849*, (Note the names of emigrants carved on the rock, including J. G. Bruff). Henry E. Huntington Library and Art Gallery, San Marino, California.

headed for California, again guided by mountain men. Soon the illustrated magazines like *Harpers Weekly*, "The Magazine of Civilization," and *Leslie's Illustrated Weekly* began to portray in vivid, but imagined, pictures the whole drama of what was becoming the largest peacetime mass migration in history. Thus, artist-illustrators joined the chorus urging Americans to go west. And one of the argonauts, James F. Wilkins, returned east to propagate his overland experiences by means of a moving panorama composed of his drawings made along the Overland Trail.[1] There, as the roll unfolded, was Chimney Rock, Courthouse Rock, Scott's Bluff, Independence Rock, Fort Laramie, Bridger's Fort, the Bear River Mountains, flooded streams, rolling rivers, towering mountains and vast deserts. Going West, Wilkins seemed to suggest, was an epic adventure and not for the weak, the timid, the faint-hearted. His best scene, however, appeared not in his panorama but in a separate painting *Leaving the Old Homestead*. Here a covered wagon stands in a rutted road beside a gothic cottage, while the old folks bid their children and grandchildren a tearful goodbye. A discarded doll lies on the ground, as does an overturned chair, while the manly husband shoulders his rifle and another companion is already climbing aboard the wagon. Such scenes must have been common, as over the drama rolled the stirring words of William Gilpin:

> Let us not forget to estimate magnanimously the unparalleled enterprise now being accomplished, under our eyes, by American pioneers. . . . Citizens each one dependent on himself alone, yet animated by a common impulse driving him irresistibly *Westward!*[2]

Such inflated rhetoric undoubtedly influenced popular Currier and Ives prints like Fanny Palmer's *Immigrant Crossing*. It certainly informed perhaps the key iconic painting of the middle period, Emmanuel Leutze's *Westward the Course of Empire Takes Its Way*, a stereochromed wall painting in the U. S. Capitol that measured a colossal twenty by thirty feet, that included just about everything in the Western experience. Executed in precise, but nearly monochromed Dusseldorf style, the mural portrayed the flow of mountain men and emigrants westward in a great horde, preceded by a Fremont figure atop the highest pinnacle, waving his hat and about to raise the American flag. Among the hopeful argonauts are, not one, but two "prairie madonnas" clasping babes to their breasts. And one woman rides atop a mule pulled by a freed black slave. One Anne Brewster asked the artist:

> "Did you not mean this group to teach a new gospel to this continent, a new truth which this part of the world is to accept—that the Emigrant and the Freed-

man are the two great elements which are to be reconciled and worked with? The young beautiful Irish woman, too, is she not your new Madonna?" The artist's face glowed, and a grim smile gleamed out under the rough mustache. . . . In the first flush of his pleasure he told me I was the first American that had understood his picture.[3]

Leutze was born in Schwabisch-Gmund, not far from Stuttgart in 1816.[4] At an early age he was taken to Philadelphia where he became a portrait painter to help support his family. In 1841, supported by patrons, he went to Dusseldorf determined to become a history painter. Raised in the free atmosphere of America, he soon became a controversial liberal in autocratic Germany. He resigned from the Dusseldorf Art Union and formed his own group, the Union of Dusseldorf Artists for Mutual Aid and Support, in direct defiance of the establishment academicians. In Dusseldorf, Leutze became a magnetic teacher for a generation of aspiring American artists such as George Caleb Bingham, Worthington Whittridge and Albert Bierstadt. He was also suspect by the increasingly repressive Prussian government. During the Rhineland revolution of 1848, Leutze painted his most famous work, *Washington Crossing the Delaware*, as a symbol of freedom to revolting workers. Thus it was not out of character when, later in life, in his *Westward the Course of Empire Takes Its Way*, he gave visual meaning to those words of Henry Thoreau, "eastward I go only by force; but westward I go free . . . we go westward as into the future, with a spirit of enterprise and adventure."

Others were less sanguine than the stay-at-home sage of Concord. Representative John Wentworth of Illinois spoke of the "dauntless spirits" who were making the overland trek. "Only think of it," he declared,

> men, women, and children forsaking their homes, bidding farewell to all the endearments of society, setting out on a journey of over two thousand miles, upon a route where they have to make their own roads, construct their own bridges, hew out their own boats, and kill their own meat; and undergoing every diversity of pain from agues, chills, sprains and bruises; where twenty miles is an average day's travel, exposed to every variety of weather, and the naked earth their only resting place! In sickness they have no physician; in death there is no one to perform the last sad offices. Their bodies are buried by the wayside, to be exhumed and defiled by the Indians, or devoured by the wolves.[5]

Occasionally it got even worse. The *St. Joseph [Missouri] Gazette* reported that one woman had "eaten parts of the dead bodies of her father and brother." "Another," according to the *Gazette*, "had seen her husband's heart cooked."[6]

Because of the hardships of life on the trail, there are relatively few eye-witness renderings of the overland experience. The most famous of these are the charming folk drawings of J. Goldsborough Bruff, former West Point draftsman who became a '49er, James F. Wilkins's surviving drawings and paintings, an illustrated diary by James W. Audubon, Frederic Piercey's precise drawings of the Mormon overland experience, and a lengthy series of paintings made in 1866 by the photographer, William Henry Jackson. The latter were designed less for aesthetic merit than to record accurately the way the westward migration actually looked, with wagon trains coursing the trail in lines abreast of one another, rather than in a long series. Though drawn while on a later wagon train, Jackson's are probably our most accurate surviving visual renditions of the experience.

Joseph Goldsborough Bruff had been a West Point cadet, a sailor, and was currently a U. S. Government draftsman in Washington, D. C. when he heard the news of the gold discovery in California. He organized 63 men into the Washington City and California Mining Association. In 13 wagons under his leadership they crossed the West to the Sierras in 120 days. In these moun-

Emmanuel Gottlieb Leutze, *Across the Continent, Westward the Course of Empire Takes its Way,* (1864). (Study for Mural, U.S. Capitol), National Museum of American Art, Smithsonian Institution, Washington, D.C., Bequest of Sara Carr Upton.

Albert Bierstadt, *The Oregon Trail,* (1869). Butler Institute of American Art, Youngstown, Ohio.

Albert Bierstadt, *Indians
Near Fort Laramie,* (1859).
Museum of Fine Arts,
Boston, M. and M.
Karolik Collection.

tains his company deserted him as winter snows set in. They never returned, and ultimately all Bruff had to show for his California adventure was a collection of on-the-spot drawings, and a matchless diary, both of which did not get discovered and published until a hundred years after the great Gold Rush.

J. Goldsborough Bruff's watercolors and pencil sketches have a distinct charm as he portrays his company cooking their food over a buffalo chip fire, or peering down from Independence Rock on a circle of wagons camped far below.[7] He also painted his company rafting across the Platte, and dead cattle abandoned by a desperate company at polluted Rabbit Hole Springs. In the main, Bruff's scenes are charming and often droll, as when he paints a companion tossed by a buffalo, but he also depicted grim scenes on the trail, which he described vividly in his diary. Bruff's folk art, like that of young James W. Audubon, son of the great bird painter, is comparable to Sam Chamberlain's scenes of the Mexican War. In their sense of authenticity they are far different from the rosy, patriotic views that generally appeared in the illustrated magazines or in Currier and Ives prints.

Among the more professional painters, portrayals of the Overland Trail experience divide up into the epic "march of empire" triumphant scenes, that are almost dreamlike, and other works depicting the dangers and tragedies of the trail that one might term "nightmare" scenes, or expressions of real or imagined scenes of hardship and terror.

Carl Wimar, *The Attack on an Emigrant Trains*, (c. 1856). The University of Michigan Museum of Art, Ann Arbor. Bequest of Henry C. Lewis.

George Caleb Bingham, *The Concealed Enemy*, (1845). Stark Museum of Art, Orange, Texas.

The most famous of the "march of empire" painters besides Leutze was his student, Albert Bierstadt. Bierstadt, who was born near Dusseldorf but grew up in Marblehead, Massachusetts, painted lurid, back-lit scenes of the Overland Trail. Often the sky is a brilliant orange created by the sun setting in the West, towards which the caravan of white-topped wagons are heading. His grandest painting of this scene is a view of a cavalcade of wagons and horsemen, together with a herd of cattle and sheep, heading westward between giant bluffs on the right and a grove of oak trees on the left. The whole scene is bathed in an eerie, cloud-banked, shimmering orange glow, as if it were all on fire, or as if a glorious future lay, in the poet Joaquin Miller's words, "Way out West in the path of the setting sun." Bierstadt painted this in 1869 after he himself had been West over the Oregon Trail and had seen a wagon train. He named the painting simply *The Oregon Trail.* In 1863 Bierstadt also painted a night scene, back-lit by a campfire with a covered wagon upon which is painted, "For Oregon." This picture, entitled *Campfire,* is less flamboyant than his sunset scenes like *The Oregon Trail* and *The Overland Trail* of 1871 where the wagons and riders disappearing over the horizon are scarcely a factor in the painting which instead seems to be an experiment in the impressionistic handling of light. By leaving the wagons indistinct as they roll over the brown prairie, however, Bierstadt catches the mood rather than the explicit facts of the westward movement. In a sense this feeling for the general mood, rather than the explicit documentary genre scene, was the strength of most of Bierstadt's overland trail paintings. Art historian Matthew Baigell points out that they match up well with the Manifest Destiny orations of William Gilpin, with which we are now familiar, passages like "Surrounded by his wife and children, equipped with wagon, ox-team and provisions, such as the chase does not furnish, accompanied by his rifle and slender outfit of worldly goods, did these harsh men embark upon the unmeasured waste before them."[8]

These later works by Bierstadt contrast sharply with those he painted on his first trip West with surveyor Frederick W. Lander in 1859. In these early works, especially *Surveyor's Wagon on the Prairie*, *Nooning on the Platte* and *Indians Near Fort Laramie*, Bierstadt seems to have been struck by the crystal clear air of the West, and to have tried to capture this shimmering, almost miragelike clarity in these paintings. Perhaps the clarity of these works is due to the fact that Bierstadt had a camera with him on this first trip. Certainly

William Tylee Ranney, *The Old Scout's Tale*, (1853). The Thomas Gilcrease Institute of American History and Art, Tulsa.

Lt. George D. Brewerton, *Jornada del Muerto,* (1853). Oakland Art Museum, Kahn Collection, Photo Credit, M. Lee Fatherree.

Indians Near Fort Laramie appears to be derived from a series of individual Indian photographs that are copied in paint, and then pasted, collagelike on a blue and green sky and prairie background. The effect of this work, in contrast to all his other work, is surreal. No art historian has as yet considered the question of deliberate *unreality* that Bierstadt seems to have injected into many of his paintings at a time when documentary realism was in vogue.

In any case, Bierstadt's work was triumphant, rather than frightening. Other artists closer to the Overland Trail period of the 1840s and 1850s projected the nightmare of Indian attack for example. In 1856 Carl Wimar of St. Louis painted just such a lurid scene, which has become the master image for countless other Indian-attacks-on-wagon-train pictures, and an inspiration to both later painters and Hollywood. The painting was entitled *Attack on an Emigrant Train,* and shows the probably doomed settlers firing their single-shot rifles in a brave attempt to fend off attacking Indians. It is possible that Wimar got the idea and some of the details for this painting from Heinrich B. Mollhausen who, one remembers, had experienced just such a plight on the wintry Kansas plains in 1851–2, before he made his way to safety in Wimar's St. Louis. Certainly Wimar himself did not have such an experience with Indian attackers.

George Caleb Bingham, too, painted a "nightmare" scene in his sinister *The Concealed Enemy* of 1845. This masterful painting depicts a Pawnee as James Fenimore Cooper had described them in his novel *The Prairie*, long rifle in hand, crouched behind some large rocks, fiercely staring down upon what is probably an emigrant train, or some trappers, invading his land. The painting resembles a similar scene by Alfred Jacob Miller, whose exhibition Bingham had seen in the Apollo Gallery in 1839.

Two more explicit Overland Trail paintings are those by the Brooklyn painter, William Tylee Ranney, who is said to have participated in both the Texan Revolution and the Mexican War. Ranney's painting of 1853, *The Old Scout's Tale,* is a genre scene in which a family camped on the prairie appears to be listening intently to advice from an old scout. The people could be members of the Bartleson–Bidwell overlanders listening to "Broken Hand" Fitzpatrick, or any one of a hundred other emigrant groups guided west by former mountain men like Dick Greenwood, Antoine Leroux, Joe Walker, or Kit Carson. One is distracted in viewing this painting, however, by the fact that the figure sprawled in the foreground bears an uncanny resemblance to former president Richard M. Nixon.

Such a distraction does not crop up in Ranney's other moving painting of this genre, *Prairie Burial.* Very European in mood, the scene is perhaps more typical of the overland experience, where far more people died of cholera and other diseases than they ever did from Indian attacks. Overland diaries describe how the dead were buried in shallow graves, their bones soon scattered by wolves and coyotes, or buried near some waterhole where the ground, and hence the digging, was soft, but which spread the cholera to the next wagon train passing through. Thus the Ranney burial scene, probably meant to be touching and sentimental, actually has overtones of menace to it.

"If Injuns an' the cholera don't git ya," one can almost hear the old scout say, then the desert, the "Journado del Muerto" or "Journey of Death," graphically and beautifully depicted by Lieutenant George Brewerton in 1853, "surely will." Lieutenant Brewerton's painting, which actually portrays the immense wastes of the Mojave Desert perhaps more graphically than any other desert painting of the American West, is distinctly germain to the "nightmare" aspects of the Overland Trail experience. Despite the existence of guides and ever more published guide-books, overlanders still got lost in the deserts west of the Great Salt Lake. One of these was a party that included William Lewis Manley, who lived to tell about it in a Western classic, *Death Valley in '49.*

Another was Sarah Royce, the mother of the future Harvard philosopher, Josiah Royce. Sarah Royce's wagon train wandered far off course into the southwestern deserts. She was a devoted, even a mystic Christian, however, and as she put it, after she prayed for help, they were saved "by the light of God and Frémont's *Travels.*"[9]

Thus, though relatively few in number, the Overland Trail paintings do form a distinct genre of dream, nightmare and reality paintings. One of the artists discussed here, William Henry Jackson, had a unique experience not shared by the others. In 1870–71, as a member of Ferdinand V. Hayen's United States Geological Survey of the Territories, he had an opportunity to traverse the old Oregon Trail again, this time with the camera, an instrument that was to make him famous. The photos he made of landmarks of vast spaces to cross and lonely prairie graves, served as a haunting reminder to people in the late nineteenth century of just what a price the common folk of America paid for a continental empire and a foothold in the promised land of the Far West.

CHAPTER **11**

THE ELDORADO VISION

On his last great venture to the New World, Sir Walter Raleigh went to Guiana in South America in search of El Dorado, the golden king who floated on a golden barge on a golden lake in a kingdom where even the family portraits were statues made of gold. Raleigh never found El Dorado. At the behest of the disappointed Virgin Queen, Elizabeth I, he lost his head instead. Dreams of gold have a way of being destructive. So thought Johann Sutter of New Helvetia, California, in January of 1848, when he rode a fateful fifty miles north from his fort to a millrace constructed by one of his hired men, James Marshall, on the American River, a stream that flowed down out of the Sierras. Marshall claimed to have discovered gold in the river on a Monday, January 24, 1848. But Sutter, who already owned a pastoral paradise that included 12,000 head of cattle, 10,000 sheep, 1,000 hogs, and 2,000 horses and mules, plus a harvest of 40,000 bushels of wheat, had misgivings. As he rode north, he remembered that the Indians had warned him that "gold was bad medicine; it belonged to a jealous demon who lived in a mountain lake with gold-lined shores." The night before his fateful northward ride he remembered this and awoke as in a nightmare that laid out the future before

E. Hall Martin, *Mountain Jack and a Wandering Miner*, (c. 1850). Oakland Art Museum, Gift of the Concours D'Antiques; Photo Credit: M. Lee Fatherree.

him. "The curse of the thing burst upon my mind," he remembered, "I saw from the beginning how the end would be, and I had a melancholy ride of it to the sawmill."[1] Sutter was right to be melancholy. As a result of the gold discovery he lost his pastoral empire, and California, swarming with goldseekers from everywhere in 1849, changed character overnight. It was not until some thirty years later that anyone tried to recapture images of pre-El Dorado California.

Anonymous, *Miner with Eight Pound Gold Nugget*, Collection Mr. and Mrs. Philip Kendall Bekeart, San Francisco.

No longer would California be seen as the pastoral paradise described by John C. Frémont, whose 1843–4 expedition had walked right over the gold in the American River. Richard Henry Dana's description of a land dotted with picturesque, crumbling missions and immense Mexican ranches became as obsolete as William S. Jewett's panoramic view of the American River Valley near Sutter's sawmill, painted in 1850. Jewett was a successful New York portrait painter when he joined a Gold Rush company in 1849. He found no gold in California, so in 1850 he established portrait studios in San Francisco and Sacramento.[2] He became California's earliest painter, and the first to paint the Valley of the Yosemite. As a portraitist of the newly rich gold tycoons, rather than as a landscapist, Jewett made enough money to buy a castle in the Pyrenees, far away from El Dorado. But his first landscape scene captured the sense of what was about to happen in California. The mountains stretch away to an infinity in the middle distance, and a river wends its way through a vast unpopulated country. But the viewer is standing on a hill looking straight down at the hamlet of Coloma that had recently sprung up around Sutter's fateful mill. To the right at the base of some tall, twisted trees, a solitary Indian looks down at the scene of change, the beginning of the end of a way of life that brought with it its own kind of curse.

Back in the East, after receiving specimens specially rushed across the continent by Marine Lieutenant Edward Fitzgerald Beale, and a tea caddy full of the yellow metal brought to him by Colonel Richard Mason, President Polk officially announced to Congress that gold had been found in great quantities in California. By the end of the year men like Horace Greeley were urging young men to hurry West. "We are on the brink of an Age of Gold," he trumpeted in the *New York Daily Tribune*. "We look for an addition within the next four years equal to at least One Thousand Millions of Dollars. . . ."

Currier and Ives, *Grand Patent India-Robber Air line Railway.* The Oakland Museum, Gift of the Oakland Museum Founder's Fund. Photo Credit: M. Lee Fatherree.

Two days later he embellished on the dream of gold in a way that would have made even Raleigh blush:

> We are all fairly afloat. We don't see any links of probability missing in the golden chain by which Hope is drawing her thousands of disciples to the new El Dorado, where fortune lies abroad upon the surface of the earth as plentiful as the mud in our streets, and where the old saying "a pocket full of rocks" meets a golden realization. The perilous stuff lies loose upon the surface of the ground, or only slightly adheres to rocks and sand. The only machinery necessary in the new Gold mines of California is a stout pair of arms, a shovel and a tin pan. Indeed many, unable even to obtain these utensils are fain to put up with a shingle or a bit of board, and dig away quietly in peace of mind, pocketing their fifty or sixty dollars a day and having plenty of leisure.[3]

The whole country began to dream of gold, to have a vision of El Dorado. This was captured in paintings like E. Hall Martin's extraordinary *Mountain Jack and a Wandering Miner,* the very epitome of the Gold Rush dreamer dreaming while high up in the Sierras. Or the El Dorado vision could be communicated by means of daguerreotypes like one portraying the successful miner holding a golden nugget the size of a cabbage. Thousands of pictures like these were sent back home, as were photographs of miners sluicing gold happily from California's shimmering rivers. Very possibly the photos and the daguerreotypes were most important in convincing people to head for California, proving in many cases that "photos do lie." But then so, too, did paintings, if anyone happened to see one. William McIlvaine's book, *Sketches of Scenery and Notes of Personal Adventure, in California and Mexico. Containing Sixteen Lithographic Plates* (1850) featured the miners digging and panning in the golden rivers of California. One of the first to be on the spot digging, he painted the scene as well, then climaxed his efforts by allowing one Russell Smith to fashion a popular moving panorama based on his drawings and paintings. The panorama was first exhibited in Philadelphia in 1850. Thus the publicity encouraging people to head for California was relentless. In the decade from 1849 to 1860 some 296,259 people took the overland route to California.[4] This did not count the large number of people who left their shops, their farms, their ranches and even their army posts to head for the gold fields by other routes. By 1850 well over 100,000 miners were combing California's hills and river valleys looking for traces of "color" or, even better, the "mother lode." In less than two weeks San Francisco's population dropped from several hundred souls to perhaps two

Charles Christian Nahl, *Saturday Night at the Mines.* Stanford University Museum of Art, Palo Alto, California, Gift of Jane Lathrop Stanford.

dozen, causing the major newspaper, the *Californian* to fold.[5] In a last editorial, the proprietor railed, "The whole country resounds with the sordid cry of gold! GOLD! GOLD!!! while the field is left half planted, the house half built and everything neglected but the manufacture of shovels and pickaxes." Shortly

William Sidney Mount, *California News,* (1850). Melville Collection, Suffolk Museum and Carriage House, Stony Brook, New York.

Charles Christian Nahl, *Sunday Morning at the Mines*, (1872). Courtesy Crocker Art Museum, Sacramento, California.

afterwards, the *Californian's* rival *The Star* also folded, and its editor dashed off for the diggings. Captain Sutter's Swiss gardener wrote:

> Exciting rumors began to spread with the rapidity of a great epidemic. Everyone was infected, and, as it spread, peace and quiet vanished. To all appearances men seemed to have gone insane . . . they were, apparently, living in a dream. Each man had to stop and ask himself: "Am I mad? Is this all for real? Is what I see with my own eyes actually gold, or is it merely my imagination? Is it a Chimera? Am I delirious?"[6]

Soon, whole flotillas of ships from everywhere on the globe—Hawaii, China, Australia, Europe and the East Coast of America—began to converge on San Francisco. Donald McKay's fast clipper ships, captained by men who used Lieutenant Matthew Fontaine Maury's "Winds and Currents Charts" set records sailing passengers around the Horn for the gold diggings. But almost any conveyance would do, from the sleek new clippers to rebuilt whalers or puffing steamers never meant for ocean travel. The Aspinwall Co. of New York got rich just hauling people to Panama's fever-ridden isthmus and up jungle rivers and over a short railroad portage to the Pacific shores. There was even Rufus Porter's " Air Line to California."[7] Porter was the founder of *Scientific American* magazine, so his visionary scheme had plausibility. He quickly signed up 200 passengers at $50 a head for a three-day trip from New York to San Francisco, "wines included." In New York he unveiled a model of his 1,000-foot long propeller-driven balloon to be powered by two steam engines. So confident was Porter that he predicted that the trip to San Francisco might take only twenty-four hours, certainly no more than five days in case of massive head winds. He called his contraption variously an "Aerial Locomotive" or an "Areoplane." Most newspapers called it "humbug," and Nathaniel Currier devoted one of a set of satirical cartoons entitled "How They Get to California" to Porter's "Aerial Locomotive" and another suggesting that the argonauts could be shot to the West Coast by means of a good stout rubber band. Currier also lampooned travel by ship. The best of these cartoons was a picture of a whale in harness towing a huge nugget of gold. The caption read, "An accurate drawing of the famous hill of gold which has been put into a scow by the owner, and attached to a sperm whale towing it around the horn."[8] Currier's whole series was replete with preposterous scenes of travel to and from California. The return journey, even for those who struck it rich, was difficult because as soon as a ship docked in San Francisco, its crew, as well as its passengers, deserted the ship. By 1850 there were already two hundred abandoned ships in San Francisco's harbor. Some of these were beached and served as semi-floating "hotels" where unwary sailors were frequently "shanghaied" back to sea duty.

The excitement of the gold discovery and the adventure of sailing to California even captured the imagination of the normally pastoral painter of Long Island scenes, William Sidney Mount. His view of a New York post office, painted in 1850 and entitled *California News,* is a masterful genre painting. One man reads Horace Greeley's *New York Daily Tribune,* while all those around him—women, a child, an old man, a black, and even a swain who points to the paper—listen intently to the news. Above their head on the wall hangs a Kentucky long rifle, symbol of a different age, while clearly evident is a large poster advertising the ship *Loo Choo,* bound for San Francisco on Thursday morning, March 1st. There is not a trace of satire in this picture. Mount, like his fellow New Yorker, Walt Whitman, was genuinely interested in the pioneers and the gold strike in California. The *Hartford Courant* for December 6, 1848, printed the day after President Polk's message to Congress, was not so enthusiastic; a gold rush would draw cheap labor from the East. Its editor reported testily:

> The California gold fever is approaching its crisis. . . . By a sudden and acciden-
> tal discovery, the ground is represented to be one vast gold mine. —Gold is
> picked up in pure lumps, twenty-four carats fine. . . . The stories are evidently
> thickening in interest, as do the arithmetical calculations connected with them
> in importance. Fifteen millions have already come into the possession of *some-
> body,* and all creation is going out there to fill their pockets with the great con-
> diment of their diseased minds.[9]

Still, companies of miners were formed daily for the purpose of what they called "seeing the elephant"—a kind of euphemism, derived from an old farm-er's story, that covered up embarrassment at so blatantly seeking easy wealth. A cartoon by McMurtrie, published as a lithograph by E. F. Butler in San Francisco, became a widely distributed view of the experience. Seeing real gold was like seeing one of P. T. Barnum's marvels.

The "elephants" and the "marvels" were of course the gold diggings and the mining camps. The towns bore picturesque names such as Hangtown, French Gulch, Bidwell's Bar, Columbia, Sonora, Downieville and Grass Valley. A number of photographs of these towns exist, such as views of Hangtown, which indeed looks sinister, or Sonora and Grass Valley, which, with their citizens proudly posing before a building on a main street, could just as well have been the subject of a George Caleb Bingham painting. But paintings or drawings of the life of the first generation of miners are rare because men who were for-merly artists were too busy digging for gold.

One of the most productive recorders of the Gold rush experience was Charles Nahl, a German who had studied in Cassel, Germany, and in Paris.[10] His mature style was strictly late German romantic or "Biedermeier," as it was called because of its fussiness and overdecoration. Charles and his half-brother Arthur arrived at the gold diggings in 1851. His first important work, done in 1851 with Frederick Augustus Wenderoth, was entitled *Miners in the Sierra.* It is a straightforward, skillfully painted view of four miners working a sluice-box on a river in a rugged defile in the Sierras. It is a cleverly composed series of balanced diagonals with the sluice-box and the stream counter-balancing one another as the eye is led deeper into the picture.

Nahl is best known for two paintings: *Saturday Evening at the Mines* and *Sunday Morning at the Mines.* In the former, Nahl shows three men measuring

out the day's "take," while a fourth makes supper over an open fire that provides, besides a candle and moonlight, the only light in the cabin. A fifth
member is asleep in his bunk, while the most dramatic person sits clutching a
whiskey bottle and grinning in a drunken stupor. Nahl used an exaggerated
glowing red light from the fireplace to lead the eye across the painting and
tie the figures together in its warm glow.

Sunday Morning at the Mines is a sprawling, masterful canvas that resembles
a frieze more than a single picture. It is broken up into groups or clusters of
miners in a genre scene that has two foci. In the center of the picture, an
insanely drunk man dances and waves his arm, slightly resembling Bingham's
Jolly Raftsman. This dancing figure, however, has to be restrained by two men
as he threatens to leap into the path of a cavalcade of racing horses that are
just then dashing through camp and, in structural terms, point our eyes toward
the profane dancing figure, who is still drunk the morning after. Played off
against him is an older, bearded man on the right middleground of the picture,
seated on a keg outside a cabin reading from a Bible, while two other miners
listen intently. In the foreground, an axe handle on a diagonal parallel with
the horse cavalcade, points toward him. To his left are two men washing
clothes, while in the far left of the painting, in front of another cabin in the
middle distance, men are brawling. Clearly Nahl meant to divide his painting
in half, showing virtue and work on the right, and vice and folly on the left.
It represents, in its sprawling, colorful detail, and most of all in its composition, a Sunday sermon at the mines by Nahl, a definitive comment on the
mining camps.

He himself moved to Sacramento, where he painted portraits, then to San
Francisco, where he made many satirical illustrations, such as Miners Brawl
and Sunday Celebrants, showing three drunken mounted horsemen inside a
saloon. Most of his satirical drawings were made in the 1850s and 1860s. They
appeared in illustrated magazines such as San Francisco's Overland Monthly and
earned him the title of "the Cruikshank of California," thus comparing him
to the most famous British artist–satirist of the day. Sunday Morning in the
Mines was painted in 1872, nearly twenty years after his actual experience in
the mining camps. But even in this picture and its Saturday Night companion
piece, the bite of satire outweighs the pull of nostalgia. Both pictures, however, have a dreamlike quality to them, almost as if we were seeing the scene
through the drunken man's eyes.

Compared to Nahl's works, Ernest Najot's Gold Rush Camp is tame and
sentimental, though Placer Mining at Foster's bar of 1851 has a dramatic

Rufus Wright, *The Card Players*, (1882). Oakland Museum, Gift of the Oakland Museum's Kahn Collection; Photo Credit: M. Lee Fatherree.

authenticity that *Gold Rush Camp* of 1882 does not, and neither of them matches the sinister rider in *A Forty-Niner Going Prospecting* painted by Henry Walton from a lithograph by Charles Nahl. In this picture the gold-seeker, riding a white horse, seems to be slipping away from camp into the Sierras in secrecy.

In 1882 Rufus Wright, a Washington, D. C., portrait painter, and later a teacher at the Brooklyn Academy, painted a masterful California scene that must have derived from his visit to the mining camps in 1857. It is called *The Card Players* and features a card game in which a grinning Chinese coolie has just "cleaned out" three Anglo gamblers in a game of poker. Clearly an anecdotal painting that resembles a Bret Harte story, the work has a singular message in that the primary loser in the game clutches a knife. It is doubtful if the "heathen Chinee" will get out of the game alive—with his winnings. This is Wright's commentary on the laws that the California legislature enacted to discriminate against the Chinese. At that very time, in the 1880s, Justice Stephen J. Field, packing pistols, was a California judge striking down those discriminatory laws and defending the rights of the Chinese under the Fourteenth Amendment.

There were other painters of the gold Rush Days, most notably Albertis Browere, whose paintings were crude and clumsy genre scenes, Eugene Camerer, an eccentric German who painted scenes of the gold fields and California towns, but whose most famous painting was *Mike Schuler's Freighting Outfit.* In this painting Camerer did show, in a near folk art manner, the difficulty of freighting supplies to the Sierra mines and towns. He signed the painting on a plaque on the freight wagon box right in the center of the picture, a sure indication that he had experience as a sign painter some time in his past.

Perhaps the best painter of all the emigrant Germans was William Hahn (1829–1887).[11] He had studied in Dresden, Dusseldorf, Naples, Paris and New York City before coming to California. The training showed, as Hahn in the 1870s painted brilliant scenes of farming in California's great central valley, a superb view of a stagecoach stop, and possibly his masterpiece, a glimpse of a group of tourists who have already "trashed" their surroundings, looking down into Yosemite Valley. He called this painting, *Looking Down Yosemite Valley From Glacier Point*.

By the end of the 1850s the day of the individual miner with pick and pan was beginning to end. A new entrepreneur class of people came into California, particularly after the completion of the transcontinental railroad in 1869. Corporate mining, that imported expert dynamite men from Cornwall and coolies from China, created a massive series of tunnels deep underground, some of which, in Nevada, Timothy O'Sullivan photographed in the world's first underground mine scenes. He wedged himself into claustrophobic spaces, and with a wet-plate camera and magnesium flares, managed to photograph the dark tunnels and the brave miners.[12] Meanwhile, other photographers were celebrating ever larger and more elaborate mining operations.

Even as early as 1851, a large mining company moved in and diverted nearly thirty miles of the American River to get at the quartz deposits below the streambed. Shafts were driven deep into the earth. One stunning photograph of such an operation shows a complex of bridges, braces and flumes spanning a cut deep into the earth. This rickety, complex structure is dominated by a mammoth hoisting wheel in a scene strangely reminiscent of Charles Willson Peale's *Exhuming the Mastodon*. Another photo that purports to be an image of progress in the machine age pictures men with huge hydraulic hoses washing away whole hillsides at the Malakoff Mine. Lakes and raw washed-away hillsides remain today as evidence of the massive scale of the hydraulic miner's devastating work. But if one catches the Malakoff diggings in just the right light they shimmer like gold even today.

By the 1870s California had grown respectable, with neat towns and fashionable mansions that resembled the lives that the argonauts had left behind: on George Caleb Bingham's "Middle Border," in New England, and even New York, for, by 1870, San Francisco had its own telegraph line and its own Stock Exchange. It was the capital of an inland empire.

CHAPTER 12

EPILOGUE
IN SAN FRANCISCO

In an 1850 oil painting entitled Telegraph Hill, San Francisco *by* an unknown artist, possibly a Chinese, the city seems to rise up out of the Bay like some giant clam about to engulf the small sailing vessels before it. It is a remarkable, almost surrealistic work that was to be almost duplicated by the Japanese in their portrayals of Commodore Matthew C. Perry's black ships off Edo bay in 1853. Perhaps the fascination of the picture lies in the fact that it portrays San Francisco as arising out of a dream, which indeed it did.

In contrast to the dearth of pictures of miners at work, there are numerous paintings and photographs of San Francisco at nearly every stage of its development, from the sleepy Spanish town of Yerba Buena, through the raucous early years of the Gold Rush days, to the crowning of Nob and other hills with a unique, fantastically inventive stick-style architecture that, on certain streets, bows outward or upward, or in towers and domes—anything to afford a view of the Bay crowded with ships, sails, and steamers bound for the Orient.

Very possibly the best views of San Francisco during the Gold Rush days were the small watercolors painted by Frank Marryat, the son of the English childrens' book author Captain Frederick Marryat. Young Frank Marryat came to California from England in 1850 "bringing a gamekeeper and blood-hounds." He soon dabbled in mining, innkeeping, acting, and he wrote an extraordinary book, *Mountains and Molehills* (1853), for which his clever paintings of San Francisco served as the illustrations.[1] He did a panoramic view from atop a hill facing Alcatraz with the harbor filled with deserted ships. In the foreground of the city view he paraded characteristic citizens: Mexicans on horseback, miners, ladies and their children, and numerous Chinese. Clearly, the polygot culture fascinated Marryat, or so he says in satirical ways in *Mountains and Molehills*. Today Marryat's early paintings or lithographs are exceedingly valuable, because they are genre scenes, done in a Cruikshank manner, that catch the street life of San Francisco at the critical Gold Rush period. He shows beached ships turned into stores and hotels, saloons, a large bookstore (larger than any today), a liquor store next to a tract or Bible society with men, women, children, dogs and horses coursing the streets. One satirical view shows San Franciscans of every stripe dealing with a muddy, flooded street. Another picture takes us inside an ornate saloon where Mexicans, Yankees, Southerners, Missouri Pikes and straw-hatted Chinese drink and perhaps gamble together. Even the dogs are admitted to this establishment where cards and bottles litter the floor, and a seated drunk pouring whiskey on his head occupies the foreground, stage right. Marryat caught the flavor of "the Barbary Coast" era.

Frank Marryat, *San Francisco Street Life.*
Lithograph. Courtesy, the Bancroft Library, University of California, Berkeley, California.

John Prendergast (Attributed), *Justice Meted out to "English Jim" by the Vigilantes, San Francisco Harbor,* (ca. 1855). Oakland Art Museum, Gift of the Concours d'Antiques, Art Guild; Photo Credit: M. Lee Fatherree.

But so did some other artists. One depicted crowds of men lined up at the post office waiting for mail from home. Another painted the great fire of 1851. Still another depicted "Fort Gunnybags," the U. S. Mint, surrounded by sand-bags and guarded by vigilantes under Mormon Sam Brannan. Two men were hanged from this structure, their deaths graphically depicted in illustrated magazines, while one painter recorded the hanging of English Jim Stuart from a gallows constructed on a ship in the harbor. He was but one of eight strung

Frank Marryat, *San Francisco Saloon.* Lithograph. Courtesy, the Bancroft Library, University of California, Berkeley, California.

up that day while the crowd cheered the vigilantes and raised the American flag.

More conspicuous than the artists in San Francisco were the photographers. C. L. Weed, fresh from Hong Kong, opened a studio there, as did Carleton E. Watkins and Eadweard Muybridge. As historian Peter Hales points out, San Francisco, almost from its beginning, became perhaps the country's most photographed city. Hales asserts that San Francisco's early photographers were "competing as much with the fabulous as with the real—San Francisco was a city written into heroic, even absurd dimensions. Newspaper accounts, booster books, advertisements by land and transportation companies, bird's eyes, lithographs, maps and dagguerreotypes all purported to define and describe San Francisco."[2] So much attention was lavished on the city by the Bay for a number of reasons. First of all, it lay at the far end of Manifest Destiny—the farthest reach of the North American Continent. Secondly, it was the gateway to the Orient and the potential great trade with China and mysterious Japan. Thirdly, it was the greatest boomtown in American history. The city was the entrepôt for the fabulous wealth that lay buried in California's and Nevada's mountains. Fourthly, by virtue of the attraction of gold, it was one of America's most cosmopolitan cities. And, due to its situation, it was one of the country's most beautiful and dramatically photogenic cities. Finally, most of its citizens were newly rich, and wished to build "more stately mansions" and to boost their instant city in the eyes of the world.

After all, what other American city, in addition to its exploding stick style architecture and its Nob Hill nabobs could boast having an Emperor? In 1853 it acquired one, Emperor Norton I. Actually the man was Joshua Norton, an emigrant from South Africa, who had made and lost a fortune in the City by the Bay.[3] When he lost his fortune trying to corner the rice market in 1853, Norton did the only appropriate thing for a San Franciscan. He proclaimed himself Emperor Norton I, Ruler of the United States and Protector of Mexico. He created no art, but was himself a work of art as he strolled grandly through San Francisco's streets clad in a Navy Commodore's costume and followed by two faithful retainers, dogs named Bummer and Lazarus. He supported his "throne" by issuing fifty-cent bonds, which were accepted all over the city, and by eating at one of San Francisco's several free lunch establishments. (In those booming days there *was* such a thing as a free lunch.) When it moved him, Norton I fired off telegrams to Presidents Abraham Lincoln and Jefferson Davis issuing instructions to them and ordering the dissolution of the

Joshua Abraham Norton, "Emperor".
Photographic Archives, California
Historical Society Library, San Francisco.

U.S. Senate. At other times he enjoyed riding the Royal tricycle and contemplating his coming marriage to Queen Victoria. In short, Emperor Norton I was an ideal symbol of booming, exotic, acquisitive—indeed imperial—San Francisco, and its citizens, steeped in illusions of sudden wealth, instinctively knew it. They enjoyed having an "emperor." He somehow expressed their dreams appropriately.

In addition to having an emperor, San Francisco was also the city where American urban photography came of age. First there were the daguerreotypists, Robert H. Vance, Fred Coombs, and William Shew. The latter made a five-part daguerrean panorama of San Francisco's crowded waterfront as early as 1852 (while Marryat was still making his lithographs). It was a stirring picture, with hundreds of tall-masted ships in the harbor, cottages in the foreground, the Sutter Iron Works clearly visible, and a rapidly growing community on a hill across the water. Hales points out that the inclusion of a half-built house and carpenter in the foreground underscores the element of rapid growth.[4] In another instance the same year, an unknown daguerreotypist put together a *seven* part panorama with figures in the foreground to define the scale and a broad sweep of the camera from hill to hill that made a dramatic frame for his 180 degree panorama. In the 1870s, both Carleton E. Watkins and Eadweard Muybridge, better known for their views of Yosemite, were also making panoramas of San Francisco, this time with wet plate cameras rather than daguerreotype apparatuses. This enabled them to sell their views in repeated printings. Of all the panoramas, Muybridge's thirteen-part view of 1878 was perhaps the most spectacular. Muybridge produced his panoramas of 1877 and 1878 with a key to each of the buildings in the picture.[5] This served two purposes: it made the panorama a much more accurate equivalent of the lithograph bird's eye city views, and it enabled one to identify his own home or place of business, etc. Thus it had a "booster" purpose.

The panoramas were grand virtuoso photographic performances, the equivalent of a Wagnerian opera or Whitman's all-inclusive *Leaves of Grass* of the same period. But the most effective and seminal visual treatment of San Francisco was George R. Fardon's *San Francisco Album: Photographs of the Most Beautiful Views and Public Buildings of San Francisco*, published in 1856.[6] According to Hales, Fardon's "*San Francisco Album* was utterly programmatic; the pictures which comprise it fall effortlessly into a few broad and obviously purposive categories: history, culture, fire protection, trade, business, and geography . . . the book was designed to allay the fears of potential investors, companies, and entrepreneurs. It addressed itself carefully to each of the prevailing mid-century prejudices about the western instant city. . . . Fardon had invented an important new nineteenth-century American phenomenon—the photographic booster book."[7]

It was only appropriate that San Francisco should be the birthplace of a new form of fantasy—the photo-documentary fantasy. After all, San Francisco was in fact the final living embodiment of Manifest Destiny, a golden dream city of great instant wealth and all cultures, perhaps a exemplar or model for the United States itself, just as Fardon's photo book became a model for all future photo-booster books. But in all the wealth, high romance and color associated with San Francisco, a guilty shadow hung over the city. It was not only the symbol, but the *product* of Manifest Destiny: a cultural phenomenon that had moved far beyond Bingham's simple Jeffersonian idyll and had wrested by force of arms half a continent away from Mexico and the Indians. Perhaps it was appropriate then, that in 1906, like the *Titanic*, San Francisco suffered a catastrophe, the great earthquake. Much of the City by the Bay came tumbling down just as an energetic president, Theodore Roosevelt, was announcing a new era of Manifest Destiny that reached out across the far Pacific and to all parts of the globe. As the city crumbled and burned, Americans, in far-off places, were assuming "the white man's burden."

Arnold Genthe, *San Francisco Fire and Earthquake: #4, View of Burning City from Russian Hill*, (1906). The Fine Arts Museums of San Francisco, Achenbach Foundation for Graphic Arts.

The irony of this seems to have escaped the anonymous photographer who opted for pathos in snapping a white-haired, bewildered product of another age, Carleton E. Watkins, being led forcibly from his burning studio, which housed his life's work.[8] It did not escape the photographer Arnold Genthe, who photographed two prostitutes walking and smiling gaily in front of his camera, as behind them the city fell in ruins and the wooden buildings went up in flames. As twin "goddesses of liberty," or a pair of "prairie madonnas," the painted ladies might well be saying, "Westward Ho!" or, better still, "Westward the Course of Empire Takes Its Way!" On that day, if one listened closely, he might just have heard—ever so faintly—the American eagle scream a kind of approval.

Part Three

IMAGES OF
GLORY

CHAPTER 13

BIERSTADT'S
MIGHTY MOUNTAINS

In the fading glow of an October afternoon in 1864, young Clarence King of the California Geological Survey stood at the brink of a four thousand-foot granite precipice overlooking the valley of Yosemite. He painted a picture in words of the scene spread out before him.

> . . . the summer haze had been banished from the region by autumnal frosts and wind. We looked into the gulf through air as clear as a vacuum, discerning small objects upon the valley-floor and cliff-front.
>
> That splendid afternoon shadow which divides the face of El Capitan was projected far up and across the valley, cutting it in halves,—one a mosaic of russets and yellows, with dark pine and a glimpse of a white river; the other a cobalt-blue zone, in which the familiar groves and meadows were suffused with shadow tones. . . . All stern sublimity, all geological terribleness, are veiled away behind magic curtains of cloud shadow and broken light.[1]

These were the words of an artist, something which perhaps made Clarence King's book, *Mountaineering in the Sierra Nevada,* a classic work of the visual imagination. But King was also a geologist, traversing the mighty Sierras—"the top of California," he called it—trying to map the landforms and recon-

Albert Bierstadt, *The Domes of Yosemite.* Chromolithograph. (1868). Courtesy Amon Carter Museum of Western Art, Fort Worth.

struct the geologic history of this majestic complex of peaks. In this recon-struction of geologic time and geologic events, Yosemite provided a matchless clue. In pursuit of his scientific quest, King made his way through "immense splintered blocks" of stone far up above Yosemite's valley, crawled out onto a jutting slab of rock, and, leaning far over the edge to gain a better view of the valley below, he commenced to imagine Yosemite's "day of creation." "It was impossible for me, as I sat perched upon this jutting rock mass, in full view of all the canons which had led into this wonderful converging of ice-rivers not to imagine a picture of the glacier period," King remembered, and he contin-ued to envision the great valley's frozen and terrifying past.

> Bare or snow-laden cliffs overhung the gulf; streams of ice, here smooth and compacted into a white plain, there riven into innumerable crevasses, or tossed into forms like the waves of a tempest-lashed sea, crawled through all the gorges. Torrents of water and avalanches of rock and snow spouted at intervals all along the cliff walls. Not a . . . vestige of life was in sight. . . . Granite and ice and snow, silence broken only by the howling tempest and the crash of falling ice or splintered rock, and a sky deep freighted with cloud and storm,—these were the elements of a period which lasted immeasurably long, and only in comparatively recent times have given way to the present marvelously changed condition.[2]

When the comparatively recent warmer ages set in, the great, gouging gla-cier and its hanging tributaries began to melt, all in concert like some mighty

Albert Bierstadt, *Valley of Yosemite*, (1864). Gift of Mrs. Maxim Karolik for the Karolik Collection of American Paintings (1815–1865); Courtesy, Museum of Fine Arts, Boston.

symphony orchestra. And as they melted, huge blocks of granite, as large as houses, came crashing and tumbling down the valley, pieces of the wall broke off, and the glacier receded, leaving giant scores and marks, pits and morains

Carleton E. Watkins, *Half-Dome from Glacier Point*, (c. 1866). Courtesy Amon Carter Museum of Western Art, Fort Worth.

all along the valley floor. A torrent rushed down from the mountains to the sea. Left behind it was the scooped-out majesty of Yosemite, that mosaic of the russet and yellow El Capitan and the sheer gray side of the Half-Dome, all that was left of a once mighty mountain after the glacier had done its work.

In that same year, 1864, it became the painter Albert Bierstadt's task to catch something of that colossal drama on canvas. He knew the difficulty of this task, because he had visited the great Yosemite Valley himself in 1863 where he spent a season making spectacular sketches in preparation for one of his giant canvases. But Bierstadt was, indeed, up to the challenge. His mighty canvases would forever popularize the same breathtaking Yosemite vistas, and immortalize the West as a sublime, natural paradise, a wonderland for the traveler, and the tourist, to discover and experience in all of its romantic splendor. King's inspirational passage might equally well have described the stirring atmospheric effects, dizzying volumes and stark contrasts of a Bierstadt painting, for these two men were kindred spirits: both the painter and the geologist had set for themselves the Promethian task of harnessing the immense western landscape in the artistic and scientific imagination, and translating it to national, and ultimately international audiences.

As the scale and ambition of western exploration increased after the Civil War, so did its pictorial representations; the sublime replaced the pastoral as the predominant image of the West in the American imagination. Instead of George Caleb Bingham's quiescent scenes of fur trappers descending the Missouri—a river they had made theirs by virtue of becoming frontiersmen—the paintings by Albert Bierstadt, Thomas Moran, and other artists trained in the European romantic tradition, pictured a different West, a West of mighty mountains that dwarfed Indian and white man alike, a West of swirling atmospheric forces, of primordial geological drama, of natural—almost supernatural—wonder.

Through the paintings by the artists who belonged to the "Rocky Mountain School," Americans became fascinated, not with the image of man living in the state of nature, but with man in dramatic confrontation with a beautiful, ageless and often terrifying nature. As a result of the popularity of his immense canvases of Rocky Mountain and Sierra Nevada scenery, Albert Bierstadt would become, for a time, the acknowledged master of this emerging tradition in western landscape painting, and the successor to J. M. W. Turner as the prime translator of the Romantic Sublime, at least to American eyes.

Bierstadt, of course, did not invent the tradition of romantic landscape painting, nor was he the first to apply the visual "language" of romanticism to

Albert Bierstadt, *Surveyors Wagon in the Rockies,* (c. 1859–60). Courtesy St. Louis Art Museum, St. Louis, Missouri.

American scenery. The English critic John Ruskin had already celebrated the painter's quest for the sublime in the works of Turner and Constable, and Ruskin's essays on mountain scenery, cloud forms and the picturesque had already suggested a means for the landscape artist to create a "transcendent" experience for his audience. Bierstadt's predecessors, such as Thomas Cole and Frederick Church, successfully created sublime, turbulent views of the American landscape. In fact, from the outset of Bierstadt's career there was a ready market for grand American landscape views. Yet Bierstadt was among the first, and certainly among the most successful painters to move the American imagination westward to the base of the Rockies, to contemplate a sublimity of much larger proportion than either Cole's exquisitive views of the Hudson River, or even Church's mesmerizing image of Niagara. Indeed, through the works of Albert Bierstadt, and later, Thomas Moran, the American West seemed to manifest, more perfectly than any other landscape in the world, John Ruskin's aesthetic principles.

A New Bedford-bred son of a German cooper who emigrated to America in 1832, Albert Bierstadt, by all rights, should have been a New England "Luminist," in the tradition of Martin Johnson Heade or Fitz Hugh Lane, his contemporaries in American art who celebrated the still Massachusetts and Rhode Island shoreline with a crystalline realist style. In fact, Bierstadt did flirt with the Luminist style before his first trip West in 1859, but clearly his tastes ran to more dramatic and monumental scenery. Undoubtedly, it was Bierstadt's training in Dusseldorf in 1853–56, and his ramblings in the Bernese Alps in 1857, with fellow American artists Worthington Whittredge and Sanford Robinson Gifford, that awakened Bierstadt's interest in the romantic potential of mountain scenery. His German training had taught him to render the classical romantic trajectory of eye and spirit into the elevated mountain vistas through a graceful arrangement of receding planes and the alternation of brilliant light with dark shadow. Even in his *Bernese Alps,* the romantic technique and structure which would later make him famous manifests itself. The pastoral foreground, populated with grazing cattle, is a diminutive setting which welcomes the viewer into a picture of grander design. Alternating bands of light and shadow lead the eye back and forth across the painting progressively into the distance, where it is left to contemplate a vision of the Alps as a soft, almost cloudy structure evanescing into the subtle shades of the sky. As Bierstadt's style matured, these cloud-like mountains would become dominating, massive forms which not only controlled the relationship between foreground and background, but broke through into the turbulent domain of the sky. Although hints of his western visions may be seen in Bierstadt's earlier European subjects, it was the experience of the Rockies that imbued his work with real force.

In 1859, after four years of study and travel in Europe and two years of dabbling with picturesque subject matter on the Eastern seaboard of America, Albert Bierstadt, by this time a handsome young man of 29 with a luxuriant beard and a purposeful gaze, was determined to strike out West in search of fresh material. His frequent tout, *The New Bedford Daily Mercury,* reported:

> It is understood that the New Bedford artist [Mr. Bierstadt] is about to start for the Rocky Mountains, to study the scenery of that wild region, and the picturesque facts about Indian life, with reference to a series of large pictures. He expects to remain more than one year, and has engaged companions, among them a photographer. We wish him all success and safe return.[3]

As it developed, his companion was another painter, F. S. Frost, and thus Bierstadt most likely took the photographs himself.

Bierstadt and Frost joined Colonel Frederick West Lander's wagon train survey of an overland passage to California, an expedition charged with the dual purpose of trail-blazing and placating the Indians en route. They departed from St. Joseph, Missouri, on May 5, 1859, and headed up the north branch of the Platte through present-day Nebraska and Wyoming. The artists were welcome members on the expedition, not only because Bierstadt had presented a letter of introduction from John B. Floyd, Secretary of War, but also because the sparing allocation for the expedition had prevented the engagement of an official artist and photographer to document the journey.

Bierstadt's intent, however, was far from documentary. His oil sketches from the journey picture a variety of interesting scenes: from stiffly posed Indians dropped into a stark planar landscape, to a study of the famous scout, Jim Bridger, to impressionistic views of land and cloudforms. Bierstadt approached the West with a somewhat different attitude than the explorer artists and photographers that preceded him. He was simply gathering images in bits and pieces which he would later compose into much larger, idealized canvases. He was a sightseer in quest of the picturesque.

Bierstadt's photographs are among relatively few pre-Civil War expedition views that have survived. They were shot with a stereoscopic camera, and it is tantalizing conjecture that Bierstadt believed only stereo vision would effectively capture the vast spaces of the West. In fact, he probably used the stereo camera because of its relative ease in the field, and perhaps in anticipation of future sale of the pictures (his brothers were early photography entrepreneurs who built a successful business selling stereo-views).

The images focused upon the camp life of the expedition, as well as upon the Sioux and Shoshone that were encountered along the way. Oddly enough, considering his intent, Bierstadt made only a few successful photographs of dramatic mountain scenery, most were fogged and poorly exposed. He lamented the problems preventing good landscape photographs: "We have taken many stereoscopic views, but not so many of the mountain scenery as I could wish, owing to various obstacles attached to the process, but still a goodly number."[4]

Perhaps because the camera provided "visual notes" on the Indians and scenery in black-and-white, Bierstadt made vividly colored oil studies during this trip, which attempted to capture the light and color of both the western sky and western landscape. These impressionistic studies, rarely finished enough for exhibition, indicate the acumen of Bierstadt's eye for natural effects, and his interest in capturing real western imagery. They would serve him in good stead in his later work of assembling his impressions of the West into large, ambitious views.

Bierstadt's first experience with the western landscape was the Great Plains,

Albert Bierstadt, *Thunderstorm in the Rocky Mountains,* (1859). Given in Memory of Elias T. Milliken by his daughters, Mrs. Edward Hale and Mrs. John Carroll Perkins. Courtesy, Museum of Fine Arts, Boston.

the rolling, endless prairies. Perhaps he felt about them as Walt Whitman did, when the poet exclaimed

> a limitless, sealike stretch of the great Kansas or Colorado plains, under favoring circumstances, tallies, perhaps expresses, certainly awakes, those grandest and subtlest elemental emotions in the human soul, that all the marble temples and sculptures from Phidias to Thorwaldsen—all paintings, poems, reminiscences, or even music, probably never can.[5]

Bierstadt reported relatively little about the expanse of prairie; it was not until the expedition struck the Wind River mountains that the landscape seemed to stir his soul. In a letter to one of the leading art magazines of the day, *The Crayon,* he wrote, "I am delighted with the scenery. The mountains are very fine; as seen from the plains, they resemble very much the Bernese Alps. . . ."[6] The numerous mountain views he painted upon his return portray the wonder Bierstadt experienced in the Wind River and Wasatch ranges much better than his letter.

Albert Bierstadt, *The Rocky Mountains—Lander's Peak,* (1863). The Metropolitan Museum of Art, New York, Rogers Fund.

Frederick Church, *The Heart of the Andes,* (1859). The Metropolitan Museum of Art, New York. Bequest of Margaret E. Dows, 1909.

In *Thunderstorm in the Rockies,* the romantic conventions of a blasted tree and overlapping, receding planes are the principal structural elements in the painting; however, the most powerful effects are created by the sky. A thunderstorm swirls around a distant mountain peak near the horizon, while clouds immediately overhead break up the intense mountain sunlight into mottled shafts and pools. The sonorous rumbling of thunder disturbs a nearby herd of deer, the only animals in the natural scene, which pointedly does not include the human figure. In this painting, produced just after his return from Lander's expedition, Bierstadt makes the viewer the solitary human witness to the unspoiled grandeur of nature. As the composition suggests, Bierstadt had carried his European vision with him into the Rocky Mountains; he visually compared the snow-covered peaks and high mountain valleys of Wyoming to the Bernese Alps. It was, to his eyes and brush, "The Italy of America in primitive condition."[7]

Bierstadt and Frost parted ways with the Lander wagon train as it proceeded beyond the Green River and through the Wasatch Range toward the Pacific. They seem content to have viewed, sketched and photographed the Rockies, and perhaps were anxious to get back to their studios to work their impressions up into finished paintings. Bierstadt's paintings completed after this first trip focus on mountain scenes and Indian encampments, both of which became elements in his first monumental work to receive critical acclaim, *The Rocky Mountains—Lander's Peak,* painted in 1863.

The famous New York Sanitary Fair exhibition of April 1864 pitted *The Rocky Mountains—Lander's Peak* against Frederick Church's equally immense painting, *The Heart of the Andes* particularly in the eyes of the critics and the public. Though only two among many paintings hung in an exhibition to benefit the Civil War equivalent of the Red Cross, the competition between the Humboldtean South American painting by Frederick Church and the North American Rocky Mountain view by Bierstadt quickly became the prime attractions of the show. They hung opposite each other in a spacious gallery which contained six hundred works of art, including Emanuel Leutze's *Washington Crossing the Delaware.* It was the midst of the Civil War, and Bierstadt's majestically nationalistic image, linked with Lander who had died a war hero, won the competition hands down.

Thousands of people came to see the show. They admired the virtuosity of the large canvases, or "earthscapes," that, even while they celebrated the romantic vistas of the American continent in vast, panoramic scale, presented at the same time nature's minute details, such as the correct leaf on the tree, the tiny birds, miniscule animals and all manner of rocks and flowers. The two paintings were, in their attention to *both* materialistic detail and romantic concerns, peculiarly American macrocosms, and the "blockbuster" pictures of their day. Viewers brought or rented opera glasses or small tube telescopes to zero in on the details of the paintings, their vision aided by the 490 gas jets which illuminated the exhibition. Bierstadt and his engraver, James Smillie, did not miss the opportunity to sell subscriptions to future reproductions of the painting. According to a contemporary account,

> the gentleman-in-waiting stands ready, at all hours, to enter in his subscription book the names of those who desire to add this combined result of Mr. Bierstadt's genius and Mr. Smillie's talent to their plethoric portfolios.[8]

Meanwhile, Frederick Church had arranged to place potted tropical plants around his picture to draw as many curious viewers as possible into *The Heart of the Andes.*

In *The Rocky Mountains,* Bierstadt became the orchestrator of a mighty, Wagnerian scene, which exaggerated the vertical thrust of the Wind River range to achieve the monumental grandeur which Americans had come to expect from their continent. It is a synthesis, as Barbara Novak has pointed out in *Nature and Culture,* of a myriad natural facts: from the snow-covered mountain summit and knife-edged peaks—the likes of which challenged the bravery of Clarence King as he cavorted in the Sierras—to plunging waterfalls, natural meadows and peaceful Indians who are reminiscent of the Westphalian peasants in Bierstadt's European views. The artist dared, not merely a literal transcription of nature, but an act of creation itself, replete with all of the creatures which, as his friend Louis Agassiz, the Harvard naturalist, would suggest, were the outward manifestations of the mind of the Diety.

Placed opposite the best that Frederick Church could offer, it was the first major painting to enlarge the western landscape to panoramic proportions. Its very scale (73½ inches by 120¾ inches) asserted that only a picture of monumental dimension could capture both the sublime majesty and the natural detail of the Rocky Mountains. His first Promethian struggle was deemed a success. Critic and art historian Henry T. Tuckerman proclaimed *The Rocky Mountains*

> a grand and gracious epitome and reflection of nature on this continent—of that majestic barrier of the West where the heavens and the earth meet in brilliant and barren proximity, where snow and verdure, gushing fountains and vivid herbage, noble trees and azure sky-depths, primeval solitudes, the loftiest summits,

and the boundless plains, combine all that is most vast, characteristic and beautiful in North American scenery.[9]

In 1863, the year before the Sanitary Fair extravanganza, Bierstadt made his second journey West, accompanied by a fellow romantic, Fitzhugh Ludlow, who was still basking in the glow of the success of his book, *The Hasheesh Eater,* in which he tested the bounds of consciousness in the service of literature. Ludlow left his beautiful (and flirtatious) wife, Rosalie, behind in order to join Bierstadt in a quest for inspiring mountain scenery. The journey took them to the Colorado Rockies, where Bierstadt found material for his next major Rocky Mountain panorama. Ludlow gushed poetically over the western mountains:

> I confess (I should be ashamed not to confess) that my first view of the Rocky Mountains had no way of expressing itself save in tears. To see what they looked like, and to know what they were, was like a sudden revelation of the truth, that the spiritual is the only real and substantive; that the eternal things of the universe are they which afar off seem dim and distant.[10]

In June, leaving Ludlow behind in Denver, Bierstadt made a side trip into the mountains near the Chicago Lakes district with William Byers, editor of the *Rocky Mountain News,* who reported the artist "in raptures with the scenery." Bierstadt christened a particularly enthralling peak Mt. Rosalie, after Ludlow's young bride. Three years later, the resulting painting, *A Storm in the Rockies—Mt. Rosalie,* had become yet another major artistic success. Meanwhile, Ludlow had been reduced to a hopeless drug addict, and the lovely Rosalie had divorced her husband to become Mrs. Bierstadt. Although Bierstadt was silent on the subject, a relationship may have already existed between Rosalie Ludlow and the painter when he named Mt. Rosalie. Possibly inspired by this, Bierstadt created a painting that represented his talents fully developed, but somehow stormy and mystical, as if it reflected his anguish over taking Rosalie away from her husband. The mountain scenery is not merely an inspiring backdrop, but has a dynamic, three-dimensional presence in the composition. Perhaps the most dramatic feature of the picture is the gathering storm about the peak of Mt. Rosalie, a storm similar to one which Bierstadt sketched on his ramblings with editor Byers in 1863. Here, in this high mountain valley, the viewer is thrust right up next to the terrifying power of a summer thunderhead. The scene pictures the meteorological processes that Ruskin described in his passages on the nature of clouds in *Modern Painters* (1847):

Albert Bierstadt, *A Storm in the Rockies—Mt. Rosalie,* (1866). The Brooklyn Museum.

Clouds, it is to be remembered, are not so much local vapour, as vapour rendered locally visible by a fall of temperature. Thus a cloud, whose parts are in constant motion will hover on a snowy mountain, pursuing constantly the same track upon its flanks . . . they are always therefore gloriously arranged.[11]

A Storm in the Rockies—Mt. Rosalie suggests that Bierstadt, like Ruskin, saw the mountains as a mighty catalyst for the enormous, unseen forces latent in the atmosphere. The clouds swirling about the peak of Mt. Rosalie seemed charged with tremendous electrical—perhaps, in light of Bierstadt's affection for its namesake—emotional energies. Although the sketching trip in the Colorado Rockies was a prime inspiration for Bierstadt, and, as it would later turn out, a fateful moment for Ludlow, the highlight of the trip lay farther to the West, in the Sierra Nevadas of California: Yosemite.

CHAPTER 14

THE WONDERS OF YOSEMITE

Set aside as a natural preserve by President Lincoln in 1864, Yosemite was one of the West's earliest tourist attractions. Frederick Law Olmsted, landscape architect of Central Park, presided as the first chairman of the preserve. Although recognized for its picturesque qualities, the original attraction of Yosemite was the unique geological features it manifested. To scientists such as Josiah Dwight Whitney, and later Clarence King, the vast granite mountainscape, visible from Yosemite's Glacier Point, a pinnacle overlooking the immense valley, revealed evidence of a great, primordial drama which took place thousands, even millions of years ago. According to King, the famous domes were created by upward surges of molten rock, which had formed a rumpled mountainscape, cut by deep, narrow valleys before the beginning of the ice age. These pre-glacial valleys charted a course for surges of later glacial flows, which scooped troughs of giant scale, creating the characteristic "U" shaped valley profile, and left hanging valleys, giant waterfalls and fallen boulders the size of houses in their wake. Tuolome Glacier, a distant vestige of ice far up the valley, and the placid, silvery stream of the Merced seemed the last traces of these powerful geological events. Like a land of the

Charles L. Weed, *The Valley, from the Mariposa Trail*, (1805). Rare Book Division, The New York Public Library, Astor, Lenox and Tilden Foundations.

Titans, in which everything was beyond human scale, Yosemite, by the 1860s, was already both a geological and a scenic wonder.

Carl William Hahn's 1874 painting of a party of pleasure-seekers perched on Glacier Point portrays a scene that most landscape painters and photographers throughout mid-century sought to conceal: Yosemite was not a remote, virgin paradise where one sat in solitude to contemplate nature's wonders. In part due to the handsome photographs made by Carlton Watkins in 1861, and the guidebooks to California and the West written by, among others, Josiah Dwight Whitney, Americans were attracted to Yosemite in increasing numbers to witness for themselves the inspiring natural wonder. Bierstadt likewise was drawn to Yosemite, first in 1863, and later in the 1870s. The panoramic images he created of the valley would be the crowning touch of his career, and would inspire a California-grown tradition of picturesque painted views in their wake.

When the Bierstadt party reached California in 1863, Fitz Hugh Ludlow was seemingly more interested in the view of the female spectators at Yosemite

than he was of the mighty valley itself. His literary account of the Yosemite
experience was quite different from the one offered by Clarence King who, a
year later, stood on the elevated brink, contemplating its ancient geological
history.

> The bachelor who cares to see unhooped womanhood once more before he dies
> should go to the Yo-Semite. The scene was three or four times presented to us
> during the seven weeks camp there. . . . No Saratoga affair, this! A total lack of
> tall trunks, frills and curling kids. Driven by the oestrum of a Yo-Semite pilgrim-
> age, the San Francisco belle forsakes (the Western vernacular is "goes back on")
> her back-hair, abandons her caquillary "waterfalls" for those of the Sierra, and,
> like John Phoenix's old lady who had her whole osseous system removed by the
> patent tooth-puller, departs, leaving her "skeleton" behind her.[1]

The four-thousand-foot-high pinnacle of Glacier Point became the scene of
stunts by these unhooped belles, as daring photographers sought to capture
such giddy foolery as dancing on the brink of Yosemite's abyss. Yet, far beneath
them in the valley below, the sublime was still serious business.

A photograph made in 1872 by the eccentric California photographer, Eadweard Muybridge, shows Bierstadt painting a study of a Mariposa Indian council in the quiet groves on the banks of the Merced. It is a loose, expressive
composition which shows that traditional native American life continued in
the valley, even as tourists flooded Yosemite's rim, looking for views. Muybridge later became famous as a pioneer motion photographer, but his early
career centered upon creating picturesque landscape views of California. Signing his pictures "Helios," Muybridge collaborated with Clarence King in the
selection of scenic Yosemite perspectives, and worked closely with Bierstadt,
perhaps even supplying him with photographs that helped him compose his
later panoramic Yosemite views.

In the latter half of the nineteenth century, photography, no less than Western
landscape painting, was becoming an aesthetic pursuit. In fact, Bierstadt and
Ludlow had seen an exhibit of Yosemite photographs taken by Carleton Watkins at Goupil's Gallery in New York before they struck out on their western
journey in 1863. Muybridge and Watkins, both residents of San Francisco,
used mammoth cameras that produced plates corresponding to Bierstadt's grand
canvases in their ambitious scale. Throughout the 1860s and 1870s, they sought
to outdo each other in creating the most breathtaking views of the Yosemite
Valley. Of the two, Muybridge was Bierstadt's kindred spirit in his desire to
create the most romantic, and evocative pictures of the landscape. Setting his

Carl William Hahn, *Looking Down Yosemite Valley From Glacier Point*, (1874).
California Historical Society, San Francisco.

camera up beneath the base of the upper falls, or at the foot of a misty rainbow
over the Merced, Muybridge plunged the viewer into the natural surroundings. In so doing, he revelled in the rich detail of trees, rocks and water. In
his elevated views overlooking the valley, Muybridge often composed his pictures without a frontal foreground, dangling himself, as well as his viewers
over the vast abyss. In such pictures as *Tenaya Canyon From Union Point* or
Valley of the Yosemite From Glacier Point, the crisp, dark rocks and vegetation
of the foreground are no more than a slippery precipice, where the viewer
seems to cling to his perch, mountaineer-style, like Muybridge himself, and
pause long enough to catch a glimpse of the infinity of space extending out
before him. Muybridge enjoyed devising inventions which would extend the
capacity of the photographer to capture the mutable image of nature. He hoped
to outdo his rival, Watkins, through the invention of a "sky shade"—a device
which allowed the differential exposure of land and sky.[2] With his sky shade,
Muybridge could capture the inspirational cloud effects in Yosemite, which
heretofore had been prevented by the extreme contrasts between light and
shadow. Like Bierstadt, whose classic Yosemite views were lit by the diffusion
of direct sunlight through clouds, Muybridge made numerous atmospheric
studies, that capture the constantly changing California sky in all of its moods.

   In contrast to the inferno of atmospheric effects which characterized Bierstadt's most ambitious Yosemite views and the daring perspectives of his com-

George Fiske, *Kitty Tasch and Friend on Glacier Point.* National Park Service, Yosemite National Park.

petitor, Muybridge, Carleton Watkins's photographs portray the valley with crystalline precision and careful, classical composition. Watkins carried both a mammoth-plate camera of his own design and a stereoscopic camera into the valley with him on his first trip in 1861. One, perhaps to capture the vast scale of the landscape through the production of a correspondingly vast glass plate negative, the other to capture the three-dimensional effects of depth and space which made Yosemite such an attraction. Following the path of C. L. Weed, who had preceded him into the Yosemite in 1859 to take a series of views, Muybridge focused upon the now famous landmarks: Vernal Falls, El Capitan, Bridal Veil Falls, as well as ingeniously arranged views from the valley floor, which used the silvery waters of the Merced to mirror the dramatic rock formations. In such photographs as *El Capitan,* the elegant formal concerns, which made him famous as a pioneer art photographer, are clearly apparent. The crisply photographed cliff, devoid of vegetation, save for minute trees at its summit, modulates upward in tone from chalky white to a gentle gray—an effect which provides a strange tonal contrast to the dark, shadowed cliffs of the background, as well as the light, clouded sky.

Cathedral Rock, in Watkins's lens, becomes a majestic formation that controls the entire frame, but, unlike Muybridge's pictures, which probe the romantic distance, Watkins interrupts the view beyond by a strong, confrontational mass. Even in Watkins's traditional panoramic vistas, such as *The Domes From*

Sentinel Dome, Yosemite, the near-spiritual extension of the eye across the distant landscape is interrupted by oddly formal concerns. The granite foreground creates a bright diagonal contrast to a dark mid-ground of pines. The domes of the Yosemite, lightly mottled in gray, are perhaps the least imposing feature of the picture.

The Watkins–Muybridge rivalry became one of the most celebrated contests in the history of American photography. It called attention, not only to the beauty of the California landscape, but to San Francisco as a leading center of art photography in the United States. Their mammoth camera views of Western landscape could hang next to lithographs and even paintings as works of art in the Victorian parlour. Muybridge and Watkins thus began to shape American tastes toward real, as well as romanticized, images of their continent. Instead of visiting the "blockbuster" exhibits of Bierstadt's and Church's panoramas, Americans began to enjoy the scenery in the privacy of their own

Eadweard Muybridge, *Bierstadt Painting in Yosemite*. Albumen print stereograph card from "The Indians of California" series, Bradley & Rulofson, San Francisco. Photographic Archives, California Historical Society Library, San Francisco.

Albert Bierstadt, *Indians in Council, California, 1872*. (1872). National Park Service, Photographed by Henry B. Bevilles, Annapolis, Maryland.

homes, thanks to the improving technology of printing and photographic reproduction.

The photographic views of Western landscape made by Watkins and Muybridge freed painters such as Bierstadt and Moran from the necessity of literal transcription of the scene. Whereas Karl Bodmer felt the responsibility of being the sole visual recorder of the frontier he witnessed, Bierstadt and Moran, who came of age in the era of photography, felt no such compulsion. Bierstadt's paintings of Yosemite pictured all of the famous geological features of the valley: Half-Dome, Bridal Veil Falls and El Capitan, but he artfully arranged and exaggerated them according to his own grandiose scheme. The responsibility of the artist was to capture the ideal sensation of the place, to recreate the effect of the scene, rather than to document it. Nowhere are his artistic liberties more apparent than in *Sunset in the Yosemite Valley*, a painting which depicts the fading glow of the sun diffused through the moist California air, as it sets behind the vertical flanks of El Capitan. The clouds extend across the valley to form a ceiling, and suddenly the viewer feels as though he is standing at one end of a titanic room, gazing into an inferno. Most viewers applauded Bierstadt's imagination, but at least one, Mark Twain, seemed to think his Yosemite view drifted too far from fact.

Eadweard Muybridge, *Teneya Canyon from Union Point,* (1872). Photograph, U.C.L.A. Collection, No. 35.

Carlton E. Watkins, *El Capitan, Yosemite.* Department of Prints and Photographs, The Metropolitan Museum of Art.

Some of Mr. Bierstadt's mountains swim in a lustrous pearly mist, which is so enchantingly beautiful that I am sorry the Creator hadn't made it instead of him so that it would always remain there. . . . We do not want this glorified atmosphere smuggled into a portrait of Yosemite, where it surely does not belong.[3]

Cheerfully ignoring such criticism, Bierstadt and Rosalie moved to California so that the artist could be close to his favorite scenery. In 1873 he built a studio on a hill in San Francisco with a panoramic view of the bay, where he threw himself into work on a series of California views. Local celebrities from the moment they arrived, the Bierstadts could often be seen at the fashionable Cliff House sipping lemonade and gazing out at the picturesque Seal Rocks and the pounding Pacific surf—a view he enjoyed enough to paint a number of times. The two years he spent in California were prolific. He finished a variety of Yosemite pictures, as well as scenes of other notable spots such as Donner Lake, King's Canyon, Mt. Brewer, Mt. Hood and the Farallon Islands. Yet perhaps his greatest contribution to the arts of the city was the role that he played as a catalyst for a developing "California School" of art, which had emerged as the principal aesthetic translator of the glories of the Far West scenery.

Bierstadt was elected an honorary member of the San Francisco Art Association shortly after his arrival in 1871. The popularity of his Yosemite views also helped bring recognition to the works of other California artists, among them, William Keith and Gilbert Munger, both of whom eschewed Bierstadt's vertical "fireworks" for more subdued, sensitive studies of the Yosemite scenery. Thomas Hill, next to Bierstadt the most famous member of the nascent California School, adopted an odd, angular brush stroke to capture his impression of the Yosemite. In contrast to Bierstadt, who often felt compelled to add lustrous sunset colors to brighten the lead gray granite walls of the valley, Hill revelled in the interplay between Sierra Nevada verdure and the cold stone domes.

Bierstadt and the other painters of the Yosemite, as well as the cadre of accomplished photographers, succeeded in turning Yosemite into a sacred space in the American cult of naturalism. The painters had created transcendental vistas, and near-mythical sunsets; the photographers had monumentalized and framed the individual landmarks and views. For Americans and European visitors, in quest of scenic and unspoiled nature, Yosemite became a haven, the successor to Niagara Falls as the favored place to confront Nature's power.

By 1871 the mighty Yosemite had drawn growing tides of pleasure seekers in search of scenic wonder, yet it still had escaped the fate of its predecessor, Niagara Falls, which novelist Henry James described in that year as

> choked in the horribly vulgar shops and booths and catchpenny artifacts which have pushed and elbowed to within the very spray of the Falls . . . [to] ply their importunities in shrill competition with its thunder.[4]

The artist and photographer, even as they celebrated the sacred qualities of the American landscape, invited their audiences to experience the wonder for themselves. At the same time they admired virgin nature in the West, they seemed, inadvertently, to hasten its demise.

By the mid-1870s Bierstadt's efforts to celebrate the Western landscape in grand, idealized views had brought him international acclaim. Awarded the Legion of Honor by Napoleon II, inducted into the order of St. Stanislaus of Russia for his services to the Grand Duke Alexis, entertained at the White House by Rutherford B. Hayes, Bierstadt became the quintessential celebrity artist.

He also became a favorite of a new monied American class that demanded his panoramic views as decoration for their New York and Newport mansions. His paintings sold for tens of thousands of dollars in the 1870s, even then princely sums for the "monarch of American landscape painting." Typical of his commercial and social success was the $15,000 commission he received from the Earl of Dunraven in 1876 to paint a view of the magnificent Rocky Mountain scenery from Dunraven's palatial hunting lodge in Estes Park, Colorado. As a result of this majestic painting, landmarks around what is now Rocky Mountain National Park were dubbed Mt. Bierstadt, Bierstadt Morain, and Lake Bierstadt, immortalizing the painter in the very landscape he had helped to make famous.

Without a doubt, Bierstadt had become the most popular Western painter of his era, yet, perhaps most importantly, his vision and imagination shaped America's attitude towards the West. When New Yorkers who had attended the Sanitary Fair of 1864 thought of the West, they thought of Bierstadt's magnificent vision of the Rockies—they imagined it a place of quiet lakes, grand waterfalls, and peaks which rose to heights rivalling the Alps in scale and beauty. No matter that these images were pieced together from multiple views, sketches and even stereoscopic pictures. They represented the very essence of the West of the imagination—a West that embodied a sense of sublime scale, of naturalistic wonder, of geological drama, and nationalistic pride which no photograph, not even one by Watkins or Muybridge, could capture.

Albert Bierstadt, *Sunset in Yosemite Valley*, (1868). Haggin Collection, Haggin Museum, Stockton, California.

Albert Bierstadt, *Seal Rocks, Farallon Islands*, (c. 1873–5). The New Britain Museum of American Art, Alix W. Stanley Fund, Connecticut, Photographer: E. Irving Blomstrann

Thomas Hill, *Yosemite Valley From Below Sentinel Dome, as Seen From Artist's Point,* (1876). The Oakland Museum's Kahn Collection; Photo Credit: M. Lee Fatherree.

CHAPTER 15

ARTIST AND PHOTOGRAPHER
IN WONDERLAND

Among the most famous tales of the Rocky Mountains related around flickering campfires at the Green River rendezvous and later told to the Forty-Niners on their arduous journey cross-continent—perhaps even mentioned to Albert Bierstadt en route to the Wind River Range in 1859— was the legend of John Colter, an old mountain man who had quit Lewis and Clark's expedition to turn trapper. On one of his forays deep into the heart of the Rockies, Colter claimed to have journeyed through a strange netherland of boiling rivers and plains of eternal fire. Rumors of a mythical "Colter's Hell" persisted down through the years, sometimes scoffed at as a tall tale embroidered by a mountain man and his friends, sometimes rejected as Indian superstition. But did it really exist? The few explorers and trappers that had been up through the headwaters of the Yellowstone River since John Colter confirmed the presence of "marvelous fountains," boiling cauldrons of mud, and a vast, silvery lake high in the mountains, from which, it was believed, waters flowed to both the Pacific and the Atlantic. Near there, the old guide and trapper Jim Bridger maintained, you could find stone trees as high as a man, and catch a trout from one stream and boil it for supper in the next.

These and other marvelous tales prompted a number of exploratory forays into the Yellowstone. The Washburn-Doane Expedition of 1870, which included a civilian party, headed by Nathaniel P. Langford, former Governor of Montana, trekked into the Yellowstone country territory, visited many of the Yellowstone sights and provided an accurate map of Yellowstone Lake and the geysers, hot springs and waterfalls in its environs. However, the drawings made by two members of the party, Charles Moore and Walter Trumbull, were only simplistic pencil sketches—the merest suggestions of the wonders that would soon be revealed to the world.

It was not until 1871 that the United States Government sent a scientific expedition into the wilderness to look for Colter's Hell. Led by the ambitious "self-made man of science" Ferdinand V. Hayden, head of the United States Geological and Geographical Survey of the Territories, its aim was to discern fact from fiction, once and for all. Hayden had seen Langford's enthusiastic lecture about the Yellowstone at Lincoln Hall in Washington, D.C., in January of 1871, which had been attended by members of Congress, among them James G. Blaine, the speaker of the House of Representatives. He surely realized that evening, as the audience sat paying rapt attention to the verbal descriptions of mud geysers and giant waterfalls, that a serious expedition to Yellowstone—and one that brought back pictorial proof of its marvels—was an imminently popular, and fundable, idea.[1]

By March 3, Hayden had secured a grant of $40,000 to lead a party to the source of the Yellowstone. Realizing the need for visual documentation, he brought with him William H. Jackson, the talented and tireless Western landscape photographer, who by that time was already an old hand at the ardures

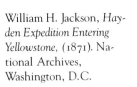

William H. Jackson, *Hayden Expedition Entering Yellowstone*, (1871). National Archives, Washington, D.C.

of trail life having accompanied Hayden on the previous year's geological survey.

Jackson, a Civil War veteran, had come West in 1866, lured by the Montana silver mines and distraught over a recently broken engagement.[2] After trying his hand as a bull-whacking teamster and a trail-riding vaquero, Jackson settled in Omaha and bought out a photography studio. Bored with portrait photography, he began to take pictures of the landscape—the building of the Union Pacific Railroad afforded him a unique opportunity. In 1870, his pictures of Western scenes caught the attention of Dr. Hayden, who offered him an unpaid position as the official photographer of the survey. His work proved so invaluable that the terms of the agreement were amended in his favor for the 1871 journey to the headwater of the Yellowstone.

Hayden had engaged Henry W. Elliot as the official artist of the expedition, but he also brought with him a frail, timid painter and engraver from Philadelphia, Thomas Moran. Unlike Jackson, Moran had never before been West,

Thomas Moran, *The Great Hot Springs, Gardiner's River,* (1871). The Thomas Gilcrease Institute of American History and Art, Tulsa.

Thomas Moran, *The Great Blue Spring, Lower Geyser Basin of the Yellowstone*, (1876). The Thomas Gilcrease Institute of American History and Art, Tulsa.

in fact he had only once ridden horseback. Born in Boulton, England, Moran, like Bierstadt, had come to America at a young age. As an apprentice to an engraver, Moran rebelled, spending most of his time painting and sketching romantic views and mythological scenes. Although never formally educated, he read extensively, particularly in the works of Romantic English poets such as Wordsworth, Shelley and Coleridge who apparently inspired some of his early artistic efforts.[3] Despite his admiration for English poetry and art, Moran felt, as did Bierstadt, that painting the American landscape was his ultimate destiny. "I decided very early," explained Moran, "that I would be an American painter. I'll paint as an American, on an American basis, and American only."[4] Perhaps this decision prompted his desire to see the wonders of the West for himself.

More at ease in the cavernous halls of the Tate Gallery in London, where he had once visited to make studies after Turner's works, or hunched over a wood-block engraving in his studio, where he had prepared the illustrative

William H. Jackson, *Upper Basins, Soda Springs, Gardiner's River,* (1871). The Smithsonian Institution, Washington, D.C.

plates for Nathaniel P. Langford's article on the Wonders of Yellowstone for *Scribner's Monthly Magazine,* Moran seemed an unlikely person to endure the mule trek high into the Yellowstone. He admitted to being, at the outset, "the perfect Greenhorn." Jackson recalled the image of the diminutive painter as "a picturesque appearance when mounted. The jaunty tilt of his sombrero, long yellowish beard and portfolio under his arm marked the artistic type, with something of local color imparted by a rifle slung from the saddle horn."[5] Yet, as the party probed into the mysterious Yellowstone, it became apparent that Hayden had made the right choice. The unlikely combination of William H. Jackson and Thomas Moran would create stirring and unforgettable images of Yellowstone's wonders. They became good friends and close collaborators, sharing a fascination with the landscape and a desire to record it for posterity in all of its bizarre splendor. For all of the doubting Thomases who refused to believe in the legendary Colter's Hell, Moran's paintings and Jackson's photographs would at last provide incontrovertible, and indeed breathtaking, evidence.

Like the Langford group before them, the Hayden survey approached the Yellowstone from the north, embarking from Fort Ellis on July 15, 1871, making their way with some difficulty over the Washburn Range (named the previous year) towards the source of the Yellowstone. Their first encounter with the strange natural wonders came with the abrupt discovery of Mammoth Hot Springs, a basin of brilliantly colored pools and geysers.

The photographer and the painter worked together, apart from the rest of the party for most of the day, accompanied by Jackson's photographic assistant and the cumbersome 400-pound load of cameras and developing equipment. Jackson credited Moran with help in framing his compositions, and Moran later admitted using Jackson's photographs for his later painted views. Both of them revelled in the marvels of Mammoth Hot Springs, where strange, almost architectural features seemed to suddenly burst from the landscape: sculpted pools of limestone rising like giant steps, one upon the other, towards a summit of fuming, sulfurous vents. This barren scape, nearly a square mile of mineral pools and limestone formations and devoid of vegetation, appeared all the more strange because of the quiet beauty surrounding it. Beyond the steaming pools lay virgin forest and vast grasslands where buffalo and elk grazed.

Jackson found so many good views in the geyser basins that he produced an extraordinary number of plates, the process hastened by an unexpected convenience. According to his account, "By washing the plates in water that issued from the springs at 160 degrees Farenheit, we were able to cut the drying time more than half."[6] His crisp black and white views of the geological features complimented Moran's watercolor scenes, which concentrated upon the vivid swirl of unusual colors.

If one could have been with Moran and Jackson one day as they sought out particularly interesting views of the Yellowstone, one might have seen the short, bearded man in high boots and suspenders as he stood transfixed at the edge of a blue-green glowing geyser pool, watching as roiling vents and hot, sulfurous cascades seemed to harbor every color of the rainbow, from magenta and bright yellow to deep greens and turquoise blues. The rising plumes of steam would pull his eyes upwards from the bizarre, molten geyserscape—towards pine trees and distant elk grazing in golden fields of wild grass and sedge. But he must have held perfectly still—long enough for the photographer, William H. Jackson, to complete his portrait. Jackson's photograph of Moran in the upper basin of Soda Springs captures the painter in his characteristic pose: gazing at the glories of the scenery. Although few of his pictures of Yellowstone ever equalled this one, the photographer often included the human figure in his pictures to provide scale to the strange formations, even perilously close to Old Faithful in eruption, where surely, the people posed at its base must have been nearly scalded by the gushing, sulfurous foam.

Unlike Yosemite, where the valley seemed to bear the scars of ancient, geological history, Yellowstone appeared to be a land in the turbulent throes of formation. Here, the artists and photographer, no less than the geologists, bore witness to the seething powers that lay just beneath the earth's crust. Instead of being oriented to the sky as on the rim of Yosemite's canyon, they wandered silently about the open mineral pools and steaming vents. In so doing, the Hayden party stood on the brink of the earth's molten interior. As Hayden and his crew sat around the campfire at night describing the day's

Thomas Moran, *Grand Canyon of the Yellowstone.* National Collection of American Art, Smithsonian Institution, Washington, D.C. Lent by the U. S. Department of the Interior, National Park Service.

measurements and speculating about the forces that led to the Yellowstone's formation, their geological enthusiasm was undoubtedly communicated to Jackson and Moran. Moran was later proud of the fact that he painted the rocks so carefully that "a geologist could determine their precise nature." Although this fact is disputable in view of his propensity for painterly, suggestive brush strokes rather than precise illustration, nevertheless, Moran's paintings for the rest of his life would bear the stamp of geological as well as scenic drama.

   The expedition camped on the shores of the placid Yellowstone Lake, which Hayden observed to be the remnant of a once-vast body of water of the post-glacial era. The scientists boated over to an island, declaring themselves the first white men to set foot on its shores. Before moving on, the members of the survey even enjoyed the trout which Jim Bridger made famous in his tales. Yet the highlight of the trip, at least for Thomas Moran, came when the explorers stopped at the brink of an immense chasm—the Grand Canyon of the Yellowstone. They had been prepared for the sight of the deep canyon with its towering lower falls by Langford's descriptions of the previous year. What shocked them was the bizarre array of colors which no pencil sketch or enthusiastic traveler's description had adequately pictured.

Thomas Moran, *The Castle Geyser, Upper Geyser Basin, Yellowstone National Park*.
Chromolithograph by Louise Prang, "Prang's American Chromos," 9¹¹⁄₁₆ x 14″.
Library, Smithsonian Institution, Washington, D. C.

As Thomas Moran stood on the brink of the Grand Canyon of the Yellowstone, gazing upon the brilliant yellows and crimsons which seemed to have erupted from the center of the earth, only to be eroded and carved into weird towers and slopes by the crashing descent of the river, he declared the scene "beyond the reach of human art." Yet, the frail, timid man with the bold paint brush may have surprised even himself in his ability to capture this, the most imposing and powerful wonder of the Yellowstone. The tints of the canyon were like no others he had seen. It was as though the dreamlike effects of his idol, Turner, had suddenly become reality in the deep recesses of the American continent.

Instead of making exact, painstaking studies of the geological formations, Moran preferred to sit and look carefully at the scene, committing its colors and forms to memory before putting them down on paper with brush and watercolor. He had an unusual ability to engrave whole features, such as the plunging falls, indelibly into his imagination.

After his return to the East, Moran moved his studio to Newark, where he set to work on an immense 7 by 12 foot painting, *The Grand Cañon of the Yellowstone*. In this masterpiece, Moran, like Bierstadt, "idealized" the composition, taking the liberty of rearranging the view for maximum romantic effect; yet he asked Hayden to inspect it for geological accuracy, a detail with which Bierstadt never bothered. After its completion in 1872, it was sold to the U.S. Government to hang in the Capitol building: a trophy that testified to the American's emerging belief that "there is no phase of landscape in which we are not richer, more varied and more interesting than any other in the world."[7] Upon viewing the painting in Moran's Newark studio, the art critic Richard Watson Gilder announced, "When I think of his carrying that immense canvas across his brain so long, I wonder that he didn't go through the door sideways, and call people to look out when they came near."[8]

Even before he produced his first large scale masterpiece, *The Grand Cañon of the Yellowstone,* Moran executed several smaller watercolors of Yellowstone's scenic wonders, including a special set for Northern Pacific Railroad magnate Jay Cooke. In 1876, the famous chromolithographer, Louis Prang, produced a limited color edition from a set of Moran's vivid aquarelles, so that the public could enjoy the scenic wonders as well. Published with a description of the discoveries by Hayden, the lavish result has been called the finest set of chromolithographs ever produced, the vivid colors of the hot springs and geysers allowing Prang to demonstrate a tour de force in the lithographer's art.

Jackson's photographs of Yellowstone country, though smaller than the mammoth *Grand Cañon of the Yellowstone,* and only black and white versions of the hot springs and geysers so beautifully rendered by his friend Moran, were no less influential than Moran's paintings to a public thirsty for visual facts about the discoveries in the West. In fact, they were the first successful photographic record of a land that had remained legend for nearly fifty years. Although Americans had come to expect flights of romantic fancy from artists such as Bierstadt and Moran, Jackson's camera did not lie. His views were the sole visual proof that "the Wonders of the Yellowstone," pictured by Moran, were indeed genuine. Jackson's photographs also provided scale to the unusual landforms and geothermal events. His compositions measured the limestone concretions, the towering eruptions and the immense waterfalls according to human scale. In doing so, they perhaps took some of the mystery out of the land once known as Colter's Hell. Reflecting upon the photographs from our vantage point of a hundred years later, our closest comparable images might be the video pictures transmitted back from the Sea of Tranquility, which showed the Moon's surface—not as a vast sea of dust, or as the miraculous crystaline caverns of Jules Verne—but as a terrain across which man could walk, and eventually drive. As is inevitable in the process of scientific inves-

ARTIST AND PHOTOGRAPHER IN WONDERLAND

tigation, Hayden's Survey of 1871 and 1872 in the Yellowstone, just like the Apollo missions to the Moon, were intended to render the unknown comprehensible to man. As Hayden's topographers carefully ascertained the altitude of Mount Washburn, measured the height of the Upper and Lower Falls, and clambered down geyser vents to understand the source of their energy, they brought a scientific perspective to one of the West's greatest mysteries, and robbed it of a little of its wonder.

The journey to the Yellowstone changed the lives of both painter and photographer. For Jackson, as he later admitted, the association with Hayden, "gave me a career." For Moran, the pictures of the Yellowstone would make him famous. An artist with a strong, almost palpable imagination, the strange landscape despite having been charged by the Hayden Survey, made a permanent impression upon him. He later recalled:

> Since that time, I have wandered over a good part of the Territories and have seen much of the varied scenery of the Far West, but that of the Yellowstone retains its hold upon my imagination with a vividness as of yesterday. . . . The impression then made upon me by the stupendous & remarkable manifestations of nature's forces will remain with me as long as memory lasts.[9]

One of the most important consequences of the 1871 exploration of the Yellowstone was the creation by Congress of the first National Park. Langford, the Park's first Superintendent, credits a member of his expedition with the germination of the idea. As he recalled in his diary, a campfire discussion regarding the potential profitability of the park ensued as the Washburn expedition prepared to leave the Yellowstone in 1870. One member of the party suggested dividing it up into sections of the "prominant points of interest [that] would eventually become a source of great profit to the owners."[10] Another suggested pooling their claims for the benefit of the whole party. Yet Cornelius Hedges, perhaps having witnessed the fate of Niagara,

> said that he did not approve of any of these plans—that there ought to be no private ownership of any portion of that region, but the whole ought to be set apart as a great National Park, and that each one of us ought to make an effort to have this accomplished.[11]

Whether or not Cornelius Hedges was the first to suggest that Yellowstone become a national park, or, as Aubrey L. Haines suggests in his book *The Yellowstone Story*, Judge William D. Kelley originated the idea in a conversation with agents for the Northern Pacific Railway, 1872 was the year that

William H. Jackson, *Mountain of the Holy Cross (Colorado),* (1873). National Archives, Still Picture Branch, Washington, D.C.

George Catlin's dream of "a nation's park, containing man and beast, in all the wild freshness of their nature's beauty!" was finally realized. Jackson's photographs and Moran's watercolors of the wonders of the Yellowstone, laid on the desks of influential members of congress were key instruments in the successful lobbying by Langford and Hayden to have Yellowstone set aside as a National Park.

In a very real sense it was the culmination of a romantic dream, for the intention was to preserve the *experience* of wilderness, nature, and especially *scenery* in its pristine state. It could not have happened a moment too soon. Even as Hayden entered Yellowstone country in 1871, claims were being staked in the area of Mammoth Hot Springs, bathers had come to the bubbling mineral pools to take the cure, and argonauts were registering claims on tracts of the surrounding countryside.

After the 1871 expedition, Jackson continued with the Hayden Survey, documenting both the scenic wonders and the scientific features of the American West. Hayden testified to the importance of Jackson's photographs:

> They have done much, in the first place, to secure truthfulness in the representation of mountain and other scenery. Twenty years ago, no more than carica-

Thomas Moran, *The Mountain of the
Holy Cross*, (1875), The Huntington
Hartford Collection, New York City.

tures existed, as a general rule, of the leading features of overland exploration.
Mountains were represented with angles of sixty degrees inclination, covered
with great glaciers, and modelled upon the type of any other than the Rocky
Mountains, the angular lines of a sandstone mesa, represented with all the pecu-
liarities of volcanic upheaval, or of massive granite, or an ancient ruin with
clean-cut, perfectly squared and joined masonry, that would be creditable to modern
times. The truthful representations of photography render such careless work so
apparent that it would not be tolerated at the present day.[12]

From his mountain panoramas, taken from the top of Colorado peaks, in
the company of Hayden's surveyors, to the nearly inaccessible prehistoric cities hidden in the elevated overhangs of Mancos Canyon which he photographed soon after, Jackson's pictures became the principal documentary images
of the discoveries in the West. His success lay not only in his technical skill
at shooting and developing in the field, at a time when even studio wet plate
photography was difficult, but also in his continual capacity for wonder at his
surroundings. The sheer variety of his pictures, from images of unspoiled nature
to shots, such as the quarrying of granite for the Great Temple in Salt Lake,
of man altering and shaping the landscape to his own ends, testified to the
vision of a man whose imagination and energy encompassed both the timeless

and the changing West, picturing it in thousands of glass plate negatives for the posterity of generations.

Perhaps Jackson's greatest accomplishment came in 1873 when, in the company of Hayden's surveyors he took the first photograph of the famous Mountain of the Holy Cross, a legend of the Spanish padres that, unlike the legendary Seven Cities of Cibola, proved to be true. After an arduous climb to Notch Mountain in the Colorado Rockies, Jackson "emerged above the timberline and the clouds," where he gazed towards the flank of the Sawatch Range at "the great shining cross . . . tilted against the mountainside."[13] The image wedded God and Nature in a single frame. In doing so, Jackson's photograph became the most famous image of an American mountain ever produced. Henry Wadsworth Longfellow, who owned a copy of the print, was inspired to write a sonnet, *The Cross of Snow* which evoked the poetic image in memorable verse:

> There is a mountain in the distant West
> That, sun-defying, in its deep ravines
> Displays a cross of snow upon its side.[14]

Jackson's old friend, Moran, was determined to paint the scene the moment he saw the photograph. Enduring the ardures of the Rockies, the painter sketched the mountain himself, and in 1875 completed a large scale version. In 1876, Moran's painting and Jackson's photographs of the Mount of the Holy Cross became the prime attractions of the Centennial Exposition in Philadelphia. Together, they represented the pinnacle of America's fascination with the Rocky Mountains as manifestations of the romantic sublime. The barren peak, emblazoned with a cross of snow, communicated what even Bierstadt's mountain panoramas had only alluded to: that the ultimate reward of sublime transcendence through nature's wonders was not a pagan polytheism, but the revelation of the Creator. "The Mount of the Holy Cross" became an archetypal image of a Christian nation, an outward sign that God himself had blessed the westward course of empire, and that the mighty mountains, indeed, were the fruits of his handiwork.

CHAPTER 16

THE GRANDEST CANYON
OF THEM ALL

Rather than return with Hayden and Jackson to Yellowstone, after the landmark trip of 1871, Thomas Moran, after completing his commissions and finishing the large Yosemite painting, struck off to the Southwest for even grander scenery. He accompanied Major John Wesley Powell on his survey of the Grand Canyon of the Colorado in 1873. More so than Yellowstone, or even Yosemite, the Grand Canyon's walls contained within their mile deep beds of strata the key to the geological history of the American West. To ride down the winding trail into the canyon was to descend into the vaults of time, counting away geological aeons with each careful step of the burro's hoof. Powell, the successor to Clarence King as the Head of the U.S. Geological Survey in 1881, had braved the gushing cataracts and muddy torrent of the river to descend the length of the Colorado in 1869. The dangerous journey had provided much more than fodder for romantic contemplation, however. Over the course of the next several years, Powell and his collaborators would use the Grand Canyon as a key to their brilliant synthesis of the West's geological evolution.

What excited Powell and the other geologists of the survey was not so much that the Canyon revealed strata of great antiquity, for the Wind River Range and the Green River district already manifested their share of Precambrian outcrops. Instead, the Canyon appeared to them a great puzzle in geological mechanics: What had formed this mile-deep cleft in the earth? What caused the broad unconformities in its structure, its 2,000 foot hanging valleys, the rifts, lava flows and transecting faults? The Grand Canyon presented one of the greatest, if not the greatest intellectual challenge to geologists of all time.

Based upon data collected on his canyon voyage, and later observations of its unexpectedly discontinuous stratigraphy, Powell asserted that the Grand Canyon could not have been formed by the simple processes of erosion commonly associated with streams flowing down the mountains towards the ocean. In a theory that his collegue Clarence Dutton would later express as the "Law of the Persistence of Rivers," Powell suggested that the Colorado river was "antecedent" in age to the deep canyon, and that, as the landscape rose in ancient times, it was cut by the stream "as a log to a saw."

The investigations of 1873 focused upon the Canyon's rim, where the broader features of the "Plateau Province," as Powell called the Grand Canyon district encompassing the western drainage of the Colorado River, could be studied. Moran, in the company of the expedition photographer Jack Hillers, was treated to views all along the sequence of the North Rim Plateaus. Among the most impressive sights was the gigantic cleft of Toroweap, where geologist Clarence Dutton wrote that men felt like "mere insects crawling along the street of a city flanked with immense temples, or as Lemuel Gulliver might have felt in revisiting the capital of Brobdingnag and finding it deserted."[1]

In the course of his expedition along the North Rim, Moran scanned the vast, eroded landscape and the distant Colorado for scenery to create a great painting to rival his *The Grand Cañon of the Yellowstone*. On the towering eminence of the Powell Plateau separated from the Kaibab, he seems to have found it. Powell described the scene:

> In the immediate foreground you look down into a vast amphitheatre, dark and gloomy in the depths below, like an opening into a nadir of hell. A little stream heading in this amphitheatre runs down through a deep, narrow gorge until it is lost behind castellated buttes. . . . The Colorado itself, seen in the distance, though a great river, appears but a creek.[2]

Here, the river angles around the promontory to reveal splendid views both up and down its course. Moran chose the cracking roof of the amphitheater as the foreground for his big Grand Canyon painting, substituting typical South-

Thomas Moran, *The Chasm of the Colorado*, (1873–1874). National Museum of American Art, Smithsonian Institution, Washington, D.C. Lent by the U.S. Department of the Interior.

west foliage for the human figure to give it scale. In his composition, he tried to "consume vast draughts of space." Fascinated with the visual metaphor of the geologist's "Rock Temples," Moran created more of a mountainscape than a canyon view—an image which emphasized verticality rather than the broad expanse of the Plateau Province through which the Grand Canyon had (in geological terms) only recently cut. Awed by a thunderstorm that he and Powell witnessed, clouds became a prime feature of the painting. In opting for meterological drama, he passed over the more significant drama of the geology. Simplifying the stratigraphy to get everything into the picture, the geological features lost definition. Some critics responded negatively. *Scribners* found in it "an oppressive wildness that weighs down the senses."[3] *The Atlantic Monthly* thought the picture "wanting almost entirely in the beauty that distinguished earlier work."[4] Perhaps the panorama was, this time, too large to carry around in his brain, or what is more likely, Moran tried to apply somewhat outworn romantic devices to a scene which defied them. Moran, despite all of his enthusiasm for the effects of the Western landscape did not have the geological vision that could capture the true drama of the Grand Canyon. It took the efforts of a very different artist to ultimately picture it correctly.

William H. Holmes, artist, ethnographer, geologist, topographer and museum curator had his own vision of the Grand Canyon, a vision not founded upon the plastic fantasies of the aesthetic imagination, nor upon the application of Turnerian principals to the American continent, but upon the "art of information" and the desire to interpret the topography in geological terms. Holmes, originally an artist and illustrator for the Smithsonian Institution, went West in 1872 with Hayden on the second year of his Yellowstone Survey. He later worked as an assistant geologist with Hayden in the Colorado Rockies in 1874, where he formed the important conception of the lacolite uplift—an important element in his friend Grove Karl Gilbert's synthesis of the geology of the Henry Mountains, and eventually a key to understanding the geological processes of the Grand Canyon.[5] In 1879 he joined Clarence Dutton on the Powell Survey of the Grand Canyon region, and was later instrumental in the creation of Dutton's famous monograph *Tertiary History of the Grand Cañon District* (1882).

Dutton's monograph was the culmination of Powell's, Gilbert's and his own research on the formation of the canyon, and, by extension, the formation of the West itself. Although he used several pictures by Moran in his text, he reproduced only one large Moran panorama in the atlas accompanying the monograph, an atlas which has often been called the most beautiful government report ever produced. It is the numerous drawings by Holmes, including a remarkable three-part panorama from Point Sublime, which actually reveal the Canyon's geological history.

According to Dutton, the actual process of erosion that produced the can-

William H. Holmes, *Panorama From Point Sublime.* One of three separate illustrations from Point Sublime in *Atlas* to Clarence Dutton's *Tertiary History of the Grand Canyon District,* (1882), Sheet XVI.

yon occurred in relatively recent geological times, most of it during the Ter-
tiary Era, when the canyon began life as a narrow outlet to a fresh-water
Eocene lake through which water poured towards its drainage in the Pacific.
Yet even before this, the Plateau Province had undergone profound changes.

As Dutton envisioned it, the story began during the Mesozoic Era, a period
150 million years ago, when much of the present-day West lay under a vast
shallow sea (the Rocky Mountains had not yet risen). Sedimentary strata were
deposited over the course of millions of years, only to be abruptly lifted and
tilted, as the Great Plains domed, and drained the Plateau Province. The
process created the beginnings of the Rocky Mountains. It was, in Dutton's
words, a period of "Great Denudation," a time when the land eroded practically to sea level, and layers of strata representing millions of years were lost,
the land planed down to virtually a smooth surface. Following this came another
long period of uniform deposition. Again, these sediments lay underwater,
sinking slowly beneath their own weight as quickly as they accumulated. With
the dawn of the Cenozoic Era 70 million years ago, the Plateau Province,
already a shallow sea, evolved into a brackish, freshwater lake, and suddenly,
episodes of uplift and denudation began to take their toll. During the middle
Eocene, which manifested itself elsewhere in the West by "immense exhibitions of telluric energy" as Clarence King described them, the Plateau Province began to expand upwards, forced by a broad lacolith deep beneath its
surface. This gigantic bubble of basaltic lava, unable to break through the
strata to the surface, elevated the whole Province, drained the huge lake, and
began to cause the disgorging channel, now the infant Colorado, to saw down
through the rising strata. With this period of uplift and fiery tumult came a
series of basaltic eruptions which forced their way through the horizontal strata.
These igneous extrusions caused massive cracks and faults, among them the
Toroweap, one of the surviving remnants of this period of upheaval.

It was not until the Tertiary period that the canyon began to take on its
present scale. The Colorado River, meandering back and forth across the basin
of the Plateau Province, eroding the earlier layers of Mesozoic strata over eons,
drained the landscape for 15,000 square miles, drawing into its erosional channel the shattered debris of thousands of vertical feet of deposited strata. The
distant Vermilion Cliffs, at some places thirty miles from the present river
bed, were "literally sawed to pieces." At the same time, the river channel
chewed deeper and deeper into the ancient sedimentary strata, its course shaped
and altered through time by the slipping faults and tumbling piles of hard

igneous rock. The erosion continued through the Pleistocene era, which manifested itself in the Southwest, not as an Ice Age, but as a rainy period: a time which hastened the process of erosion, and stripped away nearly all remnants of the deep Mesozoic beds, leaving the present canyon as a deep cleft in the much older Carboniferous and Archaean sediments.

In Dutton's *Tertiary History*, the whole process gradually unfolds to the reader as a creation story told about the marvelous landscape, a literary tour of the Vermilion Cliffs, the Toroweap fault and the series of plateaus. Holmes' drawings perfectly illustrate the entire process.

Only through his crisp panoramas can the distant edges of the Vermilion Cliffs be seen and thus the true extent of the "Great Denudation" comprehended. In superb detail, Holmes pictures the process of erosion that becomes the crux of Dutton's argument, carefully showing, in pictures such as his *Panorama From Point Sublime* how, as Dutton describes it, "Every cañon wall, through its trunk, branches, and twigs and every alcove and niche become a dissolving face."[6] By picturing not only the landscape forms, but the dip and strike of the strata themselves, Holmes is able to illustrate such important features as "The Great Unconformity," where level Carboniferous strata seem to sit practically atop tilting Archaean beds—evidence of an ancient hiatus in the depositional process. Yet it is Toroweap which is his singular masterpiece, that scene described by Dutton in such picturesque terms. Not only does Holmes capture it in all of its majesty, with Lilliputian figures standing near a rain puddle on the roof of the cliff, overlooking the inner chasm, but he shows the viewer the structure of the fault itself, displayed in the stratigraphy on the canyon's opposite wall.

For Dutton and for Holmes, the characteristic romantic vista with gathering thunderheads was not enough; the landscape told a grander story than even Moran could visualize. The history of the Grand Canyon had its own sublime character. It was nature's own narrative that the artist William H. Holmes took the trouble to render faithfully, as he painstakingly sat in the brilliant Arizona sun, drawingboard and pencil in hand, squinting through binoculars at the distant strata. Holmes somehow knew that he was limning out the West at its moment of creation and thus he needed no painterly embellishments. It was dramatic enough in its own right, a story in novelist Frank Norris's words "as big as all outdoors."

Ironically, Holmes's realist vision surpassed any photographic attempt to document the same geological features. Although Jack Hillers on the Powell Survey and Timothy O'Sullivan on the Wheeler Survey exposed some exceptional views of the canyon, none could overcome the atmospheric haze well enough to visually analyze the landscape in terms even approaching Holmes's accuracy.

It seems strange, after looking at Holmes's drawings, to turn back to the best products of Hiller's and O'Sullivan's efforts to realize that the photographers were actually still framing their shots more for romantic rather than scientific purposes. Pictures such as Hiller's *Inner Gorge of the Grand Canyon, Arizona* thrill the viewer with the bravery of the subjects perched on the brink of the 3,000-foot precipice, yet tell little about how those cliffs came to be. O'Sullivan is more attentive to documentary purpose with his pictures like *Rock Carved by Drifting Sand* and *Water Ryolites Near Logan Springs, Nevada,* yet they still appear more to be shots of natural curiosities than pictures that synthesize and illustrate geological concepts. In the art of the Grand Canyon, not only does the camera's eye fail to match the artist's, but only Holmes, who had helped to shape geological theory himself, could picture the landscape with true comprehension.

Holmes's pictures, while primarily scientific illustrations, had an aesthetic beauty all their own. Perhaps this is because they came as close as possible to representing the complex clarities of the scientific imagination itself. As such, they never rivalled Moran's more conventional painterly views of the Grand Canyon in the public imagination. In fact, few Americans outside the scientific community have ever taken the time, or had the occasion to study Holmes's stupendous drawings carefully or even to note them casually, buried away as they are in an obscure government document with the ponderous title, *Tertiary History of the Grand Canyon District.* Thus most people miss that dimension of the West of the imagination that stems from the scientific view of the West that is as old as the visions of Lewis and Clark and Peale's wonderful museum.

In addition, Holmes, an artist of information, was one of the few to rival the photographer as a documentary artist. With the growing public interest in photography as a source of information as well as art, the American landscape painters found themselves increasingly challenged by the camera, which rarely exaggerated or idealized for artistic purposes. As the end of the nineteenth century approached, Western artists—indeed all artists—would be forced to take a stance in relation to the photographer, to tell the viewers just whether or not what they showed them was true, and to justify themselves in aesthetic terms if it was not.

Whether creating extravagant, idealized visions of the Yosemite "swimming

John K. Hillers, *Inner Gorge of the Grand Canyon of the Colorado River.* U.S. Geological Survey, Denver, Colorado.

in pearly mists," or trekking through the peaks of Colorado to catch a glimpse of the Mount of the Holy Cross, or even perched on the rim of the Grand Canyon, grappling with the complex reconstruction of geological processes, the artists and photographers of Western landscape succeeded in enlarging the American vision of itself and its own continent to proportions beyond that of any other nation. The American West, where the mountains were bigger, the canyons deeper, the waterfalls higher—where one seemed closer to God's creation—became an emblem of America's pride in itself. Through their devotion to picturing Western landscape, the artists and the photographers had created a series of sacred places across the continent. Their images, with sublime trajectories, dramatic compositions and infinite detailing of natural phenomena defined the visual and intellectual processes by which citizens could best experience the American scenery. In order to preserve this experience, to set it apart, to keep it unspoiled, Congress elevated the wonders of the West to the status of inviolate precincts. They became our nation's *own* series of sacred places, sanctified by romantic and Christian and nationalistic principles. With the creation of the national park system, important parts of the West would be preserved forever as wild, picturesque and scientific marvels for future generations. Congress had legislated the difference between the sacred and the profane.

CHAPTER 17

IMAGES OF PROGRESS

Even as images of nature's western grandeur were being laid before the public, so, too, were images of civilization's progress into the vast wilderness. The triumphant march of civilization was nowhere better symbolized, or even represented, than by scenes of the transcontinental railroad being built across mountains, deserts and canyons, overcoming anything that stood in its way, while at the same time bringing the luxuries and refinements of the East to the raw oases of the West. And, along with the railroads, even ranging out ahead of them, were men of science whose daring feats in the cause of knowledge for mankind were dramatized by an intrepid group of men using still another machine—the mammoth wet plate cameras employed by official expedition photographers. These men and the railroad photographers, too, were a new breed of civilization's heroes. Trained for the most part on the battlefields of the Civil War, the photographers, like the survey engineers, did not let nature's obstacles interfere with their work. They made incredible panoramic shots from atop high mountains, using tentlike, makeshift darkrooms, and they photographed the shimmering wastes of the southwestern desert when the temperature rose so high that it boiled the collodian on their wet glass plate negatives.

The most noticeable group of western photographers, however, often accompanied by journalists, followed the transcontinental railroad, one of the greatest engineering projects of the nineteenth century.

As early as 1848, when he was advocating his "Buffalo Trail," or 38th parallel route, on which Benjamin Kern lost his life, Senator Thomas Hart Benton expressed some of the grandeur of the man-made project that would match the awesome quality of the Western landscape. "The road will be made," he declared emphatically:

> The age is progressive, and utilitarian. It abounds with talent, seeking employment, and with capital seeking investment. The temptation is irresistible. To reach the golden California—to put the populations of the Atlantic and the Pacific into direct communication—to connect Europe and Asia through America. . . . such is the grandeur of the enterprise![1]

When the transcontinental railroad was built in the late 1860s, thanks to generous land grants and loans from the U. S. Government, it was viewed in almost exactly the way predicted. Men of talent and ingenuity, like Theodore Judah, in California, and Grenville M. Dodge, operating out on the plains of Nebraska, made the dream of the railroad a reality by locating the "practicable" route that had eluded the exploring parties of the Great Reconnaissance. Then the lobbyists, financiers, and confidence men, like Thomas C. Durant and Oakes Ames, of the Union Pacific, took over, fleecing the government at every turn, but nonetheless building the mighty road. As one Missouri executive said, the American people "love to annihilate the magnificent distances."[2] And so the railroad was built, the Union Pacific moving west out of Omaha, a terminus selected by President Abraham Lincoln himself, and the Central Pacific climbing eastward over the Sierras and into Nevada's Great Basin, over a version of the Donner Pass route discovered by Theodore Judah and "Doc" Strong of Dutch Flat, California. On the western end, tunnels were blasted through the Sierras by an army of Chinese workers, using nitroglycerin, illegally manufactured at a line camp high up in the Sierras. On the eastern end it was "Five men to the 500-pound rail, 28 to 30 spikes to the rail, three blows to the spike, two pairs of rails to the minute, 400 rails to the mile—and half a continent to go 'A grand Anvil Chorus [is] playing across the plains. . . . 21 million [strokes and] this great work of modern America is complete . . . ,' " wrote an Eastern reporter in 1868.[3] Finally, of course, on May 8, 1869, the two lines met at Promontary Point, fifty-six miles west of Ogden in Utah.

Thomas Moran, *The Mirage.* The Stark Museum of Art, Orange, Texas.

In addition to an avalanche of newspaper articles, ranging from nationalistic self-congratulations to exposés of the sordid financial dealings of the Credit Mobilier, that financed the construction of the Union Pacific, the American public learned about the great road to empire from numerous illustrations in *Harper's Weekly, The Magazine of Civilization* and *Frank Leslie's Illustrated Weekly.*[4]

A.J. Russell, *Temporary and Permanent Bridges and Citadel Rock, Green River (Wyoming),* (1867–8). Yale University.

Even the *Illustrated London News* carried views of the great project. Some of these views in illustrated magazines were sheer fantasy, but others were made by journalist illustrators, like the one who accompanied Frank Leslie himself on a deluxe trip across the continent. But by far the most popular view was the Currier and Ives Print drawn for them by Fanny Palmer, entitled *Across the Continent*. Ms. Palmer clearly had *not* taken the tour across the continent. Her view showed the train puffing past a log cabin town on tracks that reached past scenic lakes and mountains, across a great plain to infinity. Settlers wave happily at the train passing by, as do a group of mounted Indians into whose faces the engine is belching smoke.

Then, too, a swarm of photographers documented the construction of the railroad. The best of these were Andrew J. Russell, Alexander Gardner (who photographed the Union Pacific and the Kansas Pacific, respectively), and William H. Jackson, a young man of twenty-three, who, in his first photographic venture, spent the year of 1869 traveling the Union Pacific, taking pictures on speculation.[5] Other photographers who photographed the railroad on speculation were Carleton E. Watkins, Eadweard Muybridge, A. A. Hart, and C. R. Savage of Salt Lake City.

A. J. Russell will forever be remembered because it was he who photographed the "Golden Spike" ceremony when the roads joined at Promontory Point. But a number of his other photographs, made with a large wet plate camera, stand out as works of surpassing symbolic beauty. His, *Temporary and Permanent Bridges and Citadel Rock, Green River (Wyoming)*, (1867–8), is perhaps his masterpiece. To the right of the picture a man and a train stand on tracks run across a temporary trestle, beside which stands a cylindrical water tank. Slanting in from the left is another track with two men on a hand-car. This track runs between two masonry piers meant to carry the permanent track. A New England salt box house stands in the far distance across a snowy wasteland, as if to testify to Yankee ingenuity. Smoke drifts out of the steam engine's smokestack towards Citadel Rock, which stands unmoved, like a nature god's throne, from which he looks down on man's mighty, though transient, efforts.

This one winter photo surely matched anything a painter could concoct. It is instructive, however, to compare Russell's *Castle Rocks, Green River Valley*, (1867–8), with Thomas Moran's rendering of the same view. Moran took a position south, or downstream, from the Castle Rocks, and placed them, in brilliant orange and yellow colors, to the right of his picture. He portrayed a

A.J. Russell, *Castle Rocks, Green River Valley*, (1867–8). Yale University.

party on horseback riding by them, as if they were a shimmering mirage. Indeed, the whole picture took on the magic quality of a mirage, which is what Moran named one of the several versions of the scene which he painted. Russell, on the other hand, snapped his picture from the west—from across the Green River—at a place, in fact, where two rivers ran together. On the right is a dark sage plain, on which one can barely make out his photographic wagon. On the left is the river, reflecting Castle Rock, and a tiny man standing beside it to indicate the giant scale of the landscape. The Castle Rock stands in the distance, not as a romantic mirage but as something solid and immovable. Though he was denied the use of vivid colors available to the painter, Russell, in this picture, managed to contrast the darkness of the sage plain on the right with the brilliant luminescence of the river reflection pointing directly at the great rock and the evening sky.

In most of his pictures, Russell included a man or some men to indicate the incredible scale of the landscape. Green River was a favorite spot for him. Another of his impressive photos, *On Mountains of Green River, South Butte in the Background (Wyoming)*, (1867–8), one tiny figure stands between two towering volcanic cores with a virtually infinite, barren, scraped landscape stretching before him. In another photo, he shows a chain of tiny men clambering up the Black Buttes of Wyoming, while a man with a mule already atop a butte, stands watching them. In still another view, Russell sought to portray the texture and solidity of a mountain into which a crew of men are laboriously carving a tunnel. As the men stand, posing with a rock cart before the dark tunnel's mouth, the wavy railroad tracks disappear into it. In nearly all of his pictures, A. J. Russell was able to infuse drama or a sense of story. He could be likened to Thomas Cole, the Hudson River Painter who did so much to dramatize the Ox Bow of the Connecticut River. This was undoubtedly no accident, because Russell, who was from Nunda, New York, began his career as a landscape and panorama painter. The Civil War changed his career; in that conflict he became a photographer for the U. S. Military Railroad Construction Corps.[6]

Nonetheless, it seems his sense of landscape painting, its techniques, and especially its proper composition, never left him. Something like this tended to be true of most of the successful Western landscape photographers, with the possible exception of Timothy O'Sullivan, who never was a painter. That is, painter or not, the photographers, as they began working in the new medium, looked back to the old in search of basic principles and nuances of composition. Thus at first, instead of the painter being influenced by the photograph, the situation was quite the opposite. The photographer was influenced by the painter.

No clearer evidence of this can be found than in William H. Jackson's work in Yellowstone in 1871, where he took his cue from the painter, Moran, and later in Colorado, from the mountaintop panoramacist, William H. Holmes. Jackson's *North From Berthoud Pass* (1873) is a striking example of this influence, and one of Jackson's best photographs, in terms of catching the "all outdoors" spirit of the West. The Colorado mountain peaks reach away to the horizon, but astride them, in an intrepid, unforgettable pose, stands Harry Yount, mountain man and later the first ranger in Yellowstone National Park.

But with no painterly influences to aid his eye, Jackson's views of the Union Pacific in 1869 become all the more interesting. For the most part, they reflect the triumph of man over nature. *Burning Rock Cut Near Green River Station, Wyoming Territory* (1869), for example, portrays a man-made canyon blasted out of a mountain. By the same token, *High Bridge at the Loop above Georgetown, Colorado* (1869), shows a train high atop a rickety bridge spanning a river gorge. In another photo Jackson portrayed a train on the outside curve of a mountain in a view from below among the rocks that had been blasted out by the roadbed crew. In these photos, scenery was subordinated to the engineering triumph that the railroad represented. Perhaps the best of these views, *Chalk Creek Canyon* (1869), revealed a railroad track curving against the wall of a canyon. The train itself, barely visible in the distance, is just

William H. Jackson, *North From Berthoud Pass,* (1873). Denver Public Library, Western History Collection, Western History Department.

about to round a turn and head right at the viewer as if defying nature itself in the image of the towering canyon wall.

By 1870, when he first joined Hayden's Survey, Jackson had developed a greater reverence for nature, upon which he was to build in all his future pictures. Accompanied this time by the artist, Sanford Robinson Gifford, Jackson made a panoramic shot from the top of Devil's Gate that caught the immense distances of the Oregon Trail as it followed the Sweetwater River winding away across a vast plain to the mountains far in the distance.[7] Here, as in his later work, nature was overwhelming, and man a mere figure in the foreground looking down upon the grandeur of it all.

A different, and more solemn, kind of grandeur was portrayed by Timothy O'Sullivan, who joined Clarence King's United States Geological and Geographical Survey of the Fortieth Parallel at its inception in 1867. The energetic King, only twenty-five years old, convinced Secretary of War William Stanton to place him in complete charge of a massive western project that, according to Stanton, was coveted by at least "four major-generals."[8] In some ways, the impetuous King, whom Henry Adams called "the best and brightest man of his generation," resembled the youthful General George Armstrong Custer. He was fearless, and he usually got results. His project was indeed breathtaking in its audacity. Let the *New York Times* of May 8, 1867, describe it:

> The section to be surveyed is a belt of land about 100 miles wide, near the 40th parallel of latitude, between the 120th and 105th degrees of longitude, or in other words, from Virginia City (Nevada) to Denver City, a stretch of 800 or 900 miles in length. This strip includes the proposed route of the Central Pacific Railroad . . . and it is the object of the Government to ascertain all the characteristics of the region which is thus to be traversed. . . . The minerals, flora and

Timothy O'Sullivan, *Sand Dunes, Carson Desert, Nevada*, (1868). Office of Chief of Engineers, Photo No. 77-KS-10, National Archives, Washington, D.C.

Timothy O'Sullivan, *Green River Near Flaming Gorge (Colorado)*, (c. 1868). Library of Congress, Washington, D.C.

Timothy O'Sullivan, *Green River (Colorado),* (c. 1868). Department of Prints & Photographs, The Library of Congress, Washington, D.C.

the fauna of the country, and its agricultural capacity are likewise to be studied and reported on. In fact all the work of nature in that wild and unknown region is to be scanned by shrewd and highly educated observers.[9]

The *New York Times* description was correct. It forgot to mention, however, that King's Survey was designed to explore and survey straight across the arid wastes of the Great Basin, leap across the Wasatch Range, that overlooked the Great Salt Lake, and terminate on the eastern side of the towering Rocky Mountains. Neither 100-plus-degree heat, snakes, mosquitoes, wild animals, mineral strikes nor hostile Indians was to delay its progress. King, in fact, revelled in the challenge. During the course of the survey he managed to chase and capture a deserter single-handed, armed only with a rifle to assault a grizzly bear in its lair to survive being struck by lightning atop a bald mountain peak, and to expose "the Great Diamond Hoax." In the latter instance, King and his men put their scientific knowledge together to locate a mesa in Eastern Colorado salted with diamonds, and thus saved many a would-be San Francisco investor from stark tragedy.

Such was the man that Timothy O'Sullivan, a veteran Civil War photographer, went to work for in 1867. O'Sullivan had been known for his almost grisly objectivity in photographing the dead on the battlefield at Gettysburg.

Timothy O'Sullivan, *Canyon de Chelly*, (1873). Library of Congress, Washington, D.C.

He was a clinical, exacting, scientific photographer with a genuine feeling for the structures of the barren rugged lands he saw all about him in the West. This is keynoted by perhaps his most famous photograph, *Desert Sand Hills Near the Sink of Carson (Nevada)*. Almost a classic of the minimal art which O'Sullivan was to espouse, this view showed his photographic wagon and horses silhouetted against a large, barren sand dune with two dark mountainside wedges framing the dune on either side. The only evidence of man was O'Sullivan's footprints in the sand leading up the dune from which he took the picture. It was one of the great matter-of-fact photos of all time. Another scene of a man in a white shirt, possibly himself, seated on a sage plain observing an alkaline water hole in the endless space of the Carson Desert further confirmed his laconic approach to photographing the West.

O'Sullivan saw it as his job to render scientific views of the landforms as exactly and intensely as possible. His dramatic *Green River Near Flaming Gorge (Colorado)* is a masterfully composed shot of a great sweeping bend of the river that yet highlighted the massive tilted and upthrust strata that formed its banks, and through which the river had cut, as it meandered through millions of years

Timothy O'Sullivan, *Ancient Ruins
in Canyon de Chelly,* (1873). Denver
Public Library, Western History
Department.

and billions of tons of rock. His scientific focus was even more dramatic in a
photo which he called simply *Green River (Colorado),* as the river is seen cutting, cutting, cutting straight down through a huge mountain of folded and
upthrust rock. As much as haze and weather permitted, O'Sullivan was able
to focus sharply on both rock formations in the foreground and in the far
distant background. The scientific image of grandeur that he produced was not
likely to appeal to tourists, however.

   In 1871, O'Sullivan joined Lieutenant George M. Wheeler's military survey
called, "The United States Geographical Surveys Beyond the 100th Meridian." Wheeler was less interested in geological structure and theory than was
King. Instead, he attempted to *ascend* the roiling currents of the Colorado
River in small boats. He and his party, which included the great geologist,
Grove Karl Gilbert, and O'Sullivan, reached a rescue party at Diamond Creek
in a state of exhaustion and near starvation. The dire circumstances of their
expedition bothered O'Sullivan not a whit. He made some of his best pictures
in the 3000-foot depth and heat of the Grand Canyon. There were two beauty

shots especially of the Black Canyon, with a brilliant sense of water reflections and the tonalities of the canyon, but in many ways O'Sullivan's most noteworthy work looked almost like a throw-away. It was a clear picture of the walls of the Grand Canyon, with the members of his party looking like tiny specks on a beach far below on the opposite side of the river. Here O'Sullivan caught all of the various geological layers that made up the earth through which the Colorado River carved its way. It was of maximum use to a geologist, as were photos of wind-sculptured rocks and evidences of massive erosion in his pictures. Something of O'Sullivan's exacting approach to his work is evident in his photograph of a Spanish inscription on Inscription Rock. Here he shot a ruler below the ancient inscription to indicate its size. The 1526 date on the inscription indicates that this expedition preceded that of Coronado.

O'Sullivan was possibly at his dramatic best in his 1873 views of the Canyon de Chelly. He photographed the towering sentinal rocks that guard the entrance

L.A. Huffman, *Taking the Monster's Robe—Skinning Buffalo, Northern Montana* (*January, 1882*). Montana Historical Society, Helena, Montana.

Arundell C. Hull, *Steve Young ("Long Steve") Hanged at Laramie by Vigilantes,* (1868).
American Heritage Center Archives, University of Wyoming, Laramie, Wyoming.

to the canyon at various times of the day until he got just the right amount of
shadow, as the huge obelisks look down upon the tiny white tents of the
expedition far below. And then, nobody has caught the mysterious spirit of
the Anasazi quite as well as O'Sullivan in his *Ancient Ruins in the Canyon De
Chelly,* a duplicate in photography of Richard Kern's drawing of 1849. In
O'Sullivan's photo, the dramatic contrast between the serene and timeless
deserted Anasazi cliff house ruins and the gigantic wind-eroded cliff wall that
hangs above it is striking. Indeed the picture is an overwhelming emblem of
the whole Southwest.

Two photos that O'Sullivan took in the Sierra Blanca Range of Arizona
were more subtle. They are of Apache Lake, a small pond hidden deep in the
mountains, surrounded by trees and brush. In the distant view, one sees nothing, but in the closer view Apache Indians—actually scouts, in this case—
armed with rifles, mingle with the rocks in the lake like sinister lizards adapting to their environment. O'Sullivan had good reason to be aware of the
Indian dangers in Arizona. A reporter carrying most of O'Sullivan's wet plate
photographs of the Grand Canyon was killed by Apaches in the Wickenberg
Stagecoach Massacre of 1873, and most of O'Sullivan's photo-plates were
destroyed.

For better or for worse, depending on the point of view, such things as
scientific railroad surveys penetrating their land, and the triumph of the transcontinental railroad, meant the beginning of the end of the wild, free life of

the Indian. Both statesmen and soldiers in Washington knew this. In fact, using the railroad and the consequent wave of emigrants as a wedge to drive out the Indians was Generals Sherman and Sheridan's conscious policy.[10] On June 17, 1868, already anticipating the construction of, not one, but two transcontinental railroads through Indian land, General Sherman wrote his politically powerful brother, Senator John Sherman: "The commission for present peace had to concede a right to hunt buffaloes as long as they last, and this may lead to collisions [with the Plains Indians], but it will not be long before all the buffaloes are extinct near and between the railroads. . . . "[11]

It was also not long before the railroad buffalo hunters became familiar sights, as they slaughtered thousands on the plains and posed proudly for photographers with heaps of bones and hides, or fields of dead buffalo as evidence of their prowess. Most famous of them all, of course, was William F. "Buffalo Bill" Cody, who claimed to have killed more than 4,280 buffalo in eight months of 1867 in his job as a hunter for the Kansas Pacific Railroad. Indeed, the railroad used the buffalo head as its totem. Every station along the line had its mounted bison head, shot by the one and only Cody himself. In the winter of 1872 Cody even took the Grand Duke Alexis of Russia out onto the plains to blaze away at the remaining herds of the great beasts. So bad was the slaughter that, in 1883, *Frank Leslie's Illustrated Weekly* published an article, "Shall the Buffalo Go?" that featured a picture of a small army of men firing at frightened buffalo from the comfort and safety of a railroad train.[12]

The Plains Indians, from the Canadian border to the Llano Estacado of Texas, took note of the splitting of the great herds into a northern and southern herd, and then the systematic slaughter of both: an effort that was bound to spell the end of the Plains Indian's nomadic life. General Sherman, in another letter to his brother of September 23, 1868, explained the emerging situation:

> The Indian War on the plains need simply amount to this. We have now selected and provided reservations for all, off the great roads. All who cling to their old hunting grounds are hostile and will remain so till killed off. We will have a sort of predatory war for years, every now and then be shocked by the indiscriminate murder of travellers and settlers, but the country is so large, and the advantage of the Indians so great, that we cannot make a single war and end it. From the nature of things we must take chances and clean out Indians as we encounter them.[13]

A great deal of the best work of America's giants of photography unself-consciously celebrated the engineering triumphs of the transcontinental railroad or the progress of the great scientific surveys that were exploring, mapping and assessing the prospects for white settlement in what was the red man's homeland. Many of these photos were copied in woodcut illustrations for magazines of wide circulation, or for illustrations in popular novels. Moran's rendering of *The Mount of the Holy Cross*, for example, was reproduced in both woodcuts and chromolithographs, as was Bierstadt's *The Rocky Mountains*, and sold by the thousands in this country and Europe. In addition, many of the photographers made stereoscopic views of the rugged Western landscape, views that graced the parlour tables of Middle America. To most Americans, the West became grand and picturesque.

The grim portrayals of the buffalo hunters only belatedly caused public concern. But about the time that travelers began to cross the continent in common coach cars, people began to be aware that the railroad had also spawned raw, rugged towns, like Laramie and Cheyenne and Corinne, Utah, a tent city near Promontory Point. Stories of the gamblers, gunfighters, thieves and prostitutes that infested these towns began to flow back to the East. In some cases the gunfighters, like Wild Bill Hickock and Wyatt Earp, became folk heroes, a status that has been carried down to the present. One photographer, Arundel Hull, however, caught the seamier side of the "civilization" that the railroads were bringing West into Indian land. Two of his photos are representative of life in the "Hell on Wheels" towns. One shows a large tent labelled "Freund's Gun Store," with a group of hard cases posing before it. The other, one of a number of such scenes shot by Hull, was a graphic view of *The Hanging of Big Steve*. Aesthetically, the photo shows a nice sense of texture, contrasting Big Steve's striped shirt with the geometric pattern of a building, behind and to his left in the background. But aesthetics in these views of dead, dangling men was hardly the point. Hull and an increasing number of other photographers were portraying the violent frontier that followed in the wake of the explorers and the railroad crews. The frontier of violence took on its most vivid character in the Indian Wars that were ultimately caused by the railroads, and to which General Sherman so casually referred. But to most of the American public, the Indian Wars represented "episodes of glory" that more than matched the "images of grandeur."

CHAPTER **18**

EPISODES OF GLORY

In 1867 a photographer wandering over the Kansas prairie came upon a grisly sight. There amidst the brush and the flowers lay the naked corpse of what had once been a United States cavalry trooper. The corpse, whose head was a battered, bloody mess, had been shot full of arrows, including one directly into its penis. Then the soldier had been gutted, his heart torn out, his arms and legs hacked to pieces such that what had once been rippling muscles were now food for flies.[1] In another photo, taken about the same time, a civilian, or perhaps a bearded scout, was pictured stretched out upon the prairie, his head again a bloody scalped mess. Beside the body, two cavalry troopers look on in dismay and sadness.[2] Back in the East, *Harper's Weekly, the Magazine of Civilization,* ran pictures of Major Joel Elliot and ten members of his command, that had once been part of Lieutenant Colonel George Armstrong Custer's Seventh Cavalry, lying naked and mutilated and bristling with arrows—the aftermath of Custer's "successful" attack on Black Kettle's village on the Washita River on Thanksgiving Day of 1867.[3]

In December of 1890, another photographer for the U. S. Army recorded the frozen body of a Sioux medicine man named Yellow Bird, whose ghost dance shirt had not protected him or his chief, Big Foot, against the Army's Hotchkiss guns or repeating rifles, as the prophet Wavoka had assured them it would.[4] Instead, the army photographer was able to record the unceremonious dumping of the Indian dead at Wounded Knee into a mass grave. Not quite a month later, on January 21, 1891, General Nelson A. Miles stood on a wintry hillside, oblivious to the blustery wind that snapped the guidons and rustled the yellow capes of the blue-coated soldiers who trooped before him, regiment after regiment. The review concluded with the trooping of the Seventh Cavalry, its band playing the late George Custer's favorite tune, "Garryowen," an Irish drinking song that had become one of the Army's universal "tunes of glory." Thus, over the graves of fallen bluecoats and Indian braves, with a band of sullen Brulé Sioux looking on from the distant bluffs, the Indian Wars that began with the massacre of most of Black Kettle's band of Cheyennes at Sand Creek in 1864 came at last to an end. "It was the grandest demonstration by the army ever seen in the West," wrote an enthusiastic reporter.[5] The Indian Wars' epitaph was not the ghastly reminders of real agony and death, but regimental colors and tunes of glory, or, better still, the brilliant scenes of the wars painted by famous artists like Frederic Remington, Gilbert Gaul, Charles Schreyvogel, Frederic Paxon, Rufus Zogbaum, and that favorite of the Anheuser Busch Brewing Company, Otto Becker.

Of all these artists, Frederic Remington was the most famous and has remained so.[6] Down on his luck after a series of business failures in Kansas City, in 1886 Remington had headed into the far Southwest, to record with his pencil and sketch pad General Nelson A. Miles's campaign against the murderous Apaches in Arizona. It was a sketch of this campaign, later sold to *Harper's Weekly, the*

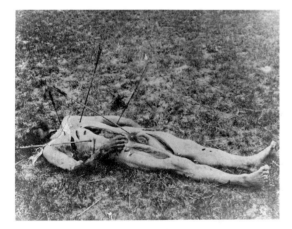

Dr. William A. Bell, *The remains of Sergeant Frederick Wyllyams, 7th Cavalry, Killed by Cheyennes at Fort Wallace, Kansas, June 25, 1876; born in England of a Good English Family. A Graduate of Eton.* Fort Sill Museum, Fort Sill, Oklahoma. Donor: Col. W.S. Nye, Pennsboro Manor, Wormleysburg, Pennsylvania.

Frederic Remington, *Through the Smoke Sprang the Daring Young Soldier,* (1897). Courtesy Amon Carter Museum, Fort Worth.

Magazine of Civilization, that started Remington on the road to artistic success. For much of his career, Remington, usually following General Miles, celebrated the exploits of the American Indian-fighting army.

By a rough calculation, Remington published nearly 300 illustrations relating to the Indian Wars in American magazines between 1886 and 1913.[7] This meant that such illustrations by the master were still being published by prominent magazines some four years after his death. And, of course, today Remington's views of the Indian Wars are by far the most often-used illustrations in books and articles on the subject. In large measure this is due to Rem-

Anonymous, *Scene on the Wounded Knee battlefield showing Big Foot lying dead in the snow. Tribe: Miniconjou Dakota,* (January 1891). Smithsonian Institution National Anthropological Archives, Bureau of American Ethnology Collection, Washington, D.C.

Frederic Remington, *Cavalry Charge On the Southern Plains* (1907). Metropolitan Museum of
Art, New York. Gift of Several Gentlemen.

ington's sure talent for bringing the old army and its troopers to life in action-
filled, dramatic scenes. As he put it, he painted "men with the bark on"—
military men of courage who faced a savage foe. In painting such stirring scenes
as *Forsythe's Fight on the Republican River, Through the Smoke Sprang the Daring
Young Soldier*, and *Cavalry Charge on the Southern Plains*, Remington left no
doubts as to where his sympathies lay. To him, the western trooper was a
flamboyant hero, fully the equal of the men who had fought in the Civil War,
but who had received more attention from the press. For the most part, too,
Remington painted the Indian battles from the trooper's point of view. If the
viewpoint in his pictures was not from behind the military lines, then it focused
directly on groups of U. S. soldiers and scouts—often, as in *Cavalry Charge on
the Southern Plains*, featuring fierce men and horses coming right at the viewer.
He knew especially the impact of the cavalry charge, which, up until World
War I and the advent of the machine gun, was the most devastating of military
tactics. In addition, Remington studied the French military painters of the
Napoleonic Wars, particularly Ernest Meissonier, whom he probably had met,
since Meissonier frequently traveled to the United States and was as interested
in cavalry and horses as was Remington. Both men were undoubtedly pleased

with one of Remington's late masterpieces, *A Cavalry Scrap,* painted in the year of his death for a New York hotel lobby. It was a huge painting (49 inches by 137 inches) that was virtually a long frieze of cavalry troopers in middle distance charging in an oblique angle towards the viewer. To the far left of the picture, Remington included some Indians just colliding with the furious cavalry charge. To many people's way of thinking, this picture was Remington's best, especially since it combined his talent for linking fully rounded action figures in a kind of artistic rhythm with his new-found ability at impressionistic painting, rather than simple illustration. Most of all, however, this large painting gave Remington's gift for the dramatic line the full freedom of the virtuoso.

In general, Remington's military paintings embodied energy, a quality so much admired in late nineteenth-century America. Even such "stationary target" pictures as *Rounded Up* and *The Intruders,* featuring wedges of men repelling an Indian attack, still seethed with a kind of potential energy, as did the seemingly relaxed *Cavalryman's Breakfast on the Plains.*

Then, too, Remington's trooper heroes, like the literary heroes of Ernest Hemingway, faced certain death stoically. Two paintings of the 1890s caught this attitude almost perfectly, *Missing* and *Captured.* In *Missing,* a captive soldier, arms bound behind his back, is marched across the canvas between two lines of Indians. *We* can imagine his fate over a slow fire, but on *his* face there is not a trace of fear. In *Captured,* what looks like the same man, bound and seated by a fire awaiting his fate, appears to be absolutely belligerent, as if daring the Indians, who are hooded phantoms, to do him in.

Thus, with his marvelous talent, Frederic Remington ran the gamut of the western cavalryman's experiences. Energy and bravery informed the tone of the pictures in the same way these qualities inform and give substance to a Hemingway novel. And behind this sense of energy and bravery in the face of danger lies the menace of death, which Remington, even more than Hemingway, captured in a kind of "fourth dimension" that was off of his canvas, but still chillingly present as a feeling that hovered over the action. But unlike the photograph of the eviscerated cavalryman, Remington's warrior heroes never really seemed to die. Sometimes they were wounded, and here and there a sanitized trooper lay face down on the ground, but in Remington's pictures there was none of the mangled horror of real death. When it came to the Indian Wars, taking his cue from a famous newspaper, he painted "all the news that was fit to paint." Though he could not know it, this made his paintings virtual icons for makers of Hollywood Western films that featured

Frederic Remington, *Rounded Up,* (1901). Courtesy Sid Richardson Collection of Western Art, Fort Worth.

Frederic Remington, *Captured,* (1899). Courtesy Sid Richardson Collection of Western Art, Fort Worth, Texas.

the cavalry, like *They Died with Their Boots On, The Plainsman,* and John Ford's famous cavalry trilogy.

In 1893 a young German-American artist, Charles Schreyvogel, visited Buffalo Bill's Wild West Show playing in New York.[8] He was captivated by what he saw, and he determined to make the West, and the Indian fighting army in particular, his subject matter. Trained in Munich, Schreyvogel never intended to pursue a career as an illustrator for magazines; consequently, his work is far less well-known than that of Remington. Schreyvogel, however, in the 1890s, and for some years in the first decade of the twentieth century, traveled west each year to sketch, collect Indian War artifacts, and listen to the tales of the trooper veterans of the now long-finished campaigns. After each trip, Schreyvogel would return to his row house in the German community of Hoboken, New Jersey, and turn his sketches into finished paintings. A methodical, sober man, he usually did two a year, using a local athlete, Stevie Schultze, and the neighborhood handyman, Grant Bloodgood, as models. Schultze, tall and muscular, looked like an Indian, while Bloodgood, with his handsome moustache, was the very epitome of the trooper. Day after day, they posed atop the roof of Schreyvogel's Hoboken home, while the painter imagined scenes of glory way out West.[9]

In one case a real trooper visited his home in the winter. Schreyvogel immediately took him to the rooftop to pose. The old trooper obliged, assuming a reclining position, pistol held up in the air in firing position. The work went on for hours, until Schreyvogel began to feel a chill. He looked up at his stoical model and saw him shaking with cold, barely able to doggedly hold onto the pistol.[10] On other occasions, Schreyvogel would hold parties at his house, and after his guests had consumed a sufficient amount of lager beer, he would persuade them to pose for him in all sorts of positions: falling, sitting astride a saddled sawhorse he used for a cavalry mount, feigning the sudden impact of a bullet or arrow, and so on. Schreyvogel eagerly made photos of these scenes, from which he then worked up his paintings.[11] His friends and neighbors were happy to oblige, and the German community of Hoboken held him in high regard. Its richest men purchased his paintings for their houses so, unlike Remington, he did not have to rush his work or make illustrations for a living, though in his early days he was often in very straitened financial circumstances. Nonetheless, it is an important fact about Schreyvogel's career that he did not have to face the often brutal competition from other painters and illustrators that Remington did. He remained largely aloof and content in the nurturing world of Hoboken.

Schreyvogel's big break came when, with some reluctance, he entered a military painting, *My Bunkie*, in the National Academy of Fine Arts annual competition for 1900. The judges awarded him the Thomas B. Clarke Prize, and his painting became famous almost immediately, though no one connected with the National Academy knew who Schreyvogel was. He himself, expecting nothing, learned of his award by reading the *New York Herald*, which featured a photograph of the picture. On January 1, 1900, the *Herald* reproduced a large photo of the painting with bold headlines, " 'My Bunkie,' Which Has Made Hoboken Artist Famous." The subhead added, "Spirited Subject and Treatment and Its Strikingly American Characteristics Are Sure to Attract Attention." Later *Leslie's Illustrated Weekly* produced a full page spread that included eleven of Schreyvogel's works. One critic, Gustave Kobbe, wrote:

> If you should ask any American soldier who are his favorite painters, he would answer quick as a flash: Charles Schreyvogel and Frederic Remington . . . both these artists have endeared themselves to our American soldiers, especially those of the old frontier army who won their laurels under Lawton and Miles, by depicting scenes of frontier life and depicting it right. Whatever the scene, one thing we may always be sure of; the accoutrements and equipment of the men depicted, be they soldiers, cowboys and Indians, will always be true to life down to the smallest buckle or button . . .[12]

Today, in the era of the electric-eye camera and the television, it is difficult to comprehend the demand for realism and accuracy in late nineteenth- and early twentieth-century America. But it was the age of newspaper and magazine journalism where competing papers or magazines often touted their pub-

Charles Schreyvogel, My *Bunkie*, (1889). The Metropolitan Museum of Art, New York, Gift of Friends of the Artist.

lications over the competition in terms of accurate reporting such as television network news teams do today. Thus in the period an aesthetics of realism developed that doomed allegorical painters like Albert Bierstadt and, at the same time, caused a face-off in the art world between the "realists" and the newer school of "impressionism" coming in from France. The realists depended upon accuracy to "the last button or buckle"—or decimal point, as was the case in American science. The impressionists insisted that, in scientific terms, the eye did not work that way. It picked up impressions of color through light striking the retina in certain ways, hence theirs was the most accurate and scientific, not to mention colorful style. Remington worked hard to become an impressionist, as the next part of this book will indicate, but Schreyvogel, with his Munich training, stuck to thick impasto landscape backgrounds that resembled somewhat the work of Van Gogh, and very realistic, unambiguous rendering of the figures in his pictures.

My *Bunkie*, which showed a furiously galloping trooper lifting a comrade aboard his horse in the heat of battle, while two other troopers on horseback covered for him, was a perfect emblem for the age. It reflected ideas of heroism derived from the recent war with Spain, and it reflected the character of com-

Charles Schreyvogel,
Custer's Demand, (1903).
The Thomas Gilcrease
Institute of American
History and Art, Tulsa.

radeship that was beginning to pervade an America that saw football, professional baseball, and other team sports blossom and provide a code of ethics for young Americans. The realism or truth-telling and comradeship of *My Bunkie* would have provided instant inspiration to the newly forming Boy Scout movement.

The issue of truth-telling came home directly to Schreyvogel in 1903 when he exhibited a painting of Custer and his aides confronting Santana, a Kiowa chief. The painting, which Schreyvogel always thought was his best, was enti-

Charles Schreyvogel, *Rescue at Summit Springs,* Courtesy of the Buffalo Bill Historical Center, Cody, Wyoming.

Charles Schreyvogel, *How Kola!*, (1901). Courtesy of the Buffalo Bill Historical Center, Cody, Wyoming.

tled *Custer's Demand.* When he saw the painting, Frederic Remington became suddenly enraged and declared it inaccurate. A newspaper war ensued, but Schreyvogel was clearly vindicated when not only Elizabeth Bacon Custer herself, but Theodore Roosevelt and Colonel Montgomery Schuyler, who was in the picture, published articles authenticating it. It so happened that Schreyvogel even possessed Schuyler's trousers, which he put on his model.

But what did Schreyvogel's Indian War paintings actually amount to in terms of realism? He got the uniforms right, but few people really died in his sanitized pictures. Some of his works were stirring scenes based on stories told to him or eyewitness descriptions of battles. He painted Buffalo Bill's role in the *Rescue at Summit Springs,* just as the great scout described it to him, though he neglected to show that one of the two female captives was brained by a squaw before Cody could rescue her. In *Attack at Dawn* he accurately portrayed the figures in the Battle of the Washita, but he had the Indians riding horses when they had no time to reach them before the soldiers struck. *The Skirmish Line* is one of his more realistic works, and *Defending the Stockade,* one of his most exciting works, portrayed an improbable scene of Indians attacking a fort, an action that had not taken place since the days of Daniel Boone in eighteenth-century Kentucky. Nonetheless, so powerful an image did the picture present that it has become a model and a mainstay for makers of Hollywood Westerns, and even for the makers of military toys, where "Fort Apache" has been a stable shelf item in toy stores for decades. Whether or not he liked toys, John Ford slept with a copy of Moffat, Yard & Company's *The Schreyvogel Prints of Frontier Life in America,* a rare volume of platinum prints, beside his bed.[13]

One of the works that Schreyvogel liked best, and which again illustrates something of the chivalric "Code of the West" that permeated America in the Progressive Era, was called *How Kola!* It was derived from a story told to him by one of General Crook's soldiers. The trooper fell behind on a winter march and was by way of freezing to death on the snow-covered prairie, when he was rescued by an Indian. Later the trooper, leading a charge in the Battle of the Rosebud, found himself about to obliterate a "redskin," when the fallen foe called out *How Kola!* or "hello friend!" The trooper recognized the Indian who had saved his life, and spared his in return. Many a dime novel hung on this tale.

There were other artists who painted the Indian Wars,[14] notably Robert Lindneux, who portrayed Chivington's dastardly massacre at Sand Creek, showing an American flag prominently displayed in Black Kettle's village, and another rendering of "Sandy" Forsythe's heroic stand at Beecher's Island in 1868. Lindneux devoted his life to turning out mediocre paintings of the Indian Wars. But all of the glory paintings—Remington's, Schreyvogel's, Lindneux's—had one thing in common: little blood was spilled and few people really died. They could have been army recruiting posters. This is what made the many views of Custer's Last Stand virtually a unique genre.

CHAPTER **19**

VIEWS OF TRAGEDY

The year 1876 was the Centennial Year. It marked not only one hundred years of American independence, but also a new era of progress. In Philadelphia at the Centennial Fair thousands of visitors gathered in the grand plaza before the Great Hall of Machines, which housed the giant Corliss Steam Engine and a host of other products of American ingenuity, including the Otis Elevator, Alexander Graham Bell's telephone and a gleaming brass Gatling machine gun.[1] Bands played the stirring *Centennial March* especially composed for the occasion by Richard Wagner. A special poem by Walt Whitman was read to the vast audience, followed by a massive chorus singing Handel's *Messiah* celebrating the Hall of Machines, Gatling Gun and all. Then President U. S. Grant and the Emperor Dom Pedro, of Brazil, stepped forward. Grant, whose administration was crumbling with scandal after scandal, was heckled briefly by the crowd, which lustily cheered the Emperor. The whole mass rose in a thunderous roar when Grant and Dom Pedro pulled a switch that started the giant engine, which in turn started all the machines in the Great Hall in motion. A new century of progress had begun. On June 25th of that same Centennial Year, Lieutenant Colonel George Armstrong Custer, out in Montana, was about to make a military maneuver that would forever erase the details of the Philadelphia Centennial Fair from the memory of the American public. As early as 1867 General Sherman, Commander-in-Chief of the Army, had written to his brother about Custer with enthusiasm:

> G. W. [sic] Custer, Lieutenant Colonel Seventh Cavalry, is young *very* brave, even to rashness, a good trait for a cavalry officer. He came to duty immediately upon being appointed, and is ready and willing to fight the Indians. He is in my command, and I am bound to befriend him. I think he merits confirmation for military service already rendered, and military qualities still needed [by the army]— youth, health, energy and extreme willingness to act and fight. . . .[2]

In that same year, despite Sherman's confidence in him, the brash Custer was court-martialed for cruelty to his men and for summarily shooting deserters. He was suspended from the army for a year and considered entering the service of the Emperor Maximilian of Mexico. Instead, in less than a year he was reinstated and redeemed himself by his winter "victory" at the Washita. More than any other officer, with the possible exception of General Crook, Custer was prepared to carry out General Sherman's strategy of pursuing the Indians relentlessly during a series of winter campaigns.

Then, all too soon, it was 1874. In the spring of that year, Custer led the Seventh Cavalry and an immense long wagon train into the Black Hills of South Dakota.[3] His ostensible mission was to confirm or deny rumors of the discovery of gold in the Indians' most sacred mountain sanctuary, and then to devise a way of controlling the swarm of miners already invading its precincts. Custer conducted his mission with a great deal of fanfare, even taking the St. Paul photographer, W. H. Illingworth, along to document the expedition as it marched along through fields of flowers and beneath sinister towering lookout hilltops. Illingworth did a good job. Alone, he bravely climbed atop the lookout sites and photographed Custer's army on the march just the way an Indian scout might see it. He also did flattering close-up shots of Custer, like a scene with Crow Scout Bloody Knife, Custer and a dead grizzly that he had shot.[4] And Custer's army did, indeed, find the rumored gold, thus starting a stampede into the Black Hills.

The fact that he had been party to the violation of the Indians' sacred sanctuary in the Black Hills may have had nothing to do with what happened in the early afternoon of June 25, 1876, at the Little Big Horn River—unless one is superstitious. There were the signs, all right. The Unkpapa Sioux Chief

W. H. Illingworth, *Our First Grizzly,* (1874).
National Archives, Washington, D.C.

Sitting Bull, in a grueling Sun Dance ritual, where blood ran down his body, had gone into a trance wherein he saw a vision of blue-coated soldiers falling head downward towards the Dakota camp.[5] His dream was recorded on the sand inside a sweat lodge not far from the main camp at Little Big Horn. Custer's scouts found it, but they dared not tell him what they thought it meant. On the other hand, Elizabeth Custer well remembered the day her husband departed from Fort Abraham Lincoln, near Bismarck, Dakota Territory. That morning a ground fog was just lifting, and the glaring sun beating upon it cast a reflection of Custer's caravan upside down upon the cloud of fog.[6] Nor should the rock carving found by Bloody Knife and his Ree scouts have been completely ignored. They had found two bulls traced out upon a rock in the valley of the Rosebud. One bull, the smaller of the two, was dead, stuck by a lance, the other, larger bull, representing the Dakotas, appeared to be shot. Bloody Knife translated the message, "Do not follow the Dakotas into the Bighorn country to which they have gone, for they will turn and destroy you."[7]

Generals Sherman and Sheriden learned about the demise of Colonel Custer and half of the Seventh Cavalry at a reunion of the Army of the Tennessee in Nashville on or about July 6, when the local paper, like all the other papers, picked up a dispatch telegraphed by J. M. Carnahan over a continuous period of sixty hours to the *New York Herald.* That paper, like the *Bismarck Tribune,* which got the story a day earlier, carried the casualty list on page one. Headlines over the black-edged columns read, "Massacre," "Horrible," "A Terrible Fight," "Great Battle With the Indians." Elizabeth Custer, at Fort Lincoln, had already heard the news on July 5th.[8]

Almost immediately, Custer's fight, and especially stories of some kind of heroic stand, became one of the great living legends of the West. Whether or not a "last stand" even took place is still not clear because only the Indians remained alive to report on the fight. Neither Captains Reno or Benteen, several miles away, nor anyone under their beleaguered command, could see what happened, beyond a huge cloud of dust and the cracking sound of guns, punctuated with yells and war whoops.

The Indian leaders survived to be interviewed by reporters, antiquarians and historians in the years after the battle. Almost to a man, they remembered Custer, with his men, standing atop the hill overlooking the Little Big Horn. Sitting Bull's account is typical:

> [Question by reporter] And Custer, the Long Hair?
> A: Well, I have understood that there were a great many brave men in that fight, and that from time to time, while it was going on, they were shot down like pigs. They could not help themselves. One by one the officers fell . . . it was said that up there, where the last fight took place, where the last stand was made, the Long Hair stood like a sheaf of corn with all the ears fallen around him.
> [Reporter] Not wounded?
> A.   No.
> [Reporter] How many stood by him?
> A.   A few.
> [Reporter] When did he fall?
> A.   He killed a man when he fell. He laughed.
> [Reporter] You mean he cried out?
> A.   No, he laughed; he had fired his last shot.
> [Reporter] From a carbine?
> A.   No, a pistol.
> [Reporter] Did he stand up after he first fell?
> A.   He rose up on his hands and tried another shot, but his pistol would not go off. . . .
> [Reporter] The Long Hair was not scalped?
> A.   No; My people did not want his scalp.
> [Reporter] Why?
> A.   I have said he was a great chief.[9]

Joseph White Bull of the Miniconju Sioux gave an even more explicit account of Custer's last. White Bull was riding with Crazy Horse that fateful day:

One soldier still alive toward the last wore a buckskin coat with fringes on it. I thought this man was the leader of the soldiers, because he had ridden ahead of all the others as they came along the ridge. He saw me now and shot at me twice with his revolver, missing me both times. I raised my rifle and fired at him; he went down. Then I saw another soldier crawl over to him. The leader was dead.[10]

Perhaps the most reverberating words spoken that day were by the Indian, Dewey Beard:

This new battle was a turmoil of dust and warriors and soldiers, with bullets whining and arrows hissing all around. Sometimes a bugle would sound and the shouting would get louder. Some of the soldiers were firing pistols at close range. Our knives and war clubs flashed in the sun. I could hear bullets whizzing past my ears. But I kept going and shouting, "It's a good day to die!"[11]

Besides the verbal accounts of the Little Big Horn Battle, the only visual records are those left by the Indians. Of these, the principal one is a long series of drawings done by the Oglala Sioux, Amos Bad Heart Buffalo, who was only six at the time of the battle, but who became the tribal historian. He records a formal opening of the battle in a confrontation between Custer and Crazy Horse and Sitting Bull, a scene that never happened. But then he plunges into detailed views of Reno's attack and its repulse, which chased Reno and his men across the Big Horn River. In Amos Bad Heart Buffalo's series, unlike the painting of Remington and Schreyvogel, death abounds.[12] Both soldiers and Indians are shot, stabbed, overrun by horses and shown grappling with one another. Bad Heart Buffalo's series is a masterful piece of primitive ledger art, influenced by white man's techniques. Other Indian views of the battle were made by Red Horse, White Bird, who drew Reno's retreat in particular, and Lame Deer, who put his record on a tanned buffalo hide, and Kicking

George Bird Grinnell and William Rowland interviewing White Bull. Photograph, Coffrin Gallery, Miles City, Montana.

Bear, who painted his version of the battle for none other than Frederic Remington in 1898.

Still, no one knows for certain just what happened to Custer and his men. The fact that no one knows, that the "greasy grass" beside the now quiet Little Big Horn will not yield up its secret, has made the battle all the more legendary and conjectural.[13] The earliest view of Custer's Last Stand to be widely distributed was William de la Montagne Cary's *The Battle on the Little Big Horn River—The Death Struggle of General Custer.* It appeared in the New York *Daily Graphic* as a full-page illustration on July 19, less than two weeks after the disaster. In this stirring newspaper picture, Cary placed Custer at the apex of a triangle with a dead soldier upside down in the foreground and Indians swirling all around him. Custer stands, left foot atop the carcass of his dead horse, wielding a saber and firing a pistol simultaneously. Cary, who went on to a long career as a Western artist, almost immediately established in the public mind the "fact" of an heroic "Last Stand," thereby creating a permanent part of American mythology. That same year Alfred R. Waud, who had ridden with the boy general in the Civil War, confirmed the "fact" of the Last Stand in an illustration for the first biography of Custer by Captain Frederick Whittaker. It appeared over the title *Custer's Last Fight,* further confirming the Last Stand image in what must have been one of the best-timed biographies in the nineteenth century.

These two pictures were in contrast to a completely imaginary lithograph of 1876 by the German-American artist Feodor Fuchs, entitled *Custer's Last Charge.* In this view of the battle there is no Last Stand, and Custer and his men, still on horseback, appear to be routing the Indians. Other artists, notably John A. Elder in a work of 1884, appeared to have followed Fuch's lead, but the concept of "doomed heroism" in the last stand characterized the vast majority of Custer paintings, just as Alfred Lord Tennyson's poem, *The Charge of the*

Kicking Bear, *Battle of Little Bighorn,* (c. 1894) [detail]. Pictograph commissioned by Frederic Remington. Courtesy of the Southwest Museum, Los Angeles, California.

Otto Becker, *Custer's Last,* (1896).
After Cassily Adams' *Custer's Last
Fight,* (1895). Also known as
"Anheuser-Busch Poster,". Courtesy
Amon Carter Museum of Western
Art, Fort Worth.

Light Brigade, forever immortalized, in a certain way, the British Charge at
Balaclava in the Crimean War.

The most ambitious of the early renditions of the Custer battle was John
Mulvaney's *Custer's Last Rally,* completed in 1881. Mulvaney, a Civil War
veteran, was seemingly always interested in military art. He studied in Dusseldorf, Munich and Antwerp with various masters of the "battle piece" genre.
He returned to America just in time to seize the opportunity of painting Custer's "heroic" last day. Mulvaney, who lived in Kansas City, worked on his
painting for two years, spending much of the time on research at or near the
battle site. Like most history painters, he wanted to "get it right." The result
of his work was a twenty by eleven foot canvas of "heroic size." Though he
had to make a few revisions, such as cutting off Custer's long, flowing locks,
which had appeared in the original, Mulvaney's painting was indeed a superb
rendition of a beleaguered Custer in a circle of soldiers, firing a pistol and
clutching a useless sabre, while, beside him his favorite horse seems to foretell
apocalypse; kneeling on his right was Captain Cook, adjutant of the regiment,
his head swathed in bandages. The picture swirls with action, portrays Custer
and his soldiers as men of dauntless, but desperate, courage, and reeks of death
all round. In this first ambitious view of the fight, Mulvaney created, or at
least played a major part in creating, the legend of the last stand. Ever after it
was agreed there was a last stand, and Custer was one of the last to stand.

Mulvaney toured his picture to Boston and New York, where even Walt
Whitman admired it extravagantly in 1881. To Whitman there was something
particularly American about Mulvaney's painting and Custer's heroic last stand.
The bard of America wrote in the New York *Tribune,* August 15, 1881, concerning the great painting:

Amos Bad Heart Buffalo, *Meeting
between Custer, Crazy Horse and Sitting
Bull.* University of Nebraska Press.

Altogether a western, autochthonic phase of
    America, the
frontiers, culminating, typical, deadly, heroic
    to the uttermost
—nothing in Shakespeare; more grim and
    sublime than either, all
native, all our own, and all a fact . . . [an]
    artistic expression
for our land and people.

William de la Montaigne Cary, *The Battle of the Little Big Horn River, The Death Struggle of
General Custer,* 1876. New York Graphic Illustrated News, July 19, 1876. Courtesy the Library
of Congress, Washington, D. C.

Amos Bad Heart Buffalo, *The Retreat of Reno's Command*. University of Nebraska Press.

Amos Bad Heart Buffalo, *Custer's Battle Field*. University of Nebraska Press.

In Louisville, a writer for the *Courier-Journal* referred to Mulvaney as "a poet of the brush who has walked out to meet the new sun of American art upon the upland lawn of the West . . ." Mulvaney became a celebrity, while H. J. Heinz bought the painting. But for Mulvaney, as for Custer, glory was fleeting. In May of 1906 a drunken "ragged derelict, uncertain of a night's lodging or a day's food," he dove to his death in New York's East River.[14]

Cassily Adams' and Otto Becker's *Custer's Last Stand,* distributed in a back-bar lithograph by the Anheuser-Busch Brewing Company, is now undoubtedly the best known of all the Custer scenes. In lithographing Adams' original

Frederick Paxon, *Custer's Last Stand,* (1899). Courtesy Buffalo Bill Historical Center, Cody, Wyoming.

Leonard Baskin, *Seated Custer.* Custer Battlefield, National Historic Site, National Park Service. U.S. Department of Interior, Crow Agency, Montana.

picture, Becker so changed and improved it that it became his own. The picture's popularity should be no surprise. It is full of gruesome, nightmarish action, including scalping and killing, set against a relatively accurate battle landscape. Bar patrons could spend considerable time discussing the gruesome and/or heroic vignettes that made up the picture. With at least 200,000 copies of the picture distributed across the land, it became one of the primary means whereby the Custer fight was fixed in the popular imagination.

Remington painted the battle at least twice—once in a somber close-up, early in his career, and once from a far off, Indian point of view. Charles Russell also saw the battle from the Indian viewpoint, while Frederick Paxon, in a mammoth, heavily researched canvas, plunges the viewer directly into the melee on Custer's last stand hill. Of all the many views of Custer's last, Paxon's is perhaps the most moving, though hardly the greatest work of art. On the other hand, arty attempts to portray the battle by such as Thomas Hart Benton, with highly expressionistic wavy figures, and Walt Kuhn, who painted only shadows confronting a fey Custer, are merely absurd, like the caricature on a hoax issue of *Time Magazine.* Still, interest by artists in the legendary battle remains alive, and ranges from Harold von Schmidt's carefully researched work of 1976 to Fritz Scholder's modern Indian version of Custer's portrait, larger than life, but spattered with a splotch and a thin red line of blood. Of all the Custer pictures, perhaps the most haunting are the line drawings done by Leonard Baskin. He portrays the principals, Sitting

Leonard Baskin, *Chief Sitting Bull.* (1969),
Custer Battlefield, National Historic Site,
National Park Service. U.S. Department
of Interior, Crow Agency, Montana.

Bull, Gall, Two Moons, Benteen, Reno and Custer in two poses, one seated
with a bullet hole in his cheek, the portrait imitated by Scholder, and one
stretched out naked and castrated as a dying Christ. Ever since he made them—
often adapting from photographs of the real characters—Baskin's haunting
views, which illustrate the Battlefield Park Guidebook, have been controversial. As art, more than any other views, they carry the same sense of mystery
and legend as the battle itself, a battle that really spelled, not Custer's last
stand, but the red man's last stand. Once they scattered before the relief forces
of Terry, Gibbon, Miles and Crook, organized Indian resistance was no more,
and simple massacre occurred at Wounded Knee, that celebrated victory of
General Miles, wherein a parade was held, tunes of glory were played, taps
was sounded, and the war was declared over. The West still maintained its
scenes of grandeur, but the days of glory were relegated to tribal memories,
with overtones of tragedy for red men and white alike.

CHAPTER 20

THE RESURRECTION
OF THE ROMANTIC RED MAN

Less than ten years after General Miles's final cavalry review at Wounded Knee in 1891, another man made a momentous decision to become the latter-day George Catlin and record the "vanishing American" or "fallen foe" for posterity. This man was Edward Sheriff Curtis, a Seattle society photographer, and instead of a paintbrush he planned to use a camera. Curtis believed that the task of photographing all of the North American Indian tribes would take about five years. Instead, the mammoth project consumed thirty years of his life, during which he visited 80 tribes, took more than 40,000 photographs, made over 10,000 recordings of Indian songs and stories on Edison's wax phonograph cylinders, and wrote twenty volumes of text to accompany a series of magnificent portfolios that added up to five hundred sepia masterworks in the art of photography.[1] As he worked away on his obsessive photographic project between 1900 and 1930, Curtis indeed became the twentieth century George Catlin. He shared many of the same feelings and impulses with Catlin. Like the earlier recorder of Indian life, he was convinced that the red man and his way of life would vanish forever, but that there was still time to record these noble people in their unspoiled state. Also, like

228

Catlin, he was a champion of the red man, and the Indians he photographed instinctively knew this and trusted him. For example, in 1912 he was admitted as a *participant* in the sacred Hopi Snake Dance ceremony. Curtis proudly described this: "Dressed in a G-string and Snake Dance costume and with the regulation snake in my mouth, I went through [the ceremony numerous times] while spectators witnessed the dance and did not know a white man was one of the wild dancers."[2]

Long before Curtis undertook his *North American Indians* project, numerous others, including William H. Jackson, John K. Hillers and a whole squadron of photographers from the Bureau of American Ethnology had traversed the West recording the Indian for science. Nearly all of these Indian photographers, from Jack Hillers to Matilda Coxe Stevenson, would have described themselves as objective observers of Indian life, though often their pictures were highly dramatic, like the Canadian R. N. Wilson's view of the Blackfoot Sun Dance with a warrior hanging by skewers through his pectoral muscles, much like the O-Kee-Pa that Catlin had described so long ago to the scorn and disbelief of Henry Rowe Schoolcraft. Other B.A.E. photographers, like James Mooney, DeLancy Gill and certainly Hillers himself made pictures of stunning beauty. An "art-science," Edward Curtis was to call it, realistically recognizing that pure objectivity in photographing the Indian was impossible.

Curtis had a special talent in this new version of "art-science," one that inevitably made the corpus of his work a new, sentimental myth of "the vanishing American." He caught the Indian's spirit and emotions close up. In almost every one of his pictures, empathy was the controlling factor. This enabled him to make matchless portraits of the Indian that revealed, if not depth of character, then the fathomless mystery of their lives. He could catch the stolid glare of Quniaika, a Mohave chief out of the stone age, the fierce pride of a decorated Piegan dandy, and the grand sense of satisfaction of Two Moons, who had ridden down Custer. He also caught the faces and wonderful dark eyes of the children and the widely varied faces of the women, from new brides to the old and wrinkled, but still prideful, squaws. With his years of practice as a Seattle society photographer, the making of portraits like *Hamatsa Emerging From the Woods—Koskimo,* a wild-looking Kwakiutl medicine man, were clearly Curtis's forte. His haunting portrait of top-knotted Bear Bull, a Blackfoot medicine man, bears an uncanny resemblance to his ancestor, Distant Bear, painted by Karl Bodmer in 1833. Curtis once wrote of the secret of his success as an Indian portraitist: "An Indian is like an animal or a little

Edward Sheriff Curtis, *Princess Angelina*. Lois Flury, Flury and Company, Seattle. Copy photography: Robert Vinnedge.

Edward Sheriff Curtis, *The Clam Digger*. Lois Flury, Flury and Company, Seattle. Copy photography: Robert Vinnedge.

child. They instinctively know if you like them—or if you're patronizing them. They knew I liked them and was trying to do something for them."[3]

Curtis also attempted to photograph Indians at work in their everyday tasks, or at ease in their villages. He did this at about the same time and with the same spirit as the Taos artists, Eanger Irving Couse and Joseph Henry Sharp, were attempting to do the same thing in their studios with brushes and paints. In many of these pictures, Curtis reverted to stereotypes. Usually the horse Indians were portrayed in borrowed finery as warlike bands, while pueblo Indians were seen grinding corn, and Northwest Coast Indians were portrayed with huge canoes, silhouetted against the sun setting over Puget Sound. These were the Indians Curtis knew best, of course, since his first aborigine photographs were of wrinkled, ageless Princess Angelina, daughter of Chief Sealth, sometimes known as Chief Seattle, the man who first sold the land upon which the city now stands. Curtis caught her wrinkled face in a portrait, but he also photographed her stooped over picking up clams along the shore of Puget Sound. His photographs, *The Clam Digger*, another one of Tulalip Indians in a boat against the setting sun entitled *Homeward,* and a third entitled *The Mussel Gatherer* won the grand prize in the National Photographic Exhibition, and in the course of a world tour of the Exhibition also garnered a gold medal.[4] These glimpses of sunset sentiment perfectly captured, not the Indians so much as the *fin de siecle* spirit of an America that had sadly, but finally solved its Indian problem. Indians were now history, as Buffalo Bill was prov-

Edward Sheriff Curtis, *Piegan Dandy*. Lois Flury, Flury and Company, Seattle. Copy photography: Robert Vinnedge.

Edward Sheriff Curtis, *Two Moons*. Lois Flury, Flury and Company, Seattle. Copy photography: Robert Vinnedge.

Edward Sheriff Curtis, *Bear Bull*. Lois Flury, Flury and Company, Seattle. Copy photography: Robert Vinnedge.

ing with his Wild West Show featuring once mortal enemies like Sitting Bull, Chief Joseph, and Gall, who had taken the lead in blunting Custer's attack.

Because of Buffalo Bill's Wild West, and because of the public's belief that the new sepia-toned nickelodeons and motion picture machines had taken them to a new dimension of moving reality, the obviously staged Indian war parties, lovers' trysts, and tribal ceremonies that Curtis photographed were taken as ethnographic reality. President Theodore Roosevelt, who wrote the foreword to the first of Curtis's twenty volumes, seemed to catch the real power of the work. He wrote, "Mr. Curtis . . . has been able to do what no man has ever done. . . . [He has] caught glimpses . . . into that strange spiritual and mental life of [the Indians]—from whose innermost recesses all white men are forever barred." This is the myth of the once savage Indian foe that Edward Curtis, the "art-scientist" created in the wake of the Indian Wars. If the Indians, in the Ghost Dance, tried to "dance back the buffalo," Curtis, "the Shadow Catcher," had brought back stone age man in the persons of the "vanishing Americans." The significance of his work is that after the bugles were blown, the guns silenced, and the war whoops a thing of the past, the Indian became "The Native American," an ancestor steeped in drama and mystery, of whom the country could be proud. Like Bierstadt's mighty mountains, the Indian was a patriotic symbol of "nature's nation." The Indian-head penny and the buffalo nickel with Chief Iron Tail on the reverse side proved it.

But just as Catlin had his nemesis in Henry Rowe Schoolcraft, so, too, did Curtis suffer an outspoken critic. He had no sooner published his first two volumes to good reviews in 1907 when Dr. Franz Boas, a professor at Columbia University, wrote to President Roosevelt himself complaining of their inaccuracy and theatricality. Curtis was perplexed because he had had his volumes scrutinized by Dr. Frederick Webb Hodge, official editor of *The Handbook of North American Indians.* Roosevelt soon appointed a scientific committee, composed of C. D. Walcott, head of the Smithsonian, Henry F. Osborn of the American Museum of Natural History, and William H. Holmes, Chief of the Bureau of American Ethnology, to look into the truth of Boas's charges. None of these men of the scientific establishment liked Boas anyway, so whatever the merits of his case, they ruled in favor of Curtis.[5] In those long ago simpler days, presidents could take a direct interest in publications like Curtis's and even the rules of modern football, as well as the by-laws of the N.C.A.A., which T. R., in concert with Yale's coach, Walter Camp, drew up.

Boas, who was the prophet of the "new" anthropology that espoused the cause of "cultural relativism," or the belief that terms like "primitive" and "savage" were ethnocentric and pejorative, felt that Curtis had presented just such a view in his volumes, which were at best patronizing and sheer fantasy. Certainly Curtis could in good conscience plead innocent to the former charges, but his relation to the charge of fantacizing was not so clear. For example, in November of 1911, frantic to raise funds to keep his project going, Curtis presented *The Curtis Indian Picture Opera* in Carnegie Hall. It was a sound and light show, featuring tinted and doctored lantern slides, a specially composed musical score adapted from his Edison phonograph cylinders by Boston composer Henry T. Gilbert, and presented as "authentic." It was a performance to rival P. T. Barnum. But Curtis suffered as he put it "seventeen kinds of hell" for it, not only because the show lost money, but also because, in Boston, in the middle of his dramatic lecture, garbled word came up from the orchestra pit that someone had died. As it turned out no individual died, only the show.[6]

But in the same year, Curtis received encouragement in the form of a review of his volumes by Harvard Professor Farabee in *The American Anthropologist.* He wrote in the fall issue:

> The author has succeeded admirably in his endeavor to make the work one which in fact cannot be questioned by the specialist, but at the same time will be of the greatest interest to the historian, the sculptor, the painter, the dramatist and the fiction writer as well as the ethnologist. . . .[7]

Edward Sheriff Curtis, *Canyon de Chelly, Navajos.* Lois Flury, Flury and Company, Seattle. Copy photography: Robert Vinnedge.

This, however, represented the old-fashioned establishment view of the romantic science tradition that had governed nineteenth-century thought. It was this romantic intellectual tradition that gave substance to Curtis's highly romantic view of the "vanishing American" that lay at the heart of an emerging mythology concerning the American Indian. Meanwhile, by the time Curtis finished his monumental task in 1930, the Great Depression made the expensive volumes unsaleable, even to large libraries, and Curtis's vision dropped out of sight, only to emerge in the "whole earth" era of the late 1960s and early '70s, when communes and "going native" became fashionable, and Curtis's photographs became totemic to millions of Americans. No matter that the poses of some of his Indians dressed in "made-in-Japan" costumes were truly embarrassing. No matter, too, that Curtis and his darkroom man, Adolph Muhr, resorted to a great deal of photographic trickery: pictures were retouched to etch out evidences of modernity, such as contemporary alarm clocks. Views were cropped for the same purpose, and to heighten drama; in addition, Curtis used an extremely wide aperture to blur the backgrounds of his pictures in which automobiles or other modern contrivances might otherwise be seen; he also disguised the fact that he used tepees and costumes of modern manufacture, and that warriors from entirely different tribes could be found wearing identical headdresses and necklaces, etc. In this case, Curtis was only employing some practices used by Catlin, Bodmer, and later on by John Wesley Powell and his Bureau of American Ethnology photographer, Jack Hillers.

Christopher Lyman,[8] in a recent work, has correctly pointed out these flaws in Curtis's work, most of which were already known to serious students of ethnology. But, to the extent that Lyman demonstrates a pattern to Curtis's trickery, namely his objective of presenting his subjects in a time-warp "ethnographic-present," Lyman succeeds in demonstrating that Curtis was indeed a self-conscious mythmaker, a creator of an aboriginal West that never was. Curtis screened out trucks, alarm clocks, even modern backdrops from his pictures in an effort to present a convincing scenario of the red men of North America, as he believed they might have looked at first white contact. Curtis was thus not an ethnologist at all, but rather an historian and mythmaker. As such, like Catlin, his works of art have had a much greater impact on society than, for example, the more scientifically pretentious Bureau of American Ethnology photographs of scenes relevant only to their specific time and place, that now lay untouched in federal archives.

Coda: Curtis lived until 1952, when he died in Los Angeles. Like Catlin, he tried and failed to sell his pictures and rotogravure plates to the Smithsonian, though, again like Catlin, he was respected by the leading figures of that institution. Instead Curtis continued to work, perhaps appropriately in view of the fact that he was a pioneer documentary film-maker, as a photographer for Cecil B. DeMille. In his latter years he refused to cease his labors. In a touching correspondence with Seattle Public Librarian, Harriet Leitch, Curtis described volumes of childrens' books that he wrote that were never published, and at the end, very much like the indomitable Catlin, he was looking forward to a cruise out of Long Beach, California, up through the jungles of the Amazon where he might see more Indians and unlock more mysteries.[9] Never mean-spirited and not to be taken lightly, Edward Sheriff Curtis was a man of imagination who, in the early twentieth century, resurrected the Indian and called attention to the fact that they might well have been or perhaps still are the profoundest of Americans.

Part Four

THE WILD
RIDERS

CHAPTER 21

FREDERIC REMINGTON:
NO TEACUP TRAGEDIES

Of all the artists who saw the West and captured it for us today, none became as famous or as important as Frederic Remington and Charley Russell. They were very different men. Remington was emphatically an Easterner from Canton, New York, who played football for Yale and made New York City and nearby New Rochelle his headquarters. Russell, on the other hand, played the role of Huckleberry Finn. The son of a rich brickmaking family in St. Louis, Charley Russell, at age sixteen, despite family misgivings, "lit out for the territory" and became a cowboy in Montana, who at first painted what he saw or remembered as a hobby or a form of storytelling that he felt would amuse his friends.

The two men became the primary visual mythmakers of the Old West. More than any other artists, their works conjured up not only the images of the West that the nation has remembered, but also the story or myth of how the West became American, and what that meant or should have meant to those who followed in the wake of the pioneers.

Moreover, together with Buffalo Bill, they created the third of America's unique, worldwide heroes. To the Indian and the Leatherstocking-Daniel Boone

Anonymous, *Remington Painting "An Indian Trapper,"* (1887). Courtesy the Frederic Remington Art Museum, Ogdensburg, New York.

figures they added the cowboy as an epic hero. Theirs, more than anyone else's, was the vision—a self-conscious vision of a frontier that they knew was passing away with a suddenness that was truly astonishing, and for the nation very sad. Like George Catlin in an earlier time, they took it upon themselves to be the keepers of its heroic memory. Remington made this mission explicit. In 1905 at the height of his career he wrote:

> I saw men all ready [sic] swarming into the land. I knew the derby hat, the smoking chimneys, the cord binders, and the thirty-day notes were upon us in a restless surge. I knew the wild riders and the vacant land were about to vanish forever . . . and the more I considered the subject, the bigger the forever loomed. Without knowing exactly how to do it, I began to try to record some facts around me, and the more I looked the more the panorama unfolded. . . . I saw the living, breathing end of three American centuries of smoke and dust and sweat.[1]

Between 1881 and 1909 Remington, as painter and sculptor, recorded the end of a world of uncommon heroism, the last days of what he called "men with the bark on." He did so in some 2,750 paintings and drawings, twenty-five bronzes, eight books, a novel, a play and countless magazine articles.[2] At one time in the late 1880s his work was appearing in nearly every mass circulation magazine. His energy was prodigious; it reflected the rhythm of the industrial age in which he lived, and it was reflected in the powerful lines and the dashing action of the figures in his paintings and drawings, as well as the force fields generated by his magnificent bronzes.

The frontier world that Remington portrayed was, like himself, more complex than it at first seemed. It was a world of melodrama and violence with death all around or else coming right at you, as in his portrayals of thundering cavalry charges or outlaws dashing for the timber with a hundred howling Indians racing close behind. And yet it was also a tragic world where individual heroism and the individual hero were fast losing their place in a machine age. Remington's imaginary frontier world was a stoic, existential world of tragedy and violence that resembled the literary world of Ernest Hemingway with its descriptions of bull fighters and tough-guy killers waiting for the end. It was a bleak world of cultural entropy. And yet there was one palpable difference in Remington's work: as late as 1909, he was still depicting a world of chivalry where, though they were fewer and fewer every year, there were still some "last cavaliers" left out West. The gallant hero in jeopardy, whether trooper, cowboy or Indian, was Remington's forte. While he was interested in realism and realistic detail, he was not interested in what the novelist Frank Norris called "small passions . . . dramas of the reception room, tragedies of an afternoon call, crises involving cups of tea."[3] For Remington, as for Norris's mentor, the French novelist Emile Zola, "terrible things" had to happen to the people of Remington's West; they had to be "wrenched out from the quiet uneventful round of everyday life, and flung into the throes of a vast and terrible drama that worked itself out in unleashed passions, in blood, and in sudden death . . ." For Remington, as for Norris and Zola, "the enormous, the formidable, the terrible is what counted; no teacup tragedies here."[4] And Remington indeed saw the vanishing of the frontier as a "vast and terrible drama" and no "teacup tragedy."

But perhaps the best way to understand Remington and his work is to realize that for much of his life he was a special kind of journalist. Raised as a youth on stories of the glories of his father's supposed Civil War exploits, Remington was part of a "post-heroic" generation. He was born just too late and it seemed the only chance for glory to match that of the Civil War heroes lay out West in the Indian Wars (as George Armstrong Custer so well understood) or else among the dashing cowboys, whose lives on horseback seemed ever so glamorous when viewed from the East.[5] Perhaps this explains why Remington left a dingy basement studio at the Yale art school, where a pedantic German professor droned on about "the economy of line" and "the probity of art," and went out West to experience life in Montana in 1881. Perhaps it also explains why the next year he tried settling in Kansas, where he imagined sheep-raising and counting coups or, in Indian fashion, chasing jackrabbits on horseback with sticks was the equivalent of the life of the cowboy and the cavalryman.

Remington, *Return of the Blackfoot War Party*, (1887). The Anschutz Collection, Denver.

A young blond giant, he entered the life of the Kansas sheepherder with zest, but he soon realized that it was not for him, especially when the parents of his eastern sweetheart Eva Caton deemed it an unsuitable occupation for a future son-in-law. Instead, at age 23, he became a secret partner in a Kansas City saloon, or common "bucket shop," as some called it. Ever the scalawag, when he returned East to ask again for the hand of the lovely Eva, he told her and her parents that he had started an iron brokerage business in the rapidly growing railroad town of Kansas City. Both Eva and her parents changed their minds then, and the Remingtons were married in October of 1884. It was only after two full blissful months of residence in Kansas City that Eva learned Remington's true business interest. Humiliated, she left immediately for Gloversville, New York, and home. Meanwhile, Remington lost his investment in the saloon and began to turn to his true interest—painting and drawing. Some of Neimeyer, his pedantic Yale art instructor's words began to seem more useful. He remembered his study of Ingres whose work epitomized "the power of the line," and he sold three of his works at Findlay's Art Store in Kansas City for $150 and two other drawings to *Harper's Weekly*.[6] Then, full of his usual confidence, he set out for New Mexico to make on-the-spot sketches of the wilder West, no matter what the danger.

When he returned to the East from his sojourn, surprisingly he found his

Frederic Remington, *A Dash for the Timber,* (1889). Courtesy Amon Carter Museum of Western Art, Fort Worth.

wife ready to take him back. Possibly this was due to financial support he received from his uncle, who actually approved of having an artist in the family. The couple settled down in a Brooklyn flat. Remington attended classes at the Art Students League in the spring of 1886, and in the summer headed for the far Southwest. There, inspired by newspaper accounts of General Miles's campaign against the fierce Apache chief Geronimo, he became an artist war correspondent, an illustrator who was the equivalent of today's photojournalists. This took him far from the sedentary delights of the studio artist whose interest was in art for art's sake.

He returned to New York from the Southwest in 1886 with a portfolio full of drawings of the remote Apache campaign. George William Curtis of *Harper's Weekly* bought one immediately, and then Henry Harper himself saw to it that the *Weekly* bought 31 more Remington illustrations, and they began to appear regularly. In addition, Remington's old Yale friend, Poultney Bigelow, purchased a number of drawings for *Outing Magazine,* and in 1887 Remington cracked the elite *Century Magazine* with a contract to illustrate Theodore Roo-

Frederic Remington, "A Texan Cowboy." Library of Congress, Washington, D.C.

Frederic Remington, *Old Time Mountain Man*. Western American Collection, Yale University.

sevelt's series of stories, "Ranch Life and the Hunting Trail."[7] With each commission Remington got better. At first his crude sketches had to be re-drawn by in-house artists like Thure de Thurlstrup. But they began to stand on their own without re-drawing, and eventually Remington was re-drawing the work of other artists. Curtis, Harper and Bigelow liked the "rugged hon-esty" of Remington's drawings, but he really captured the public's imagination with his illustrations for Roosevelt's *Ranch Life and the Hunting Trail* that came out as a popular book in 1888.

Better than anyone else, Remington focused on the social history of the West. He saw it from the beginning as a process of settlement carried on by characteristic "types" such as "an old time mountain man with his ponies," "a Texan cowboy," "a French-Canadian trapper," "the Mexican vaquero," and "the puncher," as he habitually characterized the cowboy in Western vernac-ular. He also saw the process of settlement sustained by such characteristic activities as the roundup or the calf branding or aspects of frontier military garrison life. In the latter he made monotony seem exotic and heroic without sacrificing realistic detail in his drawings. His illustrations formed a panorama, a picture gallery of Western life that was convincing and realistic to the mil-lions who saw his illustrations. He may never have actually seen the grizzled, hard-bitten "old style Texas cowman," or even the "old time mountain man," and for that matter he never participated in an engagement against Indians or outlaws, but who could doubt his images of these men, juxtaposed as they were with commonsense scenes of roping and branding and the roundup? As a young artist he hit it off well with Roosevelt because both men were historians interested in the heroic, as T.R.'s two volume work, *The Winning of the West* demonstrated. Neither Remington nor Roosevelt ever stopped being the historian of the heroic, which is why they continue to have such a tremendous impact on succeeding generations.

Many of the drawings for Remington's illustrations of the eighties, however, were based on photographs taken by the dynamic Roosevelt himself, or by L. A. Huffman, a prominent northern plains photographer.[8] Consequently, however authentic, they have a certain posed or stilted quality. Though proud of his work, Remington realized this, and began to depend less and less on the camera and more and more on his own incredible personal vision and feel for the dramatic line. In 1892 he wrote to a friend, "I can beat a Kodac [sic]—that is get more action and better action because Kodacs have no brains—no discrimination . . . the artist must know more than the Kodac. . . ."[9] Remington certainly did, and he was also able to inject emotions, such as nostalgia, into his illustrations that the matter-of-fact camera lens could never catch. "Old time," as in his famous picture *Old Time Plains Fight,* became one of his favorite characterizations of figures he observed that he knew were, or would soon be, part of history. By 1892, "Kodac" or not, he was the top historical illustrator in America. His drawings, like those in Indian tepee liners, were telling Americans "the tale of their tribe."

Albert Bierstadt, *The Last of the Buffalo,* (1888). Buffalo Bill Historical Center, Cody, Wyoming.

Frederic Remington, *Last Cavalier*, (1895). Private Collector, Cincinnati, Ohio.

Meanwhile, however, as the photo on p. 238 of Remington depicting his intense concentration on an oil painting version of a French Canadian Trapper attests, Remington also longed to be known as a serious artist. Perhaps this was due to his early success as a painter, where *Return of a Blackfoot War Party* was accepted for the annual National Academy of Design Show in 1888 and won the Hallgarten and Clarke Prizes. Moreover, his Arizona painting, *Lull in the Fight,* won him a silver medal in the Paris Exposition of 1889 while the reigning giant, Albert Bierstadt's allegorical *The Last of the Buffalo,* sadly enough, was rejected. The age of realism and realistic narration, of the kind that Remington and other journalists were popularizing, had suddenly replaced that of the romantic and the allegorical.

In the end, however, perhaps Remington's almost frantic urge to be recognized as a painter was the result of his election to the Players' Club in New York. This institution in Grammercy Park, founded by Edwin Booth, included a number of artists, among them Childe Hassam, Rollo Peters, Augustus Thomas, and Remington's favorite drinking companion, the portly Julian Ralph, with whom he once spent a drunken Christmas in Canada "hunting the lordly moose." Once he found himself among the famous artists at the Players' Club, Remington began to lose his bearings. Though he enjoyed the celebrity status of the Wild West illustrator who delivered authentic reports on the status of

Frederic Remington, *The Fall of the Cowboy*, (1895). Courtesy Amon Carter Museum, Fort Worth. Photographed by Linda Lorenz.

the "men with the bark on" and "the punchers" to effete Easterners, and played the rough and ready cowboy role to the hilt, even dressing at times in cowboy clothes, Remington still felt inferior to his artist friends at the Players' Club. Often they made him feel so by labeling him a "mere illustrator." And it did not help when, in 1890, *Harpers* mounted a full-scale publicity campaign identifying him as their authentic cowboy Western reporter, who had just returned from a narrow escape at the "battle" of Wounded Knee. The year before, in 1889, he had completed on a rare commission what he regarded as his masterpiece to date, *Dash for the Timber*. Authentic, yet full of action and color and wonderful melodramatic verve, the line of cowboys and horses hurtling through space as they fled from their Indian pursuers represented an interlocking frieze that in Remington's view, transcended the stilted classicism of the Parthenon. His desperate riders represented the wild cry of death and danger hurtling straight toward the viewer. The picture was pure theatre.

In the 1890s, building on a *Dash for the Timber*, Remington succeeded in rounding out the myth of the West with still another hero—the cowboy. He did not invent the cowboy as Western hero; that honor belongs to Buffalo Bill, if not the cowboys themselves who, like Charles Siringo of Matagorda,

Texas, began publishing their autobiographies. But in a famous meeting in
1893 in Yellowstone National Park, he convinced the young Philadelphia
author, Owen Wister, to collaborate with him in a series for *Harper's Monthly
Magazine* to be called "The Evolution of the Cowboy." It was to be the story
of the rise and fall of the great days of the open range cattle industry, where
the man who could stay all day in the saddle reigned supreme. After much
coaxing of "My Dear Wister," the series came out in 1895, illustrated by five
of Remington's most memorable paintings, including the mythopoetic collection of the world's horsemen in *The Last Cavalier* for the opener, and the
haunting winter scene, *The Fall of the Cowboy,* for the closing installment.
This series, together with the many other renditions of the cowboy that Remington made, helped to create a new, uniquely American hero. The "cow
puncher," as Remington called him, would ride forever, a symbol of American
knight errantry to the peoples of the world, as well as to generations of Americans. Remington even painted himself as a cowboy in one of his few self-
portraits.

Though he publicly scorned art schools and formal training, Remington
studied and worked hard to become the artist he felt his friends expected him
to be and to which his popular status entitled him. Knowing he had no real
training or sense of color—certainly his classicist German art teacher at Yale
had taught him none, because for him the line was all-important—in the
winter of 1886 Remington worked hard at mastering color values at the Art
Students League in New York. His surviving textbook on color theory is covered with notes and references to numerous other works on color.[10] Then,
too, his friends, particularly Rollo Peters and Childe Hassam, began to help
him by advising him to start with easier-to-paint nocturnal scenes. Actually
Remington probably found being an art student more pleasant than he expected.
In addition to tutoring from his favorite drinking companions, some of his art
teachers had actually picked up Western lingo of the sort he was to share with
T. R. Here is William Morris Hunt in his famous lectures on art: "In painting
as in pistol shooting, pay your whole attention to the object aimed at! Keep
your finger gently on the trigger, making it close slowly, deliberately, imper-
ceptibly . . . like fate . . ."[11]

While learning about color, Remington also studied the horse, in part because
he liked horses and was a good rider, but primarily because the horse was
central, not only to his Western subject matter but to every day life. Ladies
and gentlemen cantered through Central Park and mounted police rode down

robbers in the suburbs of Manhattan, even as the U.S. Cavalry chased mounted Indians across the western plains. Remington's credibility as a visual reporter depended not only on getting the clothing and weapons of his subjects set down correctly, but also on their anatomy and that of the horses involved in his pictures. One of Remington's great talents was his depiction of human and animal anatomy and movement. He confided to his friend, Julian Ralph, that he wished his epitaph to be: "He knew the horse."[12] At any rate, besides his natural eye for motion and the detail of motion, Remington also relied on the photographer Eadweard Muybridge's classic work, *Animal Locomotion*, published in *The Century Magazine* in 1882, and in book form the same year. The result of this study of Muybridge's work and other judicious uses of the camera by Remington was one of his masterpieces, *Stampede*. The relationship of the galloping horse to Muybridge's photograph is obvious. What is also obvious is the sophistication with which Remington treated the whole scene. The power of nature in the form of the storm and the lightning is paramount. But the horse, too, is part of nature, part of the storm and the stampede and the thunder and the lightning as his cowboy rider becomes a prototypical specimen of humanity caught up in danger and fate.

In addition to this philosophical dimension, Remington had also mastered several painterly techniques. He took advantage of the nocturne, but made the lightning turn everything to a color—a kind of back-lighted green. And then, in a technique identical to that of his contemporary, James McNeill Whistler, he laid on a thin layer of green paint, like a screen, that re-created in realistic fashion the rain coming down in sheets. His heroic rider was caught in one of nature's grandest sound and light shows, frozen in time by a luminous sheet of rain and a galloping horse suspended forever in mid-motion.

At about the same time, the great Philadelphia painter, Thomas Eakins, together with his students, had actually taken to dissecting horse carcasses at the Pennsylvania Academy of Fine Arts, in order to "know the horse." Eakins also made model casts of horses in motion, based on photographs, and invented a form of zoetrope, a machine, that in flashing successive photos of an animal in motion, on the inside of a rotating drum with slits for the viewer, gave the illusion of a motion picture. (Some have erroneously credited him with being the father of the modern motion picture machine.) But while Eakins was bringing all the tools of science and modern techniques of perception to bear on his study of the horse, Remington relied simply on his eye, his experience, and his intuition. One only has to compare Eakins's *May Morning in the Park* with

Frederic Remington, *The Stampede,* (1908). The Thomas Gilcrease Institute of American History and Art.

Eadweard Muybridge, *Galloping Horse* from
Animal Locomotion, (1882). The Bancroft
Library, U.C.L.A.

Frederic Remington, *Downing the Nigh Leader,* (1907). Museum of Western Art, Denver.

Thomas Eakins, *The Fairman Rogers' Four-in-Hand,* (1879). Philadelphia Museum of Art.
Given by William Alexander Dick.

Frederic Remington, *The Bronco
Buster,* (1909). Courtesy Amon Carter Museum, Fort Worth.

Remington's *Downing the Nigh Leader* to note Remington's superior talent in
painting horses.

In 1895, at the suggestion of a neighbor who noted that he drew his figures
and conceived of his compositions in the round anyway, Remington began
sculpting the horse in clay. His first attempt produced *The Bronco Buster,* a
masterpiece. Remington wrote to Wister,

> I have got a receipt [recipe?] for being *Great* . . . my oils will all get old mastery—
> that is they will look like *pale molases* [sic] in time—my watercolors will fade—
> but I am to endure in bronze. It don't decay—the moth don't break through and
> steal—the rust and the idiot cannot harm it—for it is there to stay by God—I
> am d____ near eternal if people want to know about the past. I am doing a
> cowboy on a bucking bronco and I am going to rattle down through all the ages.[13]

He was exceedingly proud to see it displayed and admired in the foyer of
the Madison Square Garden Horse Show. Now the West of his imagination
had truly become imperishable. He became fascinated with the whole process
of bronze casting and spent many hours in Brooklyn at the Roman Bronze
Works supervising the lost wax casting of his sculpted pieces. The process
seemed like magic to him, as out of the sparks and fire and the complex of
molds and wax emerged a whole new creation—an artistic entity that was
indeed "damned near eternal."

And, in a sense, for Remington, more than at first appears because of the important iconographic content of his work, the medium *was* the message. In addition to his use of photography, his studies of color and sculpture, as well as bronze casting, Remington also kept up with new printing processes, such as electrotyping and four-color offset printing. When four-color printing was invented, he knew that his style had to change from that of line-oriented illustration to highly coloristic painting if he was to survive in the magazine world, or if he was to paint artworks for direct sale. America at the time had become, in the words of one commentator, a colorful "chromo civilization."

At the same time, Remington knew without reading the census report of 1890 or hearing the historian, Frederick Jackson Turner's paper delivered at the 1893 World's Columbian Exposition in Chicago announcing it, that the real frontier, which was his reportorial beat, had come to an end.

After 1895 he retreated to an island in the St. Lawrence River where he built a summer studio, ballooned in weight to 300 pounds, and rarely went West again. Instead, he longed for a war with Spain over Cuba that would give him the opportunity once again to be the fearless artist as field reporter he had been with General Miles command in the Indian Wars. With his drawing for Hearst's *New York Journal* of the strip-search of an American woman by the evil Spaniards, he actually helped to precipitate the Spanish American War. Soon, when Theodore Roosevelt entered it with his Texas Rough Riders, it would be called appropriately in Remington's view "the Cowboys' War." But the "Cowboys' War" was not like the Plains Indian War. Wily Spanish troops shot at columns of soldiers from jungle ambush, much as the Vietnamese were to do seventy years later, and Remington's view of battle was largely confined to jungle paths and the ghastly experience of a field hospital. For an out-of-shape 300 pound, malaria-infected artist, the going was tough and Remington reluctantly had to request to be sent home. He did, however, carry on the "last cavalier" myth with his most famous painting of the war—*Charge up San Juan Hill,* thereby earning T.R.'s undying gratitude.

Frederic Remington, *The Charge of the Rough Riders at San Juan Hill,* All rights reserved. Courtesy the Frederic Remington Art Museum, Ogdensburg, New York.

Frederic Remington, *The Scream of Shrapnel at San Juan Hill, Cuba.* Yale University Art Gallery.

Frederic Remington, *Indian, Horse and Village,* (1907). West Point Museum Collections, United States Military Academy.

Frederic Remington, *The Unknown Explorers,* (1908). Courtesy Sid Richardson Collection of Western Art, Fort Worth.

Frederic Remington, *The Unknown Explorers,* (1906). Courtesy the Amon Carter Museum, Fort Worth.

Frederic Remington, *Radisson and Groseilliers.* Courtesy of the Buffalo Bill Historical Center, Cody, Wyoming.

After the Spanish American War and the turn of the century, when world-wide mechanization was taking command, it was all the more clear that the frontier West and its horse soldiers belonged to the realm of history, rather than reportage as Remington had practiced it. Buffalo Bill knew this and pitched his Wild West shows as "living history" tableaus, peopled with famous Indians like Sitting Bull and Chief Joseph. Charles Schreyvogel knew this, too, and consciously produced works like *Custer's Demand* as history paintings. After his disastrous confrontation with Schreyvogel over *Custer's Demand*, Remington must have realized not only that he had to turn from reporter to historian, but also that he had to concentrate more and more on mastering the use of color and a fashionable impressionist style.

This change proved exceedingly strategic, and also profitable. In 1903 he secured from *Colliers* one of the largest illustration contracts in American history. He was to be paid $12,000 per year for three years to do a series of centerfold illustrations that would chronicle the history of the American frontier. In addition, he could keep the original paintings or sell them as he wished. Clearly, the *Colliers* contract acknowledged him as the master illustrator of the Old West. He was its bard, its chronicler, its limner for the masses. There could have been no greater acknowledgment of his stature.

Proudly Remington set to work and executed some of his most striking paintings. But one January day in 1908, he carried some sixteen of the original *Collier's* paintings into the yard behind his studio and began tossing them onto a bonfire. He was eventually stopped by a neighbor, and a few works survived.[14]

Why the burning? Because he wished at last to erase all vestiges of Remington the illustrator. Since 1902 he had begun to master the art of impressionistic painting, and he knew now that he could do better work, or at least work that would be acknowledged by his peers. In his later paintings the wonderful magic of line gave way to the stroke of the brush, a sense of patterning on the flat surface of the canvas, and a deepening, if not dramatic, sense of color. This is evident in works such as *Against the Sunset, The Outlier* and the elegaic *Indian, Horse and Village.* But the difference between Remington the illustrator and Remington the painter is best seen in comparing two versions of *The Unknown Explorers.* The first version was painted for *Colliers* and survived the backyard burning. Its line-dominated three-dimensional character is clear. There is something about it that is very like a children's coloring book. But in the winter of 1908, Remington repainted the same picture in his new

Marcel Duchamps, *Nude Descending a Staircase No. 2,* (1912). Philadelphia Museum of Art. Louise and Walter Arensberg Collection.

impressionistic style. The sense of color defining the flat patterns that make the images emerge on the canvas, as well as the evident brush strokes are there, and together they actually enhance the mythical, the "unknown" or "lost" explorer quality of the scene he is trying to create.

And, in line with being an impressionist, subject mattered less than technique. Like Monet, whose work impressed him mightily, Remington, in painting St. Lawrence scenes, let the lily pad overshadow the canoe, which in turn need not carry historical figures like Radisson and Groseillieurs.[15] In fact, as an impressionist painter, Remington was at last free to abandon the West and its saga of glaring noonday sun landscapes forever, which he did in his second series for *Colliers.* This cost him his lucrative contract with the magazine. No matter, Remington had already arrived as a respected artist in incredibly beautiful paintings like *Evening on a Canadian Lake.*

As if in retribution for his abandoning the national saga in favor of painting as technique, Remington was struck down by an appendicitis attack in 1909,

Pablo Picasso, *Guernica*, (1937). Prado Museum, Madrid.
Courtesy VAGA © A.D.A.G.P. Paris/VAGA, New York, 1986.

at the age of forty-eight. He died in agony on his own kitchen table while the doctors furiously cut through layers of fat in a futile attempt to save his life. The newspapers mourned his untimely death as occurring just as he reached the pinnacle of his artistic development. But one wonders how untimely Remington's demise really was? He had all but abandoned his great role as myth-maker to a nation that loved the myth and the realistic way in which he presented it. And one is forced to wonder what his career would have amounted to had he lived? Certainly, impressionism by 1909 was passe. Would he have been swept aside by the Armory Show of 1913, whose works the old-fashioned T. R. called "Navajo rugs"? Could Remington, even with his comprehension of Muybridge's motion studies, have competed with Marcel Duchamp's *Nude Descending a Staircase,* or Picasso's ironic rendition of death in *Les Demoiselles d'Avignon* painted in 1909, the year of Remington's death? Or could he have translated the energy of his bronzes into the leaping flames of Vorticism? Could he have ever come to terms with "found art" such as the Dadaist's urinal, which they entered in the Armory Show? And could he have translated or re-painted, say, *Cavalry Charge on the Southern Plains* into a fashionable cubistic version, as Picasso had translated Benjamin West's 1817 work, *Death on a Pale Horse* into *Guernica,* painted in 1937, and sometimes called "the last history painting"?

Or had Remington, once he abandoned the Western saga, done all he could by 1909? Had fate as death really saved him from boredom, frustration and intolerable oblivion in later life? Had death made him, like his own Western heroes, a permanent legend? Perhaps it did.

Frederic Remington, *The Cavalry Scrap*, (1909). Huntington Art Museum, The University of Texas.

Frederic Remington, *Study, Lily Pads in St. Lawrence.* Courtesy of the Buffalo Bill Historical Center, Cody, Wyoming.

22

RUSSELL: THE COWBOY GENIUS

Charley Russell was an artist who lived his own dream, who painted himself larger than life and then lived up to that tall reputation. Consider the statue he made of himself out of wax, *Charley Himself.* There he stands, almost as if he were about to launch into a particularly bawdy yarn, perched on the bowed legs of a cowhand, hat cocked back, wearing a confident smile to match the bright red sash around his waist. "Russ is all there," wrote a reporter for the *Great Falls Tribune.* "The expression is perfect; the hat sits just as the artist wears it; the coat and tie appear most natural and the sash hangs true to the artist's everyday custom."[1]

To anyone from Montana (and to many who are not), Charley Russell is a legend: the "Cowboy Genius," the artist who painted the West the way it really was, and who knew the territory and its people like no Easterner ever could. Yet, to the uninitiated observer of his work, Russell was a talented, but by no means brilliant artist. The reason for his fame lies not so much in the virtuosity of his palette but in his ability to create authentic characters. Russell was a storyteller first and a painter second. His stories and his art created an entire world, not through the magnificent scenery of Bierstadt, the documentary genius of Bodmer, or even the dramatic instinct of Remington, but through real people seen up close. His canvases tell the stories of his friends and their adventures; bucked off a bronco, caught in a stand-off with a bear, or suffering the after-effects of a wild night in town.

Charley Russell, "the cowboy artist," was a contemporary of Remington's but he told the story of the West in his own whimsical way. While Remington was a "New York cowboy," who wore buckskins to the Player's Club, and recounted Teddy Roosevelt's exploits on San Juan Hill, Charley Russell spent most of his life in Montana Territory. He could be found, as often as not, in a Nevada City saloon, amusing cowboy friends with tales of bucking broncos, Indian women and Eastern dudes. Russell not only painted the West, he lived it; and, in the course of his career he became one of its most famous citizens.

By 1864, when Russell was born, the West was already part, though not all, legend in the American imagination. Half of its history had already been written. Artists, illustrators and photographers had been picturing the West for more than a generation. Carl Wimar, the artist who had witnessed and painted the great buffalo hunts of the Plains Indians first hand, and who lived in Charley's hometown of Saint Louis, had died only two years before Russell was born. Twenty years later Charley Russell was punching cattle on the same upper Missouri where Wimar painted his buffalo hunts.

It was the already vital legend of the Old West that captured the imagination of young Charley Russell and inspired him to "light out for the territory" at the age of sixteen.[2] Russell found life as the son of a prosperous brick manufacturer tame compared to the exploits of his famous ancestors Charles, George, William and Robert Bent, explorers and Indian traders, who founded Bent's Fort, a large adobe bastion on the upper Arkansas River in present-day Colorado.

Russell drew constantly and naturally as a child. He lined the margins of his school notebooks with pictures of knights, soldiers and Indian chiefs. When his parents enrolled him in a New Jersey military school at the age of sixteen, Russell had different plans. After a brief and less than successful academic experience, he convinced his folks to let him head West, to try his hand at cowboying.

His father arranged a position for him with the owner of a sheep ranch in Helena, Montana named Pike Miller. When he arrived in Montana, a stocky young fellow with straw-colored hair and a head full of dreams about the Wild West, Russell was as defiant of his new employer as he had been towards his parents. He later wrote of his first experience in Montana. "I did not stay long as the sheep and I did not get along well, but I do not think my employer missed me much, as I was considered pretty ornery."[3] By the time Russell left Pike Miller's sheep ranch, he was known as "Kid Russell," and folks had already been treated to his unusual talent. "He painted a few horses on the backs of some old envelopes," remembered Bill Korrell, an acquaintance of Miller's who met Russell shortly after his arrival in Montana. "Pike told me that Charley had an idea he could draw . . . that the kid had been continually running away to 'go West' . . . and that his folks had tried vainly to keep him in school."[4]

Only after quitting Miller's ranch did Charley Russell's real adventures in the West begin. Russell struck up a friendship with an old hunter and prospector named Jake Hoover a dreamer like himself, who chose the remote life of the mountain man over the companionship of townsfolk. Hoover, like Russell, had come to the West at age sixteen, in search of gold. When he and Russell met, the dreams of a strike had faded, but his love of the West remained. Hoover made his living as a hunter, providing meat for the railroad crews. Russell lived for two years with Hoover in his remote mountain cabin. "Jake had no more fear of a bear than I would of a milk cow,"[5] Russell once said. In the painting *Whose Meat?* done years later, he shows a character similar to Jake Hoover in the high country, in a standoff with a grizzly. The precipitous backdrop of the Rockies painted by any other artist of the West might have dominated the picture. In Russell's image of his old friend, the action takes center stage.

The South Fork of the Judith River, where Hoover made his home had only recently been settled by white men. The first herd of cattle to come to the Judith preceded Russell by only a year. Of the region surrounding the cabin, Russell later wrote:

> Shut off from the outside world, it was a hunter's paradise, bounded by walls of mountains and containing miles of grassy open spaces, more green and beautiful than any man-made parks. These parks and the mountains behind them swarmed with deer, elk, mountain sheep, and bear, besides beaver and other fur-bearing animals. The creeks were alive with trout. Nature had surely done her best, and no king of the old times could have claimed a more beautiful and bountiful domain.[6]

If Huck Finn had lit out for the Western territories, he surely would have found no more idyllic spot than Jake Hoover's cabin, where civilization had a

Charles M. Russell, *Charley Himself,*
(c. 1915). Courtesy the Amon Carter Museum, Fort Worth.

long way to go to catch him, and even the life of the cowboy lay miles away.
The only people with whom Jake and Charley shared their paradise were the
Indians. They were visited more than a few times by Crow and Blackfeet
hunting parties. Charley sketched one of these encounters in *A Doubtful Guest*
which shows Jake and him reaching for their rifles to greet an approaching
brave.

Russell made himself handy skinning the game that Jake Hoover shot: no
better training for an artist. While art students at the Pennsylvania Academy
in Philadelphia clustered around the pickled carcass of a draughthorse for a
chance to sketch the musculature, Charley Russell skinned dozens of different
wild species. His intimate familiarity with animal anatomy gave his art a vitality
which few other wildlife artists ever matched. Animal pose, gesture and attitude became almost second nature; he could work up a sculpture of an animal
blindfolded. Friends recall that he always had a lump of wax in his pocket that
he thumbed and worked absentmindedly while spinning a yarn. Sometimes,
to punctuate his story, he would pull the wax out of his pocket, as a perfectly
modelled figure of a bear, or deer or buffalo. Later, he took to sculpting larger
figures in clay. The result is a managerie of animals of the West. All of the
animals he came to know during his two years on the South Judith became
lively sculptures: an antelope poised to leap, a grizzly seated humanlike, on a

log, the wolf, which Russell always referred to as "the Meat Eater," the deer, the mountain sheep and, of course, Charley's favorite animal, the buffalo.

"No-one ever lived that could paint the buffalo the way Charley Russell could—I should know because I've tried,"[7] claims Ned Jacob, a contemporary Western artist. A comparison of Russell's early paintings of buffalo hunts with the efforts of previous painters such as Titian Peale shows Charley's real feel for the animal. Instead of the prancing, almost giddy flight of Peale's animal, (see p. 11) Russell's buffalo herd moves as a powerful, physical mass. He painted, drew and sculpted the buffalo all of his life, but he came to the West shortly after the great herds had disappeared from the prairies. About the buffalo, Russell once said:

> The Rocky Mountains would have been hard to reach without him. The great fur trade wagons felt safe when they reached his range. The nickle wears his picture—damned small price to pay for so much meat.[8]

To Russell, the disappearance of the buffalo from the plains became a symbol of the death of the Old West. He began to use the bleached skull of the buffalo as an icon in his pictures of the West that once was. Later the buffalo skull became his trademark, as the aging Russell came to feel like an artifact of the Old West himself.

Like few other artists before him, Russell came to know and appreciate the West as a complete environment, giving equal attention to people, animals, plants and the earth. Montana was not an exotic wonderland to be sketched and later worked into pictures for a New York audience curious about the remote Western territories. Montana, in those first two years with Jake Hoover, became Charley Russell's home, a land he loved, and a land he began to understand. This intimate knowledge and understanding would give all of his later art an authenticity and character nearly unmatched by any other Western artist.

> I stayed about two years with Hoover, when I had to go back to Saint-Louis. I brought back a cousin of mine who died of mountain fever two weeks after we arrived. When I pulled out of Billings I had four bits in my pockets and 200 miles between me and Hoover. There was so much snow, as it was April, but after riding about fifteen miles I struck a cow outfit coming in to receive 1,000 dougies from the 12Z and V outfit up the basin. The boss, John Cabler, hired me to night-wrangle horses . . . and for 11 years I sung to the horses and the cattle.[9]

Russell turned cowboy in time to join the spring roundup of 1882. This and other roundups during the 1880s provided him with the subject for his first

Charles M. Russell, *A Doubtful Guest,* (1896). Courtesy the Amon Carter Museum, Fort Worth.

Charles M. Russell, *Lone Buffalo.* Courtesy the Amon Carter Museum , Fort Worth.

large-scale paintings. In 1885 he painted *Cowboy Camp during the Roundup* for James Shelton, proprietor of a saloon in Utica, Montana: unofficial roundup headquarters. The scope of the painting suggests that Russell's ambitions had turned from small sketches and wax models to grand narrative scenes. The scene at lower right reveals the reason for Russell's popularity with the cowboys: his sense of humor. Instead of Remington's dramatic "Death in the

Charles M. Russell, *The Buffalo Hunt, Wild Meat for Wild Men,* (1899). Courtesy the Sid Richardson Collection of Western Art, Fort Worth.

Noonday Sun," Russell picked out the comic details of cowboy life as subject matter. His cowboy friends, all of whom are pictured in the painting had to laugh at the scene of a lariat sawing beneath the tail of a bronco that pitches its rider high in the air—and the rider's hat even higher. This early painting cannot conceal Russell's difficulty with perspective and his inability to create a tight composition. Its companion piece, *Breaking Camp* was Charley's first oil painting, and a much better, though still primitive, effort. He crated it up and entered it into the Saint Louis art exhibition of 1886.

The rough life of a ranch hand in Montana in the 1880s was a far cry from the series of chivalric episodes that Owen Wister depicted in his best-selling novel *The Virginian.* There were far more saloon girls than school marms this far out on the range. By some accounts Charley always beat out his companions in the race to the saloon when the cowboys hit town. The series of watercolors, *Just a Little Sunshine, Just a Little Rain, Just a Little Pleasure, Just a Little Pain,* was probably a fair likeness of cowboy life as Charley "Kid" Russell knew it.

The winter of 1886–7 was the year of "The Great Die-Up" on the northern plains. It seemed as if it snowed and blew cold forever that year in Montana. Blizzards left whole towns nearly buried with no food and shortages of such basics as flour and coal oil or wood to provide heat. The livestock fared even worse. Cattle died by the thousands, some piled up in heaps against the barbed wire fences that cut across the once open ranges. At the beginning of the

Charles M. Russell, *Cowboy Camp During Roundup,* (c. 1887). Courtesy the Amon Carter Museum, Fort Worth.

Charles M. Russell, *Breaking Camp*, (1885). Courtesy the Amon Carter Museum, Fort Worth.

spring thaw, the bitter tragedy of the long winter became apparent. Ranchers searched vainly for their herds, and found only the few, starving, emaciated cattle that had managed to survive. Charley's employer, Louis Kaufman lost an entire herd of 5,000. When his backers in Helena wrote to inquire about the condition of their cattle, Phelps returned a small watercolor by Russell entitled *Waiting for a Chinook.* The grim picture of a freezing steer confronting a pack of wolves told more eloquently than any report just how seriously the winter had affected Montana's ranchers. The small scene was soon passed around Helena, later it was widely reproduced on postcards and published in newspapers as visible evidence of the extraordinary losses suffered in the terrible winter of '86.

The few paintings and sketches Russell had done already began to make him a celebrity in Montana. The *Helena Weekly Independent* called him (for the first time) a "Cowboy Artist." The *Helena Weekly Herald* responded by branding Charley a "Diamond in the Rough . . . nurtured by true genius within the confines of a cattle ranch."[10] At this early stage in his career, Charley would take no money for his paintings; they were his way of attracting an audience.

Even though he had attained some local fame as an artist, he was still short of cash. By one account, he rode the grubline with many another out-of-work wrangler in search of a free meal. At those times, the life of an artist might have seemed even more attractive than the life of a cowboy. In 1888, the

Helena paper reported that "Mr. Russell . . . is seriously considering the propriety of going to Europe to perfect his talents in the noted art schools of the old world."[11]

As it turned out, instead of the Grand Tour, Russell headed for wilder parts. With the cattle business dead after the "Great Die Up," Charley rode north. Just over the Canadian border he hooked up with a band of Blackfeet Indians, the Bloods. Traces of Indian lore and details of Indian culture in Russell's later work testify to the profound effect his winter with the Bloods had upon him. For example, *When Sioux and Blackfeet Meet* depicts the vicious confrontation of these traditional enemies in a battle scene full of dramatic action. Russell spent long hours listening to the tribal elder, Medicine Whip, relate tales of the great Blackfeet horse-raiding parties and battles: one of these tales undoubtedly inspired this painting. Pictures of sensual Indian women from the brush of Kid Russell also hint at a romantic interlude which may have occupied his winter among the Indians. Writing later about becoming a "squaw-man," Russell relates:

> In early times when white men mixed with Injuns away from their own kind, these wild women in their paint 'n beads looked mighty encitin'. But to stand in with a squaw you had to turn Injun.[12]

Although Charley had no plans to turn Indian, he identified with their desire to keep "sivilization" at bay. In his book of yarns, *Trails Plowed Under*, Russell once admitted, "I'm all Injun but my hide; their God's my God n' I don't ask for no better."[13] Russell created his own version of the noble savage, and then mourned the inevitability of his passing. In a letter illustrated with a picture of a Blackfoot brave astride his buffalo pony, horse and rider painted for war, Russell penned:

> The Red Man was the true American. The history of how they fought for their country is written in blood, a stain that time cannot grind out. Their God was the sun . . . their church all out doors. Their only book was nature and they knew all of its pages . . .[14]

Charles M. Russell, *Waiting for a Chinook*, (1886). Montana Stockgrowers Association, Helena, Montana.

Charles M. Russell,
Just a Little Sunshine;

Just a Little Rain;

Just a Little Pleasure;

Just a Little Pain,

(1898). Courtesy the Amon Carter Museum, Fort Worth.

His old pal Teddy "Blue" Abbott, who figured prominantly as one of the riders in *Cowboy Camp During a Roundup* recalled a discussion the two wranglers once had about the life of the Indian. Russell related to Abbott in one of his famous letters:

> I remember one day we were looking at a buffalo carcus, and you said Russ I wish I was a Sioux Injun a hundred years ago, and I said me to Ted thairs a pair of us.[15]

Charles M. Russell, *Lost in a Snowstorm—We are Friends,* (1888). Courtesy the Amon Carter
Museum of Western Art, Fort Worth.

Charles M. Russell, *Fireboat,* (1918). C.M. Russell Museum, Great Falls, Montana.

Charles M. Russell, *When Sioux and Blackfeet Meet,* (1903). The Thomas Gilcrease Institute of American History and Art, Tulsa.

Russell conjured up images of the Old West, the West before the white man, more than once in his later work. He was particularly intrigued by the first contact between white man and red—the first signs of the twilight of the golden age of the Plains Indians. *The Fireboat* now hanging in the C.M. Russell Museum in Great Falls, Montana, depicts the historical journey of the steamer *Yellowstone* up the Missouri in 1832, a journey that brought George Catlin into the heart of Indian country. Russell, as visual historian, shows the event through the eyes of the Indians. One must look hard to find the tiny boat on the river. The Indians, who dominate the foreground, and who hold a fleeting hegemony over the land, look with curiosity at the puffing smokestacks, unaware of the changes which will soon be wrought.

The traditional Plains Indian buffalo hunt inspired a whole series of Russell paintings. In each, he focuses on the drama of the chase, picking out the daring brave who must sidle up to a bull galloping full tilt and kill him with one well placed shot behind the shoulder blade—a sharp contrast to the methodical slaughter of the herds by hunters armed with buffalo guns which were popularly believed to have brought the buffalo to the brink of extinction.

Russell scholar Brian Dippie has pointed out that Charley probably never witnessed a buffalo hunt, and if he did, it was not in the traditional Indian manner. His paintings were recreations of the West that was; the Indian buffalo hunt symbolized the West in its unspoiled grandeur.

Charley worked as a cowboy up to 1892–1893 if you count his trip to the World's Columbian Exhibition in Chicago where he was among the group of wranglers that accompanied a beef train all the way from Montana. Augustus Saint-Gaudens, head of the committee that commissioned the florid, neoclassical statuary and murals that graced the exhibition called it "the greatest gathering of artists since the fifteenth century." Saint-Gaudens, of course, had no notion that Charley Russell was at the event, albeit as a cowboy. He might have been shocked to know that nearly a century later more people outside of the art world would be familiar with the name Charley Russell than his own.

It was a commission received on a brief trip through Saint Louis, following his visit to Chicago that caused Charley to turned to the life of a painter full time. William Neidringhaus, a minor steel magnate, hardware store owner and cattle entrepreneur offered Russell a chance to paint what he wished and send the pictures back to Saint Louis with a bill. Nine of these paintings form the core of the Russell collection at the Amon Carter Museum. They show a vastly improved talent over the awkward *Breaking Camp.* With a few years of practice, Russell had developed dynamic compositions which focused upon central, dramatic actions: an Indian attack, a war council, a bucking bronco and, of course, a buffalo hunt. Among the watercolor techniques he had adopted by this time was the use of wet brush, which he used to capture everything from cold winter horizons to arid desert landscapes. By this time, too, Russell had begun to follow the common practice of other artists who painted Indians: he had amassed a collection of Indian costumes, decorations and artifacts which he used as models in his art to achieve realistic detail.

Charles M. Russell, *Buffalo Hunt No. 26,* (1899). Courtesy the Amon Carter Museum, Fort Worth.

Anonymous, *Mrs. Nancy C. Russell posing as Keeoma*. Courtesy Mrs. Eula Thoroughman, Fort Shaw, Montana.

Russell made Great Falls his base of operations following his retirement from the range in 1893 at age 29; however, this put him closer to his favorite haunt: the saloon. He admitted his early fondness for the bottle.

In 1895, his old friend Ben Roberts invited him up to Cascade for a visit and a place to sketch. Perhaps the Roberts family had something planned for their friend. Staying with them that fall was young Nancy Cooper, a headstrong, attractive sixteen year-old who fell in love with the handsome fellow whom no one called "Kid Russell" anymore. The two were married a year later. Their honeymoon was a 300-foot walk, hand in hand, to a small shack out behind the Roberts' house, a place they called home for the next year.

Nancy became a Montana legend in her own right. By most accounts, this young country girl was the prime mover behind Charley Russell's later success. Her first step was to ration the whiskey. Her second step was to take charge of the prices her husband got for his paintings. Shopkeepers who saw her striding down the pine sidewalks of Great Falls called her "Nancy the Robber" because she drove such a stiff deal. The name stuck, when years later she drove equally tough bargains with the New York gallery owners.

Nancy's efforts did not go unappreciated:

> The lady I trotted harness with was the best booster and pardner a man ever had. She could convince anybody that I was the greatest artist in the world, an' that makes a feller work harder. Y'u jes' can't disappoint a person like that, so I done my best work for her . . .[16]

With a little bit of money in their pockets, the Russells moved into Great Falls, and took up residence on the best street in town, Fourth Avenue North. Charley used the dining room as a studio—an arrangement that was not entirely satisfactory. Nancy set her heart on building him a real studio, and in 1903

Charles M. Russell, *In Without Knocking*, (1909). Courtesy the Amon Carter Museum, Fort Worth.

she saw to it that they had the money to build a log cabin, using what was handy: telephone poles. Not since the days in Jake Hoover's cabin was Russell so happy with the accommodations. Stepping across the threshold of Charley's cabin was like stepping into the Old West: his Indian paraphernalia hung ceremoniously around the walls, saddles, boots and bridles propped up for modelling—this is where Charley Russell really began to create his world.

All of his old friends populated the series of works which he produced in this studio: Jake Hoover, Teddy Blue Abbott, his old grub-line buddies, even his Blackfoot brothers. The wild life was more of a memory now, but as the rich imagination of Charley Russell reached back into the past for inspiration, the scenes and the tales got better.

His story-telling, second nature to Charley Russell, gave the paintings their vitality. Yet, no longer were his works mere illustrations of a yarn he was spinning over a bottle of whiskey. The pictures began to speak for themselves. *In Without Knocking* is one of Russell's most explosive action paintings, inspired by a story his wrangler companions once told him about one particularly wild night on the town. Leaving Russell to tend the cattle, the five cowboys, identified as Henry Keaton, the Skelton brothers and Matt Price rode into the town of Stanford, Montana on the eve of a long trail ride and neglected to dismount before entering the saloon. Looking at the painting one can almost hear the cowboys telling Russell later about the whirlwind of dust and poker cards, the horse that put its hoof through the sidewalk, and the whoops and gunshots which accompanied their revelry. Although the event occurred in the early 1880s, Russell told the story on canvas more than 26 years later, after decades of laughing about it with his friends. His memory supplied a much better picture then one he had painted of a similar scene years before. Charley called that one *A Quiet Day in Utica*.

The time that "Big-nosed George" held up the stage between Miles City and Bismark, became the subject for another of Russell's visual folk-tales. In *The Hold Up*, George, his prominent trademark poorly concealed by a bandana, holds a gun on the terrified passengers: a gambler, a prospector, a schoolteacher, the widow who ran the Miles City boarding house, and a Chinaman. Among them stands an Easterner, Isaac Katz, whose recent luck at faro had earned him several thousand dollars which he had sewn into the lining of

Charles M. Russell, *The Holdup (Big Nose George)*, (1899). Courtesy the Amon Carter Museum, Fort Worth.

his clothes. The bandits found his winnings, and the money of all the other passengers as well. "Big-Nosed George" eventually paid for his crime. He was lynched by the furious citizens of Rawlings, Montana, and his hide was used to make a pair of ladies shoes and a horse quirt.

The adventures on the Montana frontier of Russell's youth grew larger and more entertaining in the telling. In Russell's later years, when Americans were beginning to mourn the passing of the Old West, The "Cowboy Artist" was translating some of his best recollections into ambitious canvases of the cowboys he knew so well. Paintings such as A *Tight Dally and Loose Latigo, The Cinchring, Mussellshell Roundup, Wild Horse Hunters* and *Smoke of a .45* create an absorbing episodic narrative which follows Charley Russell's friends through thick and thin across the wide-open spaces and little cowtowns of frontier Montana. They capture the frontier as he knew it, and wished it to be remembered.

In 1904, the Russells visited "The Big Wigwam": New York City. Nancy rented a little basement gallery off Bryant Park to show off Charley's work, but she soon found it more profitable to carry the paintings around to the dealers directly. Evidently Charley had time during the day to look at art, and to paint a little, but New York never suited him. He even took a dislike to the New York saloons: "The bar tenders won't drink with you even," he said. "Now I like to have the bartender drink with me occasionally, out of the same bottle, just to be sure I ain't gettin' poison. . . ."[17]

Charley also took exception to New Yorkers' taste in art. "They are all daft on the impressionist school. In one gallery I saw a landscape they were raving about. Color! Why, say, if I ever saw colors like that in a landscape I would never take another drink."[18]

Despite his protests, the work Russell did after his trip East had a brighter, stronger palette. The vivid color of the sky in such works as *Kit Carson and his Men* reveal Russell's ability to absorb other techniques and translate them to his own distinctive subject matter. A closer look at the painting reveals a detail not apparent in reproduction: Russell's newfound command of oil glazes. While impressionists revelled in daubing raw pigment on the canvas to create optical effects, Charley Russell rediscovered the use of thin, layered coats of oil paint, glazes, to create a richness and depth in his art. He could only have learned this through close study of older works, perhaps even Renaissance art, which he must have seen in New York. At the same time, Russell began to use the much more lurid colors that you could now buy in tubes. He liked the

My 3d 1907

Friend Sid fur fere you will worry about me I am droping you a line I intended leaving here sevrn weeks ago but I cant brak away from Rockeyfeller an his bunch every time I try an make a git-away he invites me up to have crackers an milk with him he shure hate to see me leave John sends his regards to the bunch an wanted me to remember him to Piano Jim an W A Clark with best wishes to friends your friend C M Russell

Me an Jack

Charles M. Russell, *Letter to Friend Sid from New York.* Courtesy the Amon Carter Museum, Fort Worth.

brilliant blues, the blue-greens and the sunset oranges. To an Easterner they looked like Maxfield Parrish's fantasies, but to Charley these new colors were just the thing to capture the drama of sunrise and sunset on the hills and mesas of Montana.

Indeed, throughout the 1890s and early 1900s Russell's work had begun to reflect a growing sophistication in composition as well as use of media. Almost entirely self-taught and not disposed to learn art from a book, Charley Russell's sudden mastery of a wide range of artistic techniques is nothing short of remarkable. By 1905, ten years after he was fashioning little wax figurines in a Montana saloon for a round of drinks, Charley Russell's bronze, *The Scalp Dance* was selling in Louis Tiffany's alongside Frederic Remington's *Bronco Buster* and Augustus Saint-Gaudens's *Diana.* The Wild West, rendered in the free and fluid style of Russell or the dynamic vorticism of Remington, had achieved a level of immortality: the icons of Cowboy and Indian—products of the American experience—rivalled the classical dieties of Greece and Rome in the American imagination.

Russell's growing national fame made him one of Montana's favorite sons. In 1911, the efforts of his friend Frank Lindeman led to his consideration for a major public commission: a monumental mural for the chamber of the House of Representatives in the State Capitol in Helena, Montana. That Russell had

Charles M. Russell, *A Tight Dally and Loose Latigo,* (1920). Courtesy the Amon Carter Museum, Fort Worth.

Charles M. Russell, *Smoke of a .45,* (1908). Courtesy the Amon Carter Museum, Fort Worth.

Charles M. Russell, *Letter from Charles M. Russell, Pasadena, California to Friend Phil Goodwin, April 10, 1920,* Stark Museum of Art, Orange, Texas.

Charles M. Russell, *Carson and His Men,* (1913). The Thomas Gilcrease Institute of American History and Art, Tulsa.

never painted a mural of that scale was a mark against him, despite his popularity. The legislative committee was attempting to decide between the New York muralist John Alexander and himself, when Russell appeared before them and said: "If you want cupids and angels and Greek godesses, give this New Yorker the job. If you want a western picture, give it to me."[19] He received the commission.

Austin Russell, the artist's nephew was visiting him at that time. In his biography of his uncle, he recalls the problems posed by such a large painting. For example, when Charley heard that the committee wished the mural to be done in fresco, using egg tempera and plaster, he was shocked.

> "Egg!" said Charley. "Squeeze it out of the hen, I suppose, instead of a tube. Well you can come along and hold the hen. When I holler 'Egg!' you squeeze her." [20]

Russell persuaded the committee to accept the painting on canvas, however to accommodate the 25 by 12 foot work in his studio he had to raise the roof. An illustrated letter sent to the artist Phillip Goodwin shows the elaborate rig and long handled brush that Russell built to finish the job.

The completed work is an historical painting which some regard as his masterpiece. A swirl of Indian horsemen with upraised lances seem to spin out from the canvas, against a backdrop of Montana's "Big Sky" and rising river mists. To the far right is the subject of the painting: Lewis and Clark meeting the Flathead Indians at Ross' Hole. Like so many of Russell's historical paintings which depict the early contacts between the white man and Indian, the mural is painted from the Indian's point of view. As Russell tells it, the encounter occurs as a minor event in the life of the free riding tribesmen, few of whom would live long enough to understand the significance of the event.

Although the panoramic proportions of *Lewis and Clark Meeting the Flathead Indians at Ross' Hole* make it reminiscent of Russell's early narrative effort *Cowboy Camp During the Roundup,* the masterful mural bears little trace of the naivities which characterized Russell's earlier work. The bald green hills and simple blue sky of *Cowboy Camp* have been replaced by distant mountain crests gently illuminated by the approaching dawn and the early morning cloud forms which cling to the wooded hillsides. Russell has given up the bird's eye view for a perspective that places the viewer in the midst of the action astride an Indian pony. His colors now are deep, rich and realistic, and the complex forshortening problems posed for himself by the central figures is solved as

Anonymous, *Charles M. Russell in Studio, Great Falls, Montana*, (1911–1912). In background painting titled *"Lewis and Clark Meeting Indians at Ross' Hole."* Montana Historical Society.

skillfully as Frederic Remington's masterpiece, *Downing the Nigh Leader*, executed about four years earlier. Not only would the mural guarantee Russell some measure of artistic immortality, but it insured him a perpetual place in the heart of all future citizens of his beloved adopted state, Montana.

Although Russell professed a reticence for leaving Montana, he and Nancy traveled to New York a number of times as his reputation grew. In 1914, they made their tour of Europe, visiting Paris and London. His commentary on the trip can be followed in his *Paper Talk*, illustrated letters which he sent to his friends. Created for the amusement of his old cowboy pals these letters later became treasured documents of his particular slant on the modern world. In commenting on the state of art appreciation in London, Russell's humor is in rare form. Speaking of an abstract painting on view in London's Tate Gallery, shown to him by a knock-kneed English art critic, Russell writes:

> he led me up to something that looked like an enlarged slice of spoilt summer sausig and said this is not disintegration of simultaneousness but dynamic dynamism. An it did look like that. Another he showed as near as I could make from his talk represented the feeling of a bad stomach after a duck lunch . . .[21]

Beginning in 1920, the Russells began to vacation in Southern California, where they sometimes stayed with fellow cowboy artist, Edward Borein, who

Charles M. Russell, *Dynamic Dynamism*, (Letter from England). Museum of Western Art, Denver, Colorado. Photograph by James O. Milmoe.

had given up the life of the vaquero to illustrate for *Sunset* Magazine. Russell called California "the birthplace of Bunko and bungalos . . . a beautiful country all right but . . . strictly man made."[22]

Life in California became more fun as Nancy saw to it that they met the stars of Charley's favorite form of entertainment: the movies. Russell's fellow Montana cowboy and writer friend, Wallace Coburn had left the range to star in the 1916 film adaptation of his poem, *Yellowstone Pete's Only Daughter*. It may have been through Coburn that the Russells became friends with a number of other stars: Douglas Fairbanks, Mary Pickford, William S. Hart, Harry Carey, Sr. (who himself had been a real cowboy with the 101 Ranch) and others. Russell was fascinated with the way movies conjured up another time and place in the imagination. To his friend Douglas Fairbanks he sent one of his most famous examples of "Paper Talk":

> We meet again Douglas Fairbanks, alias D'Artagnan, tho only on paper. . . . But Doug don't forget our old west. The old time cowman right now is as much history as Richard, The Lion Harted or any of those gents that packed the long blade and had their cloths made by a blacksmith. You and others have done the west and showed it well but theres lots of it left . . .[23]

The popularization of the West did not bother Russell, for to him, the West had always been a form of entertainment. Now, suddenly, it was being appreciated by ever-growing audiences. As he put it in a letter to his friend George W. "Buck" Conners, a star in Buffalo Bill's Wild West Show: "[T]hese days aney body that knows and loves the old west seems like an old friend."[24] As early as 1910, some of Russell's old cowboy buddies had moved into show business. Ed Botsford, who rode with him in the spring roundup of 1888 con-

Charles M. Russell, *We Meet Again, Douglas Fairbanks*, (1921). C.M. Russell Museum, Great Falls, Montana.

vinced Charley to ride with him again in 1910, in the opening parade of the Wild West Show in Madison Square Garden, where Botsford was now a featured performer.

Charley Russell's alter ego in the entertainment business was one of the first performers to popularize the distinctive style of Western storytelling and homespun philosophy which had been Russell's stock in trade: Will Rogers. Rogers and Russell met as young men on the train to New York, both headed east to seek their fortunes. They remained friends for the rest of their lives as

Charles M. Russell, *Charley Russell and Friends*. Montana Historical Society.

each, in his own way, became an ambassador of Western wit. Russell immortalized Will Rogers in bronze, depicting the slim cowboy astride an equally lanky mount, a smile on his face, and one hand on his famous lariat. Will Rogers's testament to Charley Russell was the introduction to *Trails Plowed Under*, a posthumously published collection of Russell's Western tales. In it he wrote to his old friend: "I always did say you could tell a story better than any man that ever lived."[25] *Trails Plowed Under* (1927) was the last of three books that Russell wrote himself featuring still another alter ego that may have been inspired by Will Rogers—or Teddy Blue for that matter—that of "Rawhide Rawlins," a name straight out of the comic pages, but a man of the open range who not only told stories but frequently seemed to offer a commentary on Russell himself and the changing ways of his life. Rawhide Rawlins was one part nostalgia and one part Charley's social conscience. He enabled Russell to speak words he could never bring himself to say out loud to strangers:

> Speakin' of cowpunchers. . . . It put me in mind of the eastern girl that asks her mother: "Ma," says she, "do cowboys eat grass?" "No, dear," says the old lady, "they're part human," an' I don't know but the old gal had'em sized up right. If they are human, they're a separate species.[26]

Charley Russell lived until 1926, time enough to witness the emergence of the Taos Society of Artists, cubism, the 1913 Armory Show, and the birth of modernism. It never caused him to change his art, for he felt no need to. His reputation had been built on painting folklore and history, as well as things he had experienced—in creating and maintaining the myth of the Old West. The Old West and its pioneer people who lived mainly through nostalgia were as real to him as they were to his many admirers in his own time and even more so today when superhighways run over the trails plowed under.

In both Charley Russell's and Frederic Remington's art, the landscape of the West was an inspiration but not in the same way it was to the grand romantic painters of the Rocky Mountain School. Nature and nature's creatures, sometimes benign and sometimes treacherous, are more directly related to the actions and predicaments of human figures "with the bark on," whether engaged in raucous play or mortal combat. Both artists, a Westerner and an Easterner, were interested in the way the West was peopled, the way Indians lived before the white man, the way explorers opened up the West, the way the settlers populated it. Their pictures—closeups of decidedly human dramas—document and enlarge the life of the West, not simply its grandiose geography. As such, they embody the myth of the West more perfectly than perhaps any other artists.

Frederic Remington's spirited images of battle enlarged the Western experience to monumental proportions, while Charley Russell's comic pictures of the life of the cowboy reduced it to human scale. His cowpokes and Indian braves became old friends. Even the animals of the West, when rendered by Russell's hand, became less threatening and more alive.

In *Charley Russell and Friends,* he pictures the characters that made him famous: the cowboys and Indians riding together across the empty Montana plains. He sits on his horse in the same painting—his persona as much a work of art as theirs—they are as real as himself.

Few artists have ever created characters which assumed lives of their own, who transcended their makers to take their place in the imagination long after the artist has passed away. Perhaps only Walt Disney surpassed Charley Russell and Frederic Remington in the ability to give birth to such vital and unforgettable characters. Like Disney, the fundamental ingredients of their artwork: action, nobility, humor, personality and stirring narrative embedded their characters forever in the American imagination.

Whereas the human figures in the art of Bierstadt and Moran were dwarfed by the lofty peaks of the Rockies, or the monumental buttes of Green River, Russell and Remington brought the viewer up so close to people as to reveal all that one needed to know about their lives and to record their adventures in relation to the old West. They asserted the struggle of man for survival in a rugged land that was nonetheless a land of surpassing beauty because it was unspoiled. Both men came late to the pioneering saga that characterized men and women's experiences in the Old West, and both artists were forced at times to paint history rather than direct experience. But "Kid Russell" did, after all, roam with both the Indian and the cowboy, and Remington did bivouac with the punchers and the cavalry at the tag end of a dream. They were close enough to the frontier process to know it and to feel it deeply. Russell put it most simply: "Any man that can make a living doing what he likes is lucky, and I'm that. Any time I cash in now, I win."[27]

Even Rawhide Rawlins couldn't have said it better.

Part Five

PLAY THE
LEGEND

CHAPTER 23

THE AMERICAN
SCOUT TRIUMPHANT

On the night of December 16, 1872, the boisterous audience at Chicago's popular playhouse, the Amphitheater, witnessed a poorly acted melodrama that had been written in four hours, starring two men who had never before appeared on the stage. No one could have known that "The Scouts of the Prairie" was a performance that would change American entertainment forever—it was the first "Western."

By all accounts, Act II, scene iv was the most entertaining. Cale Durg, played by Edward Zane Carroll Judson, alias Ned Buntline (the author of the play) manfully struggles to free himself and the lovely Hazel Eye from the bonds of their Indian captors. Both seem doomed to be roasted at the stake, the victims of Wolf Slayer, the treacherous Ute. As the Indians circle around Durg and Hazel Eye, stacking wood about their moccasins, and chanting their "Death Song," even the eyes of the musicians in the orchestra are glued to the awful scene. The brave trapper scornfully hurls insults at his red captors: "Burn ye cursed dogs, burn!" Their reply: "Death to the Paleface!" elicits boos and hisses from the audience. An Indian maiden, Dove Eye, played by the Italian danseuse (later famous for introducing the can-can to America) Mada-moiselle Morlacchi suddenly whirls on the stage in the nick of time, slashing

Anonymous, *The Cast of "Scouts of the Prairie": Buntline, Cody, Morlac-chi, Omohandro* (1872). Courtesy of the Buffalo Bill Historical Center, Cody, Wyoming.

Durg's and Hazel Eye's bonds. As the audience gasps, Durg struggles with his captors vowing, "We'll fight Ye all." From offstage comes the cry, "Death to the Redskins!" Buffalo Bill and Texas Jack have arrived to save the day![1]

Buffalo Bill is a sure shot. The Amphitheater echoes with the sound of his six-guns, the dying cries of the savages and the cheers of thrilled onlookers. Texas Jack handles his whirling lariat to deadly effect, lassoing the Indians. Together, the brave scout and skillful cowboy dispatch the last of the renegades, at least until Act III. The curtain closes to thunderous applause, not because the story is so good or the acting so professional, or even the drama so intense. They clap because they have been treated to the sight of two real-life heros in action: Buffalo Bill and Texas Jack. As the Chicago *Herald* critic put it, "Everything is so wonderfully bad it is almost good."[2]

By 1872, Buffalo Bill, William Cody, had already become a media personality, due in large part to Ned Buntline's dime novel, *Buffalo Bill, King of the Border Men* serialized in the *New York Weekly* in 1869, consisting of a fabric of tall tales which borrowed (some say exploited) the name of Buffalo Bill for the entertainment of thousands of readers. It was the first of more than 550 published accounts of Buffalo Bill's adventures in the West, most of them the product of overactive and sensational literary imaginations. Yet, Cody's real life, in many ways, was more exciting. Even before Buntline met Cody, he had become the most famous scout in the West, the pride of the Fifth Cavalry, the hero of the Summit Springs Rescue, a man who, by age 26 had already lived the life of Western adventure.

He was born in 1846, in LeClaire, Iowa, and by age 13 he had already made his first journey across the Western Plains, in the company of a wagon train.

Robert Lindneaux, *First Scalp for Custer*, (1928). Courtesy of the Buffalo Bill Historical Center, Cody, Wyoming.

In 1860, at 15 years old, he became a Pony Express rider, laying claim to the third longest trip of the service: 322 miles. He joined the cavalry in 1864 and served as General William Tecumseh Sherman's scout and dispatch bearer.

In 1867–8, Cody worked as a hunter for the Kansas Pacific Railroad, hunting buffalos to feed the rail crews on their drive westwards towards Promontory Point. It was his skill as a marksman, and his claim to have shot 4,280 buffalos that earned him the nickname "Buffalo Bill."

Cody returned as the chief of scouts to the Fifth Cavalry in time to engage in several notable Indian fights. At the battle of Summit Springs he particularly distinguished himself, scouting the route for a successful surprise attack on an Indian party holding two white women hostage, and also capturing the horse Tall Bull in the fray, a mount that would later win him hundreds of dollars in race purses.

Buntline met Cody at Fort McPhearson, Kansas in 1869. He was there, as Cody recalled, to deliver a temperance lecture. Buntline borrowed Buffalo Bill's name, and something of his dashing character, to create "Buffalo Bill, the King of the Border Men" for the *New York Weekly*. The rest became entertainment history.

Texas Jack Omohundro, like Cody, was a legendary army scout. It had also been his lot to join the Texas trail drives, where he learned to rope wild

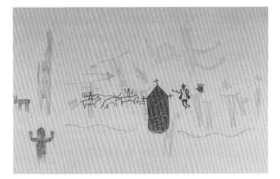

Forest Kirkland, Copy of Indian Cave Painting, Pressa Canyon, Texas. Copy made July 13, 1937. Courtesy of Texas Memorial Museum. Acc. no. 2261-8, University of Texas, Austin.

Anonymous, *Republic of Texas $2.00 bill,* (1841). Courtesy Dorothy Sloan Rare Books, Austin, Texas.

longhorns with a rawhide lariat, risking his life on the dangerous journey from the Panhandle to Kansas. Although their exploits were genuine, both men had been popularized as heros of the dime novel, their fictional personae responsible for hundreds of daring rescues and incredible adventures on the Western Prairies.

Ned Buntline, whose real name was E. C. Z. Judson, on the other hand was a notorious scoundrel. Jailed as a deserter from the Union Army, indicted for inciting racial riots in St. Louis with the "Know Nothing" party, a bigamist and, ironically, a temperance reformer, Buntline had found his milieu as dime novelist and showman.

Buntline, it must be admitted, had his hand on the pulse of America. Taking his cue from the success of Buffalo Bill as dime-novel hero, he proposed, in 1872, to bring the real character before the American public. Entreating Cody to leave his position as scout for the Fifth Cavalry, he lured him East to Chicago with promises of enormous profits. He was not far wrong. Although Cody blew his lines, and was initially terrified of the stage, he was an overnight success. The show played for years, and gave birth to the career of one of America's greatest showmen.

"The Scouts of the Prairie" was a landmark production, even though Catlin's Indian Gallery had earlier brought real Western types to the American public, presenting authentic Indians performing dances and songs. But "The Scouts of the Prairie" was different. It was not educational, factual or informative. It played solely upon the fanciful imagination and the evolving mythology about the frontier. In doing so, Buntline's new show founded all of the archetypal features we now associate with the Western novel, the Western film and the Western television series: brave heroes fighting against overwhelming odds, using their skills at gunplay and roping to subdue the Indians and save the beautiful maiden.

Without even knowing it, Buntline also invented the cowboy as media star. Texas Jack, with his deadly lasso, was the first known performer to use the lariat on stage. He was the archetypal cowboy, though referred to, like Cody, as a scout. After the first successful season of "The Scouts of the Prairie," Texas Jack and Buffalo Bill parted ways with the untrustworthy Buntline, and continued the touring show themselves. The star of the show's terpsichorian interludes, Madamoiselle Guiseppina Morlacchi, married Texas Jack, and, through the winters of the early 1870s the trio appeared as the "Buffalo Bill Combination," one of the most unusual entertainment troupes of the late nineteenth century.

For Cody, the summer months were spent scouting in the West under the command of the Fifth Cavalry. In this manner, fact and fiction about the West became inextricably intertwined. In 1876, agitation among the Plains tribes came to a head with the Custer Massacre. Cody, scouting for a troop in Wyoming when he learned of the disaster, claimed to be the first to avenge Custer's death, with the taking of the scalp of Yellow Hand, the Cheyenne Chief. In an episode that would become one of the most famous sequences in his Wild West show, Cody met the chief abruptly in the course of pursuing a small party of Indians, a few weeks after the battle of the Little Big Horn. Yellow Hand and Buffalo Bill fired at each other in unison, but the Indian's bullet missed the mark. In a grisly exhibition that would later offend certain towns in which his show played the following year, Cody proudly displayed Yellow Hand's scalp and war bonnet, undoubtedly effective publicity for his evening performances of "The Right Red Hand; or Buffalo Bill's First Scalp for Custer." By this time, Texas Jack and his wife had split off from Cody's company to form their own successful troupe.

By 1883, Buffalo Bill had evolved from a famous scout into a skillful showman. He had come to understand the public thirst for entertaining images of Western adventure. His shows brought real Indians and real Anglo heroes, like "Wild Bill" Hickock to the stage. In that year he again capitalized upon the popular character of the cowboy. Only two years earlier, President Chester A. Arthur reported to Congress that parts of Arizona territory were being terrorized by "armed desperados known as 'Cowboys.' "[3] That same year, 1881, *Leslie's Illustrated Weekly* pictured a cowboy, characteristically at the head of a stampede of longhorns, cracking his bull-whip. The columnist wrote:

> The cowboy is a distinct genus. He is unlike any other being. . . . His pet is his horse; his toy a revolver; a source of intense pride, his hat—a broad-brimmed straw or wool affair. Leather leggings are worn over his pantaloons, and heavy top boots, with high heels and enormous spurs, protect his feet. His lariat is composed of eight pliable rawhide thongs, plaited into a rope forty feet long and half an inch thick. With this he can almost lasso a streak of lightning.[4]

By this time, the cowboy was already a romantic "type," on the way to becoming a Western folk hero.

If Ned Buntline had "invented" the cowboy as media hero, by introducing Texas Jack and his lariat to the stage in 1872, the image of the cowboy had already taken shape over the course of previous centuries. Most scholars agree that the cowboy actually evolved from the Spanish vaquero, who herded the longhorn across the arid trails of the Southwest, as early as the sixteenth century. In fact, the earliest known picture of a vaquero is in an Indian rock painting dating back to the Spanish era, probably eighteenth century. Clearly drawn in ochre on an overhanging cliff in Pressa Wash, Valverde County, in far West Texas, is a pictograph showing a Spanish mission church, a raffish conquistador in eighteenth-century garb of frock coat, pantaloons and frilled cuffs, and nearby, two cowboys in ten gallon hats, astride their mounts, one lassoing several longhorns. The scene is witnessed with some amazement by an Indian shaman also painted on the cave wall.

The picture of the cowboy and the longhorn was already a characteristic image in Texas when the Republic put it on its $2 bill in 1841, five years after the Texas Revolution of 1836. The rough cowboy, with a high hat, wielding a lasso with one hand and handling a cowpony in the other, symbolized the economic future of the new Republic. This was forty years before Charley Russell took part in the spring roundup in Montana, and more than thirty years before Ned Buntline introduced Texas Jack to the stage.

The cowboy figured prominently in the next transformation of Buffalo Bill's Combination: "Buffalo Bill's Wild West." His melodrama, in which each performance featured the brave scout vanquishing the Indians, always had overtones of nationalism. In 1882, Buffalo Bill siezed an opportunity to present the "Old Glory Blowout," a wild, outdoor extravaganza celebrating the Fourth of July. It took place outside of North Platte, Nebraska, where Cody had purchased a ranch, and his wife Lulu had supervised the construction of a house as large as their newfound wealth would allow.

Handbills were printed, advertising prizes for expert riding, roping and shooting, the contests to be held at the North Platte racing grounds. Contemporary accounts claimed that: "The attendance was unprecedented . . . the whole country for a radius of over one hundred and fifty miles being temporarily depopulated."[5] Although organized as a gesture of civic pride, the enormous success of the "Old Glory Blowout" gave Cody the idea that a touring show, featuring cowboys, broncos, sure shots and recreations of his past exploits on the prairie would draw large paying crowds. His showman's intuition was correct.

Although expensive as a business venture, and initially difficult to arrange, the traveling exhibit, "Buffalo Bill's Wild West" took America by storm. The early posters for the show describe many of the featured performances. One of them shows Buffalo Bill in full color, as he recreates a desperate Indian surround, in which he and his scouts hold off marauding savages with their dead aim. It was a direct copy of one of Frederic Remington's magazine illustrations. Other prints picture scenes of cowboy fun: "Saddling a Bucker" (1885) *precedes* Frederick Remington's similarly composed *Collier's* print of the same theme, by almost twenty years. "A Bucking Bronco" (1885) shows a cowboy with hat flying, atop a mount with its head down and kicking feet in the air: almost the exact image that became a favorite of Charley Russell's.

In 1884 Annie Oakley, "Little Sure Shot," joined the Wild West show. A star performer with Cody for the next seventeen years, she delighted the crowd with remarkable feats, such as shooting a dime from her husband's fingers, cutting a playing card in half edgewise with a single shot, and bringing down two clay pigeons after leaping over a table and seizing her gun while the targets were in the air. No less amazing to the crowd were Cody's own feats of marksmanship from astride a galloping horse, and those of his adopted son, Johnny Baker, who shot targets while standing on his head.

As it evolved over the course of twenty years, Buffalo Bill's Wild West began to encompass all things Western. It reached back into Western history and folklore to resurrect Cody's exploits with the Pony Express, his role in the Summit Springs Rescue, and the Killing of Yellow Hand. In these historical incidents, Cody often sought to include authentic detail. He purchased the original Deadwood stage, and recreated the wild dash of cowboys as they saved it from the attacking Indians.

Cody also brought before his audiences the wildlife of the West. In recreating "the Great Hunt of the Plains" he assembled buffalo, elk, deer, wild horses and cattle. One year, his cowboys showed off their skill at roping and riding buffalo. One account suggests that this dangerous stunt stopped when the cowboys convinced Buffalo Bill to ride Monarch, the largest buffalo bull in the herd. After one painful tumble and two weeks in the hospital, Cody dropped the buffalo riding sequence from the repetoire.

"Some of my best friends were Indians," Cody once claimed. They were, from his early days as an Indian scout. When he turned performer, he got his "old friends" to star in the grand spectacle that would make him famous—the Wild West show—in which he packaged the frontier experience and sold it for a nickle a head from Topeka to Paris. A featured performer in 1885 was the famous chief and spiritual leader of the Sioux, Sitting Bull. One of the chiefs instrumental in the Little Big Horn, he drew throngs of curious onlookers who paid to see the Unkpapa chief ride out to take his bow during the performance. Sitting Bull always considered Cody a friend. In an ironic twist of fate, the trained horse Cody gave him featured prominently in his death just before the Battle at Wounded Knee in December of 1890. In the final confrontation with the U.S. Seventh Cavalry under the command of General Nelson Miles, Sitting Bull defiantly refused to surrender. The famous chief was gunned down. At the crack of the assassin's pistol, his white horse, the trained mount from Buffalo Bill's Wild West, went through a macabre "dance" which included kneeling on the ground, oblivious to his master's fate.

Despite the occasional intrusion of reality, or, more likely, because of it, "Buffalo Bill's Wild West" became, not only a national, but an international success. In 1887, Buffalo Bill played before Queen Victoria in London on the occasion of her Silver Jubilee. The European crowds, already exposed to the adventures of Buffalo Bill and the American West through dime novels and the London Illustrateds, delighted in finally seeing the real thing. The gallant figure of the old scout, now 41 years of age, seated astride his horse, bowing before Queen Victoria and the world, left an indelible mark in the European imagination. The famous French artist, Rosa Bonheur, even painted his picture which appeared on a poster linking Cody with the great Napoleon himself. Europe, like America, became infected with a fascination for the Wild West, a West that was fast disappearing.

Cody's show, under the astute business guidance of his partner Nate Salsbury, grew to become an even greater equestrian extravaganza with the introduction, at the World's Columbian Exhibition of 1893, of "the Congress of Rough Riders of the World." This show included Arabian Horsemen, Russian Cossacks, Mexican Vaqueros, Argentine Gauchos and representatives of the most famous cavalries of the day—The First Guard Uhlan Regiment of German Emperor Wilhelm II, Chasseurs à Cheval de la Garde Republique Français and the 12th Lancers, the regiment of the Prince of Wales himself—all depicted on the marvelously complex posters which sought, like Buffalo Bill himself, to include a little bit of everything. This expansion of the show to include military horsemen from all over the world, and even a dramatization of U.S. Marines lifting the seige of Peking during the Boxer Rebellion indicated that Buffalo Bill, like his friend Theodore Roosevelt, visualized worldwide imperialism as merely an extension of the Western spirit of Manifest Destiny. Thus, as it grew, Cody's extravaganza, used the Western metaphor to express other attitudes, political and emotional, of the times in America.

A visitor to "Buffalo Bill's Wild West and the Congress of Rough Riders of the World," show could have seen virtually the same performance as captured by Thomas Edison on film in 1894, when he was casting around for entertaining subjects to document with his new invention: the kinetoscope, the world's first true motion picture camera.

As crowds of 20,000 rose to their feet and watched from grandstands decorated in patriotic bunting, the Cowboy band struck up the "Star Spangled Banner" a tune that kicked off the show. From one end of the colosseum-like enclosure, the Grand Review of the Congress of Rough Riders of the World began: cavalry troops from all nations paraded to rousing cheers from the crowd. Miss Annie Oakley followed, demonstrating, among other tricks, her ability to shoot backwards, taking aim with a mirror. After her, a spirited horserace pitted a cowboy, cossack, a vaquero, an Arab and an Indian against each other: a contest calculated to settle the dispute over which nation had developed the greatest natural horsemen.

Soon, the history lesson began. Buffalo Bill, dressed in fringed buckskin finery, sporting a neatly trimmed beard and mustache, trotted out before the adoring audience. First, he demonstrated the famous Pony Express ride. Other performances included the rescue of a trail of covered wagons from marauding Indians. Later, Buffalo Bill chased a small herd of his namesake ungulates around the arena, shooting blanks. Then the crowd cheered the rescue of the Deadwood Stage by Buffalo Bill and his cowboys, but the climax of the show came at the very end: The recreation of the Battle of the Little Big Horn. With all the Cavalry and Indian actors on the playing grounds at once, the audience was treated to an unparalleled spectacle: the clash of hundreds of horsemen, in what was billed as "Custer's Last Charge"—a "Last Stand" not being quite dramatic enough. The backdrop was a huge panorama of the Dakota hills, rendered with surprising realism, surely the largest Western painting to

Bucking Bronco, Courtesy: Musee des Arts
Decoratifs, Paris.

Frederic Remington, *A Bucking Bronco.*
Yale University.

date. Against this scene, mock combat on horseback, and finally hand-to-
hand fighting, reduced the struggling troops to a mere handful, setting the
scene for what truly must have been one of the most melodramatic stage deaths
of all time.

Buffalo Bill's Wild West spawned many imitators, as shows featuring frontier exploits, trick shot artists and cowboys rivaled the traveling circus in popularity. Buffalo Bill himself maintained a rare, symbiotic relationship with the

Anonymous, *Buffalo Bill's Wild West, Ambrose
Park, South Brooklyn,* (1893). Courtesy of the Buffalo Bill Historical Center, Cody, Wyoming.

Anonymous, *Sitting Bull with Buffalo Bill.*
Denver Public Library, Western History
Collection, Western History Department.

other popular media of the day, from dime novels to illustrated newspapers.
Feeding upon each other, as well as upon Buffalo Bill's imagination about
Western adventure, the popular literature developed archetypes of Western
life: the rough-hewn cowboy, the renegade Indian, the intrepid scout. Buffalo
Bill brought all of these to life in his Wild West Show. It was unique, not only
in its scope and ambition, but because it brought authentic figures from the
West before the American public, blurring the distinction between make-
believe drama and reality. As crowds cheered the rescue of the Deadwood
Stage, or the valiant efforts of Custer at the Little Big Horn, battles became
colorful dramas, proving grounds for courage. Such an attitude, which Buffalo
Bill not only played upon, but perhaps helped to foster, led to the lionization
of Teddy Roosevelt and his Rough Riders, who, by the way, were named *after*
the equestrian display in Buffalo Bill's show. Even the art of Frederic Remington and Charley Russell must be viewed in the context of Buffalo Bill's
popularity during the era in which they worked. Without Texas Jack, and
later, "The Great North Platte Blow Out" of 1882, no one might have cared
whether Montana produced a "Cowboy Artist," and art patrons might have
hesitated before investing in a bronze depicting such an odd theme as wild
cowboys "Coming Through the Rye".

CHAPTER 24

COWBOYS AND CAMERAMEN

It was the closing extravaganza to Buffalo Bill's Wild West depict-ing the Battle of the Little Big Horn that would inspire ambitious historical recreations in a newly emerging visual medium: motion pictures. Although brief Westerns, such as Edwin S. Porter's *The Great Train Robbery* (1903) followed closely on the heels of the pioneer kinetoscope peepshows, none rivalled in scope Buffalo Bill's 1913 epic film production, *The Indian Wars Refought.* By this time, the aging William Cody, past his prime as a showman, and suffering from financial losses brought on by, among other things, an unsuccessful mining venture, joined forces with the Essenay Company of Chi-cago to form the Colonel W.F. Cody (Buffalo Bill) Historical Pictures Com-pany. Its purpose was decidely ambitious: to document, in as historically accurate terms as possible, the Indian wars of the West.[1]

Cody enlisted the support of none other than General Nelson Miles, the commander at Wounded Knee, and a stickler for absolute historical accuracy. Granted the use of the U.S. Cavalry through the course of production, Miles and Cody went back to the actual scenes of the Indian battles. Miles boasted of the unique nature of the production:

We expect this will be one of the finest records in the government archives. I understand nothing of the kind has ever been attempted before. Having these officers of my own staff there will make it a splendid thing. It will be a regular reunion on the ground where we fought and bled together. . . . Some of the Indians will be there who fought against us. They will fight again, but there will be no bullets. All that is over.[2]

Miles may have spoken a bit too soon. Although relations between the Indians and the Cavalry were largely cordial during the production, tempers began to run higher as the time for filming the Wounded Knee sequence approached. Chief Iron Tail, himself a veteran of the Indian Wars, and later the immortal profile on the Buffalo Nickel, reported a rumor that some of the Indian actors were planning to fire real bullets in the upcoming recreation. Although Cody pacified both sides, the actual filming of the event was itself, a heart-rending spectacle. *Motion Picture World* reported:

> During the entire taking of the picture, the squaws chanted their death song as they did years ago when they saw the brave warriors fall under the rain of bullets. Many of them broke into tears as the vividness of the battle recalled that other time when lives were really lost and everything was actual.[3]

It is a tragedy of American visual history that all but the final reel of Buffalo Bill's movie was lost.

Cody was not the only one to use the movies to picture the historical and ethnographic past. In 1915, the Indian photographer, Edward S. Curtis, produced *In the Land of the Head Hunters,* a dramatic story of Northwest Coast Indian life which used real Kwakiutl people, and attempted to recreate their traditional houses, war canoes, ceremonies, dances and dress. Although not produced with a pure documentary intent, the film has become a priceless artifact which not only preserved Native Americans' image of their own past, but also established the ethnographic film as a movie genre—one that helped to launch the careers of men like Robert Flahraty, who gained immortality with *Nanook of the North,* shot on Baffin Island. Charged with the responsibility of acting out their traditional culture, rather than becoming mere cultural specimens in the present, Curtis's Kwakiutl actors gave powerful, and sometimes authentic, performances.

Like Buffalo Bill, D.W. Griffith was fascinated with recreating the glories of the U.S. Army. His father, a Civil War veteran, Griffith grew up on his father's stories of Gettysburg, Antietam and Bull Run. His *Birth of a Nation,*

Anonymous, Title page from A *Texas Cowboy or Fifteen Years on the Hurricane Deck of Spanish Pony*, (1885). The Barker Texas History Center, The University of Texas at Austin.

Anonymous, *Bronco Billy Anderson in Early Western*, (1907). Chicago Historical Society, Chicago.

produced in 1914, attempted a recreation of the Civil War on the scale of Buffalo Bill's *The Indian Wars Refought*. Perhaps the most famous moment in the history of battles on film, however, was a time when moviemakers refused to wait until history had been made. In 1914, Mutual Film Corporation's Harry Aiken, the producer of *Birth of a Nation*, made an agreement with Pancho Villa for exclusive footage of his campaign. The famous revolutionary actually delayed his attack on Ojinaga so that American cameramen could get into position to film the casualties as they fell.

But what of that most famous genre in American film, the Western?

The Western was alive and flourishing by 1915. In fact, it was in the process of growing into the greatest "myth machine" the world has ever known. Over and over again it told the story of a modern knight errant in countless variations of a morality play that took place, either in majestically scenic settings that recalled the dawn of creation, or at rude outposts or towns symbolically just beyond the fringes of civilization. Though the cavalryman, the scout, the mountain man, and even occasionally the Indian, figured as heroes in some Westerns, by far the most prominent hero was the cowboy. The cowboy's lineage as a popular hero goes back to Buffalo Bill's Wild West, and even to Texas Jack's lariat-swinging stage roles. It was given a boost by none other than Theodore Roosevelt in his widely read book of 1888, *Ranch Life and the Hunting Trail*, wherein T. R. portrayed himself as an heroic cowboy. Then, too, as we have seen, the man that illustrated Roosevelt's book, Frederic Remington, in 1893, talked the Philadelphia author, Owen Wister, into writing a magazine series, "The Evolution of a Cowboy," in which both men saw the puncher as "The Last Cavalier." Wister went on to write what has been considered the quintessential Western, *The Virginian*, published in 1902 and made into motion picture versions countless times. Meanwhile, the cowboys themselves helped to create their own myth. In 1885 Charles Siringo published *A Texas Cowboy, or Fifteen Years on the Hurricane Deck of a Spanish Pony*. A bit later, in 1899, C. C. Post published *Ten Years a Cowboy*, with an addenda by "Tex Bender, the Cowboy Fiddler," and shortly afterwards such works as Andy Adams, *Log of a Cowboy*, and "Teddy Blue" Abbott's *We Pointed 'Em North*, became famous accounts of cowboy life. They carried on the mythic tradition in the guise of realism. In short, the cowboy helped tremendously to create his own mythical stature as the heroic man on horseback. The cowboy writers, in their autobiographies, made the long cattle drive up out of Texas to Sedalia and Caldwell and Dodge City as much an epic as the covered wagon trek over the Oregon Trail. But in this case it was not the scout or the wagonmaster who was the hero. It was the cattle-driving cowboy who sat "tall in the saddle." In addition to these cowboy autobiographies, the ubiquitous dime novels, such as those written by Ned Buntline, were sold by the hundreds of thousands, and city kids longed for the life of the open range, while country boys thrilled to the promise of a cowboy adulthood as they read the often-forbidden literature out behind the family barn. And if Buffalo Bill's Wild West did not bring all this to life, then Miller Brothers' 101 Ranch traveling extravaganza or half-a-dozen imitators did. But nothing compared to the inspiration supplied by motion pictures and television.

Some idea of the impact of the Western on American youth has been eloquently described by movie historian Don Graham, who grew up on a *farm*, not a *ranch*, near the tiny north Texas town of Lucas, now a suburb of Dallas near the site of the famous T.V. ranch, "Southfork." "We never tired of Westerns," Graham remembers,

> We saw what the Texan brought to town; and we went back to our grandfather's house in the country and shot it out. We staged mock gunfights; we rode stick horses; most of all, in tireless repetition, we postured to get the draw, the walk, the look just right.
>
> Such was the dream life I lived through Westerns. It bore little relation to my actual life on a Texas farm.[4]

In a sense, the first Western also bore little relation to the West. As Bronco Billy Anderson, the first cowboy star, relates it, the making of *The Great Train Robbery* in 1903 was almost an afterthought. Down on his luck, Bronco Billy went to see Edwin S. Porter, a maker of short 50-foot mutascope or nickelodeon films, hoping for a part in one. He entered a gathering of men drinking coffee and eating doughnuts while lamenting the quick demise of the movie business. One of these men was Porter. But it was another, who now remains anonymous, who suggested that Porter make a longer "story" movie. Bronco Billy chipped in, "Yeah, I think that's a good idea, Porter. Why don't you give them longer pictures, give them something they can sink their teeth into."[5] Another member of the group added to this thought. He said, "Say, you know, Porter, I was in a play once, a sketch, rather, called *The Great Train Robbery*. And it went so well that they finally wrote it into a five-act play. And it went much better then. It was longer, more meaty, and the audience seemed to like it better."

Once again Bronco Billy chimed in, "Porter, that's it."

After such a genesis, the world's first Western, based on a stage melodrama, was shot on a siding of the Delaware and Lackawanna Railroad near Dover, New Jersey. Bronco Billy, who could not ride a horse, had only a small part in the film, but he took a proprietary interest in it, going to see its impact on an audience at a lower East Side Fourteenth Street theatre, and then scouting out the house when it opened to an uptown crowd at 42nd Street. After seeing the "rousing reception" the picture got at both houses, Anderson said to himself, "That's it. It's going to be the picture business for me. . . . No more stage for me. No more posing [for magazine covers]. I was going to stick to the picture business until I got a foothold, as far as I could go in it."[6]

Porter's film, with its train made to seem in motion by means of a moving painted background seen through the open mail car door, and its switch cuts from one scene to another, was a revolutionary advance in moviemaking, but its impact on Bronco Billy was even more important. He went on to become the first cowboy star. A short, beefy man with a prominent bladelike nose, Anderson was an unlikely hero, but he consciously made himself into a recognizable and lovable character. As he put it when describing his role in his earliest pure Western, *Bronco Billy and the Baby* (1907),

> I tried to make the premise as simple as possible and to characterize and dramatize the leading character. I always wanted him to do things the public would like. Even though he committed a robbery, see, I had him amend for it by doing something [good].[7]

Bronco Billy went on to form the S. & A. (Essanay) film company with a man named Skoor, who had invented a movie machine called the Kenodrome, a great improvement on Edison's early machine, and the Polyscope of William Selig. Billy took a small film company with him to Niles, California, a canyon thirty miles from Oakland. There he ground out hundreds of two and three reelers, like *Shootin' Mad,* where he played a rough, tough lovable character. In the process he even learned to ride a horse tolerably well.

It is interesting to note that, in a genre usually downgraded for its lack of subtlety, from the very beginning the cowboy heroes always added a dimension of complexity to their roles. In Billy's case it was the bad man with a sentimental "heart of gold." This type of character, of course, goes back to the sentimental heroes and heroines of Bret Hart's fiction, and it was at the time a fashionable character portrayal in family magazines like *The Saturday Evening Post,* from which Anderson admitted pirating Peter B. Kyne's story "Bronco Billy and the Baby." Thus, the stage melodrama and the mass circulation family magazines, with their realistic illustrations, provided primary inspiration for the development of the Western and its heroes.

The next big cowboy star was Tom Mix, who, in addition to making up a fantastic background story of his life, also ushered in the era of the glamorously dressed cowboy. He was the first of the white-hatted heroes, togged out in white satin shirts, hand-tooled holsters and boots, and with his own trick sidekick horse, Tony. According to Mix, he was born in a log cabin near El Paso in 1880. His mother was part Cherokee and his father was a captain in the Seventh Cavalry. He was nearly adopted by Buffalo Bill, attended V.M.I., was a lumberjack, a veteran of the Spanish American War, the Philippine campaign, the Boxer Rebellion, the Boer War, a sheriff in Kansas, Oklahoma and Colorado, as well as a Texas Ranger. He also faced a Mexican firing squad for helping the rebel forces of Francisco Madero, and he rode with Pancho Villa on the great Ojinaga raid. As Mix once said to his pal, the stunt man director, Yakima Canutt, "What the hell. They're here for entertainment. So I give them a reel out of one of my pictures."[8]

Tom Mix was actually born in Mix Run, Pennsylvania.[9] At an early age, he learned to ride very well, and when the Spanish-American War broke out, he enlisted in the Army, which, ignoring his talents as a rider, assigned him to the artillery. Eventually he went A.W.O.L., and technically became a deserter. That did not stop him from joining "The Cowboy Brigade" that rode up Pennsylvania Avenue to celebrate Theodore Roosevelt's inauguration in 1905. But Mix's greatest early days were with Miller Brothers' 101 Ranch. As

Anonymous, *Tom Mix in "Fighting for Gold,"* (1919), Tom Mix Bio File, Prints and Photographs Division. Library of Congress. Washington, D.C.

he put it, "I could name hundreds of incidents and scenes in my pictures that really had their origin along the banks of the old Salt Fork River."[10]

Mix made most of his pictures for the Selig Polyscope Company, and they earned him a fortune and two ranches, one near Prescott, Arizona, and the other at Newhall, California, near those of cowboy stars Harry Carey, Sr., and William S. Hart. He made his first picture, a documentary, *Ranch Life in the Great Southwest,* in 1909 in Colorado. In fact, most of his early pictures were shot there, or at his Diamond S. Ranch near Prescott. By the time Tom Mix reached Hollywood, where he built an immense mansion in the Hollywood Hills, he was already a star. He had several ex-wives, a barrel full of money, and a fancy wardrobe to prove it. He frequented the Old Waterhole Saloon on Hollywood Boulevard and Cahuenga Avenue, a prime hangout for would-be cowboy movie stars. There he set an example for fancy Hollywood cowboy dress that went back to the fantasies of Buffalo Bill. One observer remarked,

> No one can escape the foolishness of the place. Just let a cowpuncher come in off the ranges to Hollywood where somebody wants him to ride a bucking bronc, and he isn't there twenty-four hours before he begins trying not to act like a cowboy. He puts on a huge two-gallon hat, which nobody would know what to do with on a real cow range—wears fancy boots which torture his feet. He doesn't

Selig Motion Picture Co. Poster, *The Moving Picture Cowboy.*

know what they are for; but he knows in a dim, dumb way that they go with acting like a cowboy.[11]

One presumes too, that, like the historian-to-be Don Graham, they "postured to get the draw, the walk, the look just right." In Tom Mix's Hollywood, outrageous play-acting, illusion and conspicuous consumption were the standards of the day. Mix realized this and enjoyed every minute of leading parades on his horse Tony, endorsing toy cap guns and cowboy suits, as well as the children's radio program, "Tom Mix and His Ralston Purina Straight Shooters."

Mix affected the role of a straight-shooting, hard-riding, but humorous character. He did most of his own stunts, rarely got the girl in the end, preferring his horse Tony instead, and was a generally jovial hero. He projected happiness on the range, a role later embellished by such singing cowboys as Gene Autry and Roy Rogers. One of his best surviving pictures, however, pokes fun at Hollywood's illusions. Made in 1915, it was called *Bill Haywood, Producer.* It was the story of a cowboy who assembles his "pardners" and their lady friends and attempts to make a movie. In pure slapstick fashion the scenery collapses all around them, horses charge right through false-front buildings, riders tumble in a heap and get into a fight, the camera blows up, and finally the "cowboys" decide moviemaking is too dangerous, so they will all go back to cowboying.

Despite their sometimes clumsy comedy, Tom Mix's movies, like Buffalo Bill's Wild West Show, were soon among the first to be distributed all over the world, as were those of a similar comic cowboy favorite, the trick riding, youthful Hoot Gibson. It was the silent era, so it was relatively simple to substitute foreign language titles and dialogue cards for the English-language ones used in the States.

Tom Mix lived the gaudy Hollywood life of the twenties to the hilt with fast cars and fast women, and a mansion to boot. But by 1929, when talking pictures came in, his career was nearly over. One could almost hear the laughing echoes of his one-time co-star, Texas Guinan, by then queen of the New York speakeasies, saying "So long, sucker!" as Mix left town with the Sells-Floto Circus. Though his movies were Saturday matinee box office draws all through the thirties, he made only one picture during that period, a 1935 Western serial. In 1940, he drove his flashy car at top speed onto a washed-out bridge near Florence, Arizona. His neck was broken, some say by a suitcase full of twenty-dollar gold pieces.[12]

Real entrepreneurship had entered the business of making motion picture Westerns with Thomas Ince and George Washington Miller. Ince was an executive of the Bison Motion Picture Company. In late 1911 he arrived on the West Coast, looking for a suitable place to infringe on Thomas Edison's motion picture camera patents with impunity. By that time, Edison's agents had reached Chicago and even penetrated Colorado, where they invariably destroyed the opposition's cameras and film. As luck would have it, just about the time Ince found the ideal moviemaking 20,000-acre hideaway in Santa Inez Canyon in the hills above Malibu, the Miller Brothers' 101 Ranch Wild West Show was in Santa Monica. Soon Ince and the Miller Brothers joined forces, giving Ince all the cowboys, horses, cattle, wagons, stagecoaches, and other Western paraphernalia he needed to make Westerns. He also got Tom Mix, Buck Jones, Mabel Normand and the 101 cowboys and Indians in the bargain.[13] Soon a Western town set, as well as living quarters, were built, together with a complete village of tepees for the Indians, somewhat removed. Ince modestly called the whole movie hideout Inceville. It was the motion picture equivalent of Robber's Roost or the Hole-in-the-Wall. The only Edison agent who ever approached it via its one canyon entrance looking out on the Pacific, was soon sent packing by the hard-bitten cowboys, some of whom were already hiding out from the law.

Anonymous, a still from *Hell's Hinges,* (William S. Hart, guns drawn), (1916), Academy of Motion Picture Arts and Sciences, Beverly Hills, California. Blackhawk Photos or Films, Davenport, Iowa, or Killiam Shows, New York.

As an organizer and producer, Ince was a genius who foreshadowed the studio moguls of the 1920s and '30s. By February of 1912, Ince had produced four Westerns, based loosely on history, which seemed to give them the "class" lacking in some of the Bronco Billy and Tom Mix films. The magazine, *Film Fancies,* in its February 24th issue, gushed, "The world has gone wild over the 101 Bison pictures. Critics who have seen Mr. Ince's work proclaim him the Belasco of the moving pictures business. . . ."[14]

But perhaps the smartest thing Ince ever did was to sign his onetime New York roommate, William S. Hart, to a $125-per-week contract. Hart soon became one of the brightest stars in the galaxy of Western movie heroes. He brought in a new style, which some movie historians have called "realism."[15] Though he was not born in the West, Hart traveled across the country and into the West with his father, a flour miller, whom Hart called "a white gold pioneer."[16] As a boy, Hart intended to go to West Point, but at the age of fifteen he became an actor. He was intensely interested in cowboys and the West, however, so he studied their ways carefully and learned to ride like a veteran cowhand. In time, he came to know some of the real Western celebrities, such as Wyatt Earp, Bat Masterson, the outlaw, Al Jennings, the cowboy detective, Charles Siringo, and Sheriff Bill Tilghman. In fact, he carried on extensive correspondence with them and other fading heroes of the Old West. One of the saddest of these letters is a missive from a sick and nearly blind Wyatt Earp asking to borrow fifty dollars so that he and his wife could leave town.[17] In addition to writing to these men of the Old West, Hart collected their guns and other paraphernalia, which he actually used in his movies. His two proudest possessions, however, were his pinto pony, Fritz, whom he loved more than he loved human beings, and a portrait of himself on Fritz painted by his old friend, Charley Russell. He and Russell became fast friends during Charley's visits to Los Angeles, where, as Kid Russell, he knew Harry Carey, Sr., of Newhall, as well as his artist friend, Edward Borein, who lived up the coast at Santa Barbara. While Nancy Russell mostly hob-nobbed with Douglas Fairbanks, Mary Pickford, Rudolph Valentino and other glamour figures, Charley liked to "ranch it" in Newhall with Carey, Will Rogers, Bill Hart, and their cowboy friends. As a writer, as well as a painter, he of course picked up a great number of authentic Western tales from Hart, who knew the real characters. Hart was also able to use Russell's cowboy knowledge in writing, directing and producing his own pictures.

For some time Hart made pictures, such as *The Bargain* and *The Passing of Two-Gun Ricks,* for Ince. In fact, he made or starred in some forty-five such pictures. In 1916, under the direction of Charles Swickard and Ince himself, Hart made perhaps his most famous picture, *Hell's Hinges.* It was the morality tale of a minister and a Western town gone bad—so bad that it was beyond redemption, and could only be consigned to the flames of hell. Under the steely eyed, two-gun direction of Bill Hart as Blaze Tracy, that is exactly what happened. Tracy first shoots down the chief villain, then deliberately sets the town on fire, while rescuing the heroine and burying her murdered brother. The town burning scene, specially directed by Ince, was perhaps the most spectacular movie fire before Selznick burned Atlanta in *Gone With the Wind.*

Meanwhile, Hart developed still another distinctive cowboy persona—the grim-faced gunfighter who seems the personification of evil at first, but then comes on like an avenging angel—In short, the very model of today's Clint Eastwood, one of whose movies, *High Plains Drifter,* is actually a remake of *Hell's Hinges.*

Hart knew enough old gunfighters and lawmen to know that there could be a kind of de-humanizing coldness about them because of the nature of their work. And over the years, he must have discussed this with them often, just as he passed on tips to Charley Russell and his paper-boy protégé, Joel McCrea.

In 1924, Ince and Hart came to a parting of the ways, curiously enough over the continued use of Hart's favorite horse, Fritz. After that, Hart wrote, produced, directed and distributed his own pictures. He also had directors Cliff Smith and John August as part of his team. In addition, at Newhall, just below his souvenir-filled mansion, he maintained a miniature Inceville, consisting of sets, corrals, horses, cattle and cowboys. Thus, in one vertically integrated, self-contained unit, Hart could make his own pictures, which he did very often. Today Hart's Ranch is a well-preserved state park. It is probably the last place one can see just how the old-time moviemakers functioned and lived.

In 1925, just as Gary Cooper was appearing as an extra in a Tom Mix film, and Mix himself was starring in a poor adaptation of Zane Grey's *Riders of the Purple Sage,* William S. Hart made his last picture, *Tumbleweeds.* Based on a story by Hal Evarts in *The Saturday Evening Post,* this was intended to be an epic version of the Oklahoma Land Rush of 1889. The best part of the movie was the grand spectacle of the land rush itself, with racing horsemen, rumbling wagons, tumbling buggies, and even a man on a high-wheeled bike, all dashing to claim land on what was The Cherokee Strip. Ultimately, it failed as a movie because of the melodrama that Hart injected into it, but it succeeded as spectacle, *and* it was in keeping with a new wave of Westerns, first sparked by Ince, that celebrated American history as myth and a grand national saga. During the twenties, in addition to Irving Willat's Texas cattle drive epic, *North of 36,* both Thomas Cruze's *The Covered Wagon* and John Ford's *The Iron Horse,* the story of the Union Pacific, became classics for all time, while introducing entirely new filming techniques.

A new age was coming, and though he was only in his fifties, Hart knew it and he retired gracefully on the wealth he had made from the "picture industry." In 1939, however, he remade *Tumbleweeds* with sound and music, and gave it the proper distribution that it failed to get in 1925. In a special prologue, Hart explained the epic qualities of the movie and the period in history that it depicted, his voice full of reverence for the Western past whose images he had done so much to project to millions. In rich imagery he saluted "the long lines of cattle" moving in a cloud of dust and glory along the horizon, led by a now-riderless pinto pony, his faithful horse, Fritz, who in a "low whinney' calls upon Bill to join him one last time. Then, removing his hat, Hart looked straight into the camera and, somewhat prematurely, delivered his own obituary seven years before he actually died:

> My friends, I loved the art of making motion pictures. It is as the breath of life to me. But through those hazardous feats of horsemanship that I loved so well to do for you, I received many major injuries. That, coupled with the added years of life, preclude my again doing those things that I so gloried in doing. The rush of the wind that cuts your face . . . the pounding hooves of the pursuing posse. Out there in front a fallen tree trunk that spans a yawning chasm, with a noble animal under you that takes it in the same low, ground-eating gallop. The harmless shots of the baffled ones that remain behind, and then, the clouds of dust through which comes the faint voice of the director—"Okay Bill, okay. Glad you made it. Great stuff, Bill, great stuff. And say, Bill, give old Fritz a pat on the nose for me, will you?" Oh, the thrill of it all! . . . Adios, amigos. . . . God bless you all . . . each and every one.[18]

The early motion pictures had succeeded in molding for all time and for all places on the planet the archetypal cowboy as the archetypal American.

25

PICTURES TELL THE STORY

The heyday of Western movies early in this century also became the heyday of Western illustration. Western pulp fiction, which had made Buffalo Bill famous in the 1870s and '80s was still going strong after the turn of the century. With dramatic titles and vivid, sometimes lurid pictures of Western adventure, dime novels and adventure magazines promised, like the movies, a brief moment of escape from everyday concerns. The West in fiction became a setting for bravery, chivalry, romance and excitement. Consequently, the cover art was calculated to evoke the myths of the old West, never mind the real thing.

The late Nick Eggenhoffer was only one of many illustrators who drew and painted for the covers of Western pulp fiction, yet his art is interesting because it refers as much to the tradition of the art of the West as it does to the West itself.

Eggenhoffer, born in 1897, grew up in Germany, where Buffalo Bill had made a lasting cultural impression with his European tours, and the novelist Karl May had popularized the American frontier in his widely read series of Westerns. Before coming to America at age 16, Eggenhoffer remembered going to the "Kinos" to see films of Buffalo Bill's Wild West Show. After his arrival in America, Eggenhoffer undoubtedly saw the popular printed art of the day as well, because his first published illustration, for the cover of *Western Story Magazine* in 1920 looks remarkably like Remington's *Downing the Nigh Leader*. Eggenhoffer also used Charley Russell's art as a model for his illustration and painting; famous Russell images such as his buffalo hunts, *Kit Carson and his Men* and *The Jerkline* were used by Eggenhoffer, becoming iconographic elements that, to those familiar with the tradition of Western art, directly recalled the earlier images. Compositions we now might consider mere copies, were actually visual "echoes" that enriched Eggenhoffer's work as they did the work of many later Western artists. These "echoes" kept powerful images of the West alive in the imagination, and in so doing, they referred the viewer back in time to earlier art, and also reinforced the already strong archetypes of the myth of the old West.

Western illustration reached its peak, not in the dime novel or on the covers of Western pulp magazines, but in a newly emerging popular medium around the turn-of-the-century: the ten-cent magazine. During the 1890s, well designed and lavishly illustrated magazines such as *Collier's* and *The Saturday Evening Post* began to replace *Harper's* and *Leslie's* as America's premier form of entertainment. They were distinctive both graphically and editorially. The stories they featured ranged from adventure tales to society dramas, by authors like Jack London, Frank Norris, Rudyard Kipling, Owen Wister, O'Henry, Edith Wharton, Booth Tarkenton, Mark Twain, Will Rogers and Emerson Hough. The illustrators were no less accomplished: Maxfield Parrish, Edwin Austin Abbey, Frederic Remington, Howard Pyle, Charles Dana Gibson—all were famous and sought-after artists.

How publishers such as Cyrus Curtis, the genius behind *Ladies Home Journal* and owner of *Saturday Evening Post* or James Wannemaker, department store

Newell Convers Wyeth, Illustration for *The Saturday Evening Post* story, "The Three Godfathers," by Peter B. Kyne.

Newell Convers Wyeth, *Bronco Buster,*
(1902). Oklahoma Museum of Art.

visionary and publisher of *Everybody's* were able to package so much high
quality writing and illustration in a weekly magazine, at a price considerably
lower than the 35 cent cost of competitors such as *Harper's* and *Century,* was
then, and still is, something of a mystery. Looking at the flood of new magazines such as *McClures, Munsey's, The Saturday Evening Post, Collier's, Cosmopolitan, Overland* and *Everybody's,* Scottish critic and writer William Andrews
declared, "There is nothing quite like them in the literature of the world, no
periodicals which combine such a width of popular appeal with such serious-
ness of aim and thoroughness of workmanship."[1]

One way they did it was through an explosion in periodical circulation that
brought vast economies of scale. Where as the combined circulation of the
earlier and more expensive illustrated magazines, *Harper's, Century* and *Scribner's* was less than 600,000 in 1885, twenty years later, a single illustrated
magazine, *The Saturday Evening Post* alone exceeded that figure in circulation,
and the combined circulation of the new ten-cent illustrateds exceeded 5 million.[2]

Another important factor was the reduction in the expense of pictorial
reproduction. Woodblock prints, the stable of the earlier illustrateds, was a

skilled, labor-intensive trade. In the 1880s the introduction of the "Ives process," now known as the half-tone, allowed editors to duplicate a black and white drawing or painting photographically, without the costly intervention of hand engraving. Color process printing, which had done so much for the art of Frederic Remington, opened up marvelous, new expressive avenues for other artists as well. Perfected around the turn of the century, it used a separate photographic plate for each primary color and allowed a cheaper, and ultimately more accurate, reproduction of the original.

Some scoffed at the public appetite for pictures. The editor of the *Bauble*, which kept itself aloof from the competition among "picture papers," remarked that "Modern publishers seem to think that the eye measures the depth of the popular mind." How right he was! In the scant thirty years from 1875 to 1905, American media immeasurably expanded the depth, variety and sheer volume of the public's visual experience. Visiting the Sanitary Fair to see a panorama by Albert Bierstadt could no longer compete with going to *The Great Train Robbery* on Saturday night, and being able to see photographs, drawings and read direct reportage from the all over the world in *The Saturday Evening Post*, let alone being able to enjoy the large, full-color posters advertising Buffalo Bill's Wild West!

It was in this charged, visual environment that Western illustration flourished. The West had already become a visual and literary genre in and of itself. The cowboy, thanks to Buffalo Bill, was one of America's most familiar characters, and the dime-novel had already widely popularized his daring adventures on the frontier. Owen Wister's *The Virginian* is a typical example of the post-1900 Western tale. Published in 1902, it was part nostalgia for the disappearing West, and part romantic "corn-ball," the kind of "cowboy goes a-courtin' " material which made for good page-turning by young and old alike; it was light entertainment. The illustrations by Remington and Russell lent the novel a vitality and authenticity that it might not have had if the text had to stand on its own. Despite this, it was extremely popular, remaining continuously in print for more than fifty years, and inspiring first a melodrama, then a movie and finally, in the 1960s, a television series.

Remington and Russell both profited from the growing interest in illustration; Remington signing his *Collier's* contract, and Russell contributing to the pages of *The Saturday Evening Post*. However the Western illustrators that followed in their wake were not of the same, self-taught type. N. C. Wyeth, first in the line of the famous American painting family, was typical of the "new" Western illustrator. First, as his 1903 cover for *The Saturday Evening Post* suggests, he was the inheritor of a long, visual tradition. The archetypal bucking bronco that graced both Charley Russell's first major painting, *Breaking Camp,* as well as an 1885 Buffalo Bill poster became part of an elegant, stylized cover composition: the cowboy's quirt breaking the double heading line of the masthead, the bronco's coiled hindquarters about to kick a story title off the page. What it lacked in originality of subject it made up for in energy and design.

Wyeth was no cowboy artist; he was a New Englander who had fallen in love with Remington's West and determined to become a Western illustrator himself. In this endeavor he was remarkably successful. Wyeth picked up where Remington left off in the use of strong colors for emotional effect, spirited figure compositions and a viewpoint that managed to put his audience in the thick of the action. Although Wyeth may have come by these talents and artistic insights naturally, they were discovered and refined by the greatest teacher of illustration in America, a man who either directly or indirectly inspired almost every Western artist and illustrator in the twentieth century, Howard Pyle.

Pyle himself made few, if any, pictures of the American West. His specialties were medieval romances, fairy tales, fantasies and historic subject matter. In contrast to his chief rival, Charles Dana Gibson, Pyle eschewed the light, airy imagery of the gay '90s for massive, dark, even mysterious forms. Around the turn of the century he assembled an elite cadre of his most promising students to create a school of illustration. Located at Chadds Ford, Delaware, in the Brandywine River area, it would become known as "The Brandywine School," a place where illustrators such as N. C. Wyeth, W. H. D. Koerner, Frank Schoonover, Allen True and Harvey Dunn studied under Pyle's's unusual curriculum—a curriculum that shaped not only their own talents but the entire direction of Western art and illustration forever afterwards.

Pyle, a large-framed man who might have stepped out of one of his own powerful drawings, was peculiarly philosophical about illustration. A Swedenborgian mystic, he often stressed to his students the importance of vivid mental visualization. The purpose of his teaching was to "strike sparks from the imagination." He cared little about such traditional topics as how the paint was applied to the canvas. What he searched for in his students' work was a creative way of telling the story. According to contemporary Western artist John Clymer, who considers himself "third generation Pyle," the master

Newell Convers Wyeth, *Hahn Pulled his Gun and Shot Him Through the Middle,* (1906). Stark Museum of Art, Orange, Texas.

would tell his students, "It didn't matter how you put paint on a picture. It's what you had to say in the picture. How clearly you said it—how much you involve yourself with each person that was in your painting."[3]He de-emphasized the slavish copying of images from models, insisting that this made for "dead" pictures. Instead he urged his students to immerse themselves in their chosen subject. In a sense he was the Stanislavsky of American Art; he taught "method painting," demanding that his students intimately understand the subject. Afternoons at Chadds' Ford might thus find two students paired off with broadswords, clanking across the floor of the old mill studio in mock combat.

It was surely this insistence upon "communing" with the subject that prompted N. C. Wyeth's first trip West in 1904, two years after joining Pyle's school. Perhaps on the recommendation of fellow Pyle student Allen True, a native of Colorado and later an accomplished Western muralist, Wyeth took the train to Denver, a cattle and mining metropolis on the dusty plain east of the Central Rockies. Exposed to the real thing, "The *great* West," Wyeth finally had a chance to tote a Colt 45, sport angora chaps, hunt rattlesnakes and see a "bronco busting" contest in Denver, where he witnessed the legendary black cowboy Bill Picket "bull-dogging" a steer to the dust by biting its lip. Wyeth's illustrations, most notably his series of vertical compositions for *McClure's* in 1906, capture the color, drama, excitement, as well as the majestic western landscape in a way that might even have made Frederic Remington jealous. In *Hahn pulled His Gun and Shot Him Through the Middle*, the audience follows a cowboy as he runs headlong into destiny at the wrong end of a six-shooter. *Listen to what I'm Tellin' Ye!* captures the tough look of the Colorado saloons that Wyeth liked to frequent in his angora chaps. By the look of the regulars, the young New England illustrator was lucky to leave in good health. In these and other pictures, Wyeth took his audience on the wild ride of a vivid, Pyle-trained imagination. As his work matured, Wyeth branched out beyond Western subject matter. He is perhaps best known today as one of America's greatest children's book illustrators, his masterpiece being *Treasure Island*.

Several of Wyeth's comrades at Pyle's studio were artists who likewise fell in love with Western illustration, and devoted much of their careers to it. W. H. D. Koerner was born in Germany, but grew up in the Midwest. He came to Chadds' Ford after some experience as a professional illustrator for the *Chicago Tribune*. Under Pyle's guidance, he would become a regular in the stable of *The Saturday Evening Post* illustrators and a specialist in Western and outdoor themes. His most famous work is undoubtedly *Madonna of the Prairie*, a

W.H.D. Koerner, *Madonna of the Prairie*, (1922). Courtesy of the Buffalo Bill Historical Center, Cody, Wyoming.

picture that became the cover of *The Saturday Evening Post* in 1922, announcing Emerson Hough's serial, *The Covered Wagon.*

Although Pyle students Frank Schoonover and Allen True—both devotees of Western illustration—made frequent contributions to *The Saturday Evening Post,* the favorite seems to have been Harvey Dunn. The West was also his specialty but he preferred picturing the world of sod-busters and pioneers rather than cowboys and shoot'em-ups, maybe because he was the son of a Dakota sod-buster himself. Dunn took to Pyle's teachings more than any of his colleagues. His trade mark in *The Saturday Evening Post* was his imaginative compositions that threaded their way through the text: a dashing speedster might wind its way from the top of the page to the bottom, dodging paragraphs. Dunn illustrations broke borders, did unexpected things, turning the printed sheet itself into a visual adventure. Oddly enough, his paintings, relegated to rectangular canvases, revealed none of Dunn's characteristic vitality. Perhaps he thrived on the challenge of layout and design posed by the magazine work.

Harvey Dunn, like Howard Pyle, was a gifted teacher. He followed in Pyle's footsteps and opened an instructional studio in New Jersey, which attracted younger illustrators. Hired later by the Grand Central School of Art, Dunn carried the torch of Howard Pyle's unique philosophy, by emphasizing imagination over copying from life, immersion in the subject, and, above all, a strong narrative thread to the picture.

This latter element was perhaps the most vital aspect of Pyle's teaching. Each of his students, whether working in the Western genre or not, was a master at *narrative* art. Because they were trained to create images that accompany and amplify fiction, the narrative mode was a natural one. Later, as American art in the twentieth century moved away from narrative art towards abstraction and realism that recorded the immediate, rather than the imagined experience, telling a story with a picture would become practically obsolete and Pyle's teaching seemingly dead.

On the West Coast, a different school of Western illustrators emerged even as the "Brandywine" artists threatened to practically monopolize the field. Unlike the students of Howard Pyle, each of which bore the unmistakable stamp of their master, the group of California illustrators, most of whom lived in the Los Angeles area, practiced widely different styles.

Charley Russell used to visit Edward Borein's Santa Barbara studio on his summer vacations with Nancy. Self-taught like Russell, Borein contributed frequent pictures to a new magazine founded in 1898, *Sunset. Sunset* was the promotional organ of the Union Pacific Railway, and thus had a vested interest in evoking images of a picturesque West. Borein's rough and tumble sketches of cowboy life—expressive, and like Russell's, anecdotal—fit its image perfectly. *Harper's, Collier's, Century* and *Western World* also took his work.

Frank Tenney Johnson and Victor Clyde Forsythe shared a studio in Alhambra, California, where Forsythe worked as a cartoonist and painter, and Frank Tenney Johnson painted his characteristic night scenes of the Santa Fe trail, some of which became cover art for works by one of the most famous Western pulp novelists of all time: Zane Grey. Artists who made their living as illustrators regarded their product in somewhat different light than painters who stuck to "fine art." Hal Shelton, an accomplished painter, map-maker and illustrator who hung around Frank Tenney Johnson's studio as a youth in California, recalls how the artist would "price" each painting. "People liked to buy pictures with white horses," Johnson would tell him. "If I paint a picture with one horse in it—it's a two-hundred dollar picture. If I paint the horse white, it's a four hundred dollar picture."[4]

An acquaintance of Frank Tenney Johnson, and a close friend of Edward Borein was the artist Maynard Dixon, surely the most original of all the California painters, and one of the most distinctive of Western illustrators. As a young man, Dixon sent his drawings to Frederic Remington, who in 1891, wrote to him, "You draw better at your age than I did at the same age—if you have the sand to overcome difficulties you could be an artist in time."[5] The time was two years later, when he published drawings of cowboys in the popular San Francisco magazine *Overland Monthly* which called him "the coming rival of Frederic Remington."[6] Dixon began to live up to this reputation, with a dynamic cover illustration of a rearing horse for the cover of *Harper's Weekly* in 1902, and illustrations for books such as Jack London's *Men of Forty Mile* and *Son of the Wolf.* He did his most dramatic work before 1910 for *Sunset Magazine.* The distinctive design of the magazine called for stylized color covers—images tied into the Western theme, but modern in their "look." Dixon's evolving style perfectly fit the bill. He drew traditional Western subjects—cowboys, Indians, landscapes and explorers—but he simplified their forms. During this creative period in California, he explored visual themes to which he would return in later years. The October 1905 issue of *Sunset* pictures an Indian in a blanket standing on a mesa, his back to a vast, desolate landscape. Ten years later, this picture would become his famous painting, *What an Indian Thinks.* Dixon flourished in California, but after moving to New York to join

Maynard Dixon, *What an Indian Thinks.*
Sunset Magazine version. Yale University
Library.

Maynard Dixon, *Earth Knower,* (c. 1932). The Oakland Museum. Bequest of Abilio Reis.
Photo , M. Lee Fatherree.

Maynard Dixon, *Open Range*, (1942), Museum of Western Art, Denver. Bernard O. Milmoe, Photographer.

Norman Rockwell, *Gary Cooper as "The Texan,"* (1931), Museum of Western Art, Denver, Colorado; Photography by James O. Milmoe.

the hordes of other illustrators, he became disillusioned with the hackneyed imagery of the frontier, an image which had, by 1912, drifted farther and farther away from fact. As he put it, "I'm being paid to lie about the West. I'm going back home where I can do honest work." Dixon thus took one of the most creative professional detours in Western art, devoting himself to re-examining the sky, land and people of the Southwest with a remarkably fresh vision. He became a master at portraying the archaic. Dixon addressed the Indian tribes in a manner reminiscent, yet not imitative of Paul Gauguin's Tahitian paintings, simplifying, primitivizing and, to a large extent, philoso-phizing. His *Earth Knower* describes a primordial relationship between the Native American and the earth: the sculpted folds of the Indian blanket rythmically echoing the eroded hills of the background. Even more significant are his studies of the Western skies. In Dixon's *Open Range,* the clouds are immense and powerful, yet silent, the subject of contemplation by, of all things, a cowboy. Instead of copying the wild rider popularized by Remington, or even Russell's comic cowpoke, Dixon fought against stereotypes to create an image of the solitary rider in the "Big Country": a person who is moved more by the western landscape than he is by the prospect of the saloon at the end of the trail. It may have been inevitable that Maynard Dixon, who sought to mon-umentalize the American West, rather than to reduce it to a series of illustra-tions and anecdotes, would become a muralist.

It is also not surprising, with the emerging film industry in Southern Cali-fornia in the early twentieth century, that art and film would ultimately mix. Victor Forsythe formed friendships with Walt Disney, Gary Cooper and Will Rogers, while some artists, like painter Carl Oscar Borg, the Swedish illustra-tor and landscape painter, actually worked as set painters and art directors. In point of fact, many of the early Western films were taken straight from the pages of *The Saturday Evening Post,* inspired by pictures and pulp fiction.

Other film-makers also adapted successful Western serials, the most notable of which was Emerson Hough's *The Covered Wagon,* made into a ten-reel extravaganza in 1923 by director James Cruze. The huge production not only brought to life W.H.D. Koerner's iconic illustrations of pioneer life, but, staged as it was in the barren landscape of Nevada, it captured the authentic char-acter of the pioneer experience—perhaps better than Hough's story itself. *Tumbleweeds,* William S. Hart's swansong, was likewise adapted from a *Sat-urday Evening Post* story, a short tale by Hal Evarts.

As writers, artists, film-makers and playwrights all drew from each other's work in the early twentieth century, they reinforced images and stereotypes of the West that had evolved during the previous century. Unlike an earlier generation of illustrators, many of those who drew for the ten-cent magazines never experienced the adventure on the frontier the way Russell and Remington did. If the Wild West was on the wane, the myth of the West was in ascendance, and sometimes it was the mythology alone that inspired artists like Nick Eggenhoffer and N.C. Wyeth to become illustrators. Norman Rockwell's 1931 cover of *The Saturday Evening Post* may have summed up the golden age of Western illustration and movies most effectively. Gary Cooper sits before his makeup artist, on the set of *The Texan*. In a vignette typical of Norman Rockwell's humor, the tough cowboy has been reduced to a meek actor, his lips colored with lipstick, waiting to be made-up for the camera. The only tough guy in the scene is the make-up man. Rockwell points out that the Wild West had by 1931 passed mostly into the realm of myth and illusion sustained by the magic of film.

CHAPTER   26

_____

COWBOYS CREATE HISTORY

As a frigid November wind swept across the Sonora plains, three cowboys sat huddled around the warmth of a single campfire, sharing company and conversation. They had come down to Mexico together, to help a friend work some cattle. It was, as one of the comrades later remembered, "An old time type of roundup. Those *vaqueros* sure showed us how to handle a rawhide *riata* and sit up straight on a bronc."[1] As they pulled off their boots and stretched out their sore bones after a long, hard day on the range, their conversation turned to a favorite subject, art.

All three cowboys were artists. Joe Beeler, a native of Oklahoma with part-Cherokee heritage, was also a veteran of the Hollywood movie scene. After art school he had worked for "Fats" Jones in the 1950s decorating movie sets—a line of work he gave up to become a painter.

John Hampton was an enthusiastic Westerner, even though he was born in New York City. A pulp magazine illustrator and cartoonist, Hampton had made enough money drawing the comic strip "Red Ryder" to stake himself to a small ranch in New Mexico. It was hard to tell that this rugged man with a jauntily tilted Stetson and a long cowboy drawl was a transplanted Easterner. As he put it, "The stork dropped me on the wrong range."[2]

Charley Dye was born in Colorado in 1906, when Bill Picket was still bull-dogging steers. A heavy-set man with a quiet Western wit, Dye later remarked that "I could not recall a time when I was not at home on horseback, or that I didn't portray the life I led with pen and pencil."[3] Dye took his natural talent to New York City in 1936, where he began to study with Harvey Dunn, Howard Pyle's prize pupil. Like his teacher he became a successful magazine illustrator, doing everything from floorwax advertisements to his favorite subject: Western life. Dye had returned to the West by 1960, taking up residence in Sedona, Arizona.

As the three friends sat around the fire that cold night in 1964, they speculated about ways to preserve that special feeling of camraderie that all of them shared not only as participants in the life of the West, but as special interpreters of it. Theirs was then, and still is, a kind of "cowboy counter-culture" that resists or ignores the new movements and trends in art, preferring instead the traditional life of the cowboy, and the simple narrative realism of bygone times. What they needed was an organization of like-thinking "cowboy-artists," people who would enjoy roundups and trail rides as much as easel painting and illustration. That night, the idea of the Cowboy Artists of America was born.

At the first meeting of the Cowboy Artists of America at Bird's Creek tavern in Sedona, Arizona, the credo of the organization was hammered out over several rounds of Coors beer. In the main, the CAA was formed to "perpetuate the memory and culture of the Old West as typified by the late Frederic Remington, Charley Russell and others; to insure authentic representation of the life of the West, as it was and is . . ." as well as to "conduct a trail ride and camp-out in some locality of special interest once a year . . ."[4] The upstart organization, like many other associations of artists, was born in the spirit of iconoclasm. Charley Dye spoke with pride about belonging to the new CAA: "It's not like being a whore in black stockings like some of these big painters."[5]

By swapping black stockings for a weathered pair of cowboy boots, the Cowboy Artists of America became "big painters" in their own right. The organization now has a museum in Kerrville Texas, which attracts tens of thousands of visitors annually. Joe Beeler, as well as other members of the CAA, holds workshops in painting, thereby living up to their promise to "perpetuate the memory and culture of the Old West." Yet what is perhaps more interesting is the culture of collectors that has emerged in the West, the broad-based interest in realistic and narrative images of the old West in the tradition of Russell and Remington. Now, more than twenty years after the founding of the CAA, the Western Art auction circuit is eagerly awaited each summer, not only by artists, museums and galleries, but also by collectors, for whom cowboy art auctions have become special social events.

Although important sales are held in Phoenix, Houston, Denver, Sun Valley and the mecca of Western Art, Great Falls, Montana, until recently a prestigious ceremony kicked it off: the awarding of the coveted Prix de West by the Cowboy Hall of Fame in Oklahoma City. The National Association of Western Artists, NAWA, a splinter group that swerved from the original CAA, awarded a $100,000 prize each year to a single Western artist. The award also included a trip to Europe, as well as virtually guaranteeing publicity in the numerous Western Art magazines: *Persimmon Hill, Southwest Art* and *Artists of the Rockies and the Golden West,* to name only a couple.

The collectors of "contemporary Western Art" as it is now called, range from cowboys themselves, who now, more than likely can only afford a print of a poster by a member of the CAA, to cattle men, oil barons, even movie stars. A common bond shared by collectors of this genre is a love of the Old West, and a sense of heritage that somehow the cowboy artists have been able to capture. Instead of being an art form that describes the West to a remote audience, contemporary Western Art is mostly a regional phenomenon, speaking to people who feel a kinship with the West itself.

A common bond among most contemporary artists of the American West— working in the "narrative-realist" mode—is a strong commitment to history and tradition. This manifests itself in many ways, perhaps most directly in their subject matter.

John Clymer, a member of the Cowboy Artists of America and the National Association of Western Artists, is another Harvey Dunn student who has continued to keep the teaching and philosophy of Howard Pyle alive by visualizing and painting scenes of America's frontier past. A native of the Northwest, Clymer and his wife have traced the entire course of the old Oregon Trail, as well as Lewis and Clark's route, using historic diaries and accounts. This immersion in the landscape of the past has provided Clymer with authentic settings for many of his paintings. In *Narcissa Whitman Meets the Horribles,* he pictures a scene from a pioneer woman's diary describing a meeting with the Nez Perce Indians on the west side of the Continental Divide. The landscape is oddly prosaic, not the kind of romantic scenery one might expect in a Bierstadt painting or even a picture by N.C. Wyeth: Clymer shows the *real* place. According to Clymer, "I went there and I knew exactly what the landscape looked like, and it made me feel much closer to the subject than if I had just stayed at home . . . I wanted to feel and imagine what it would have felt like to her to have been there."[6] Because of Clymer's insistance on using the real locations, the viewers of his paintings are taken on a trip back into time, which becomes all the more authentic through his commitment to accurate historical detailing. His historical paintings are vivid imaginings, in the true spirit of Howard Pyle, yet he strives above all for accuracy. According to Clymer, "I think that history paintings, if they are not as correct as you can make them, they're not worth doing."[7]

Other Western artists such as Tom Lovell, Frank McCarthy and Howard Terpening also paint history striving, as does Clymer, for authenticity. McCarthy, another former Hollywood scene painter is, in fact, at his best when he imitates dramatic movie stills in a photorealist manner, such as his famous cavalry painting *Leading the Charge* (1984). One element common to all of their pictures is a definite narrative theme. Perhaps because of its strong foundation in illustration and motion pictures as well as its inspiration by those original "cowboy artists" Remington and Russell, Western history painting strives to engage the viewer in a story or an anecdotal moment. The past has become a rich visual playground for Western artists. At its worst, Western history painting devolves into saccharin nostalgia. At its best, it uses all of the techniques of the illustrator's and historian's trades to transport its audience into another place and time, leading them through the eye into a contemplation of the vanished frontier. Yet, good or bad, all of the historical art of the American West follows the lead of Frederic Remington, responding to the same imperative to record the "wild riders and the vacant lands [that] were about to vanish forever." For artists like John Clymer, as well as for Frederic Remington, the West is a panorama which the artist witnesses as it unfolds, the immense saga of many peoples and many places and many events, great and small that have shaped, and will continue to shape the dreams of a great many Americans.

One fact confronting contemporary Western artists is that Western Art, as a genre and a vision, is no longer new. Any chosen subject, whether it be Lewis and Clark, a Plains Indian buffalo hunt, trappers in the Rockies or a cowboy roundup, has accumulated myriad visual precedents, extending back in time to the paintings by Titian Peale, Alfred Jacob Miller and George Catlin. Rather than hiding such historical precedents, many Western artists make overt references to them. Like Nick Eggenhoffer who borrowed compositions from Remington and Russell, the Western artists have become willing

John Clymer, *Narcissa Whitman Meets the Horribles*, (1985). Collection of the Artist, Teton Village, Jackson, Wyoming.

vehicles for the perpetuation of compelling Western images, unafraid to take from the past and to re-work or replicate archetypes. This tendency towards replication is perhaps the most jarring or unusual facet of modern Western art, because it flies in the face of the usual mandate that an artist must offer an original, not a derivative image. We Americans like our artists to break from the images of the past, rather than to imitate them. Oddly enough, in other cultures (one is tempted to call them "traditional" societies) such as ancient

Frank McCarthy, *Leading the Charge*. Cowboy Artists of America Museum, Kerrville, Texas.

Greece and Rome, as well as dynastic China, aesthetic replication was all-important. To today's tradition-oriented Western artists, who are recording history—even legend—replication is equally important to the central message of the artwork. The message is not how innovative the individual artists may be, but how memorable, how worthy of preservation and rememberance, is the image he creates. Thus, the modern Western painters are not simply carrying on a dialogue with dead artforms of the past, they are keeping the "narrative-realist" mode alive, putting it to use the way Remington and Russell did, refusing, to let the art of the Wild West, as well as the life of the Wild West, slip into the forgotten shadows of the past.

Michael Coleman is a skillful painter in gouache, also the favorite medium of nineteenth-century Western artist Henry Farny. Farny, a contemporary of Frederic Remington, worked on an intimate scale, creating crisply realistic images of Plains Indian life. Coleman has adopted Farny's stylistic trademarks: the Plains Indian subject matter and tight, precise brushwork, keeping the master's aesthetic alive. Like Farny's pictures, Coleman's works have a rational, almost geometric composition, created by the planar bands of land and sky. His work is popular not only because of his skill as a painter, but because he has resurrected a much admired technique by an artist whose original works sell for extremely high prices.

Henry Farny, *Indian Encampment*, (1901), Anschutz Collection.

What Coleman does with scenes of American Indian life, painters such as Wilson Hurley and Michael Mahaffey do with the Western landscape. Both are representational artists who continue to paint what has now become an archetypal image in American landscape art: the Grand Canyon. Thomas Moran and William H. Holmes did not drain all of the inspiration from the famous North Rim vista; in fact, perhaps due in part to their early efforts, the Grand Canyon has been continuously painted and photographed for the better part of a century. Some artists, like the dedicated watercolorist Gunnar Widforss have spent their entire lives painting the canyon, trying to encompass the vast expanse within a single frame. Others, like the photographer Elliot Porter have discovered the beauty of nature's detail. In a sense, Hurley and Mahaffey have "inherited" the canyon from these earlier generations of painters—every picture they do reverberates with the visions of those who have come to this dramatic spot before.

Hurley, working with the now-traditional gigantic canvas, has followed Moran's lead in keying his paintings to the moods of the sky. Yet, instead of simply imitating Moran's theatrical thunderstorm effects, Hurley brings a unique facet of understanding to the subject. A former airforce pilot, he has a meteorologist's vision of the skies, understanding the atmospheric forces which drive the gathering clouds. Hurley usually chooses to picture the canyonland skies in their characteristic summer mood: suffused with the haze that William H. Holmes so skillfully evaporated in his scientific drawings. The accurate depiction of atmosphere and light governs the creation of Hurley's paintings, keying the tones of the rock to starkly realistic grays and yellows rather than torrid reddish hues.

While Wilson Hurley works with subtle brush strokes and thin glazes to capture the effects of land and sky from the rim of the Grand Canyon, Michael

Wilson Hurley, *West from Cedar Ridge, Grand Canyon*. Museum of Western Art, Denver, Colorado.

Mahaffey plunges his viewers into the abyss, selecting views which occasionally echo the sensitive photographs by Elliot Porter of the now-flooded Glen Canyon. Mahaffey has developed an unusual technique called "stain-painting." As you approach one of his pictures from a distance, it looks like a photorealist mural. Yet, up close, the banded sandstone cliffs and rippling water dissolve into an insubstantial pattern of colored blots on un-primed canvas. For Mahaffey, the dialogue with tradition occurs not so much in the pictorial image, but in the act of painting the Grand Canyon itself. A student of all Grand Canyon art, from Moran to the present, Mahaffey sees the act of returning to the canyon to paint as a celebration of the continuing power of the landscape to inspire artists, even after generations have been there before. For years, Mahaffey hosted the bi-annual "Grand Canyon Paint-Off," in which twenty or thirty painters would spend a day together at the canyon, each producing a work that was judged at the end of the day. It mattered little who won or lost. The final judgment was made by a friendly park ranger. The process of painting this grandest of all American sacred places is akin to a renewal rite, an aesthetic ceremony which is all the more powerful because it is part of a long and continuing tradition. One might say that the Grand Canyon is to Western landscape artists what Mount Fuji is to Japanese painters.

Ned Jacob is a Denver-based artist who specializes in rapid, expressive paintings of Indians. As a young man he struck out West for Montana and lived with the Blackfeet, working for a time as a clerk in a reservation trading post. In the course of his development as an artist, he sketched many of his friends among the Blackfeet, only to find out that, for certain families, he was only the latest in a long line of artists who had portrayed them. Descendants of Iron Shirt, who posed for Karl Bodmer, and ancestors of Buffalo Bull's Back Fat, who sat for Catlin's famous painting, were still alive in the 1950s when Ned Jacob began to sketch. Separating him in the course of history from Karl Bodmer and George Catlin were generations of artists with vastly different visions: Paul Kane, John Mix Stanley, Charles Russell, the ethnographic painter Joseph Henry Sharp, and even the illustrator Winold Reiss, who had spent a lifetime with the Blackfeet, taken an Indian name, and whose ashes were scattered by the tribe at the foot of the Rockies after his death in 1953. Ned Jacob found himself part of a generations-long chain of artists and subjects who, together, had created a sequence of images through a century and a half in time, recording the changes, as well as the continuities in Blackfeet Indian

Harry Jackson, *Sacajawea*,
(1980). Harry Jackson,
Wyoming Foundry Studios,
Cody, Wyoming.

history. Their culture had changed, but then again so had his.

One man who embodies the defiant attitude of the new Western artist is the Wyoming-based sculptor Harry Jackson. Asked to join the CAA and the NAWA—rival factions in the current world of Cowboy Art—he declined both, after previously being prevented from showing at the CAA exhibit, writing:

> For My Cowboy Artist Friends
> (On bein' Throwed Out o' the CAA)
>
> I was proud when you ast me to join ya
> And was proud when ya tells me ta git
> Fact, I'm proud to be with er without ya
> 'Cuz I never bin broke to the Bit . . .[8]

Despite his disaffiliation, Harry Jackson is perhaps the best known of the Cowboy Artists, not only because of his well-known sculpture of John Wayne, but also because of a large corpus of work that seeks to monumentalize the mythology of the Old West in traditional, yet unusual ways.

Harry Jackson, *The Horseman, (Sculpture of John Wayne on Willshire Blvd.,* (1984). The Great Western Financial Corp., Beverly Hills, CA. and Harry Jackson, Wyoming Foundry Studios, Cody, Wyoming.

Born in Chicago in 1924, Jackson, like many other Western artists, ran away to the West as a young man to become a cowboy. His art took a modern turn when he moved to New York in 1946. Once a devotee of the abstract expressionist, Jackson Pollack (himself a Westerner, born in Cody, Wyoming), Jackson gave up a promising career as a member of the New York School to become a realist painter and sculptor. His creations, like the monumental statue of "the Duke" entitled *The Horseman* in Hollywood, are oftentimes shocking, even revolting to contemporary critics. He paints his bronzes, an heretical act to most, but one which Jackson finds attractive and unusual in today's world, when most outdoor sculpture is abstract and reveals the materials from which it was made. Modern "purists" in this vein have taken their cue from the mergence of a machine culture in America and from the principles of the Chicago skyscraper school of architecture. They forget that the much admired classical statues of ancient Greece like those of Phidias were originally painted in vivid colors.

The sculptor is at his best when working with simple, almost elemental schemes. In Jackson's *To the Gods* (1961), a Plains Indian astride his horse is rendered with the looseness and simplicity of an Archaic Greek figurine, almost taking on the character of a prehistoric votive artifact. In a primal image, horse and rider are lifted vertically towards the sun by a central staff, the Indian "tree of life" or cosmic axis motif.

Jackson's *Sacajawea,* a larger-than-life monumental sculpture at the Buffalo Bill Historical Center in Cody, Wyoming is one of his best known works. The image of the Shoshone Indian woman, Sacajawea, guide and heroine of the Lewis and Clark expedition has, like an ancient votive figurine, been reduced to elemental forms. Jackson observes: "I must simplify, yet without letting any superficial sense of mannerism or mere stylization be suggested."[9] The result is one of the most powerful modern sculptures of an American woman. Her massiveness and strength, like the haunting figure on Mrs. Henry Adams's tomb in Rock Creek Park by Augustus Saint-Gaudens, is created by the voluminous folds of her garment, and focused by her determined, frontally symmetrical gaze.

Like other Western artists, Jackson is a traditionalist. Jackson's John Wayne sculpture may be his most ambitious revivalist project of all: returning to the traditional monumental equestrian statue within an urban context, at a time when it is decidely unpopular among critics to do so. Situated as it is upon a major urban thoroughfare, Wilshire Boulevard, of a city which owes most of its fame to movie heroes, the John Wayne sculpture must be seen in the long tradition of other public equestrian statues: from the Renaissance bronzes by Donatello, Verrocchio and Leonardo, to nineteenth-century American works in the same tradition, among them Augustus Saint-Gaudens's statue of General Sherman, situated at the base of Central Park in New York City. Jackson's art, as Western art, reaffirms older images and traditional values. Through his efforts and the efforts of others, the West has come to stand, not for America's future, its Manifest Destiny, but for its rich pioneer past—a past that celebrates the role of the American Indian as much as the role of the American cowboy. As artists like Harry Jackson, some good and some bad, continue their exploration of the American West through art, they create and perpetuate archetypes in the American consciousness which draw upon generation upon generation of earlier Western imagery for their power and meaning. Sometimes, as with the making of Sacajawea, this process is conscious. Other times, as with the derivative imagery of Nick Eggenhofer, it is most likely unconscious. Either way the image of the West persists, and continues to keep dreams alive.

By selecting images and subject matter already explored by earlier generations, Western artists like Harry Jackson and others seem to be asserting that the West is beyond the scope of a single artist's comprehension. The images of the West take on a life of their own and work their way into the artist's vision, capturing another artist in turn, transcending the individual imagination, and passing into what a psychologist might call the "collective unconscious."

Although American art critics have long demanded that a painter swerve from influence and strike out into new visual terrain, denying his links with the past, or rendering them impotent through ironic mannerism, Western Art is clearly different. The Western artist has willingly become a human medium for the development and perpetuation of the culturally sustaining history, myth and legend about the West—for him (or for her), aesthetic novelty now has no special lure. Although painters in a traditional mode, this attitude places Western artists in a counter-cultural stance. Some artists, like Harry Jackson, thrive on this position. Some Western artists simply ignore the art world, and do their own work.

On a high granite outcrop outside of Custer, South Dakota, a young man sits behind the wheel of a bulldozer. With his right hand he yanks the throttle back, creeping the machine slowly forward with its load of shattered fragments. Watching the pieces as they bounce and tumble off the granite cliff face, you can just barely recognize the outline of a gigantic horse and rider. The sculpture *Crazy Horse*, was begun by Korczak Ziolkowski in 1948. His vision: Crazy Horse and his mount, galloping full speed across the sacred Indian landscape of the Black Hills. When it is complete, and no one knows when that will be, the statue will be a fully three-dimensional image of the famous Indian Chief, 641 feet long and 563 feet high. Mr. Ziolkowski has died, but his family has continued his work. In a very real sense, this work of art will thus transcend the lifespan and vision of a single person; the image of the Indian chief will live for an estimated 10,000 years. As his son and other members of the Ziolkowski family work the bulldozer through the course of their lifetimes, they will help to preserve an iconographic tradition which stands in defiance to the ebbs and flows of aesthetic fashion, and seeks to impress upon the very land itself a diagram of what we, as relative newcomers to the West, hold as important to remember.

27

WESTERNS MAKE HISTORY

Norman Rockwell's 1931 Saturday Evening Post cover of Gary Cooper being made up for *The Texan* could just as well have been a view of Cooper in 1929, not only the year of the Great Crash, but also the year he starred in the first sound version of that immortal tale of cowboys without cows, *The Virginian.* Cooper was surrounded by talent. Richard Arlen was his sidekick and Trampas, the villain, was played by Walter Huston in a black mustache! In the famous scene when Trampas calls the Virginian "a son-of-a——," and Cooper, in a low voice, his pistol in Huston's stomach, says "When you call me that, smile." Huston, as the villainous Trampas, merely giggles and leers. But as the years rolled on, Westerns took on another, more serious, dimension. They still had sappy comic cowboys, and even singing and yodeling cowboys, but more and more they made use of history, or rather, they created a history, and even a landscape, for the American West that was nothing if not a full-blown saga of horseback heroism in the great scenic outdoors.

The film maker, John Ford, in a 1962 film, *The Man Who Shot Liberty Valance,* put the creation of history something like this. There sits an elderly

James Stewart as Western Senator Ransome Stoddard, surrounded by attentive newsmen, telling the real story of his path to fame. For the first time,
Stoddard, the lawyer-dude, cuffed into glory because he rid the world of the
villainous Liberty Valance (Lee Marvin) in a shoot-out, reveals that it was
not he, but his deceased friend, Tom Doniphan, who shot Valance from ambush.
The gentlemen of the press listen, then close their notebooks on the Senator's
story. Stewart, as Stoddard, says in disbelief, "You're not going to use the
story?" The chief editor of *The Shinbone Star* then says it all: "This is the West,
sir. When the legend becomes fact, print the legend."

From 1936 onward, legends as history abounded. While Don Ameche as
Alexander Graham Bell, was inventing the telephone and Spencer Tracy, as
young Tom Edison, the lightbulb, Gary Cooper as Wild Bill Hickock was
getting his lights shot out by Jack McCall on the Deadwood City set of Cecil
B. DeMille's *The Plainsman*, a movie that "purely disgusted" William S. Hart.
But in that same year, 1936, James Cruze came back to tell the story of *Sutter's
Gold*, and King Vidor helped celebrate the Texas Centennial in Dallas by
premiering *The Texas Rangers*, allegedly based on fact, but actually derived
from historian Walter P. Webb's book of the same name. The film was supple-
mented by a comic-book history of Texas called, appropriately, "Texas Movies." It was hard to tell which got top billing at the Dallas Centennial fair,
Vidor's *Texas Rangers*, a giant hot-air balloon of a bloated Texas Ranger, the
comic book history that recorded triumphs over "the greasers," or Sally Rand,
the daring fan dancer. Some say the 1936 Centennial fair marked the first true
definition of the Texas character.[1] Others delay that moment until 1960, when
John Wayne, in a coonsksin cap, directed and acted in a Yale University
financed version of *The Alamo*, authentically recreated at Happy Shahan's
ranch at Brackettville, Texas. So authentic was this recreation of an historic
place that most tourists prefer it to the real Alamo in downtown San Antonio.
No matter, somehow the movies had made history and Americans were learning from them.

In 1937 Joel McCrea, Bill Hart's paperboy, starred in *Wells Fargo*, and then
in '39 came back as the hero of De Mille's big budget *Union Pacific*, that
competed with Henry King's *Jesse James*, starring Henry Fonda and Tyrone
Power. That same year saw Errol Flynn don Western garb in *Dodge City*, and
James Stewart and Marlene Dietrich making history in *Destry Rides Again*. On
and on went Hollywood's moviemakers, creating American history for millions. Billy the Kid was celebrated and dissected many times over. Judge Roy

Anonymous, Still from *She Wore a Yellow Ribbon*, (1949). Depicts Sergeant Tyree galloping. Courtesy William Howze, Amon Carter Museum, Fort Worth.

Bean made "law west of the Pecos" more important even than the Texas Rangers, though not the Lone Ranger. Western Union, the Pony Express, Custer's Last Stand, (where "They Died With Their Boots On") and the Gunfight at Tombstone's O.K. Corral were indelibly imprinted as all-important epic events by the movies on the public imagination. As late as 1969, we were learning about Butch Cassidy and the Sundance Kid, speculating as to whether Butch and the Kid *really* did die in a shootout in—Bolivia? Back in 1963 we learned from several master directors *How the West Was Won*, though not from whom. That had to wait until Arthur Penn's classic *Little Big Man* in 1971, made at a time when "the good Indian" was all the rage. In Penn's film we learned our history, humorous as it got to be, from an unimpeachable source: the total recall memory of Jack Crabbe, who was 120 years old, and had, as it were, lived through it all. Penn, like the editor in *Liberty Valance*, printed the legend, but it was all backwards with a crazy Custer and a heroic Indian chief,

Frederic Remington, *Downing the Nigh Leader*, (1907), Museum of Western Art, Denver.

who kept saying, "It's a good day to die." This had a much profounder effect on the public than Ralph Nelson's *Soldier Blue*, Robert Altman's *McCabe and Mrs. Miller,* (which wasn't very "American" anyway), or Eliot Silverstein's *The Ballad of Cat Ballou,* in which, for the first time in a Western, a cowboy was mean enough to cold cock a horse and thus upstage, perhaps for the only time, Jane Fonda. That one-punch knockout landed Lee Marvin an Academy Award.

Perhaps the greatest cinematic maker of Western history, however, was John Ford. In his career, that spanned fifty years, Ford made fifty-four Westerns.[2] While many of these were two- and three-reelers, made for Universal Pictures and usually starring Harry Carey, Sr., Ford also made some astonishing Western epics, such as one is tempted to say that he created the genre. But the Ford Western should be seen first of all as part of a total picture of American history that he eventually filmed. The critic, Andrew Sarris, wrote:

> No American director has ranged so far across the landscape of the American past, the world of Lincoln, Lee, Twain, O'Neill, the three great wars, the Western and trans-Atlantic migrations, the horseless Indian of the Mohawk Valley and the Sioux and Comanche cavalries of the West, the Irish and Spanish incursions and the delicately balanced politics of polyglot cities and border states.[3]

Orson Welles argued that schools would do well to show Ford's films as their regular course in American history,[4] while Peter Bogdanovitch, a director himself, concluded, "What Ford can do better than any film-maker in the world is create an epic canvas and still people it with characters of equal size and importance. . . ."[5]

John Ford first came into prominence with his well-researched tale of the Union Pacific, a film called *The Iron Horse.* This was released in 1924, the year after Cruze's epic, *The Covered Wagon.* One still from Ford's film, which shows the joining of the rails at Promontory Point in Utah in 1869 is identical to Andrew J. Russell's famous photograph, taken on the spot at the time, except that Ford included Russell and his large wet plate camera, as well. This is significant, because virtually all of Ford's history films, including his Westerns, reflect his use of old photographs and paintings by the masters. While Ford claimed that he just walked onto the set and placed his actors through sheer instinct, it is clear that he had a remarkable visual memory for authentic or seemingly authentic historical scenes that he had seen in other media. With regard to *She Wore a Yellow Ribbon,* he admitted to Peter Bogdanovitch, "I tried to copy the Remington style there—you can't copy him one hundred percent—but at least I tried to get in his colour and movement, and I think I succeeded partly."[6] In this particular instance, Ford not only got in Remington's blue and yellow cavalry colors, he also caught the tremendous energy of Remington's lines in the dashing movement of his riders. Sergeant Tyree, who serves as scout and messenger, racing madly across vast stretches of desert landscape, conjured up the lead figure in Remington's famous painting, *Cavalry Charge on the Southern Plains,* and in so doing he made Tyree seem to stand for a whole regiment of thundering cavalry. Thus, in a sense, when he made his epic films, Ford based them on images that, whether really correct or not, had been deemed correct by his viewing public for a long time.[7] Irish Catholic himself, he employed the Scottish Realist's principle of "associationism" in his films. That is, a scene in his films usually conjured up in the viewer's mind a scene that he or she had witnessed somewhere before, maybe even in an entirely different context. This gave Ford's epic films a feeling of reality and factual allusion when, in fact, he was really spinning out his own ideas and myths.

In 1939 Ford produced what many regard as the greatest Western of all time, *Stagecoach.* Written by Ernest Haycox, it is the story of a group of people, not unlike Chaucer's Canterbury pilgrims, heading via stagecoach through an Apache uprising to Lordsburg, New Mexico. In the film John Wayne, as the outlaw, Ringo, emerged as a star, while Thomas Mitchell received an Academy Award for playing a drunken doctor. The stagecoach indeed contained "pilgrims" with the sinners, an outlaw, a drunken doctor, a gambler and the town prostitute outnumbering the saints. The story of these outcasts sustains its religious tone when one of its passengers has a baby in the rude confines of a stagecoach stop in the middle of nowhere, and she is helped by two of the sinners, Doc and Claire Trevor as the Mary Magdalen figure.

Stagecoach was also the first of Ford's films to be made in the almost surreal grandeur of Monument Valley. As such, the location, with its mesas and buttes and sky-high volcanic cores standing out against the sky, became a character in the film. Monument Valley served several functions; it took the action out of the mundane and familiar, thus making clear that the story was legendary, and because of its monumental scale, by comparison it also suggested that the characters in the story were larger than life, however commonplace their station in society might be. More than any other director, Ford was conscious that a Western should include the Western landscape. And, as the stagecoach raced across this barren panorama, chased by Indians, Ford also duplicated in his chase frames one of Remington's greatest paintings, *Downing the Nigh Leader*. This allusion caught the Remington spirit of energetic melodrama acted out on a bare stage under the maddening glare of a noonday sun.

In addition, Ford was conscious of frontier people on that barren stage as being isolated and sometimes outcasts from crowded, built-up society. They were either community builders—families starting over again in the spirit of Frederick Jackson Turner—or total outcasts who represented an ambiguous view of the frontier culture that they saw beginning to grow up around them. Often the only order out in the middle of nowhere was a military order which sheltered, but sometimes conflicted with, the order inherent in the families at the lonely outposts.

The question of legend and order came up again in Ford's 1946 Western, *My Darling Clementine*. Here the focus is upon the famous Earp brothers and the town of Tombstone, Arizona, with the climax of the gunfight with the Clanton family at the O. K. Corral. Once again, the mimetic, or realistic, qualities of the film were striking. Ford lavished more attention on his sets in this film than he had in any other. At the same time, he brought a Rembrandt-like sense of chiaroscuro to the scenes, filming many of them in dimly lit interiors or outside at night. These scenes contrasted with a community building scene in which a fund-raising dance takes place in the bright sunshine on the wooden floor of what is to become the town church. Ford used the same kind of chiaroscuro technique in *The Man Who Shot Liberty Valence*.

Ford actually knew Wyatt Earp who, along with Harry Carey, was probably the genesis of the film. The director recalled,

> I didn't know anything about the O. K. Corral at the time but Harry Carey knew about it, and he asked Wyatt and Wyatt described it fully . . . as a matter of fact, he drew it out on paper, a sketch of the entire thing. Wyatt said, "I was not a good shot, I had to get close to a man . . ." So in *My Darling Clementine*, we did it exactly the way it had been. They didn't just walk up the street and start banging at each other; it was a clever military maneuver.[8]

Joseph Secker and Michael Wilmington, in their discussion of the film, go on to point out that, while Earp may have choreographed the climactic gunfight accurately, John Ford played fast and loose with history in other parts of the film. Earp did not meet Doc Holliday in Tombstone; Doc came with him from Dodge City. Moreover, Holliday did not die in the gunfight, but in bed of tuberculosis eighteen months later. Old Man Clanton was not even at the

O. K. Corral; he was killed much earlier during the Earp's long feud with the Clantons, who did not steal a cattle herd from the Earps, described in the film as the causative factor in the feud. And finally Virgil, not Wyatt Earp, was the town marshall.[9] "When legend becomes fact, print the legend."

Ford continued his history lesson in his "Cavalry Trilogy": *Fort Apache,* 1948, *She Wore a Yellow Ribbon,* 1949, and *Rio Grande,* 1950. Though he had worked with him before in *Stagecoach,* in the Cavalry Trilogy Ford "discovered" a new star, John Wayne. Wayne had appeared along with Montgomery Clift in Howard Hawks's *Red River* (1948), easily the best cattle drive epic ever made. In that film Wayne played the tough, tyrannical leader of the drive, while Clift played his scrawny protégé: a surrogate son with whom he eventually has an epic fist fight, ostensibly over the herd and the men, but actually over actress Joanne Dru, in one of Hollywood's most obvious bows to *Oedipus Rex.* The film was excellent, and so was Wayne. After seeing Wayne in *Red River,* Ford told Hawks, "I never knew that big sonofabitch could act."[10] Then he quickly signed him up for the key roles in all three of the cavalry pictures.

Fort Apache starred both John Wayne and Henry Fonda, heretofore Ford's mainstay as a hero. In this case Fonda, as Colonel Thursday, played a surrogate George Armstrong Custer. Like Custer, Colonel Thursday lusted for glory after the Civil War was over. Against advice from John Wayne as the veteran frontier soldier Captain York, he orders his cavalry troopers to charge a horde of Indians screened behind a huge cloud of dust. This proves to be a major blunder, as Colonel Thursday and all his men are trapped on a small knoll in a box canyon by a horde of Apaches under Chief Cochise, with whom Captain York had formerly been on good terms. Clearly, in his mad desire for glory, Colonel Thursday has committed his men to a massacre. Then in an alternative scenario to that of the Custer fight, Captain Kirby York (John Wayne) rides through the cloud of Indians and appears to have saved the mad Colonel. But to his credit in York's eyes, Colonel Thursday refuses to be saved and stays on to die with his men. The movie ends with a foreshadowing of the "print the legend" scene in *Liberty Valance.* A group of newsmen is interviewing Colonel York, who discusses the now-famous Thursday's Charge, a painting of which, described by the reporters, hangs prominently in the White House. According to John Baxter in *The Cinema of John Ford,* this is a clear reference to John Mulvaney's *Custer's Last Rally,* which Walt Whitman saw in 1881 and described in terms identical to the movie dialogue.[11] Knowing the real story,

Colonel York, without a trace of bitterness, declares, "No man died more bravely, nor brought more honor to his regiment." At that very time, the regiment rides by outside the Commandant's office and "The Battle Hymn of the Republic" comes on the sound track, suggesting that whatever Colonel Thursday did, his successor, Colonel York, does not wish to be seen as a folly and a waste of lives. "The Battle Hymn of the Republic," a hymn of glory, endows the foolish action with nobility. Again, as in virtually all Custer paintings, legend triumphs over reality. "They died with their boots on."

By the same token, *She Wore a Yellow Ribbon* opens with an evocation of the Custer tragedy. "Custer is dead and around the bloody guidons of the Seventh Cavalry lie the two hundred and twelve officers and men he led. . . ." The narrator goes on to say that the whole Western frontier is ablaze with Indian uprisings. These uprisings swirl all around the Southwestern fort in *She Wore a Yellow Ribbon*—a fort that is a good 2,000 miles from the Little Big Horn. In this film, that is so evocative of, not only Remington's paintings, but also those of Charles Schreyvogel and Charley Russell, there is an elegaic note. John Wayne, as Captain Nathan Brittles, is about to retire. He has led his last patrol that takes him to a burnt out ranch and corral, where he witnesses the death of an old adversary in arms, Trooper Smith, who had been a brigadier general in the Confederate Army. Trooper Smith is buried with full Confederate military honors. This underscores the extent to which John Ford respects ritual and the sentiment attached to it. The same sort of sentiment appears shortly afterwards when at muster the men present Captain Brittles with a gift, "a brand new silver watch," as Brittles ironically refers to it. There is not a dry eye among the ladies witnessing this ceremony. But Ford perhaps went too far when he portrayed Captain Brittles at the grave of his wife and two daughters against a lurid red sunset that could only have been derived from the palette of Karl Wimar, the 1850s St. Louis painter. By now we know that this is definitely the end of something *we*, as well as Brittles, do not want to come to an end. On the other hand, when hoping to head off an Indian War, Captain Brittles and the heroic Southerner, Sergeant Tyree, visit the hostile Indian camp, we learn that retirement does not disturb old chief Pony-That-Walks one bit. "Too late, Natan, too late," he says in an immortal line, "We go fish and hunt buffalo together." The chief is prepared to melt into the glorious landscape and become part of nature. Captain Brittles refuses the old chief's eloquent offer and instead, in the few hours of command left him, leads his men in an attack on the village pony herd and the village that prevents an

Indian War. In Ford's terms, pacifism is no good. There is such a thing as a "good war," or, in the context of 1949, a "preventive attack."

Rio Grande, in which Wayne reverts to his role as Colonel York, is more of a domestic squabble. His son, Jeff, is initiated into the regiment with no favoritism shown by his father. Maureen O'Hara, as Kathleen, the Colonel's estranged wife, arrives to get *her,* not *their,* son out of the army. *Their* son, however, proves himself a hero. Colonel York is wounded while rescuing the garrison's children from the Indians, and Maureen O'Hara is reconciled to him with the strains of "I'll Take You Home Again Kathleen" sounding in the background, absurdly sung by a military quartet (The Sons of the Pioneers). This indicates not only the degree of Ford's Irish sentimentality, but also the way in which most of his films make effective use of familiar, clichéd and terribly sentimental songs such as "Kathleen," "She Wore a Yellow Ribbon," and "The Battle Hymn of the Republic." His use of music complements Ford's Catholic emphasis on the importance of ritual and honor, as well as his evocation and renewal, in terms of meaning, of very familiar paintings to key his scenes.

Most modern critics regard *The Searchers* (1956) as Ford's masterpiece because of its ambiguity and its use of nature as an even more central factor than it had previously been. Essentially the story of Confederate veteran Ethan Edward's (i.e., Ethan Allen, the Deist, and Jonathan Edwards, the staunch Puritan, combined) indefatigable five-year search for two nieces captured by the Comanche Chief, Scar, on the Texas frontier, which Ford still films in Monument Valley, it pits the savagery of one civilized man against the relative civilization of the so-called savage, Scar. True, Scar has horribly murdered Ethan Edwards' brother and sister-in-law, with whom Ethan was secretly in love, and has captured and driven to the point of madness some white women, but still Ford indicates a certain sympathy for Scar because of his love for the captured girl, Debbie (Natalie Wood), whom he has made one of his wives. The Texas Rangers attack Scar's village. Debbie's cousin, Martin Pawley (Jeffrey Hunter) rescues her from Scar's tepee. Then Ethan enters and savagely scalps Scar. He also chases the frightened Debbie to kill her because she has been soiled and "Indianized" by Scar. Will he actually kill Natalie Wood? Well—no. Instead, he picks her up in his arms in the most humane of gestures and gently carries her home. This is not Ford's plot. The movie is rather closely based on a long story by Alan LeMay that first appeared in *The Saturday Evening Post.* What seems to give the movie its profundity is the ending in which Ethan brings Debbie home to the Jorgensen Ranch, now his only home,

Harry Jackson, *The Marshal*, (John Wayne as Rooster Cogburn in *True Grit*. Harry Jackson, Wyoming Foundry Studios, Cody, Wyoming.

but then turns his back and, symbolically framed by the doorway, walks off to the desert and nowhere, a figure of the past whom the Civil War and the personal tragedy of the Indian massacre have made rootless and an obsolete savage, himself. He will vanish like the Indians. This is a far cry from Ford's earlier glorification of the cavalry in his trilogy. It casts forward to the non-violent messages of *The Man Who Shot Liberty Valance* (1962) and *Cheyenne Autumn* (1964).

John Ford's Western films are, however, the twentieth century equivalent of Frederic Remington's paintings. They resurrect the story of the Old West, the days of "men with the bark on" in such a way as to convince a generation and several American presidents that he was portraying, not only history, but the American character, as well as the glorious manifest destiny of a tough, but humane and sentimental, America. And in the character of John Wayne, he created a giant-sized hero who embodied these values of rugged, but decent, individualism. John Wayne's finest moment came, however, not in a John Ford picture, but in Henry Hathaway's *True Grit* (1969), which earned Wayne his only Academy Award.

In *True Grit*, some say Wayne played himself, but then he always did, in whatever movie he appeared. He became *sui generus*, and perhaps had *True Grit* not come along, he would have been best remembered as Captain Nathan Brittles with his "brand new silver watch." But the character of portly, one-eyed, hard-drinking Rooster Cogburn, as he charged single-handed, like a knight-errant of old, into a band of outlaws, made the association between man and character unforgettable. It was the epitome of tough, independent-minded honor and chivalry that the movie character John Wayne invariably portrayed, and with whom generations of Americans invariably identified. If he always played himself, by the same token he also played what millions deemed to be the quintessential American. Not only on the fragile celluloid of the movies does Rooster Cogburn as John Wayne ride, but he rides forever in the extraordinary painted bronze statue created by the sculptor, Harry Jackson. In fact, like some equestrian hero out of real life, who might adorn Central Park or the Washington, D. C. Mall, equestrian bronzes of John Wayne dominate the John Wayne Airport in Orange County, California, as well as previously mentioned Wilshire Boulevard, the latter courtesy of the Great Western Financial Corporation. You will find no similar statue of Texan movie star Audie Murphy, World War II's most decorated hero. Instead, we cast the legend which has become reality.

No discussion of the Western and history can quite end with John Ford and John Wayne, powerful mythmakers though they were. Somewhere between their era and the present, the Western died. Gradually it ceased to carry a clear message, and a kind of diffusion of meanings became attached to the Western, such that with the coming of the anti-hero Westerner in *McCabe and Mrs. Miller*, the bomb-loving Slim Pickins in *Dr. Strangelove*, and the new-style sky cavalryman, Robert Duval, in *Apocalypse Now*, a kind of moral entropy almost destroyed the Western.

Call the roll of television Westerns, for example, that once dominated the media and now are as dead as Bronco Billy: *Rawhide, Wagon Train, Gunsmoke, Wyatt Earp, The Rifleman, The Rebel, Bat Masterson, Sugarfoot, Maverick, Have Gun Will Travel, Nichols, Big Valley, High Chaparral,* and *Bonanza* (now only a steak house). The only television Western that remains is that saga of affluence and chicanery at "Southfork"—*Dallas,* and J. R. is a worldwide symbol of America, who takes us right back to that original British caricatured image of the shrewd, not quite honest, Yankee from backward America: Uncle Sam.

On the other hand, the announcement of the death of the Western, as

Mark Twain might have put it, is perhaps premature. During the straight-forward Western's slide toward oblivion, the work of one man, much concerned with moral ambiguities, kept the genre at least breathing. This was Sam Peckinpah, actually born in Fresno in 1925, but who claimed to be from Coarsegold, a mining town of 800 people high up in the Sierras, just under the shadow of Peckinpah Mountain. Sam Peckinpah learned the moviemaker's craft writing episodes of television's *The Rifleman*, starring Chuck Connors. His first feature movie, *The Deadly Companions* (1961), largely took place on a desert and was unremarkable. But in that same year, 1961, he also directed a new classic, *Ride the High Country,* that seemed to reflect the trend of the Western, if not the mood of the country. It was the elegaic story of two aging gunfighters, brilliantly played by Joel McCrea and Randolph Scott. The two gunfighters agree to go up into the high country to bring down a shipment of gold, for a price. One of them, a former sheriff, McCrea, intends to keep the bargain, while Scott, his partner, intends to make off with the gold. The story opens in a turn-of-the-century town down in the lowlands, where a young man riding a camel is constantly beating the town's fastest horsemen in races. It is time to get out of town, so he joins the two aging gunfighters.

Halfway up the mountain they meet a young woman and her fundamentalist father, whose house is covered with Biblical slogans he never in his mean spirit follows. The girl runs away and joins the gunfighters and their young protégé as they climb high up to Coarsegold. There she, dressed like the nineteenth century's Lotta Crabtree and riding a mule, gets married to one of several loutish brothers in a brothel. The wedding is a farce, and so is the marriage, as all the brothers feel they should share the bride. So the aging gunfighters, their young sidekick, and the girl take off down the mountain with the gold. Meantime Scott attempts to steal gold from McCrea. Halfway down they find the brothers have gotten ahead of them, killed the girl's father, and set up an ambush at her farm. A shootout takes place, the brothers are killed, but so is the honest Scott McCrae. Filled with remorse, while McCrea utters Peckinpah's father's favorite Biblical line, "I will go into my house justified," Scott declares he didn't mean to keep the gold anyway. McCrea responds, "Shucks I knew that."

Despite its simple plot, Peckinpah's *Ride the High Country* is replete with religious symbolism. But it wasn't nostalgia or even religion that kept the Western alive. It was violence. In 1969 Peckinpah made *The Wild Bunch,* starring William Holden, Warren Oates, Ben Johnson, and Ernest Borgnine as still another set of old gunfighters and border veterans who get caught up in the Mexican Revolution on the Diaz side in 1910. In perhaps the bloodiest, most violent Western of all time, if one excepts *Bonnie and Clyde,* the Wild Bunch is totally wiped out while trying to save a Mexican compadre, but in the process they destroy an entire town, killing, in a vivid manner, what looks to be half the Mexican army. The final killing scene lasts for nearly half-an-hour. *The Wild Bunch,* with its violence, during the height of the Vietnam protest movements, appealed to American youth like no other movie. It seemed to use the Western as a vehicle to symbolize the American presence in Vietnam in the persons of the Wild Bunch who destroyed, more than they helped the Mexican cause.

Possibly Peckinpah himself realized he had gone too far in other violent movies: *Straw Dogs,* wherein Dustin Hoffman in Cornwall does indeed demonstrate that, though his wife may be sodomized, at least his home is his castle, and the follow-up film, *Bring Me the Head of Alfredo Garcia,* starring Warren Oates, who romps through Mexico, carrying a smelly, fly-catching severed head in a sack.

But the violence-monger and arch symbolist, Peckinpah, redeemed himself with one lovely, gentle parable of a movie that chronicled the whole of Western experience, *The Ballad of Cable Hogue* (1969). Left to die in the southwestern desert between the town of Dead Dog and Lizard City, prospector Cable Hogue lasts out a sandstorm, finally gets down on his knees and prays to God, and consequently finds the only water for miles and miles around. In *The Ballad of Cable Hogue,* Peckinpah's sense of the fable, or rather, history as fable, reveals itself in extraordinary ways. Peckinpah himself declared, "*The Ballad of Cable Hogue* for me is an affirmation of life. It's about a man who found water where it wasn't. It's also about God."[12]

Once he finds water, Hogue, like an American Adam, begins to build his Eden out of scraps that fall from passing wagon trains. He also finds his Eve, a saloon girl named Hildy, elegantly played by Stella Stevens. But revenge against those who deserted him is always on his mind. A passing, lecherous preacher cannot talk him out of it. Neither can Hildy, who finally leaves him to seek a rich husband in San Francisco. But as Hogue sits beside the trail, all of the Western experience passes before him in epic fashion. To sustain himself he sings this song, which is one of three that structure the rhythm of the film:

> Let tomorrow be the song you sing
> And yesterday wont mean a thing

Make today your next day's dawn
And you'll still be here grinning when the
sun goes down.

This and the other songs, like the lilting love song, "Butterfly Morning,"
were composed by Richard Gilliss, whom Peckinpah found singing his own
songs in a bar and hired on the spot to compose the music for his picture.[13]

Some things went wrong on the location, which was Nevada's Valley of
Fire. Peckinpah fired 36 people, which brought about 119 Labor Relations
Board violations. He also imported some town prostitutes to the set, and the
whole company came down with V.D., which they euphemistically called
"Apple Valley fever."[14] But at last Cable Hogue gets his revenge on the two
men who left him to die in the desert. He kills one, and in the spirit of the
Good Book, forgives the other; in fact, he turns his whole Eden over to him
and is preparing to seek out Hildy when, like magic, up she drives in one of
the first automobiles ever seen in the West. Hildy, in fancy clothes, looks like
a butterfly as she races to Hogue. But alas, the car, clearly representing progress, runs over Hogue, and he dies. As he is dying he has his preacher friend
lay on a eulogy that could just as well be meant for the passing of the Western
pioneer:

> Cable Hogue was born into this world nobody knows when or where. He
> came stumbling out of the wilderness like a prophet of old. Out of the barren
> wastes he carved himself a one-man kingdom.
>
> Some said he was ruthless, but you could do worse, Lord, than take to your
> bosom Cable Hogue. He wasn't really a good man, he wasn't a bad man. But,
> Lord, he was a man! He charged too much, he was as stingy as they come. Yes,
> he might have cheated, but he was square about it. Rich or poor, he gouged them
> all the same. When Cable Hogue died, there wasn't an animal in the desert he
> didn't know, there wasn't a star in the firmament he hadn't named, there wasn't
> a man he was afraid of.
>
> Now the sand he fought and loved so long has covered him at last. Now he
> has gone into the whole torrent of the years, of souls that pass and never stop. In
> some ways he was your dim reflection, Lord; and right or wrong, I feel he is worth
> consideration. But if you feel he is not, you should know that Hogue lived and
> died here in the desert, and I'm sure Hell will never be too hot for him.
>
> He never went to church, he didn't need to. The whole desert was his
> cathedral. Hogue loved the desert, loved it deeper than he'd ever say. He built
> his empire, but was man enough to give it up for love when the time came. Lord,
> as the day draws toward evening, this life comes to an end for us all. We say

"adieu" to our friend. Take him, Lord, but knowing Cable, I suggest you do not take him lightly. Amen.[15]

And so, in a sense, with a few exceptions, the Western came to an end. As this is written, it shows signs of reviving. Though it no longer dominates the "silver screen," it seems to be alive and well in another guise. Has Cable Hogue come alive as a balladeer? Is the rage for "country and western" music, that created Houston's Gilley's, with its mechanical bulls, and Forth Worth's "Billy Bob's, the Largest Honky Tonk in the World," with its real bulls for singing "urban cowboys" to ride, a sign that the West and the "Western" thrives in a different form? Has the trail driver become the truck driver, his Mack Truck cap the new ten-gallon Stetson? Does the West live again in resurrected form in the personae of Jerry Jeff Walker, Emmy Lou Harris, Billy Joe and Waylon? And have Willie's heroes really "always been cowboys"? Are "cowboys *special*"? As representative Americans they seem to be.

Part Six

OTHER VOICES, OTHER WESTS

CHAPTER 28

ESCAPE TO TAOS

In the crystalline brilliance of an early September morning in 1898, a short, bespectacled rider, struggling to balance both himself and a broken wagon wheel atop his particularly obdurate mount, descended into the valley of Taos, New Mexico as if into a forgotten paradise.

> I started down the mountain on what resulted in the most impressive journey of my life. . . . The color, the reflective character of the landscape, the drama of the vast open spaces, the superb beauty and severity of the hills, stirred me deeply. I realized I was getting my own impressions from nature, seeing it for the first time, probably with my own eyes, uninfluenced by the art of any man. Notwithstanding the painful handicap of the broken wheel I was carrying, New Mexico inspired me to a profound degree.[1]

When Ernest Blumenschein packed up his newly fixed wagon wheel for his return journey to a stranded buckboard and an awaiting artist companion, Bert Geer Phillips, he had already decided to stake his artistic claim to this aesthetically virgin land.

353

In the course of the next thirty years, due to his efforts and those of a circle of artist comrades who came to New Mexico in the wake of his "discovery," the remote hamlet of Taos, where time stood still and life seemed as fresh and as simple as it might have been a thousand years ago, would become yet another version of the West of the imagination: a West that had little to do with cowboys or thunderstorms in the Rockies, but a terrain that nonetheless became as profoundly mythical as any Western dream that had preceded it.

Phillips and Blumenschein, friends from their art school days at the Paris Académie Julian, had taken a vacation from their work as studio artists in New York to seek new material. They had traveled southward from Denver on a buckboard painting tour of the West that ended with a broken wheel on the steep precipice of a mountain road just north of the Taos valley.

The inspiration for their quest had been the vivid tales of a previous visitor to New Mexico, a fellow student at the Académie Julian, Joseph Henry Sharp. Sharp, an accomplished illustrator who had come to Paris to hone his skills at painting, entertained his fellow American students with stories and sketches of the pueblo country which he had visited while on commission for *Harper's Weekly* two years previously in 1893. The stories of exotic Indian dances and stark desert scenery seemed infinitely more interesting than what Blumenschein remembered as, "the hackneyed subject matter of thousands of painters . . . lady in negligée reclining on a sumptuous divan; lady gazing in a mirror; lady powdering her nose; etc., etc.,"[2] which the Académie instructors forced upon their students. Four American graduates of the Académie Julian, Ernest L. Blumenschein, Joseph Henry Sharp, Bert Geer Phillips and Eanger Irving Couse would become the nucleus of the Taos art colony, a colony which, one may argue, lives on to this day.

From Blumenschein and Phillips who were later joined by Sharp and Couse, the New Mexico art colonies of Taos and Santa Fe grew in ever-widening circles to include some of the most famous artists, writers, composers and photographers of the early twentieth century. The group included John Sloan, Robert Henri, Andrew Dasburg, Georgia O'Keeffe, D. H. Lawrence, Mary Austin, Paul Strand, Leopold Stokowski and many others whose vision and talents helped shape the culture of the twentieth century.

A number of the original Taos artists, like Ernest Blumenschein, spent their winters in New York or Chicago teaching, illustrating and painting, saving their money to rent a picturesque adobe house on the outskirts of Taos during the summers which were spent roughing it with no running water, or other

conveniences. They freed themselves from the trappings of civilization, if only for a few months of the year. Life in the West agreed with them; the rural delights of New Mexico were pleasantly and inspiringly foreign, a stimulus to creative work. Riding through the sage, packing their paints up in saddlebags and heading for the mountains, setting up their easels on the rooftops of ancient pueblos, the painters adopted Taos as a kind of Western Walden Pond, just far enough from civilization to inspire the aesthetic appreciation of wilderness.

New Mexico loosened their palettes and inspired freer compositions. They revelled in impressionistic images of piñon and sage on the remote flanks of a New Mexico hill, the vibration of blue-purple shadows against the tawny walls of adobe architecture. Even the native costumes inspired exuberant patterns of color in works such as Sharp's *Sunset Dance—Ceremony to the Evening Sun*, a painting in which all of the attributes that attracted the artists to New Mexico are structured into a series of receding planes, beginning with the ethnographic present—Indians clustered around the courtyard—to the Christian

Joseph Henry Sharp, *Sunset Dance—Ceremony to the Evening Sun*. Berry-Hill Galleries, New York.

Bert Geer Phillips, *Broken Wagon, September 4,* 1898. The "Broken Wheel," near Taos, New Mexico. Ernest L. Blumenschein and Bert Phillips. Courtesy Museum of New Mexico.

church, from which the artist leads the viewer back through time, as well as space, to the traditional Taos pueblo and plaza, where native ceremonies have been held for five centuries, and finally to the swell of the mountains beyond— hills which protect the sacred blue lake of the Taos Indians—their traditional source of life and rejuvenation. Above all is the constantly changing and evolving New Mexico sky, with the warm brilliance that inspired Blumenschein.

The New Mexico painters, and the other artists who shared their inspiration, became the prime translators of a rarefied Western experience which saw the environment and its peoples through eyes nurtured by the highest level of artistic training, and minds enriched by everything from revolutionary socialist politics, to the literature of D.H. Lawrence. With few exceptions, their's was not an art directed at the popular media, to be published as illustrations in *The Saturday Evening Post* and *Collier's;* they came to Taos to leave their mark on the art world of New York, Chicago, Paris and London.

Taos Society of Artists on Couse's Porch, (c. 1915–16). The Thomas Gilcrease Institute of American History and Art, Tulsa.

Left to right: Bert Phillips, Herbert Dunton, Joseph Henry Sharp, Oscar E. Berninghaus, E. Irving Couse, Ernest L. Blumenschein.

Anonymous, *Bert Geer Phillips Painting Indian Girl in Studio*. Museum of New Mexico, Santa Fe.

The Taos Society of Artists first met in 1915: a group of six painters, who had been working together on and off since Blumenschein first rode into the Taos Valley. In their charter, they expressed the intention of "bringing before the public through exhibition and other means, tangible results of the work of its members."[3] It was an alliance among a cadre of artists in order to get their work exhibited and accepted, and it was a closed organization. To become a member required three years work in Taos, proposal by two members, and, originally, a unanimous vote of the society.

For several of the Taos artists the essence of the Western experience was the contemplation of the American Indian. In numerous works by Couse, Sharp and Phillips, one finds the Native American stripped of the trappings of white culture. In these depictions of idealized, handsome models (one is tempted to say specimens), we see the painter's quest for the ideal image of "Indianness." No matter that the noble savage was a theme thoroughly explored by previous generations of artists. Sharp and Couse both believed that they had no higher calling than to document, and at times recreate the fleeting vestiges of man in his natural state.

In Sharp's *A Corner of My Studio in Taos* the viewer can sense the gravity of the artist's mission. Sharp stares forth from his mirror with an intent gaze that fixes both the viewer and the Indian models, who are posed, silent and still, at the opposite end of the room. Sharp's studio was his personal ethnographic laboratory, where Indians could be made to wear traditional clothing and simulate traditional tasks. The products of these ethnographic sessions, such as his untitled picture of two seated Indians with drums, reveal figures posed with the grim stiffness of a photographic subject, as if the long process

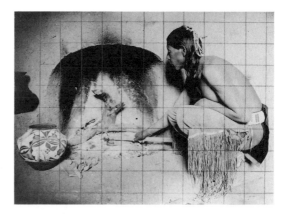

Anonymous, *Ben Lujan Posing for Couse (With Grid)*, (1917). Couse Family Archives, Couse Enterprises, Ltd.

of exactly recording the pose robbed the scene of any genuine vitality.

Sharp's studio abutted the house of Eanger Irving Couse, whose interest in the Native American subject was no less intense. In Couse's hands Indian culture became a romanticized, perhaps even nostalgic, reverie. In an untitled painting showing an Indian with a red blanket the Indian model is rendered with a sensuousness reminiscent of the erotic salon nudes of his teacher and mentor at the Académie Julian, William Adolphe Bouguereau. Yet, in contrast to the classic nymphs and acadian pastorales which dominated his teacher's work, Couse adopted the American Indian as a symbol of lost innocence and natural eroticism. Couse rarely departed from the classical mode of study-

E. Irving Couse, *The Drummer.* Museum of Western Art, Denver. Photographer: James Milmoe.

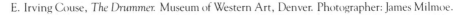

Joseph Henry Sharp, *The Bow and Arrow Maker.* Courtesy the Gerald Peters Gallery, Santa Fe.

ing and rendering his subjects. In a photograph of the artist in his studio, Couse uses a gridded frame to analyze the figure as if a rational framework could provide some insight into the mystery of Native American consciousness.

Couse and Sharp not only shared a common wall, they shared Indian models, such as Ben Lujan and Jerry and Jim Mirabal, who became the primary actors in the romantic tableaux of the noble savage promulgated by both artists. Rather than casting them in heroic dramas, Sharp and Couse preferred to depict the Indians engaged in everyday tasks. The squatting figures, absorbed in such traditional activities as fire-starting, arrowmaking and weaving, became popular subjects; in fact, Couse's paintings were widely reproduced on Santa Fe Railroad calendars and posters. While both artists were interested in the ethnographic past, the world of the Indian before the white man, the native American in traditional dress, doing traditional tasks, Irving Couse's paintings went beyond Sharp's in their attempt to take the viewer deep into the mind if not the soul of the red man. Couse removed the Indian to an idealized domain, where the figures were illuminated by the flickering, primal light of the hearth: a technique which created a compelling, nearly mythical world.

The extent to which the original members of the Taos society of Artists were interested in preserving the vestiges of Native American culture is revealed by their expressed intention to promote, among other things, "ethnology and archaeology, solely as it pertains to New Mexico and the states adjoining."[4] Indeed, New Mexico at that time was becoming an archaeological, as well as an artistic, paradise. In the wake of the dramatic discoveries of cliff dwellings by Adolph Bandolier, and Richard Wetherill's excavation of the immense, multi-storied Pueblo Bonito in Chaco Canyon, archaeologists such as Edgar Lee Hewett, founder and director of the Museum of New Mexico in Santa Fe, had begun surveys and excavations in the hope of reconstructing the prehistoric continuum. Although earlier research had focused upon the dramatic architecture of the ancient Southwest peoples, later scientific investigations into common objects of prehistoric life caused the ancient cultures to be delineated by terms such as "Basketmaker I, II, III and IV," which identified a series of ancient cultural horizons across the far Southwest. This focus upon the prehistoric activities of daily life manifested itself as much in the paintings of Eanger Irving Couse as it did in the reports of the School of American Archaeology (now the School of American Research) in Santa Fe, which was founded in 1907 by Hewett. Couse's paintings thus suggest more than a passing familiarity with the work of his contemporaries in archaeology.

The other Taos artists did not need to dress their models in Indian garb and paint them in the studio. Native American culture was alive and teeming all around them. The Taos Pueblo, a scant three miles north of town had been continuously inhabited in the traditional manner since the fourteenth century. The Taosenos, although Christianized by the Spanish, still celebrated the annual cycle of ceremonies: the Green Corn Dance and Rabbit hunt, Deer Dance, Turtle Dance. At these moments, it was not the artist, but the Indian who was in control. One of the early Taos artists, Oscar Berninghaus was particularly intrigued by the Indian Rabbit Hunt, and, in his swirling paintings of the ceremonial chase across the desert, the viewer feels the artist caught up in spirited movement, unwilling and unable to freeze the subjects for painstaking study.

The magnificent pageantry of the pueblo ceremonial dances inspired particularly daring compositions. In *Moon, Morning Star, Evening Star* by Blumenschein, the viewer seems to stand, with the artist, on the flat roof of an adobe pueblo, overlooking a plaza filled with the moving, costumed forms of the celebrants, some dressed in the spreading antlers of the deer, as if living representatives of a paleolithic cave painting. All bow for a moment in deference

Bert Geer Phillips, *Penitente Burial Procession.* The
Thomas Gilcrease Insti-
tute of American History
and Art, Tulsa.

to a sole figure standing amid the fruits of sacrifice, who raises his face and
breathes smoke toward the rising sun. At the top of the painting looms a
celestial icon as real, for a spellbinding instant, to artist and viewer as it is to
the Indian believers. At the bottom of the picture, their hands clasped in
Christian prayer, a minority of the worshippers kneel before the tabernacle of
the saint whose nominal feast day marks the dance's occasion.

Other Taos and Santa Fe artists also seemed at their best depicting the
Indian and Hispanic ceremonies. In *Penitente Burial Procession* Phillips explored
the scene before him with somber expressionism. One is tempted to believe
that the artists, absorbed by the powerful emotion and sacred energies of these
ceremonies, temporarily suspended their trained objectivity in favor of a generous expressionism that moved in sympathetic rhythm to the peoples they
observed. The carefully receding planes of three-point perspective were par-
tially abandoned, and exhuberant patterns of color, figures and costumes took
its place. Yet, despite the liberties they took in their paintings of native ceremonies, the inability of this first generation of Taos and Santa Fe artists to
abandon the narrative, figurative and documentary modes left a true understanding of the primitive hopelessly beyond their grasp. For primitive Indian
art was one of abstraction and symbol, not representation. Of all of the early
Taos artists, only Ernest Blumenschein seemed to grasp this. In such paintings
as his *Sangre de Christo Mountains* of 1924, Blumenschein painted a representational scene, but the composition as a whole was dominated by an abstract
design: two cylindrical mountains cut by the slash of a snow-covered village.
In *Moon, Morning Star, Evening Star,* the abstract design of the painting was

Ernest L. Blumenschein, *Moon, Morning Star, Evening Star.* The Thomas Gilcrease Institute of American History and Art, Tulsa.

Ernest Blumenschein, *Sangre de Christo Mountains.* The Anschutz Collection, Denver.

Ernest Blumenschein, *Ourselves and Taos Neighbors*. Stark Museum of Art, Orange, Texas.

Walter Ufer, *Hunger*. The Thomas Gilcrease Institute of American History and Art, Tulsa.

an oval, topped by the sacred circle. Because he spread his paint on with a thick impasto, the abstraction that underlay his work could easily be missed at first glance, but it was there all the same. Alexandre Hogue wrote of Blumenschein's work:

> To enjoy [the overall decorative design] of a Blumenschein we must forget subject matter and revel in fantastic shapes and harmonious color. The Indian understands these attributes far better than our own people, who are too often prone

to order their art tempered with the ignorance that calls for a photographic slav-ery to the details of nature.[5]

In the latter phrases of this statement, Hogue could have been talking about the representational art of Sharp, Couse and Berninghaus, or the "pretty" hollihock pictures of Bert Geer Phillips. The Taos Society of Artists was hardly united in its approach to art. But Hogue had written to praise Blumenschein, not to bury Sharp, Couse and Berninghaus—or so it would seem.

While Couse and Sharp, and to a lesser extent Berninghaus and Phillips, tried to capture Indian life in representational forms, either by conjuring up dim visions of the past, or by making do with the genuine fragments of the present, other Taos artists found the layering of cultures in the small New Mexico community more interesting.

Walter Ufer took exception to the patronizing and overly romanticized Indian paintings by his fellow Taos artists which depicted the native American as "a curiosity—a dingleberry on a tree."[6] He felt that the real story to tell in his art was the constant process of adaptation and assimilation which he saw before him in Taos. He felt the Indian was crushed by the onslaught of Spanish Christianity and then by a mechanized American culture. Ufer observed, "The Indian has lost his race pride. He wants only to be an American. Our civili-zation has terrific power. We don't feel it, but that man out there in the mountains feels it, cannot cope with the pressure."[7]

Ufer's cynicism about the degradation of the Indian through cultural assim-ilation is often concealed by his aesthetic sophistication. If Couse and Sharp painted in an academic, if somewhat unimaginative style, Ufer was a genu-inely innovative artist. *Hunger* shows an Indian family imploring a Spanish crucifix to relieve their hunger—a hunger perhaps brought by the Spanish class system which relegated the Indian to poverty. Ufer's bold patterns and daring cropping of the foreground figures emphasizes the drama of the subject. Ufer, a Chicagoan who came to Taos in 1914, held firm socialist convictions. Not only was he a member of the Industrial Workers of the World (IWW), but he was a host to Trotsky during the Russian revolutionary's brief visit to the Southwest, en route to Mexico.

Ernest Blumenschein, though less politically motivated, was equally fasci-nated by the social and cultural inequalities he found around him. His explo-ration of these themes became one of the most famous paintings produced by the Taos Society. *Jury for a Trial of a Sheepherder for Murder* (1936) depicts the polling of a jury composed of Hispanic men, who have just convicted a young man of their own class—a shepherd—of second-degree murder. The decision had been particularly painful, for the young defendant, a member of the penitente society to which some of the jurors belonged, had been surprised by a hiker who stumbled upon him in the mountains. In a more traditional society, the crime might have gone unpunished. Tried in an Anglo court, under U.S. law, the jury had to condemn him. Blumenschein's powerful composition, his insightful portraits of the jurors, and the mysterious details—such as George Washington, depicted as blind justice at the top, as well as a lurking, spectacled figure in the background—make it a haunting image, reinforced by a powerful abstract composition which imprisons all, jury and sheepherder in a cubelike cell. Published in *Time* magazine, the painting became emblematic of the newly emerging identity of Taos as a crucible of a new strain of American Art. Ufer voiced a belief that many of the Taos artists shared: "I believe that if America gets a national art, it will come more from the Southwest than from the Atlantic Board. . . . Gradually, and with the Indian here, I believe we can give much to American Art in the future."[8]

Unfortunately for these Southwest revolutionaries, the artistic battles they were fighting had, for the most part, already been won in Europe by such artists as Vincent Van Gogh, Henri Rousseau, Paul Gauguin and Henri Matisse. The Taos artists stressed fundamental principals of good figurative painting: dynamic composition, color and form. Blumenschein urged his students to "Ask yourself when contemplating your work: are the masses large? Is your design vigorous? Are your proportions or spaces beautiful in their relations?"[9]

He also seems invariably to ask: Does the work have a philosophical or psychological underpinning, as in *Jury for a Trial of a Sheepherder?* Blumenschein's rules and broad primitive masses of color, like Van Gogh's, represented a stage on the road to abstraction. Few of his Taos neighbors got the message. Perhaps the only artists to absorb his lessons were the dapper sophisticate Victor Higgins, who lived at the other end of town, and Herbert "Buck" Dunton, a student of Blumenschein's at the Art Student's League, who had moved to Taos at his teacher's suggestion in 1912. In daring compositions by Dunton, such as *Sunset in the Foothills* (currently in the collection of the Stark Museum in Orange, Texas) we see the echoes of the master. The strong, almost abstract, pattern of sage and piñon against the New Mexico soil dominates the subject in a perspective which has been tipped to nearly an aerial view. The thick, fluid impasto lends the image a presence and monumentality similar to the canvases of his teacher who urged formal discipline, not philosophical principles.

The first generation of Taos artists—Blumenschein, Phillips, Sharp, Couse,

Ernest Blumenschein, *Jury for Trial of a Sheepherder for Murder,* (1936). Museum of Western Art, Denver. Photography by James Milmoe.

Berninghaus, Dunton, Ufer and Victor Higgins—often referred to as "Los Ochos Peintures," enjoyed extraordinary success as a result of their work in the Southwest. For several of them, the primary goal of achieving recognition as artists, not merely illustrators, had been reached. In the first three decades of the twentieth century, their paintings were shown in the most prestigious institutions and exhibitions in the country, indeed, in the world: from The Art Institute of Chicago to the Venice Biennale. Several of the original Taos artists became members of the National Academy; more than one received the Logan Award from the Grand Central Galleries. For example, in 1929 it was awarded to Blumenschein for *Adobe Village Winter.*

These Taos artists were successful in another respect: in their paintings of Indian culture they had extended the myth of the primitive to the native peoples of the Southwest, evoking a subtle influential image and demonstrat-

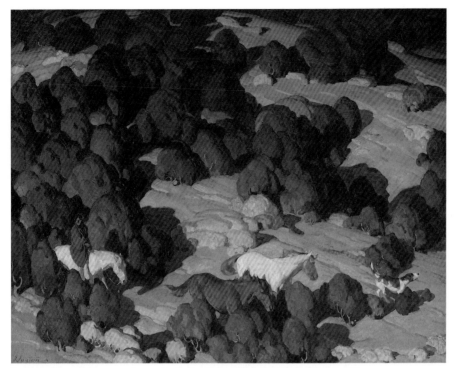

Herbert "Buck" Dunton, *Sunset in the Foothills*. Nelda C. Stark, Orange, Texas.

ing to their peers in the art world that the mind and soul of the primitive were both present—indeed accessible—to the artist who made the pilgrimage to Taos. To a particular circle of intellectuals and literati in New York, disillusioned with modern, industrial society, and stimulated by the writings of Freud and Jung, which stressed modern man's need to rediscover his primal self, the lure of New Mexico was irresistible.

CHAPTER **29**

LEFT BANK ON
THE RIO HONDO

Mabel Dodge, the "Bohemian Queen" of Greenwich Village, political activist, radical columnist, free-thinker, Freudian advocate and pioneer
supporter of birth control, held some of the most famous avant-garde soirées
of the pre-war era in her apartment on lower Fifth Avenue. She numbered
among her friends, Gertrude and Leo Stein, John Reed, Walter Lippmann,
Max Eastman and Lincoln Steffens, Andrew Dasburg, Alfred Steiglitz and
Georgia O'Keeffe. In 1913, she had been an active sponsor of the Armory
Show, which shocked the world of American art by introducing it to abstraction.

Yet, by 1917, Mabel Dodge felt she had tired of the world of the "movers
and shakers," a world of her own making. She declared:

> Little by little I ceased to attend meetings that required my presence as an influ-
> ence for change. I just lost interest in that fabricated puppet, Mabel Dodge, as a
> creature of importance for her Time, and I longed only for peace and more peace.[1]

Strangely, she found that peace in the dark, primal paintings of Eanger
Irving Couse, which she had seen exhibited in New York. A devotee of every

artistic principal that rejected the romantic figurative tradition in which Couse
painted, Mabel Dodge was not inspired so much by his painting, but by the
simple, primordial world that it implied. For the rest of her life, E. Irving
Couse's fiction, a product of Bouguereau's Parisian training, and the rational
grid of realism, became her reality.

Mabel Dodge visited Taos in 1917 with her artist husband Maurice Stern.
While he had come for aesthetic inspiration, she had come for spiritual rejuvenation. She found it in the person of Tony Luhan, a Taos Indian who
assisted her in her quest for "the power of the mystic." Mabel, who claimed to
have seen Luhan's face in a dream vision before they met, became a frequent
visitor to his home in the Taos pueblo. She would sit with him for hours,
watching him squatting before the adobe hearth, performing the daily routines
of Pueblo life—E. Irving Couse's painting's incarnate. But unlike Couse, Mabel
sought not simply to observe the world of the Indian, but to embrace it. She
took Tony Luhan as a lover, and eventually a husband, casting aside Maurice
Stern and her Greenwich Village persona to give herself fully to the world of
Taos. She remembered: "My life broke in two right then, and I entered the
second half, a new world that replaced all the ways I had known with others,
more strange and terrible and sweet than any I had ever been able to imagine."[2] Rather than enter the world of the Indian, she removed Tony Luhan
from it. Together they oversaw the construction of Mabel's Taos mansion: an
eclectic adobe and wood structure that took the step-wise, mountainous massing of the pueblo and fractured it into an entertaining variety of arbors, porches,
picture windows and decorative screens, topped off by a majestic adobe and
glass cupola with a 360-degree view. All around their mini-pueblo were dove

*Big House, Los Gallos, Taos, (Mabel
Dodge Luhan's Taos House)*, Beinecke
Library, Yale University.

Victor Higgins, *Daisy Mirabal,*
(1931), Los Angeles Athletic Club
Art Collection.

Andrew Dasburg, *New Mexican Village,* (1926). Collection of Museum of Fine Arts,
Museum of New Mexico, Santa Fe.

Raymond Jonson, *Earth Rhythms*, (1925). The Jonson Gallery of the University of New Mexico, Albuquerque, New Mexico.

cotes on high poles signifying her new love of gentleness and nature. The "Big House" as it was called, became the new center of her cosmos, and the capital of Mabeltown.

Despite her mystical communion with the primitive world, and the shedding of the husk of her activist life, Mabel Dodge succeeded in moving a large part of her Greenwich Village salon to Taos, and with it, the seeds of expressionism, cubism and abstraction that eventually came to dominate the New Mexico art scene. She became a channel of modernist force. It was not enough to simply experience the joys of primitivism herself, she felt compelled to introduce it to others as well.

Her most famous convert to New Mexico primitivism was novelist D. H. Lawrence. She drew Lawrence to her, convinced that he alone had an intuitive understanding of the Indian spirit, and that, once in Taos he could communicate his experience through literature. She later wrote in her account of Lawrence's New Mexico sojourn, *Lorenzo in Taos* (1932):

> Of course it was for this I had called him from across the world—to give him the truth about America: the false, new, external America in the east, and the true,

primordial, undiscovered America that was preserved, living, in the Indian bloodstream.[3]

Lawrence and his wife Frieda arrived at the train station in Lamy, New Mexico, on a September day in 1922. They were met by Mabel and Tony Luhan who had taken to dressing in expensive riding pants and driving the motorcar in daredevil fashion down the dusty, New Mexico roads. The Lawrences were whisked off to their first Indian experience, perhaps not quite the sort that Mabel would have wished. Walking to an Indian village late at night, wrapped in a Mexican blanket, his spirit acutely sensitive to the powerful cultural differences which separated him from the Indians, Lawrence stood outside of a kiva, unwilling to enter, satisfied simply to observe his own emotional response. Lawrence later described the encounter in "Indians and an Englishman":

> I shall never forget that first evening when I first came into contact with the Red Man, away in Apache country . . . it was something of a shock. Again something in my soul broke down, letting in a bitter dark, a pungeant awakening to the lost past, old darkness, new terror, new root-griefs, old root-richnesses.[4]

Like Mabel, he immediately felt the fundamental ancient kinship with tribal man. Unlike her, he believed one could never leap the gap. His essay continues:

> I do not want to live again the tribal mysteries my blood has lived long since. I don't want to know as I have known in tribal exclusiveness . . . I stand on the far edge of their fire light, and am neither denied nor accepted. My way is my own, old red father. I can't cluster at the drum any more.[5]

Mabel Dodge, so eager to dominate, influence and channel the creations of the artists around her own campfire, had built Lawrence and Frieda a small, pink adobe house across the open field from the Big House, close enough so that Lawrence and she might collaborate on the great New Mexican novel. But not even that distance could prevent the inevitable clash of strong personalities. Lawrence regarded Mabel's attempts to prove the mystic as somewhat foolish. He wrote:

> White Americans do try hard to intellectualize themselves. Especially white women Americans. And the latest stunt is this "savage" stunt again. White savages, with motor-cars, telephones, incomes and ideals! Savages fast inside the machine; yet savage enough, ye gods![6]

Mabel was on the cutting edge of the emerging cult of the primitive, which had only recently seized upon the creations of a virtually illiterate Spanish painter, Pablo Picasso, who himself sensed the expressive potential of African and Oceanic masks to characterize society's deep-seated relationship to tribal man. Yet Lawrence was ultimately more interested in the fundamental energies and motivations of modern man, whose soul had to somehow accommodate the complexities of contemporary culture, than he was in the spirit of the primitive, which he understood, but which he refused to try and share. It was modern man whom Lawrence bared in his indulgently fleshy paintings illustrating his notorious novel, *Lady Chatterly's Lover,* that were exhibited and then banned in London in 1929. The small field that separated Mabel's Big House from the small pink adobe guest cottage where Lawrence resided had become a force field of intense wills, charged with the resistance of two conflicting notions of modern man and the primitive, and enhanced by emerging sexual jealousies. Frieda Lawrence took steps to prevent the intellectual and physical seduction of her husband which she sensed was in the making the moment they arrived in Taos. She and Lawrence departed in late autumn for a small ranch, deep in the New Mexico hills, where they spent the frigid winter in close contact with nature.

With Andrew Dasburg's arrival in Taos in 1918, at Mabel Dodge's invitation, the first generation of painters, with their dreams of pioneering a uniquely American Art, became distinctly "old guard." Dasburg, an American with cubist, futurist and synchromist tendencies picked up while studying in Paris during the early part of this century, had been one of the radical new artists to exhibit in the 1913 Armory Show.

His paintings fractured the landscape and architecture of New Mexico into Cezannelike compositions, reducing the romantic draughts of space to crisp, interwoven surface planes that wriggled before the eye across the canvas. The same shadows of the pueblo architecture, once lustrously rendered in impressionist blues and purples by Sharp and Blumenschein, became mere prismatic angles in Dasburg's work, useful for creating optical cubist effects. The magnificent Sangre de Christo Range, that had inspired Blumenschein on his first descent into the Taos Valley was reduced by Dasburg's brush to a mass of seething paramecia that denied the timeless quietude of the landscape and replaced it with an expression of the artist's own jazz-like sense of rhythm.

Most of the Taos Society painters were horrified, but one of them, Victor Higgins, was inspired. Rare in his ability to absorb, experiment with, and translate new aesthetic styles, Higgins seized the new visual language that Dasburg and later modernist visitors to Taos offered, and used it expressively. His *Indian Composition* juxtaposes the sensual, rounded nude form of an Indian woman with the vibrant, geometric background of a cubist setting: an impossibly exploded chair, and overlapping planes of rugs and blankets which, by extending behind and below the figure at once, serve to deny any three dimensional reality except the absorbing curves of the figure. In Higgins's painting we see two worlds in collision: the romantic image of the Indian created by the pioneer artists of Taos and represented by the central figure, and the cubistic fusion of both space and time, imported by Andrew Dasburg, represented by the wildly patterned background.

Raymond Johnson, another of the modernists, used an overtly musical metaphor as the basis for his New Mexico paintings. Johnson, a proponent of Wassily Kandinsky's theories about art and psychology, proclaimed of the new modern tradition: "It is the subconscious mind speaking through the conscious that we want." His *Earth Rhythms* series, painted in the early 1920s, analyzes the New Mexico land forms with a surrealistic formula that treats the swell and circumference of each hill as the basis for a visual improvisation that rhythmically celebrates the land as an assembly of shapes, not space. Indeed the nearly claustrophobic composition seems fundamentally opposed to the vast expansiveness of New Mexico, as if the artist had exposed his subconscious to the viewer, only to reveal a discomforting, compulsive imagination.

John Marin, who painted in New Mexico during the summers of 1929 and

W.W. Newcomb, *Indian Rock Art of Texas*, (1967) University of Texas Press, Austin, Texas.

John Marin, *Canyon of the Hondo, New Mexico*, (1930). Denver, Colorado. The Anshutz Collection,

Marsden Hartley, *New Mexico Recollection*, (1922–23), Archer M. Huntington Art Museum, The University of Texas at Austin. Lent by James and Mari Michener.

1930, was perhaps less rigid than Raymond Johnson in his desire to apply modernist iconography to the Southwestern landscape. He was more akin to D. H. Lawrence in his intuitive understanding of the Indian perspective. In *Near Taos—New Mexico* he exploded the conventional view of the plains and mountains outside of Taos, adopting a format that points to the four corners of the Indian cosmos, and centering the picture upon the sacred mountains. The dashing, diagonal strokes deny the illusion of depth, and instead reinforce the importance of the surface. The paper itself has become the site of a ritual act, not unlike the sacred sand paintings of the Southwest tribes, which are likewise often framed with abstract directional motifs.

Marsden Hartley, the cerebral theorist of the American modernist movement, appeared in New Mexico in 1919, stalking the streets of Santa Fe in a dark, dramatic fedora. He affected the crude, naive brushstrokes of the Fauvists to paint his version of the stark desert scenery. Like many of the New Mexico artists, chief among them John Sloan who organized the first major exhibition of Indian art as art, not cultural artifact, Hartley was intrigued by the similarities and differences between the modernist vision and the primitive vision, a topic on which he published an article in 1922 entitled "The Scientific Aesthetic of the Red Man."

The modernists had shifted their attention from the people of New Mexico to its landscape; however, by this time, the landscape was no longer the *subject* of their focus, but a point of conceptual departure for their forays into abstraction. The place and its people no longer fascinated the aesthetes of Taos and Santa Fe, they became more intrigued with documenting personal experience. Indeed, Stuart Davis, who had come to Santa Fe at John Sloan's urging in 1923, twenty-five years after Ernest Blumenschein's first exhuberant enchantment with New Mexico, declared that he found nothing there to paint. Instead he went back home and devoted himself to abstractly painting a machine, an eggbeater, over and over again until he got it right.

For all of the admiration the original artists of Taos had for native art, and for all the love they had of the natural surroundings of Taos, they remained only observers of the world of the primitive. Although they were avid collectors, they did not understand and embrace its fundamental lessons of native American art; its patterns, its starkly planar forms. The later abstract artists that came to Taos did. Like Mabel Dodge, who married into the Indian world rather than being content to observe it, painters such as John Marin, Marsden Hartley and Victor Higgins embraced the elemental principals of an art which denied conventions of time and space, and reduced the visual world to notational motifs orchestrated into bold pattern.

By attracting a circle of artists, writers and literati, Mabel Dodge had created "an oasis of 20th century culture in a vast desert of primitive nature"— perhaps not her original intent. Instead of getting away from it all, she had brought it all with her. Altering the peaceful world of "Los Ochos Peintures," she became the director of a modernist drama, in which the players sought to probe with her beneath the surfaces of reality to discover fundamental truths. Taos, she wrote:

> is the setting that can still in us the confusion that so often gathers there. Taos has the quality of a place in which to . . . find God. In Taos, one could create the condition, the form of discipline that is the tuning of an instrument of harmony which we must be to find ourselves, the power of the mystic.[7]

It may have been, as Lawrence insisted, a "comic opera played with solemn intensity," but it was a fertile setting for the development and evolution of a profoundly influential tradition in American art which brought the myth of the American West from the setting for the noble savage to an image of a homeland of heightened aesthetic awareness, where the landscape is itself so beautiful that for the artist (as Georgia O'Keeffe once declared), "half your work is done for you."[8]

CHAPTER 30

WHAT HAVE YOU DONE
WITH YOUR LAND

Just as the Taos Modernists began to ignore the surface contours of the land, so, too, did the inhabitants of the Great Plains, that vast prairie ocean that had once belonged to the Indian, then the cowboy. By the twentieth century, from the bleak Dakotas to the plains of West Texas it had become the domain of the sod-buster and the agri-businessman, whose army of tanklike tractors and combines was annually turning "the sea of grass" into millions of rows of seed-implanted dirt that would become dust in a little more than a decade.

In imagining the West, we sometimes forget that, after the Indian, the cowboy, and the buffalo had pretty much gone, the farmer became its characteristic citizen. He fit right in with what Henry Nash Smith, in his important book, *Virgin Land,* called "the myth of the yeoman farmer" with his "sacred plow" and his naive belief that "rain followed the plow."[1] As the sturdy yeoman, the Western farmer at the turn of the century was merely an extension of an agrarian myth that had held America in its grip since the days of Thomas Jefferson. Just as Jefferson envisaged the sturdy yeoman on his independent, fee-simple, family-owned farm as the backbone of democracy, so, too, did

377

Thomas Hart Benton, *Boomtown*, (1928). Memorial Art Gallery of the University of Rochester. Marion Stratton Gould Fund.

Thomas Hart Benton, *Cattle-Loading in West Texas*, (1930). Addison Gallery of American Art, Phillips Academy, Andover, Massachusetts.

most Americans in the first decade of the twentieth century, despite the fact that just at this time the country was turning demographically into an urban nation.

In the public mind the sturdy yeoman, who moved with his family out onto the Great Plains, was still another in the sequence of heroic pioneers who had made America great in comparison to all other nations. And, mesmerized by railroad and real estate promoters, the public at large, and the yeoman farmers in particular, looked upon the plains, with its rich soil, as a kind of American Eden, where both virtue and riches abounded. People moved by the thousands onto the plains in a steady march of "progress" that dwarfed the Oklahoma land rush of 1889, with its "Sooners" engaged in a mad dash for Indian lands.

In the beginning, armed with barbed wire, windmills, and a superficial knowledge of dry-farming techniques, plus the aid of a wet cycle, the yeoman had phenomenally good years. These lasted through World War I when, as far as they were concerned, it was high plains wheat that won the war. For over thirty years the yeoman expanded his operations, mechanizing more and more, borrowing more and more, and moving out into the land of little rain beyond the 100th meridian, a population shift that Major John Wesley Powell, head of the U. S. Geological Survey, had warned against as long ago as 1879, when he published his book, *Report on the Lands of the Arid Regions of the United States.*

As this movement, ever westward into the high plains, took place, the myth of the West, the tale of the tribe, changed. The cowboy became the gunfighter and badman—like Trampas in Owen Wister's archetypal Western novel, *The Virginian* (1902)—while the little man, the yeoman with his family and the accoutrements of fixed civilization, became the hero. The motion pictures just coming into vogue dwelt on this topic from *Hell's Hinges* in 1916 to *Shane* and Michael Cimeno's box office disaster, *Heaven's Gate*, as late as 1953 and 1980, respectively.

Moreover, this aspect of the Western saga was not neglected by the artists and image-makers, from the painter Thomas Hart Benton's visual hymns of praise as he traveled through the West and painted in the 1920s, to the producers of that charming movie *The Wizard of Oz*, that premiered in 1939. In the latter, a motion picture that turned from black and white dramatically into technicolor, Judy Garland as the heroine, Dorothy, along with her little dog Toto, are swept up out of a John Steuart Curry Kansas landscape by a tornado, and deposited in the wonderful kingdom of Oz that, with its lush geometric green fields and its yellow brick road, resembled nothing so much as an enamelled landscape painted by the Iowa artist, Grant Wood.

Even Walt Disney got in on the act with his short cartoon, *Mickey Mouse's Band,* in which Mickey and his musicians, who insist on playing the "high falutin" "William Tell Overture," while Donald Duck quacks away at the farmer's anthem, "Turkey-in-the Straw," are also swept up in a tornado, from which they come tumbling down playing Donald Duck's humbler tune. During the whole period from World War I to World War II, Americans were swept up, intellectually and artistically, in a paradox of cross currents. On the one hand, Paris and its atmosphere of modernism attracted a host of artists, writers and intellectuals from all across the land, but on the other hand the same period saw "the rediscovery" of America by these expatriates and others of their kind who stayed home. This phenomenon began in the 1920s and gained momentum with federal support in the 1930s.

Artists as various as Thomas Hart Benton, Grant Wood and Jerry Bywaters studied their craft in Paris, usually at the Académie Julian, then in New York at the Art Students League, returning to America, thus rejecting European Modernism in favor of seeking their roots in America's native ground. Benton, for instance, went through a Cubist phase, then a Synchromist phase. Grant Wood made constructions of "found art," as did Marcel Duchamp and Man Ray. Both became painters of the American scene who self-consciously dealt with the themes of American history, myth, and folklore. Thomas Hart Benton of the famous Missouri Bentons, aided by the caustic critic Thomas Craven, became the most outspoken. He declared that he had rejected "modernist dirt" in favor of American soils and an American style that was uniquely his own.

In 1925 Benton began wandering through the interior regions of the United States, painting characteristic pictures of small town America[2] and, in so doing, extolling its virtues and its energies. Perhaps his two most famous Western scenes of the period were *Cattle-Loading in West Texas,* about which he wrote nostalgically but also prophetically, "The pioneer West has gone beyond recall . . . on the trails to Wichita and Dodge City, where the hard-riding boys of the old days used to drive their long strings of cattle, the tractors and the combines are chugging."[3] And, in his other important Western picture of the period, Benton painted the oil-boom town of Borger as the generic Western "happening." He called the picture appropriately *Boomtown.* In it a wedge of "civilization" seems driven into the heart of the small town by the oil fields in the background that are characterized symbolically by a huge cloud of greasy, menacing black smoke. And at the crossroads of the town a sinister modernity has taken over; prostitutes roam in front of a new movie house, a uniformed man stalks a woman with a knife while, on the other hand, land deals are made in the middle of the street at the same time town louts are fighting. All this may not have been so different from the Wyatt Earp days at Dodge City, or Wild Bill Hickock's Deadwood, except that instead of horses, automobiles and machinery had taken over. At about the same time, the environmental critic Siegfried Gideon published a book whose title fit the situation perfectly—*Mechanization Takes Command.*

Benton himself wrote about the West:

> The West, like all other parts of our country, is in a state of rapid change. . . . A great number of people in the West . . . cling to the bucking, shooting, yelling glamour of the past. Even in the society grooves of the new western cities the older male members hanker for the tough days that are gone. . . . It is not only among the old boys either that this condition holds. Every true westerner likes to think of himself as a fellow who could nonchalantly guide a hot stallion to a skittish mare or perform adequately with a herd of fear-stricken cattle.

But he added:

> In the new cities with their shiny skyscrapers, their golf clubs, community churches, and cultural forums, an intensely cultivated feminine gentility expresses concern with another kind of past. Socially ambitious women take aggressively to establishing the respectability of their backgrounds. No hot stallions or smelly cowboys for them.[4]

Benton's *After Many Springs* is another example of his view of the West. It portrays a farmer plowing his field in the background, but the foreground is dominated by a tree and lush, colorful foliage that bespeaks the earth's primal energy. This lushness splits open, however, and the earth opens up, revealing a human skull and a rusted six-shooter: remnants of the dark, sinister past of the cowboy pioneers, who had first conquered the land. The painting has nostalgia for the pioneer days in it, but it also has something full of menace about it, as if the earth possesses an almost human sense and is guarding its secrets, awaiting a time for revenge. Viewers who saw the painting in 1940 knew that revenge was the Dust Bowl.

Benton went on to paint a prodigious number of pictures, all characterized by wavy, expressionistic figures reminiscent of El Greco, whose works he had carefully studied. And even when he was extolling the virtues of the American scene, there was something sinister, or at least sardonic, about his paintings. Perhaps he learned this from the great Mexican masters, Diego Rivera, Jose Clemente Orozco, and Alfaro y Sequieros, whose work he admired because, being a Marxist at the time, he naively believed it grew "out of their native soil."[5] He saw no ironies in their twisting and caricaturing of history, not even in Rivera's mural that portrayed Cortez as a hydrocephalic dwarf. For Benton, as for most of the American Scene painters, expressionism was all, and sometimes they resorted to overstatement, or at least what Middle America regarded as overstatement.

Benton also turned to painting what Sherwood Anderson had called in *Winesburg, Ohio* small town "grotesques"—usually people sexually frustrated by the fundamentalist religion that dominated such towns. On the one hand, he could paint such a religiously positive picture as *The Lord is My Shepherd* and, on the other hand, he could paint such negative and psychologically twisted views as *Persephone* and *Suzannah and the Elders*. Both pictures are dominated by explicitly painted female nudes set down in lush settings near a substantial body of water. In *Susannah and the Elders* the nude female is being observed by some farmers, surely Benton's application of the Bible's lesson to the Bible Belt. In *Persephone* the aspect of the grotesque is even worse because the naked young woman is being surreptitiously observed by a gnarled and grotesque old man peeping around a gnarled tree. Both pictures suggest the sexual repression that Benton detected in Western rural life. During the 1930s Benton, like a number of other writers and artists, managed to link Marx and Freud in his portrayal of Middle America.

His murals at New York's left-leaning New School for Social Research, organized like the rotogravure pages of the Sunday newspaper, were widely admired, as were his Indiana murals. But his mural for the Missouri State Capital at Jefferson City drew heavy fire for its realistic portrayals of politicians, like Boss Pendergast "whose organization voted dead men" in the process of hijacking the state government, the James boys, a black version of Frankie and Johnnie, early traders corrupting the Indians with whiskey, slavery, lynching, the ever-present sinister black smoke, the rear end of the Missouri mule, and a mother irreverently changing the diaper on a bare-bottomed baby while one of the state's politicians (actually Boss Prendergast) was speaking to a small multitude. Ironically, only the person who posed for the bare-bottomed baby is alive today to comment on the mural, and he seems to like

Thomas Hart Benton, *Section of Mural for the Missouri State Capital.* Missouri Division of Tourism, Jefferson City, Missouri.

Thomas Hart Benton, *After Many Springs.* Museum of Western Art, Denver.

it just fine some fifty years later. but Missourians were furious with it at the time, eliciting perhaps the only extended explanation of his work that Benton ever made.

> The theme of the painting is the evolution of society in the State of Missouri. This theme does not demand the presentation of specific characters or events emphasized in historic record. It calls simply for a depiction of the ways people lived and the changes they effected on the environment as Missouri developed. . . .
>
> My first choice of any particular group of historic facts has been determined by two things. First by its similarity or near relationship to facts which I have experienced myself, directly. This is because things immediately and directly known by the artist can be made to appear more lifelike in his work than things he only gets by hearsay. . . . The second thing that determined my choice was the manageability of facts in the logic of this pictorial scheme.
>
> I think any of you can see that the objects painted on these walls are not just slapped on arbitrarily. . . . The "realness" of this work depends on a lot of abstract adjustments of lines and planes and gradations of color. These adjustments cannot be disturbed without causing me a lot of work, without, in fact, making me do this thing all over.[6]

By and large, Benton, with his distinctive, colorful combination of El Greco forms and his Mexican mural style, was a booster of the American scene, once he got over his flirtation with Marxism.

Thomas Hart Benton, *Persephone*, (1938–39). On loan to the Nelson-Atkins Museum of Art, Kansas City, Missouri. From the Benton Testamentary Trusts.

Grant Wood, *Daughters of Revolution*, (1932), The Cincinnati Art Museum, The Edwin and Virginia Irwin Memorial and V.A.G.A., New York, 1986.

People did not see Kansas' John Steuart Curry in quite the same way. Though Curry, who moved from Connecticut back to the Midwest of his birthplace, thought he was painting scenes of his childhood, Kansans objected to such pictures as *Tornado, Hogs and Rattlesnakes* and *Baptism in Kansas*. The latter seemed to portray Kansans as religious fanatics, while the former indicated that the state was a distinctly hostile environment. Eastern seaboard critics agreed with the Kansans, but for the wrong reasons. They lumped Curry and Benton and all artists who painted west of the Hudson River and who did not subscribe to the abstract tenets of Modernism as "Regionalists"—a pejorative intended to suggest the limited interests of American Scene paintings. European-oriented, the New York School cared nothing about the West, except Taos, and they did not think the myth of America was especially relevant, except in a crypto-fascist sense, because it paralleled certain "native land" and "native peoples" statements that Adolph Hitler was making at the same time, especially at Nuremberg and the 1936 Olympics. At the very least, the so-called Regionalists were regarded as chauvinists and woefully behind the times.

But one of these regionalists was harder to figure. Grant Wood, though he had studied in Paris and absorbed the tenets of modernism, had defiantly opened an art school in Cedar Rapids, Iowa. With Curry, he enjoyed posing in plain old overalls for newsmen.[7] Hardly a son of the soil, Grant Wood was probably the cleverest manipulator of the American myth since Benjamin Franklin. His paintings of the Iowa countryside featured wildly unrealistic polished fields with neat geometric furrows and a plow usually standing innocently in the foreground. Was he painting Iowa as the land of plenty its boosters claimed it to be? Or was he slyly kidding these boosters in pictures like *Arbor Day*, where schoolchildren are planting a lone tree in a schoolyard about to be cut away by erosion? And did he admire Herbert Hoover so much in 1932 that he felt compelled to paint an antiseptic, almost surreal picture of his birthplace? And what did he mean in such pictures as *Daughters of the Revolution*, a picture of three turkey-wattled women holding teacups in front of a reproduction of

Grant Wood, *American Gothic,* (1930). Courtesy of The Art Institute of Chicago, Friends of American Art Collection.

Emanuel Leutze's *Washington Crossing the Delaware,* and his immortal painting of his sister and the local dentist, *American Gothic?* Were these touting the Midwest and the Great Plains people? Or was he having fun, creating a land of Oz and an absurd "Emerald City" at their expense? His 1939 masterpiece, *Parson Weems' Fable,* a parody of Charles Willson Peale's *The Artist in His Museum,* should have provided a clue. There stands Wood in eighteenth-century garb, pulling back a tasseled curtain to reveal, not a museum, but a myth or fable, that of little George Washington and the mutilated cherry tree. Washington is a miniature adult with a Gilbert Stuart head and a brand new hardware-store hatchet. The cherry tree is loaded, not with cherries, but tassels like those on the curtain, and the whole landscape is sterile and surreal, suggesting a dream, or better still, the American subconscious. Wood, more than Benton, who now seems rather clumsy in his utterances, made a career out of poking fun at the American Dream and the idea of a land of plenty in the midst of depression and drought, where farmers daily lost their farms to the auction block. He saw, as in *American Gothic,* the American Dream as one of sheer hypocrisy, absurdly put forward as the truth. But to this day Iowans and scholars alike still believe he meant to pay homage to the land of plenty[8] in which he found himself surrounded by bigots and hounded by pseudo-intellectuals where he taught at the University of Iowa.

Another group of regionalists were less concerned with sly satire than they were with the Dust Bowl, which was the consequence of the farmers moving

Grant Wood, *Parson Weem's Fable,* (1939). Courtesy the Amon Carter Museum, Fort Worth.

out onto the arid high plains west of the 100th meridian. One of their spokesmen, Jerry Bywaters of Dallas, articulated their belief in John Dewey's maxim
that art was "a mode of interaction between man and his environment."[9] A
number of artists who have become known as "The Dallas Nine" painted Dust
Bowl scenes in vivid ways that complemented and reflected the striking work
of Farm Security Administration photographers like Dorothea Lange, Arthur

Solomon D. Butcher, *John Curry Sod
House Near West Union in Custer
County, Nebraska,* (1886), Solomon
Butcher Collection. Nebraska State
Historical Society, Lincoln,
Nebraska.

Rothstein, and Russell Lee. In 1935 the multi-talented Pare Lorentz made a government-sponsored feature motion picture about the Dust Bowl called *The Plow that Broke the Plain*.[10] It premiered in the White House in a special show-ing for F.D.R. himself.

Day after day the winds blew across the high plains and carried the topsoil of the "Grant Wood" plowed-over fields with them. On May 9, 1934 a dust storm blew 350 million tons of soil eastward across urban America. By evening twelve million tons of dust had covered Chicago, and at noon on May 10, Buffalo, New York was completely darkened by dust. But that was not the worst. In March of 1935 the old cattle town of Dodge City was almost totally darkened by dirt blowing on the wind. And "The Great Blow" came in April of 1935 with huge billowing black clouds rolling over town after town.[11] The F.S.A. photographer, Dorothea Lange, was on the high plains in those years and photographed the almost total obliteration of Dodge City and Liberal, Kansas, and she also caught the "Black Blizzard" in Prower, Colorado as late as 1937.

As a result of the Dust Bowl and the agricultural depression, the Federal Resettlement Administration, in a survey of forty hardest-hit counties, deter-mined that the population had decreased by three percent in the 1930–35 period, but between 1935 and 1937, 34 percent of the people left the high plains. Over 300,000 people made the trek to California in rattletrap cars piled high with children and treasured family possessions.[12] This represented a new Western migration that compared in numbers almost identically with

Dorothea Lange, *The Great Blow of 1934*, Library of Congress, Washington, D.C.

Arthur Rothstein, *Fleeing a Dust Storm, Cimarron County, Oklahoma,* (1936).
Library of Congress, Washington, D.C.

those who went overland to California in the Gold Rush of 1849–50. This comparison was not lost on the novelist John Steinbeck, whose novel, *The Grapes of Wrath* was made into the key motion picture of the era. It portrayed the Joad family as modern-day pioneers heading West in a virtual caravan of migrants along Route 66. The Oklahoma songster, Woody Guthrie, composed a lyric to fit the situation. He sang, as did many at the time:

> We loaded our jalopies and piled our families in
> We rattled down the highway to never come back again
> I'm goin' down the road feelin' bad.[13]

Writers like John Steinbeck, songwriters like Woody Guthrie, and the folklorist Pete Seeger, as well as moviemakers like Pare Lorentz and John Ford, who directed the motion-picture version of *The Grapes of Wrath* helped to

Dorothea Lange, *Migrant Madonna*, (c. 1936). Library of Congress.

Arthur Rothstein, *A Bank That Failed, Southwest Kansas*, (1935).
Library of Congress, Washington, D.C.

Arthur Rothstein, *Stock Watering Hole Almost Covered over by Erosion, Cimarron County,* 1936.
Library of Congress, Washington, D.C.

Dorothea Lange, *Tent City: Tulare, California,*
(1938). Library of Congress, Washington, D.C.

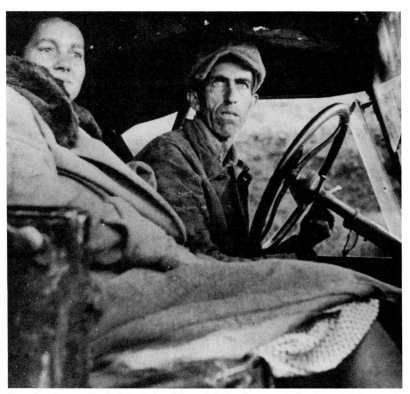

Dorothea Lange, *Ditched, Stalled and Stranded,* San Joaquin Valley (1935), Library of Congress, Washington, D.C.

fashion a new version of the myth of the West that nonetheless harkened back to the old values and even images portrayed in the paintings of Thomas Hart Benton. In fact, John Ford's art director on *The Grapes of Wrath* remembers deliberately trying "for that Thomas Hart Benton look" [14] in the film. But the major mode of expression in a period dominated by social scientists, newsreels, and picture magazines like *Life* and *Look* was, as Professor William Stott has pointed out, "documentary expression." [15] Even mythmaking had to have the verisimilitude of the photograph or be buttressed by graphs, charts and statistics. Pragmatically oriented university departments of sociology and economics flourished as brain-trusts sprang up all over the country to aid in overcoming "dust, drought and depression."

In early 1935 Rexford Guy Tugwell, head of the Resettlement Administration, commandeered Roy Stryker to head up a team of documentary photographers that would go out into the field and photograph conditions of rural and urban poverty that would serve to educate the people about the most pressing of the nation's problems. Tugwell soon departed, and with him the Resettlement Administration, which was replaced by the Farm Security Administration (F.S.A.). By that time, Stryker had assembled a crack team of photographers: Walker Evans, Ben Shahn, Margaret Bourke White, John Vachon, Russell Lee, Arthur Rothstein and Dorothea Lange, who at the time was just terminating her marriage to the Western artist, Maynard Dixon.[16] This group of photographers between 1935 and 1943 made some 270,000 pictures,[17] plus Lorentz's two motion pictures.

Of the group, Arthur Rothstein and Dorothea Lange in particular concentrated their energies on the heart of the Dust Bowl country in western Oklahoma, Kansas and the Texas Panhandle. Their photographs documented in a vivid way the Dust Bowl experience. Arthur Rothstein's *Fleeing a Dust Storm, Cimarron County, Oklahoma,* made in Oklahoma in 1936, showing a man and boy dashing for a half-buried root cellar, was one of the most famous pictures of the period, along with Lange's photo of a gaunt farm woman, hand held to her head in a pose of despair, entitled *If You Die, You're Dead.* The two photographers followed Stryker's instructions and constantly focused on human interest and pathos.[18] Lange would picture a migrant madonna while Rothstein snapped a view of a farm auction or the eviction of sharecroppers. Both photographers also got at one of the causes of the Dust Bowl problem. They pictured neat rows of turned-over soil, dust-covered farms, rusting disc harrows, and the abandoned "sacred plow" that had indeed "broken the plains." The plow, the windmill, the abandoned sharecropper's cabin, the ghost towns with failed banks or land offices, rotting machinery and battered old cars were prominent symbols in their photographs, as were cattle dying of thirst in views even more vivid than Charley Russell's famous snowstorm picture of 1886, *Waiting for a Chinook.* Rothstein's *Stock Watering Hole, Cimarron County, Oklahoma* was a particularly apt view of cattle in dire straits, while in Lange's *Top-O-the-World Farm, Coldwater, Oklahoma* pictures, satire and irony abound.

Lange, in particular, made a series of pictures of Oklahomans migrating to California that provided the documentary basis for Steinbeck's *The Grapes of Wrath.* In 1938, especially, she followed migrants westward, composing studies of families starting out looking scared and bewildered in overloaded flivvers, to scenes of their breakdowns and camps along the road, or visits to gas stations and stores where only the compressed air was still free, and on to views of their plight in California as virtual wage slaves in the cotton fields, and squatters in squalid farm labor camps. Her camera caught children working in

Alexandre Hogue, *Dust Bowl,* (1933). National Museum of American Art, Smithsonian Institution, Washington, D.C. Gift of IBS Corporation.

the fields, rudimentary F.S.A. camps, and armed California vigilantes and police ready to break up strikes and roust troublemakers. She even photographed "Okies" who had returned from California to the squalor of their Muskogee sharecroppers' cabin declaring, "People aren't friendly out there." When he wrote *The Grapes of Wrath* and *In Dubious Battle,* the story of a California fruit pickers' strike, Steinbeck, working with the F.S.A. photographers and field camp managers, had plenty of documentary and personal experiences upon which to rely. Meanwhile, through the medium of documentary photographs, Dorothea Lange and Arthur Rothstein, along with Russell Lee,[19] who came to the region a bit later, but whose pictures such as *Christmas Dinner* were equally graphic, told a story that became forever part of the myth of the West. They showed human pathos, fear and bewilderment graphically, but they also did much more. They documented human dignity and the human spirit in the face of poverty and natural disasters in such a way as to evoke the whole social history and all the subtle nuances of the westward movement, whether it be in the 1830s or the 1930s. They evoked an epic quality in the ordinary American that the painter Thomas Hart Benton had also been reaching for with brush and canvas.

Alexandre Hogue, *Erosion No. 2—Mother Earth Laid Bare*. Philbrook Art Center, Tulsa.

Jerry Bywaters, *Oilfield Girls*, (1940).
Archer M. Huntington Art Gallery,
The University of Texas at Austin. Archer
M. Huntington Museum Fund, 1984.

Russell Lee, *Christmas Dinner, Smithfield, Iowa,* (1936). Library of Congress, Washington, D.C.

Of the other Regionalists, Alexandre Hogue of the Dallas group was clearly the most powerful and accomplished painter. Beginning his career as a Taos artist and protégé of Ernest Blumenschein, Hogue, who grew up in Denton, Texas, really found his milieu in painting the Dust Bowl. His 1933 painting entitled *Dust Bowl* made the farm country seem like a World War I battlefield with its bare sand dunes and barbed wire bathed in an eerie violet light, split by the sun bursting like a star shell over the whole scene. His *Drouth Survivors* (1936) that pictured wire, sand dunes, a rusted tractor and dead cattle with only the rattlesnake and the prairie dog alive, so offended the Chamber of Commerce of Dalheart, Texas, that it took up a collection of $50 to purchase the painting and destroy it. Hogue declined the "generous" offer and sold the picture instead to the Musée National d'Art Moderne in Paris.[20] Among Hogue's other masterpieces of disaster was *Drouth Stricken Area,* almost a cartoonlike vision of a lonely cow trying to drink from a water tank filled with sand while a patient vulture looks on. This picture reflected Rothstein's photograph, *Stock Watering Hole, Cimarron County, Oklahoma.* But Hogue's most powerful picture was *Mother Earth Laid Bare* (1938). According to Hogue, it echoed stories his mother had told him about the "earth mother" who lived just beneath the surface of the ground.[21] In the painting we see the earth eroded away on a farmstead in such a way as to reveal the contours of a nude sleeping woman.

In the foreground is an ugly plow that, in a sense, began the rape of "mother earth."

Hogue's Dust Bowl paintings were rivaled by William Palmer's climactic *Dust, Drought and Destruction*, Joe Jones's *American Farm*, which portrayed a farm house marooned on a last ridge in a sea of eroded land, Otis Dozier's *Jackrabbits*, a surreal scene of giant jackrabbits standing out on a barren plain, and Jerry Bywaters's haunting *Old Field Girls*. The latter painting, which depicts two girls, one an experienced woman of the world dressed in slinky black, and the other a naive cowgirl about to hit the road to the oil fields in the distance which are polluting the land, added the dimension of social dislocation, even in booming regions, to the picture of the 1930s. Bywaters, the leading spirit of the Dallas art group that became famous in the Texas Centennial of 1936, was greatly influenced by El Greco and other Spanish masters whose work he had studied in Europe, and by the Mexican muralists, with whom he had worked.[22] All of the "Dallas Nine" were inspired by a visit and a series of lectures delivered by Thomas Hart Benton in 1935. But, congregated on Alice Street in Dallas, these artists did not think of themselves as especially linked to the Regionalists, who were Midwesterners in their eyes. Founders of the *Southwest Review*, they had spokesmen like Walter P. Webb, J. Frank Dobie and Henry Nash Smith, who considered the Southwest as a unique region unto itself, with Dallas and Texas as its central focus.[23] But for the talent and civilized drive of those who espoused this view, it might have been considered another garden variety of chauvinism. Still the works of Webb and Smith spoke to the world, as did the paintings of Hogue and the murals of Bywaters, while the new Dallas Museum of Fine Arts attracted such as Gertrude Stein, Salvadore Dali, and George Grosz as lecturers and admirers of Southwestern culture even in the Depression and Dust-Bowl days.

All of this new regional consciousness that sprang up in the 1930s and could be noted in post office murals across the land, had special meaning for the West. It revived the myth of the West and it added new characters and nuances of spirit to the story. It was especially important as a series of art forms— paintings, photos, lithographs, films—that deliberately spoke to the masses, rather than the avant-garde elite of an art world that was rapidly distancing itself from the people. The arts of the 1930s in America were in many ways mythmaking propaganda, but they were also democratic propaganda, designed to reach out to the common man to evoke his sympathies and to bolster his courage in a time of crisis. They added a vivid, but more important, a useful dimension to the West of the imagination.

CHAPTER   **31**

THE INDIAN RENAISSANCE

In the twentieth century, the Native American has moved from the oft exploited subject and symbol in Western art to become a creator of his own vision, and a narrator in his own right, of the Western experience. The commanding *ouevre* of the contemporary American Indian artists Fritz Scholder and T. C. Cannon, as well as the monumental panels of history and myth by the emerging talent, Randy Lee White, present a very different story than that told by the Cowboy Artists of America. In fact, the cowboy artists and the American Indian painters have emerged as parallel, and at times rival, traditions in contemporary Western art, each with its own techniques, its own visual language, its own historical roots and its own distinct culture.

At its best, the work of contemporary Indian artists embraces the multiplicity of Native American cultural and artistic life. Forced—perhaps more than any other American social group—to respond to myths and stereotypes, to explore their past, to deal with the dual identity as both modern American and Indian, Native American artists have brought the contemplation of the Indian experience into the art gallery, demanding that the viewer explore with the artist the multifarious threads of his influence, and begin to understand the history of the West from his point of view.

Quite unlike contemporary realist painters, the American Indian painters trace their prime influences back to roots in modernism and abstraction. The early history of American Indian "fine art" painting is a curious one indeed, and reveals the extent to which the Native American Indian artist operates in an environment of heightened self-consciousness.

Twentieth-century American Indian art emphatically did *not* evolve gradually out of the traditional tribal crafts which such painters as E. Irving Couse and Joseph Henry Sharp were so fond of including in their nostalgic paintings of Indian life. Before the 1930s the U.S. Government intentionally pursued a policy of assimilation which discouraged organized attempts at preserving tribal languages, religious ceremonies and art forms. American Indian life had changed and evolved so rapidly in response to shifting political and economic circumstances over the previous century, that relatively few traditional arts remained intact and vital, and those that did were rapidly becoming the object of exploitation and influence by the new tourist trade. Navaho sandpainting, for instance, had long functioned as a sacred art created only by a trained Navaho priest in temporary materials. The invention of a means to cement sand and pigment permanently to a masonite panel turned it into a secular artform.

Although Karl Bodmer may have been the first artist to encourage Indians to use the white man's materials of pencil, paper and watercolor to express themselves as artists, it was not until the turn of the century, in the environs of Santa Fe, that the first group of Indian artists using non-traditional materials and subjects was formed and received broad recognition. In fact, the group of San Ildefonso painters known as the "Self-Taught Painters" developed a creative, symbiotic relationship with members of the Santa Fe artists colony in the early decades of this century, while the latter was in the throes of evolution towards modernism. Observation and appreciation of the work of the early non-traditional American Indian painters became fundamental to the philosophical underpinning of Southwest modernism, and, in many ways, the early Indian artists could be said to have painted exclusively in that style.

Edgar Lee Hewett, the tireless creative force behind so many of the cultural institutions of Santa Fe, provided the seeds of inspiration to painter Crescencio Martinez, a brother-in-law of the famous potter, Maria Martinez, when he commissioned him to do a series of watercolor paintings of Indian ceremonies around 1910. In *Deer Dancer* the costumed dancing figure is painted very differently from how he might have been by, say, a member of the Taos Society of Artists. In Martinez' version of what would eventually become a famous subject in Indian painting, the hunched pose of the deer dancer, as he leans forward on his two staffs, is rendered with little expressive character. Instead, Martinez gives great attention to symbolic detail—diamond motifs, frets, zig-zags and eagle feathers—all of the identifying features of the dancer's costume which have real meaning in the context of the ceremony. Although the torso is shifted at a slight angle to the viewer's frame of reference to accommodate representation of both arms, the overall effect of the picture is two-dimensional and stylized. Perhaps most importantly, Martinez felt no need to place the figure in representational space: we see no plaza, no groundline, no shadows. Although Martinez produced relatively few paintings before his death in 1918, he established the stylistic basis for nearly half a century of American Indian painting.

Hewett commissioned other San Ildefonso painters as well, among them Awa Tsireh, Crescencio's nephew, and Julian Martinez, his brother. Working together, the painters developed specific stylistic themes and motifs and in doing so, they created a series of paintings that captured the imagination of several members of the Santa Fe artists colony who had begun, around 1920, to become disenchanted with realism as a viable expressive mode. Both writer Mary Austin and poet Alice Corbin Henderson, wife of American "Fauvist" William Penhallow Henderson, purchased and promoted works by these artists, as did John Sloan, who organized a New York exhibition of works by the "Self-Taught Painters" in 1920. Sloan collaborated with Oliver LaFarge on an ambitious national traveling exhibition of contemporary and traditional Indian arts in 1931. "The Exposition of Indian Tribal Arts," called by them "the first exhibition of American Indian Art selected entirely with consideration of esthetic value,"[1] sought to analyze both traditional and non-traditional Indian art in modernist terms. Rather than comparing the San Ildefonso painters to realist artists, Sloan and LaFarge asserted that

> The Indian artist deserves to be classed as a Modernist, his art is old, yet alive and dynamic; but his modernism is an expression of a continuing vigor seeking new outlets, and not like ours, a search for release from exhaustion.[2]

As this quote from their lavishly designed and illustrated catalogue of the 1931 exhibition suggests, Sloan and LaFarge hoped to find in the work of the new Indian painters a kind of "natural" modernism, which owed no allegiance to outside influences and styles, and did not have to undergo the turmoil of learned departure from realism. The intense enthusiasm with which the Santa Fe artists greeted the newly evolving art tradition is reflected in numerous

Julian Martinez, *Seven Kiva Dancers*, (1924). Gerald Peters Collection, Santa Fe.

articles published about the Indian painters in the local newspaper, as well as in *El Palacio,* the journal of the Museum of New Mexico. The white artists waited with barely concealed anticipation to see what techniques for representation of space might emerge, what colors the native artists would choose, what subjects would interest them. They recognized that, in its stylization and abstraction, the Indian painting, even to educated eyes, resembled the brazen

Crescencio Martinez, *Eleven Figures of the Animal Dance.* Museum of Fine Arts, Museum of New Mexico, Santa Fe, New Mexico.

mock-primitivism of such sophisticates as Stuart Davis and Marsden Hartley, and indeed may have actually influenced them.

In one sense, these early champions of American Indian painting suffered from a kind of pathetic fallacy; they believed that the motivations and intentions of the Indian artists coincided with their own. In fact, it is likely that the early San Ildefonso painters were less motivated by a desire to express themselves as artists than they were by the growing market for this new art form. Although marred by a paternalism we now find distasteful, the early efforts of the Santa Fe artists to develop and market Native American painting not only generated much needed income for the painters, but planted the seeds of an aesthetic self-consciousness quite apart from the traditional ceremonial artist's role within the tribe, and laid the groundwork for the eventual adoption of this new means of expression of the Native American experience in the twentieth century.

Dorothy Dunn, artist, teacher and art historian, is widely and properly credited with the institutionalization of American Indian painting. In 1932, shortly after the completion of the national tour of the Exposition of Indian Tribal Arts, she founded an instructional studio at the Santa Fe Indian School. Awa Tsireh and Julio Martinez, as well as Jack Hokeah—a member of the group of five young Oklahoma Kiowa artists who had also received early encouragement as artists—painted a mural for the school; thereby symbolically, as well as actually, passing on their visual heritage to the following generation of Indian painters. The founding and early growth of the Santa Fe Indian School occurred in a newly emerging political climate of tolerance, and even encouragement, of traditional Indian culture. The Meriam Report of 1928 had urged the stimulation of Indian art by the U.S. Government as both a source of revenue for the Indians and a means of cultural expression. In 1933, the Wheeler-Howard Act, in large measure drawn up by anthropologists like Hewett, became the prime instrument of the Indian New Deal. The Indian New Deal attempted to reverse the process of assimilation into white culture and to encourage the development of the reservations as viable economic and cultural communities that preserved tribal integrity and all of the symbols that expressed it.

The development of an active Native American painting tradition fit well with the new governmental attitude towards tribal groups. Dorothy Dunn's philosophy of instruction prompted her to encourage not only a distinctively non-white basis for her student's art, but a foundation in his or her own tribal traditions, lest they become too acculturated by the process of schooling away from their home reservation.

Allan Houser, *Apache Girl's Puberty Rite*. Museum of Northern Arizona Collections, Flagstaff, Arizona.

Although Dorothy Dunn's "studio" style seems now almost embarrassingly clichéd in its extreme stylization and lack of innovation, it must be seen in the context of the time in order to understand both its appeal to the white patrons who purchased the art, and also to the Indians themselves, who had come to regard themselves as modern visual artists.

What seems now to be naive simplicity was regarded at that time as refreshing primitivism, a stronger and more visceral aesthetic response than well-schooled realism. The lack of individualism in the school's products was actually perceived by the Santa Fe aesthetes as the reflection of a tribal consciousness, in which, as Mabel Dodge Luhan put it, "Virtue lay in wholeness instead of dismemberment."[3] The distinctive flatness seemed to connect the Indian painter's work to the parietal art of the ancient pueblos, which had begun to come to light in the 1930s due to Hewett's archaeological investigations. Instead of criticizing the artist for employing overly used visual clichés, such as isolated sprays of vegetation to represent the environment, the Santa Feans regarded these as analogues to the evolving stylized visual notations of John Marin, and ultimately of Wassily Kandinsky. Yet, perhaps the fundamental appeal of the products of Dorothy Dunn's studio was the potential the students had to express the Native American consciousness in terms which modern American painters could understand. In order to encourage the evolution of a Native American style, Dorothy Dunn refused to allow her students to imitate the work of realist artists, even disallowing conventional perspective. She insisted that

In spite of the fact that many young artists . . . ask to be taught drawing and design "like American artists do," the Indian schools must refuse to do so. they must do everything possible through a thorough study and intelligent handling of the situation to help the children recover, maintain and develop their own art.[4]

Dorothy Dunn further believed that her Indians students painted best from memory, rather than from life, as if the vitality of their art and meaningfulness of the symbol would well up from the subconscious mind of the artist; a near Jungian ideal.

Perhaps the greatest success of the Studio was in fostering the re-emergence of American Indian art as fine art. Dorothy Dunn helped American Indians regard themselves as artists, and validated the use of traditional themes and symbols in the context of the new medium of watercolor and oil paint. Although many of the artists who attended the Santa Fe studio subsequently gave up art, two of its alumni became successful and well known artists: Oscar Howe, who was later to introduce strains of cubism and futurism to Indian painting, and Allan Houser, whose massive, now almost archetypal images of Indians rendered in stone ultimately derive from the mastery of the simple clichés of his Santa Fe studio instruction. In Houser's *Apache Girl's Puberty Rite* we see the best and worst features of the studio style in a single painting. Flattened, stylized, almost naive, the figures reflect the standardized visual vocabulary of the school. Yet Houser works within these formal strictures to introduce expressive pose and gesture, even anecdotal narrative, such as the non-traditionally dressed Indian man at right, who pinches a baby's cheek while the ceremony takes place. The sharp contour lines and frieze-like stiffness become a context for expressing a gentle, human rhythm. The elegant focal point of the picture, the presentation of a flower to the girl who has come of age, becomes an understated ceremonial act—rare restraint for a studio style work.

Although extremely important as the first major institution devoted to the instruction of American Indian art, the Santa Fe Indian School failed as an institution to carry the visual language of Indian painting much beyond the forms already in use by the San Ildefonso artists before its opening. Although one perceives in the precisely visualized and rendered images of the students the thorough development and exploration of a singular visual style, it lacked the vitality and innovation to be truly powerful. One of the failings of the school perhaps lay in the fact that it was really too small to create a nurturing context for art. Unlike their untrained predecessors, the students at the school had little occasion for interaction with the Santa Fe artists' colony, and perhaps their art suffered because of it. If there was a dearth of nourishing artistic influences, the school also lacked the supportive tribal context in which the more traditional art forms had evolved. The result is a kind of stasis and sterility which characterized the art of the Santa Fe Studio, and against which a later generation of American Indian artists vigorously rebelled.

The Institute of American Indian Art, the successor to the Santa Fe Indian School, was founded in 1962 in Santa Fe in the political context of a pan-Indianism which sought a locus for the training of Indian students from a broad range of tribes, and which ultimately created the wider sphere of interaction and exchange of ideas that made possible the vital Indian art of today.

Not only did the IAIA attract Indian pupils from all over the country, but, with the later support of the Rockefeller Foundation, it differed fundamentally in its objective to train studio artists. The art of both the pupils and the teachers of the IAIA became the product of a much wider sphere of influence than its predecessor institution. Not only did teachers like Fritz Scholder introduce students to a broader range of influence, but, by painting in a style outside of the traditional Indian mode, an action for which he was initially severely criticized by "traditionalists," Scholder awakened Indian painters to their potential role in the broader context of American art.

During the first decade of its existence, perhaps the strongest influence on the art and experience of the students at the Institute was the political activism of the 1960s and early '70s. As early as 1966, Santa Fe had been the location of a political confrontation between the National Congress of American Indians and the Bureau of Indian Affairs over the issue of governmental consultation of the tribes. With the Indian occupation of Alcatraz in 1969, the Trial of Broken Treaties march on Washington and subsequent occupation of the Bureau of Indian Affairs in 1972, and finally the demonstration and shoot-out at Wounded Knee in 1973, a radical Indian activism had taken shape which, although sharing certain features with the civil rights movement of the 1960s, differed in its attempt to react against assimilation into white American culture and sought, instead, to achieve political status as a separate nation within America.

For some Indian artists of this era, particularly Billy Soza War Soldier, a student at the IAIA who participated in nearly all of the activist demonstration mentioned above, art become a tool of personal and political expression. In his *FBI-Death* of 1979, and *Death From Above*, (1970) the American eagle, simultaneously a sacred bird to the Southwest Indians and the symbol of U. S. might, has become the harbinger of doom. Although "Indian," Soza War Soldier's art participates in the broader movement of political art that appeared throughout mid-century America in response to specific social and political issues. In its free use of American Flag iconography and stenciled lettering, it resembles the encaustic canvases of Jasper Johns much more than the placid, nearly craftlike pictures of the earlier Santa Fe Indian School artists. Although most powerfully evident in Soza War Soldier's work, this stylistic contrast between old and new, traditionalists versus modernists holds as a true aesthetic division between students of the two successive institutions.

The life of Billy Soza War Soldier, a fugitive from justice after a shoot-out in Albuquerque in 1973, embodies a myth about the American Indian which was widely popularized in the Hollywood production which became a national cult film, *Billy Jack*. The movie was shot on location in and around Santa Fe, and a number of IAIA students participated in the production—perhaps even Billy Soza War Soldier himself.[5] Its half-Indian hero is forced to live outside the law, a victim of persecution, but nevertheless a strong, willful character who fights back. Through the persona of Billy Jack, the nation saw the Indian as a symbol of the struggle against social injustice, and, more than that, sympathized with the kind of emotions which would later characterize Billy Soza War Soldier's paintings.

The counter-cultural energies of Billy Soza War Soldier's paintings found more subdued and slightly altered expression in the art of other Indian painters, who preferred a more sophisticated criticism of the treatment of the Native American, instead of Soza War Soldier's frontal assault. One of the Institute's most accomplished graduates was T. C. Cannon, a Kiowa/Caddo who served in Vietnam during the late 1960s while Soza War Soldier was demonstrating with the American Indian Movement. Although paintings such as *Village with Bomb* (1972) indicate Cannon's willingness to make overt political statements with his art, he clearly places art before politics. *Two Guns Arikara* is a portrait of an American Indian seated in the unlikely context of a Matisse-like room of vibrant color and pattern. Cannon's debt to pop art is obvious in the optical boldness of the painting. The figure seems almost bound, not only by the stiff, upholstered chair, but by the arbitrary patterns and colors of the picture itself, both products of European tradition. The image of the nineteenth-century Plains Indian is wrenched from his romantic, noble savage context; objectified, and ultimately monumentalized by the artist.

Cannon's almost cartoonlike portraits of American Indians seem to stand in sharp contrast to his serious, reflective verse. In his poetry, he gives full rein to the subtleties and shades of emotion about the past that the strong, flat colors of his art seem to shut out.

these days i am falling into guises of the
eversmiling native who has his eyes on the beyond.

i refuse to shed tears for my shortcomings
    anymore.
i am comfortable and sane and smiling
running towards the arms of god this evening.

dammed if I'll let this get us down.
let's shine on the world for a long time
even if we are beyond the voice and ear of
those that proclaim us the dreamers of some
dismissed religion.[6]

Cannon's poetry suggests we read his paintings as ironic pictures of himself and other Indians. If we do, they seem to project a near-gallows humor. They bring the traditional image of the American Indian into a surreal and arbitrary visual context, the world of his modern-world descendant, T. C. Cannon.

In 1978, Cannon lost his life in an automobile accident, his last vision at the moment of death predicted two years earlier in a sketchbook verse:

all i know is that you . . . my friends
will be far away when i die . . .
. . . none will see my final grimace of pain
and smile of diamond clenched teeth bones
on that final bed of sand and cactus
out there where it gets lonely in the
early summer rain.[7]

The sophisticated aestheticism of T. C. Cannon owed much to the teaching of Fritz Scholder, perhaps the most famous contemporary Indian artist. More than any other Indian artist, Scholder is acutely aware of the power of the mythology of the Old West to shape attitudes towards the Indian. Many of his paintings such as *Indian Cliché*, are ironic dialogues with images that helped to define the Indian in the American consciousness. James Erle Fraser, designer of the buffalo nickel, produced the classic image of the Indian in defeat, *The End of the Trial*. In Scholder's lithograph, the bronze is reduced to a simple outline, as if to suggest the hollowness of the stereotype.

More often, as in the art of T. C. Cannon, Scholder's social criticism is

T.C. Cannon, *Two Guns Arikara.* Aberbach Collection, New York.

T.C. Cannon, *A Remembered Muse, (Tosca).*
Courtesy Nancy and Richard Bloch, Santa
Fe.

T.C. Cannon, *Village with Bomb*, (1972). Aberbach Fine Art, New York.

disguised in bright, expressive terms, its symbolic power yielded to the viewer only after careful reflection. Like Cannon, who freely quoted Matisse in his canvases, Scholder used the strange modern surrealism of Francis Bacon in many of his early paintings, perhaps most powerfully in his portrait of George Armstrong Custer. The general is rendered as a grotesque, his face a contorted stain of white and green, ritually slain once again by the artist who has dripped a bright slash of red into his heart. The portrait attempts to rewrite Western history, to change Custer from a hero to a villain.

In *Super Indian No. 2* Scholder borrows the massing of Leonard Baskin to create seemingly comic juxtaposition between the large Indian in ceremonial garb and the tiny pink ice cream cone in his left hand. Scholder describes the event portrayed in the painting:

He tried to ignore the hoard of ugly tourists as he left the others. In the old days there were few white watchers along with the old professional Indian lovers. Now it has turned into a carnival. He stepped up to the red, white and blue concession stand and ordered an ice cream cone—a double-dip strawberry.[8]

In choosing to paint in outrageously non-traditional Indian style, with expressive, flamboyant strokes and defiantly modern colors, Scholder might even see himself as *Super Indian No. 2*; an Indian no longer willing to maintain his traditional identity even for the "old professional Indian lovers."

Even Georgia O'Keeffe is not immune to Scholder's incisive wit. His *Giant Bloom #2* is an obvious parody of her large flower paintings. Perhaps more than any other living Western artist, Fritz Scholder is aware of the extent to which images write history. His paintings are both criticisms of past presumptions by white artists about the Indian, as well as attempts to leave his own mark upon the myth of the West. He does it humorously, boldly with little trace of the radical edge which touched the Institute of American Indian Arts in the 1960s.

Humor has become an increasingly dominant mode for contemporary Indian artists, perhaps in reaction to the weighty self-importance which has characterized much of the work of their predecessors in Western art. Harry Fonseca's *Coyote Meets Lone Ranger in the Western Desert* steps beyond Scholder's dialogue with Western fine art and photography to deal with the manner in which television has shaped attitudes toward the West. Fonseca recognizes cartoons and serials as powerful "myth cycles," and he has chosen, as a painter, to create his own. His protagonist is not the Lone Ranger (or Tonto, for that matter), but a wily and cool coyote, a pop-trickster figure which doubles for the artist himself, and who confronts the Lone Ranger as an equal.

Soza War Soldier, Cannon, Scholder and Fonseca, as well as accomplished painters such as Alfred Young Man, George Longfish and Kevin Red Star, all explore the personal meaning of being an Indian in contemporary American society. They have rebelled against the necessity felt by Dorothy Dunn to keep the Indian artist free of outside aesthetic influences in order to maintain a purity of primitive consciousness and expression. Living in a pluralistic society, moving on and off the reservation, exposed to different styles and influences, as well as different cultures, contemporary Indian artists have sought to develop a complex visual language of expression which uses native art in ironic, modern contexts. There is no single, coherent ethnographic present for the contemporary Indian artist, only a cultural history which has been radically altered, a liminal role in the national identity, and an objectification as a mythical noble savage or "natural environmentalist" rather than as a multifaceted personality. The extent to which the Indian artist is able to capture these strange cultural roles in his art, and to communicate them effectively to his audience is the extent to which his art has real influence.

One of the most sophisticated contemporary Indian painters is Randy Lee White, who lives just north of Taos, New Mexico. His large, powerful canvases have a presence that recalls the paintings of the abstract expressionists, yet White's paintings are a maze of complex iconography that demand semiotic deconstruction. The viewer must be familiar with the entire trajectory of Plains Indian drawing and painting to read the individual pictures in his *Messianic Memoirs,* in which the sticklike figures of late nineteenth-century Plains Indian art are combined with Christian imagery, and a fictionalized persona of Crazy Horse to create a personalized "myth cycle." Unlike many other contemporary Indian painters, White's images are narrative, but they tell their story in the pictographic language of the Plains Indian "ledger drawings," rather than the realism of Western figure painting. In such paintings as *Custer's Last Stand—Revised* White imagines that the Indian Wars of the past continue to be fought in confrontations in the present.

In *Custer's Last Stand—Revised,* vengeance is being wrought upon unscrupulous used-car salesmen who sold the Sioux some useless, gas-guzzling automobiles. The salesmen become Custer's soldiers, defending themselves against an Indian surround: their rational, square-shaped forts contrasted to the chaotic, open range of the Indians. Like Scholder, who ritually dispatches Custer in his painting, White re-lives the triumph of the Little Big Horn, in *Custer's Last Stand—Revised.*

In other episodes of *Messianic Memoirs,* White becomes, himself, a savior of the Indians. He celebrates a figure who embodies iconographic features of both Christ and Crazy Horse. He has absorbed and digested both Christian and Native American symbols, mixed them up with the persistent presence of the historical past which charaterizes the Indian experience, and translated all of this through his art. The result embodies a rich complexity that has only begun to be unwoven by its admirers, such as this rendition of Crazy Horse or Christ ascending into heaven.

Although the traditional studio painting style is still practiced, the more sophisticated, perhaps more worldly style brought forth by the Institute of

Harry Fonseca, *Coyote Meets Lone Ranger in Painted Desert,* (1978). Courtesy of the artist.

Randy Lee White, *Custer's Last Stand–Revised,* (1980). Elaine Horowich Galleries, Santa Fe.

Fritz Scholder, *Portrait 1876-1976*, (Portrait of
Custer). Museum of Western Art, Denver. James
O. Milmoe, photographer.

Fritz Scholder, *Super Indian No. 2*, (1972). Courtesy of Nancy and Richard Bloch, Santa Fe, New
Mexico.

American Indian Art now dominates as the most serious form of artistic
expression by American indians. In its expressionism, its fascination with
iconography and symbolism, its humor and sophistication, it is a product of
its troubled and creative times in which Native Americans have sought to
reject even the positive stereotpyes placed upon them by whites, and to search
for their own identity in the melange of cultures, symbols and styles at their
disposal.

32

MONTEZUMA'S RETURN

*There is a moving scene in Elia Kazan's film, Viva Zapata, star-*ring Marlon Brando, in which white-clad peasants by the thousands stream down from the mountains and out of the jungles to give aid to the revolutionary leader, Emiliano Zapata. As they do so, the rank and file Mexicans give identity, not only to Zapata and the Revolution, but also to themselves. There is no one hero, only the people for whom, it is clear, Zapata has become, with his white horse, his sombrero, and his brooding Indian face, a legendary surrogate. Something very like this has been happening, in artistic terms, among the large Hispanic population, particularly in the Southwest from Los Angeles, California to Austin, Texas.

In the barrios, or largely low-income Hispanic housing projects, whole neighborhoods have come together in a voluntary group effort to create murals on building walls that were once defaced by graffiti. Along one of the Los Angeles aqueducts, that runs through the city's east side—the largest concentration of Mexican people north of the border—the local citizens have painted an entire history of the Mexican-American experience. This stunning mural, that runs for perhaps a mile, is called *The Great Wall of Los Angeles.* In San

Diego the y-shaped supports under the bridge to Coronado are similarly decorated. Thus, the most ubiquitous, most noticeable modern Mexican-American
art is a public and political art that re-interprets, not only Mexican history,
but also the North American experience of the Hispanic immigrant.

Perhaps the most striking of these "art-of-the-people" projects is the Casiano Homes Project in San Antonio, Texas. As recently as July 1978, the
Community Cultural Arts Organization was formed. Though it has a leader,
Anastasio Torres, at this writing, the decisions as to which buildings on which
to paint murals and the subject matter of the murals is arrived at through group
discussion, which includes even schoolchildren for whom the murals serve as
inspiration as well as lessons. Since 1978, the San Antonio Community Cultural Arts Organization has completed some ninety murals, many of them the
products of the childrens' own imaginations. The first of the murals was painted
on the side of a building covered with graffiti, where teenagers had come to
get high on spray paint-sniffing. After laying a coat of white paint over the
graffiti, the muralists laid on an extraordinarily powerful scene of paint-sniffing
and its deleterious effects, both on the individual and on the whole Hispanic
culture. In the foreground sits a youth, his body set against flames and his head
surrounded with skulls. Running diagonally to the right behind him are examples of the kinds of Mexican heroes with whom he has lost touch in paint-
sniffing: a World War II hero, a hero of the Revolution, and an Aztec ancestor. They float in a cloud of yellow, as if in a dream. According to Anastasio
Torres, that mural still stands as painted and "it hasn't been tampered with."[1]
In addition to admonishing reform among Hispanic youth, the Collective
envisages the murals as inspirational messages, not only to the community,
but to "the world at large."

Clearly the mural form harkens back to the modern successes of Rivera,
Sequieros and Orozco, indeed, even further back to the pre-Columbian mural
works such as those still visible at Bonampak in Yucatán, that so inspired the
native peoples. Thus, the form itself takes the viewer back to an ancient tradition. One series is called "The Aztec Series." It begins with a mural called
Mestizos, that portrays the Indian side of the Mexican-American heritage. A
powerful Aztec chief, Montezuma perhaps, is shown rising out of an ear of
corn; arms outstretched, he seems to be worshipped by two sea serpents. Some
versions of the origins of the Aztec corn warrior suggest he came from out of
the sea, other versions have him descending from the sky. Still another mural
in this series, entitled *The Greeting,* portrays Cortez meeting Montezuma on

Mestizos, Casiano Homes Project,
San Antonio. San Antonio Com-
munity Cultural Arts Organization.
Photograph courtesy Dr. Ricardo
Romo, The University of Texas.

Gregorio Cortez Mural, Casiano
Homes Project, San Antonio, San
Antonio Community Cultural Arts
Organization, Photograph Courtesy
Dr. Ricardo Romo, The University
of Texas.

Paint Sniffing Mural, Casiano Homes Project, San
Antonio. San Antonio Community Cultural Arts
Organization. Photograph Courtesy Dr. Ricardo Romo,
The University of Texas.

Pancho Villa-General Pershing Mural, Casiano Homes Pro-
ject, San Antonio. San Antonio Community Cultural
Arts Organization. Photograph courtesy Dr. Ricardo
Romo, The University of Texas.

Luis Jimenez, *Progress I*, (1973). Courtesy Luis Jimenez, Hondo, New Mexico.

Luis Jimenez, *Progress II*, (1977). Courtesy Luis Jimenez, Hondo, New Mexico.

peaceful terms. It suggests that a merger of Spaniard with Indian on peaceful terms would have been far better than *The Conquest*, portrayed in a related mural. In many cases a great deal of research into Aztec history and legend lies behind these murals. In fact, they amount to a re-writing of Mexican and Mexican-American history, taking cognizance of legends like that of the two volcanoes that overlook Mexico City, which are seen as god and goddess.

Most of the relatively modern Mexican heroes are represented, including Benito Juarez, seen driving the French from his native land, Zapata in a sombrero, flanked by two versions of the Mexican eagle, and an incredible, humorous view of a giant-sized Pancho Villa, holding a miniature General Pershing in the palm of his hand in front of an American flag. Villa also rises like a mountain above a realistic portrayal of Pershing's soldiers. More modern heroes who appear on the project's walls, including a World War II Medal of Honor winner, very probably form the famed Texas 36th Division that fought in Italy during that war. And the contemporary lettuce strike leader, Caesar Chavez, occupies a prominent place on a wall as well, flanked by the stylized black eagle of La Raza Unita, the Chicano political party.

Still another of the heroes of history portrayed is that of Gregorio Cortez, a poor Texas farmer who shot a sheriff in self-defense and then led the largest manhunt in Texas history. Cortez's feats of horsemanship are legendary, as is the sense of Texas justice miscarried as he finally turned himself in and was jailed for a crime he didn't really commit. This story only underscores the political dimension of the muralist movement, which is tinged with sarcasm as well as inspiration. Most recently, in 1982, Moctezuma Esparaza Productions of Los Angeles, with the help of the National Endowment for the Humanities, released a feature motion picture based on the life of Gregorio Cortez as seen through the various ballads concerning his feats and his plight. Cortez is played by Edward James Olmo, who has his final moment of stunning cinematic power when he walks from the Gonzales, Texas, jailhouse to board a train that will take him to a long-term prison sentence at Huntsville. *The Ballad of Gregorio Cortez* has been called "the best film ever made about Texas." This is perhaps an overstatement, but at least it did add a Mexican view of the heretofore hallowed Texas Rangers to our tapestry of history. It also, along with the film, *Seguin,* has signaled the beginning of a small but talented Chicano film-making movement that promises to destroy such stereotypes as that of the Cisco Kid, a "fancy Dan" Mexican style "Lone Ranger," played by Leo Carillo in the 1930s. In a sense, in a collective *film* enterprise the wall murals are beginning to take on motion and depth of character in motion pictures and on television screens.

Two further murals, both of which are religious, merit consideration. One is extremely powerful and called *Holocaust.* It portrays a man in the middle ground frantically clutching a large cross, while in the foreground, in front of some cactus, stands a diapered baby, who may or may not be born, with a ray of light shining down upon him, while the whole mural seems to be an explosion. The other mural, not so powerful but rather gentle, shows Our Lady of the Rosary arising out of a tree of life on a pink cloud. She provides inspiration to the women of the Hispanic community, and, at the same time, clearly indicates that for Chicanos, religion is also political.

Expressionistic murals are clearly the mainstream of today's collective Chicano art, but individual painters have also made their mark. Back in the sixties, a local Austin painter, Mel Casas, painted *Humanscope Number 51 Auto-Erotic,* a brash seduction scene in the back of a car. While he was painting this, the sculptor, Luis Jimenez, created a statue of a woman making love to a Volkswagon bug in what critic and Jimenez's dealer at the time, Dave Hickey, terms "the transmissionary position."[3] It was supposed to be an "image of the American Dream," but it turned into an irreverent version of "Leda and the bug." There were other Chicano artists who have been more subtle. Jesse Trevino's photo-realist painting, *Los Santos de San Antonio* (1980), is at one and the same time a study of light and its impact on the reflective surface of the window of a store selling religious objects, and also, because it places these objects through reflection against the gleaming skyscrapers of San Antonio, it is an ironic comment on the city and its power elite. Amado Pena of Austin, Texas, once the revolutionary poster artist of the Crystal City, Texas, lettuce strike, has recently, through visits to Santa Fe, rediscovered his mother's Indian heritage, and today he paints works that dramatize in vivid colors and wonderfully powerful lines, his mestizo heritage.

But the important Hispanic artist today is Luis Jimenez,[4] best known for his sculpture that ranges from the life-sized Reginald Marsh-style cutouts of *Honky Tonk,* to his glitzy, powerful fibreglass statues of *The Vaquero* (1976), *The Sodbuster* (1982), *Progress I, 1973,* and *Progress II, 1977.* All of these works are part of a series which Jimenez claims are true reinterpretations of our Western heritage—modifications of the iconic paintings of Frederic Remington, Charley Russell, and Thomas Hart Benton. *The Vaquero,* once displayed among the tall buildings on New York's Fifth Avenue, recalls the cowboy's vaquero

Mel Casas, *Humanscape No. 51, (Auto-Erotic)*. Courtesy of Mr. Robert Wilson, Houston, Texas. M. Lipscomb, Photographer.

heritage. It now stands as a delight and inspiration to Mexican American children in Houston's Moody Park in the heart of the barrio.

The Sodbuster, created for the city of Fargo, North Dakota, is a white-bearded farmer pushing a plow across the plains behind two substantial oxen. Interestingly enough, his plow unearths fossils and arrowheads, relics of older tenants of the land and former cultures, whose "trails" have been "plowed under," in Charley Russell's words. *Progress I* shows a tired—indeed exhausted—Indian atop a worn-out horse on top of a buffalo whose eyes gleam red, and who surges with power. The buffalo, in fact, is trampling on a leaping coyote while a rabbit races before it. Beneath the coyote is a cowskull, Charley Russell's unmistakable trademark. The face and head of the buffalo are also unmistakably those of a stylized Chinese temple dog. In Jimenez's work, traditions do clash, or as in *Progress II,* a cowboy atop a blue vaulting horse roping a surging Longhorn cow—not a steer—satirizes the whole Wild West tradition of Remington and Russell, whom Jimenez believes to be the most iconically powerful of Western artists. In another irony, Jimenez, like Remington, has found a way to immortalize his work in inexpensive modern fibreglass rather than old-fashioned bronze. Luis Jimenez continues to upset city fathers with his art. Uncertain as to whether to regard his latest creation, *Southwest Pieta,* as sincerely religious, though it is a man holding an erotic dying woman in his arms, rather than Mary holding Christ, the city of Albuquerque removed the statue from tourist-oriented Old Town to the Mexican barrio.

Luis Jimenez, like T. C. Cannon, Fritz Scholder, and the artists of the "Indian Renaissance," deals in the irony and satire that is fashionable in the mid-twentieth century. He has also created, in the fibreglass statues of Western icons, a deconstructive vision of the Old West that is above all, public art. His large sculptures, like so many of the works of the recent modernist movement, are meant to be seen by the masses, not hidden way in the homes of the rich. They represent an ideology in and of themselves. They also harken back to the 1960s love affair with popular culture, from obscene comic books, and Andy Warhol's *Brillo Boxes* to flashy custom cars. Many of the works of that period were designed to shock middle-class Anglo-Americans. In Jimenez's case, his sculptured works had that objective too, but they also grew out of his work in his father's's electric sign company, and, more importantly, his utter fascination with automobiles. About the same time that Tom Wolfe, in his *Kandy-Kolored-Tangerine-Flake-Streamlined Baby* was touting electric sign-makers and California custom car designers as the great unsung artists of our age, comparing them to the sculptor, Brancusi, Luis Jimenez was glitter-spraying low riders with the same youthful exuberance that now informs his works of sculpture. Some Western artists who portrayed the country and its epic history sought timelessness and transcendence, but Luis Jimenez, like Billy Soza War Soldier and even Charley Russell, is very much a part of and for his time, making myths out of spray-painted fibreglass.

CHAPTER 33

THE TRANSCENDENT WEST
OF GEORGIA O'KEEFFE

While many artists were documenting the history of the West from varying points of view, whether it be that of the cowboy artist-illustrator, the Mexican American, the documentors of the Dust Bowl disaster, or the shooting stars of "the Red Man's Renaissance," only one twentieth-century artist envisioned the kind of transcendent West that so captivated Albert Bierstadt in the nineteenth century. This was Georgia O'Keeffe from Sun Prairie, Wisconsin.

O'Keeffe managed since the second decade of the twentieth century to create on canvas a West that is uniquely her own, one that features the earth and the sky rather than the tale of any tribe, red, brown, or white. This makes her work seem to exist beyond historical time and in Biblical terms, like the earth that "abideth forever." Her paintings present a modernist view of the West that is at the same time still in the mainstream of American representational art.

O'Keeffe's story is well known.[1] Born in 1887, she studied variously at the Art Institute of Chicago, at the Art Students League in New York under William Merritt Chase and Kenyon Cox, the University of Virginia with Alon

Bemont, Columbia Teacher's College with Arthur Dow and at the famous 291 Gallery with Alfred Stieglitz, whom she married in 1924. Her experience and training were thus at the very center of the American Modernist movement, and yet, in the end, she must be best known for her very special view of the American West. From William Merritt Chase she must have acquired her love for color, from the works of Wassily Kandinsky suggested to her by Bemont, her sense of form and pictorial rhythm, and from the great connoisseur of Japanese art, Arthur Dow, both a sense of calligraphy and the functionalism of the minimal so characteristic of the Japanese print. But, like that other great master of recent times, the architect, Frank Lloyd Wright, O'Keeffe really acknowledged no antecedents. Always she strove for independence. Perhaps that is one reason why the wide-open spaces of the American Southwest appealed to her more than New York City and the Stieglitz family seat at Lake George. Of the latter she declared, "There wasn't anything to paint there."

Amarillo, Texas was the part of the West that O'Keeffe saw first when she taught art there in the years 1912 to 1914. At the time Amarillo was still a rough Texas cattle town where there were more saloons than churches, or schools, for that matter, and cowboys still settled grudges on main street in traditional gunfighter fashion. In fact, O'Keeffe remembered especially the day one Beal Sneed gunned down a man who ran off with his wife, and the man's banker father for good measure, and then was acquitted by a jury of his peers after ten minutes deliberation. Tempting though it might have been to a cowboy illustrator-artist like Charley Russell, O'Keeffe did not paint the incident or even the memory of it. She was more interested in the land, the vast rolling contours of the Staked Plains and the sky that could be seen for 360 degrees in every direction. In the years 1912–14, and later 1916–18, when she taught art at the West Texas Normal School in Canyon, Texas, twenty miles south of Amarillo, O'Keeffe, usually using watercolors, painted the prairie and the sky. Some of her most striking works depicted the glow of the lights of Canyon disbursed in a kind of halo by the dust that still hung over the prairie at night, or the strange green, red and yellow rings of the evening star, as she perceived it in her own special way. The Palo Duro Canyon also fascinated her. She saw it as a burning, seething caldron, almost like a blast furnace full of dramatic light and color. Then there was the red stormy sky pierced by blazing yellow lightning bolts, which she painted as late as 1954. While many, including Frederic Remington, who said he would rather rent out Texas and live in hell, complained about West Texas and its lack of amenities, Georgia O'Keeffe loved it. On the plains of Texas O'Keeffe combined all of the elements of her training into the first phase of her own distinctive style.

Few identified it with Texas at first. The colorful star bursts of watery light, the seething caldron of color, and the thin calligraph done with a Japanese brush and appropriately titled *Blue Lines* when they appeared in her first "solo" show at Alfred Stieglitz's Gallery in April of 1917, were labeled "delicately veiled symbolism for 'what every woman knows.'" [2] A reviewer for the *Christian Science Monitor* went on to say, "Now perhaps for the first time in art's history, the style is the woman." And indeed much of O'Keeffe's paintings, from views of Jack-in-the-pulpits and clam shell configurations to views into the inside of New Mexican churches, seemed to incorporate with intensity images of the phallic, both male and female. O'Keeffe vehemently denied it, of course, when critics occasionally made allusions to the theme, but the fact was that the sexual allusions were there, in fact they were very much a part of "the style that is the woman." O'Keeffe was always liberated.

In the summer of 1917, traveling to Colorado with her sister, Claudia, O'Keeffe first saw New Mexico. "I loved it immediately. From then on I was always on my way back." But it was not until twelve years later, in 1929, that she made the trip again. By that time she had married Alfred Stieglitz and spent most of her summers on Lake George, which is where she first took up painting mammoth flowers that filled the canvas. On May 1, 1929, however, traveling with photographer Paul Strand's wife, she headed out for New Mexico. It was the beginning of a life-long adventure in the Southwest. That summer she was "captured" by her old friend Mabel Dodge Luhan, who shipped her luggage directly from Santa Fe to Taos. O'Keeffe and Beck Strand were put up in the same Pink House across that "force field" meadow from Mabel's house that once sheltered D. H. Lawrence. For much of that summer O'Keeffe was engaged in "art talk" with the numerous celebrities that Mabel brought in, or else pressed into service as an intermediary between Mabel and Tony Luhan, who were quarreling constantly, especially when Luhan went back to living with his Indian wife.

From 1929 on, O'Keeffe spent the summers in New Mexico, despite protests by Stieglitz, who stayed behind at Lake George. At first she stayed with the Pack family at a dude ranch called Ghost Ranch. There she met the photographer Ansel Adams in 1933, and began a life-long friendship, which was appropriate because, more than any other artists of the twentieth century,

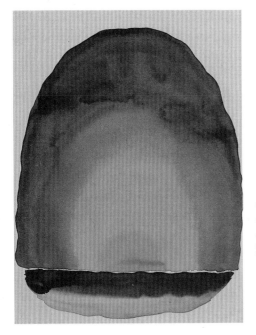

Georgia O'Keeffe, *Light Coming On the Plains II*, (1916-18). Courtesy the Amon Carter Museum, Fort Worth.

Georgia O'Keeffe, *Grey Hills*, (1942). Indianapolis Museum of Art, Gift of Mr. and Mrs. James W. Fesler.

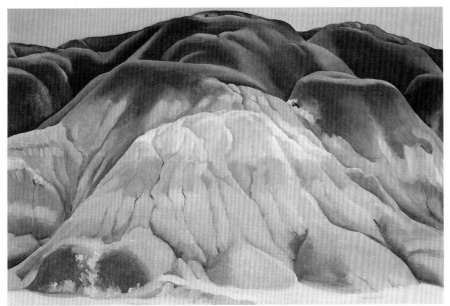

they focused on the enduring qualities of the Western landscape. In 1937, in a letter to Stieglitz, O'Keeffe described something of the joy she received from the New Mexico landscape. It was a "perfectly mad looking country—hills and cliffs and washes too crazy to imagine all thrown up into the air by God and let tumble where they would. It was certainly as spectacular as anything I've ever seen—and that was pretty good—the evening glow on a cliff much higher than these here in a vast sort of red and gold and purple amphitheatre while we sat on our horse on top of a hill of the whitish green earth."[3]

It was spectacular landscapes such as this that kept O'Keeffe coming back. And it was such landscapes that she painted. Her favorites, the "Grey Hills" and the "Black Mountain," red and yellow cliffs that swept down in cascades of color, "the White Place," red and orange hills folded and wrinkled by eons of time until they looked like a mummified animal carcass, the Pedernal looking down on these same wrinkled red hills, and one of her masterpieces *Red Hills and Bones*. Here she joined those twin symbols of time that meant so much to her in one picture. The bone that lay across the foreground loomed enormous and as pre-historic as Charles Willson Peale's mastodon femur discovery 140 years earlier.

In 1931 she had bought a Model A Ford and taught herself to drive. The car made her more mobile than dude ranch horses, and it was especially good for painting out of the heat of the sun. O'Keeffe had torn out the passenger seat and put the driver's seat on a swivel so that she could turn around, rest her easel on the back seat, and see the hills framed by the wide windows. When it got too hot for painting she could take a nap in the shade under the high-standing car. The Model A became a kind of personal triumphant drama for her, as was the acquisition of her own place, the Rancho de los Burros, which she acquired in 1928, together with "a mountain all her own" to paint. The small ranch, without electricity or running water, was acquired by the sale of just one of her paintings.

After she acquired the ranch, O'Keeffe began to collect bones—animal skulls in particular—that she liked. She often took these back East with her to have something of the Southwest to paint during the dreary New York winters. This resulted in her famous skull series in paintings like *Ram's Head with Hollyhock* (1935), *Summer Days* (1936), a deer skull accompanied by flowers looming against the clouds above the distant red hills, and *From the Faraway Nearby* (1937), a very elaborately horned deer skull placed in front of similarly lined distant hills. This series was not necessarily a hymn to Western wildlife, though it did recall the days when New Mexico must have teemed with wild game, and hence the series was as nostalgic as anything Remington ever painted. In these works, O'Keeffe also played on the ambiguous difference between the bones in the foreground and the hills in the background, and between the live flowers and the dead skulls. In each picture, her draftsmanship was precise and perfect, endowing the skulls with an eerie sense of a life of their own. Her favorite was *Cow's Skull-Red, White and Blue* (1931), which, in a puckish mood, she deemed "The Great American Painting" to go with "The Great American Novel" that, according to her, everyone was trying to write in those days.

Skulls were not her only bone paintings. She also did a series on the pelvis which formed an ideal frame for whatever colored sky she chose to place behind it. And color is as much a part of her art as anything could be. This also became evident in the penitente cross series that she painted. There are black crosses virtually blotting out a seething, bubbling hot landscape, as if the crosses themselves were aflame, and there are white crosses with cool maroon backgrounds. O'Keeffe was inspired not only by the crosses that she came across atop lonely hills and mountains, but also by the crucifixions, or penitente ceremonies, that she surreptitiously observed.

In 1945 O'Keeffe decided to move closer to a town, albeit none of the townspeople spoke English, and she refused to learn Spanish. In that year, however, after a struggle with the Catholic Church, she acquired a house in the historic northern settlement of Abiquiu. Then she began painting a series of views of a door in the wall that fascinated her. It was this "door series," together with her "flower series," that the Indian artist Fritz Scholder parodied in some of his paintings. O'Keeffe, however, admired the stark geometry, just as she admired the geometry of the church at Rancho de Taos, in much the same ways that the photographer, Timothy O'Sullivan, had admired a similar Spanish church in Santa Fe in the 1880s.

In the 1960s, during the time of the Chicano uprisings in New Mexico's San Luis Valley, she painted the road that ran past her house to Tierra Amarilla, the scene of the occupation of the county courthouse. She painted the road in the same style that she used in her first works of 1917: the thin curved lines of the Japanese calligrapher. And finally, like Maynard Dixon in his spectacular *Cloud World,* she turned to painting only the sky in her largest painting, which is twenty-four feet long and eight-feet high. It is a view of the geometry of clouds as seen from an airplane flying above them, and in the distance you can see the curvature of the earth.

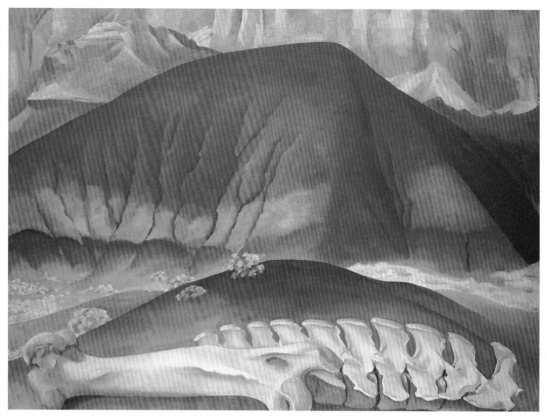

Georgia O'Keeffe, *Red Hills and Bones,* (1941). Philadelphia Museum of Art, The Alfred Stieglitz Collection.

From this description of her work, it should be clear that the modern master, Georgia O'Keeffe, had, over a period of 73 years, seen or envisioned a West of the imagination apparently different from any who came before her. Her vision remained in the representational tradition necessarily espoused by Western artists, and, though clearly modernist, it defied classification as cubist, expressionist, or even surrealist. Art critics have not yet been able to dream up a label for her unique style. But in one of its many contexts, that of the West of the imagination, it does have profound meaning. O'Keeffe's Western work underscores the enduring, timeless quality of the Western experience in a way that the ethnographic Taos painters, like Sharp and Couse, reached for but could never quite grasp. The lady from Sun Prairie's vision reached back, beyond history, beyond even the thousand years of ethno-history, to the ageless vision of the geologist. She presented a twentieth-century version of those great illustrated reconstructions of the vast geological prehistory of the

West so characteristic of the dazzled visions of the scientists who first saw the
"Great Denudation" that marked the Grand Canyon and the Paria Plateau as
far as the pink cliffs of Zion and Capitol Reef, or that "stunned imagination"
of the survey party that first saw in 1873 the Mount of the Holy Cross shining
white in the sun, deep in the mountain fastness of western Colorado. In short,
O'Keeffe's paintings make one realize how very recent and how very relevant
the historical era of the American West has been in comparison with the
transcendent eternities she has portrayed.

Georgia O'Keeffe is not the last artist to be fascinated by the West. The
tradition of Western art goes on today in even stronger and more varied terms.
Vast alluring open spaces in the West have attracted the grandiose imagina-
tions of a new group of highly representational artists—the earth sculptors.
Michael Heizer has carved his own deep, perplexing man-made canyons in the
Nevada desert and he has placed the pseudo-primitive pyramids that so resemble those of ancient Mexico out in lonely isolation on the Western landscape.
Christo has created a "running fence" of cloth panels across a part of Califor-
nia from the mountains to the sea. Robert Smithson has left the Great Salt
Lake with a massive, enigmatic spiral jetty. And in a desolate spot near Que-
mado, New Mexico, Walter de Maria has actually made a place where we can

Cristo, *Running Fence*. Gianfranco Gorgoni, Contact Press Images, Inc., New York.

literally bring lightning from the skies. Using stainless steel poles planted in the ground over a vast area, like Benjamin Franklin in days of old, he has rediscovered the lightning rod, but on such a vast scale that its attractions of lightning patterns form a thing of beauty that is at the same time awe-inspiring, like the West itself, a never-ending source of wonder for so-called civilized man today. An act of modern engineering, *Lightning Field* also hearkens back to the sacred technology of the Southwest Indians and their rain dance. It is thus significant, that all of these new, even "radical" earth sculpture forms that see man attempting to dominate, control, or even duplicate the earth and nature itself, actually harken back to very old traditions. They call up a new primitivism and they re-emphasize nature's forces as Western art has always done, because first of all, the West is a place and then it is also a state of mind. Nothing recalls this more dramatically than Ansel Adams's mysterious, god-like self-portrait, a shadow of a man's image in the holy environment of de Maria's *Lightning Field.*

As we come to the conclusion of our survey of the many forms of Western art, it is important to ask the question what have we, or can we learn from it? What can we learn about America and about Americans as well? Western art, as we have seen, embodies many themes and contains, like the West itself, many possibilities. Take nature itself. From the beginning, a large number of Western artists have formed the culmination of a romantic naturalist tradition that reaches back beyond the European romantics like William Wordsworth to a pantheism beyond the edges of history. By creating an object, usually one that condenses a visualization of nature into a single frame, Western artists have created a series of sacred spaces in the American landscape where people go to match their views with artists like Bierstadt and Moran, to effect, like Ansel Adams most recently, the ultimate, sublime connection between art, nature and God.

By the same token, science and Western art have always gone hand in hand, from Titian Peale's early excursions onto the vast prairies to the engineering of the current earth works. A closer look at the symbiotic relationship between science and art reveals a profound process at work, clearly visible in the lithographs of the Great Reconnaissance. The scientific artist, in attempting to render the exact forms of nature, inevitably transforms them. It is a vivid example of physicist Werner Heisenberg's very modern "Uncertainty Principle."

In another vein, Western art forms a fascinating laboratory for examining continuity in art. Through a period when novelty and innovation in art have been fashionable, Western art as narrative or documentary realism, an art of high information content, runs closer to the great, lasting traditions in world art where representation and replication were ideals. One immediately thinks of the classicism of ancient Greece and Rome, but one could also look to the Maya and the Aztecs in this hemisphere and to China and India in the Far East. American Western art, because it is still a living tradition, gives us matchless insight into the way continuities have dominated the great artistic traditions. For example, almost all Western artists today acknowledge having been inspired by the work of earlier artists, like Frederic Remington, and most acknowledge personal masters and mentors like the artists of the Renaissance; indeed, in such close-knit groups as the Cowboy Artists of America, they have

Walter De Maria, *The Lightning Field,* Copyright © Dia Art Foundation, 1980. Photographer: John Cliett.

Ansel Adams, *Self Portrait, Monument Valley, Utah, 1958.* Courtesy of the Trustees of the Ansel Adams Publishing Rights Trust, Carmel, California. All rights reserved.

attempted to duplicate the "Renaissance School" master and apprentice experience.

Western art, in some forms, from drawings to photographs, has also been the driving force behind nineteenth- and early twentieth-century anthropology, which in turn, is but one scientific expression of a sophisticated cult of primitivism. Some forms of Western art, from the works of George Catlin through the drawings of Richard Kern, to the works of the Taos painters, have induced a desire to transcend the role of colonial observer and to immerse oneself in the consciousness of another culture. We can also see how this works as we look closely into the twentieth-century arts of the American Indian and the Mexican-American. As we do so, we ourselves are anthropologists on a great adventure.

But we can also trace, not only the dreams, but the disillusionments of modern, even enforced "primitivism" as we observe its effect on the Native Americans themselves. This is an important story, an episode and a process that happens nowhere else in quite the same way.

And Western art, with its creation of a series of heroes and heroic events—men like the cowboy and events like Custer's Last Stand—has shown us several of the many ways in which a civilization digests and interprets cultural experiences. The downtrodden, working-stiff cowboy proletarian is incredibly glamourized in almost all artistic media, except the still camera that often reveals the harsh realities of his life. By the same token, Custer's Last Stand, in all its painted variations, is essentially a nineteenth-century version of *Apocalypse Now*. These paintings are like a rationalization or digesting of the unpleasant experiences associated with a battle or a war that was lost.

The nineteenth-century West, because of the many government surveys, and because of its exotic landscape and exotic native peoples, was one of the prime foci of early photography. Indeed, many Western artists were also accomplished photographers. In no place else is there quite the same opportunity to study the process of the cross-fertilization of two, and if we include the movies, three art forms as well as the divergent courses they also took. Indeed, this sense of cross fertilization in the arts has been one of the many themes in this book.

Western art also seems, to the distant observer, if not also to many Americans, to represent what is distinctive about American civilization. While there have been many frontiers around the world, there has been only one American West. The heroic Western adventure has seemingly made our culture distinctive in the eyes of observers around the world. People tend to conjure up visions of the "wild riders and vacant lands," of cowboys and Indians, when they think of Americans. The cowboy and the Indian are both universally recognized as archetypal heroes in the world wide cultural and political imagination.

Thus, Georgia O'Keeffe's twentieth-century transcendent vision should only serve to remind us of the immensely poetic, landscape that has been and still is the West. And all the other artists and photographers and image-makers through whose eyes we have seen the many Wests that together make up the great saga of human experience on this continent should underscore the importance of myth. They should serve to illustrate just how myth or the story of a people—the tale of the tribe—weaves together the many strands and layers of complex human experience into one understandable story that inspires the people or the tribe to go on as one into succeeding epochs, sustained by an increasingly timeless tradition. It should also be clear that this myth or story that we tell ourselves about the historic Western experience has become part of that experience. Hence, in describing the myth, we are also describing a perceived reality that has profoundly affected both Western and American behavior patterns and values. This powerful, basic story to which new elements are added as time passes also has had a life of its own in oral ties, music and the written or printed word, but it has also been reified and carried along by the artists and image-makers. It is this dimension of American experience, one so often lost in the litter of art criticism on one hand the so-called "Real West" history on the other that ignores social and psychological realities, that we have sought to present. It should be clear by now that the awesome Western landscape and the incredible historic experiences that rise up in our collective memories like ghosts from some vivid past have provided inspiration not only for generations of artists, but also for generations of Americans, red, brown and white. Thus the West lives on, even today, in the hearts of most Americans. Now we have only to ask, as we move toward the year 2000: What new myths will the West engender?

NOTES

Introduction

  1. Quoted in Arthur Moore, *The Frontier Mind* (New York, London, Toronto, 1957), p. 11.

  2. Samuel Flagg Bemis, *A Diplomatic History of the United States* (New York, 1953), pp. 181–2.

  3. Bernard DeVoto, *The Course of Empire* (Boston, 1952), pp. 248–9.

  4. Material on knowledge of the Missouri River is based on Abraham Nasatir, *Before Lewis and Clark*, 2 vols. (St. Louis, Mo., 1952), passim, William H. Goetzmann, *Exploration and Empire* (New York, 1966), pp. 15–16, Gary Moulton, ed., *Atlas of the Lewis and Clark Expedition* (Lincoln, Neb., 1983), passim.

  5. Antonio Gerbi, *The Dispute of the New World* (Pittsburgh, 1973), passim.

PART 1.

Chapter 1.

  1. Edgar P. Richardson, Brooke Hindle, Lillian B. Miller, *Charles Willson Peale and His World* (New York, 1982), p. 142. For an account from Peale's autobiography see Charles Coleman Sellers, *Mr. Peale's Museum* (New York, 1980), pp. 79–80.

  2. Ibid. passim.

  3. Richardson, Hindle and Miller, *Charles Wilson Peale and His World*, p. 122.

  4. Ibid., p. 119.

  5. Donald Jackson, ed. *The Letters of the Lewis and Clark Expedition* (Urbana, London, 1962), pp. 16–21, 23–24, 36–61 ff.

  6. This account of the Long Expedition is based on the following: Edwin James, *An Account of an Expedition from Pittsburg to the Rocky Mountains, Performed in the Years 1918 and '20*, 2 vols. and *Atlas* (Philadelphia, 1822), Goetzmann, *Exploration and Empire* and Roger Nichols and Patrick Halley, *Stephen Long and American Frontier Exploration* (Newark, Del., 1980).

  7. Quoted in William H. Goetzmann, *Army Exploration in the American West, 1803–1863* (New Haven, 1959), p. 40.

8. See Stephen H. Long Map, 1823 with Great Plains labeled "Great Desert" reproduced in Carl I. Wheat, *Mapping the Transmississippi West* 6. vols. (San Francisco, 1958), vol. II, opposite p. 80.

9. Patricia Trenton and Peter Hassrick, *The Rocky Mountains, A Vision For Artists in the Nineteenth Century* (Norman, Okla., 1983), p. 20.

10. Barbara Stafford, *Voyage into Substance: Art, Science, Nature and the Illustrated Travel Account, 1760–1840* (Cambridge, Mass., and London, 1984) passim.

11. Trenton and Hassrick, op. cit., p. 28.

12. Nichols and Halley, op. cit., p. 162.

13. See Jessie Poesch, *Titian Ramsey Peale, 1799–1885 and His Journals of the Wilkes Expedition* (Philadelphia, 1961) for a biographical account of Titian Peale.

CHAPTER 2.

1. Unless otherwise stated, this account of Catlin's life is based upon Marjorie Catlin Roehm, *The Letters of George Catlin* (Berkeley and Los Angeles, 1966), Harold McCracken, *George Catlin and the Old Frontier* (New York, 1959), William Treuttner, *The Natural Man Observed, George Catlin's Indian Gallery* (Washington, D.C., 1979) and *George Catlin, Letters and Notes on the Manners, Customs and Conditions of North American Indians*, 2 vols. (Dover reprint, New York, 1973).

2. Treuttner, p. 70.

3. George Catlin, *Letters and Notes*, I, pp. 2–3.

4. For a discussion of McKenney's Indian Gallery see Herman Viola, *Thomas L. McKenney, Architect of America's Early Indian Policy 1816–1830* (Chicago, 1974).

5. Quoted in Treuttner, p. 107.

6. Treuttner, p. 92.

7. Catlin, *Letters and Notes*, I, pp. 56–7, II, pp. 196–200.

8. For Catlin's 1867 description of the O-Kee-Pa ceremony see John Ewers, ed., George Catlin, *O-Kee-Pah*, reprint from original (New Haven, 1967).

9. Ibid.

10. William H. Goetzmann, *Exploration and Empire*, p. 190.

11. Catlin, *Letters and Notes*, I, p. 4.

12. See organization in George Catlin, *A Descriptive Catalogue of Catlin's Indian Gallery . . . Exhibiting at the Egyptian Hall, Piccadilly, London. . . .* (London, 1841)

13. John Cullum, MS, "Lecture on the Manners & Customs of the North American Indians. Illustrated By the Costumes Worn By Them" (London, 1841). See Treuttner, p. 138. MS courtesy of William Reese.

14. Catlin Correspondence with Sir Thomas Phillipps, MSS Thomas Gilcrease Institute of American History and Art, no date, but probably late 1850.

15. McCracken, pp. 202 ff.

16. Roehm, p. 326.

17. Catlin's travels in South America are described by him in *Episodes from Life Among the Indians and Last Rambles*, Marvin C. Ross, ed. (Norman, Okla., 1979), see especially Itinerary from Catlin's 1871 Catalogue, Appendix B, pp. 344–5. This Itinerary can also be found in Catlin Correspondence, Gilcrease Institute. But the date of his departure for South America appears to be 1854, not 1852 as Catlin implies in his *Itinerary*. See his letters of May 3, 1854 from Paris, and November 27, 1854 from South America, especially the latter. Catlin correspondence, Gilcrease Institute. We are especially indebted to Nancy Anderson at the National Gallery of Art for calling our attention to this discrepancy in dates.

18. Ross, *Last Rambles*, p. 10.

19. Ibid., p. 345.

20. The best biography of Humboldt in English is Douglas Botting, *Humboldt and the Cosmos* (New York, 1973).

21. Catlin to Sir Thomas Phillipps, MS, Gilcrease. Bruxelles Nov. 3, 1857. Though deaf, Catlin heard a sound "not unlike the drawing of a violin bow across one of the strings."

22. Quoted in Goetzmann, *Exploration and Empire*, p. 189.

CHAPTER 3.

1. For biographical data on John Mix Stanley, see Julia Ann Schimmel, *John Mix Stanley and Imagery of the West in Nineteenth Century American Art* (PhD. Diss., 1983).

2. William H. Goetzmann and Becky Reese, *Texas Images and Visions* (Austin, Tex., 1983), pp. 10, 54–5. Also see Schimmel, pp. 211–12.

3. Unless otherwise stated, details as to Paul Kane's biography are based on J. Russell Harper, *Paul Kane's Frontier* (Austin, Tex., and London, 1971).

4. Ibid., see esp., p. 213.

5. For biographical details of Captain Seth Eastman, see John Francis McDermott, *Pictorial Historian of the Indian* (Norman, Okla. 1961), Chapter IV.

CHAPTER 4.

1. Unless otherwise stated, biographical details concerning Prince Maximilian and Karl Bodmer are based on Goetzmann and William Orr, *Karl Bodmer's America* (Lincoln, Neb., 1984).

2. Quoted in Davis Thomas and Karin Ronnefeldt, *People of the First Man* (New York, 1976), pp. 200–201.

CHAPTER 5.

1. Ron C. Tyler, ed., *Alfred Jacob Miller: Artist on the Oregon Trail* (Fort Worth, 1982), p. 51.

2. Unless otherwise stated, biographical details concerning Alfred Jacob Miller are based on Ron C. Tyler, ed., *Alfred Jacob Miller: Artist on the Oregon Trail* (Fort Worth, 1982) and Mae Reed Porter and Odessa Davenport, *Scotsman in Buckskin* (New York, 1963).

3. David L. Brown, *Three Years in the Rocky Mountains,* reprinted from the Cincinnati *Atlas* of 1845 by Edward Eberstadt & Sons, 1950.

4. Brown, p. 10.

5. Tyler, p. 37.

6. Ibid., p. 38.

PART 2.

CHAPTER 6.

1. Zenas Leonard, *Narrative of the Adventures of Zenas Leonard . . .* , John Ewers, ed., under the title of *Adventures of Zenas Leonard Fur Trader* (Norman, Okla., 1959), p. 89.

2. Ibid., pp. 94–5.

3. E. Maurice Bloch, *George Caleb Bingham, The Evolution of an Artist,* 2 vols. (Berkeley and Los Angeles, 1967), Ch. V, p. 89n.

4. Quoted in Bloch, I, pp. 144–5.

5. The "key" to the characters in *The County Election* made by Oscar Potter is in the collection of the Arrow Rock Historic Site. But see also Bloch I, p. 146n.

6. Bloch I, p. 145.

CHAPTER 7.

1. Richard Henry Dana, *Two Years Before the Mast,* Modern Library Edition (Boston, 1840; New York, 1936), p. 176.

2. Ibid., p. 134–5.

3. For biographical details on James Walker, see Peggy and Harold Samuels, *Illustrated Biographical Encyclopedia of the Artists of the American West.* Also see Howard R. Lamar, ed., *The Reader's Encyclopedia of the American West* (New York, 1977), p. 1233.

4. For biographical details on Theodore Gentilz, see Dorothey S. Kendall and Carmen Perry, *Gentilz, Artist of the Old Southwest* (Austin, Tex., 1974).

5. See James Patrick McGuire, *Herman Lungkwitz, Romantic Landscapist on the Texas Frontier* (Austin and San Antonio, Tex., 1983).

6. Samuel Ratcliffe, *Painting Texas History* (PhD. Diss., The University of Texas, 1985), Ch. II, p. 3.

7. Ibid., II, pp. 6–7.

8. Dan Kilgore, *How Did Davy Die?* (College Station, Texas and London, 1978), passim.

9. Ratcliffe, II, p. 6.

10. Ibid., II, p. 13.

11. Kilgore, passim.

12. Ratcliffe, II, p. 14.

13. Cecelia Steinfeldt, *The Onderdonks: A Family of Texas Painters* (San Antonio, 1976).

14. Ratcliffe, II, pp. 21–2.

15. Biographical details on William Huddle can be found in Pauline A. Pinckney, *Painting in Texas, The Nineteenth Century* (Austin, 1967), pp. 186–209 deals with the major painters of the Texas Revolution. But see also William H. Goetzmann and Becky Reese, *Texas, Images and Visions* (Austin, 1983), pp. 26–7, and Ibid., pp. 34–5.

16. Ratcliffe, Ch. II, p. 38.

CHAPTER 8.

1. *A Catalogue of the Collection of American Paintings in The Corcoran Gallery of Art, Vol. I, Painters Born Before 1850* (Reprint edition, Washington, D.C., 1974), pp. 52–3.

2. For biographical information on Woodville see, Ibid., pp. 115–6.

3. William Gilpin, *Mission of the North American People. . . .*, rev. ed. (Philadelphia, 1874), p. 130.

4. Quoted in William H. Goetzmann, *When the Eagle Screamed, The Romantic Horizon in American Diplomacy* (New York, London, Sydney, 1966), p. 61.

5. Ronnie C. Tyler, *The Mexican War, A Lithographic Record* (Austin, Tex., 1973), pp. 15–16.

6. Quoted in Tyler, p. 27.

7. Ibid., p. 23.

8. Chamberlain's many adventures are recounted in Samuel Chamberlain, *My Confession: The Recollections of a Rogue* (New York, 1956), passim.

9. Quoted in Tyler, p. 19.

CHAPTER 9.

1. Material concerning the overland parties and Frémont's exploits is derived from William H. Goetzmann, *Exploration and Empire* (New York, 1966), pp. 169–78, 240–9, 266–70.

2. See Goetzmann, *Exploration and Empire*, pp. 333–52, Bernard Smith, *European Vision and the South Pacific 1768–1850* (Oxford, London, New York, 1960), passim, and Barbara Stafford, *Voyage into Substance* (Boston, 1984), passim.

3. Goetzmann, *Exploration and Empire*, pp. 266–70. For a more recent and complete account of Richard Kern's activities, see David J. Weber, *Richard H. Kern, Expeditionary Artist in the Far Southwest, 1848–1853* (Albuquerque, 1985).

4. See picture, Weber, p. 92.

5. Goetzmann, *Exploration and Empire*, pp. 281–93, 303–31 presents a synopsis and evaluation of the Pacific Railroad Surveys. A more complete treatment is in Goetzmann, *Army Exploration in the American West 1803–1863* (New Haven, 1959), pp. 262–337.

6. The Pacific Railroad Reports can be found in 33rd Cong. 2d Sess., *Sen. Exec. Doc. No. 78*, 1855, and variously until 1861. For a bibliographical description of the reports, see Henry R. Wagner and Charles L. Camp, *The Plains and the Rockies*, 4th ed., rev., enlarged and edited by Robert H. Becker (San Francisco, 1982).

7. Barbara Novak, *Nature and Culture, American Landscape Painting, 1825–1875* (New York, 1980), p. 137.

8. Goetzmann, *Army Exploration in the American West . . .*, 379–92, and illus. at back of book.

9. Daniel Boorstin, *The Americans: The National Experience* (New York, 1965), p. 223.

CHAPTER 10.

1. *An Artist on the Overland Trail, the 1849 Diary and Sketches of James F. Wilkins*, John Francis McDermott, ed. (San Marino, Calif., 1968), see espec. pp. 3, 6.

2. Gilpin, op. cit.

3. Quoted in Barbara S. Groseclose, *Emanuel Lentze, 1816–1868: Freedom Is the Only King* (Washington, D.C., 1975), p. 61.

4. For biographical details see, ibid., espec. pp. 27–33.

5. John D. Unruh, Jr., *The Plains Across* (Urbana, Chicago and London, 1979), p. 51.

6. Ibid., p. 49.

7. *Gold Rush, The Journals, Drawings and Other Papers of J. Goldsborough Bruff . . . April 2, 1849—July 20, 1851,* Georgia Willis Read and Ruth Gaines, eds. (New York, 1949).

8. Quoted in Matthew Baigell, *Albert Bierstadt* (New York, 1941), p. 56.

9. Ralph H. Gabriel, ed., *Sarah Royce, A Frontier Lady, Recollections of the Gold Rush and Early California* (New Haven, 1932), p. 3.

CHAPTER 11.

1. William Weber Johnson, *The Forty-Niners* (New York, 1974), p. 26.

2. Biographical details in Peggy and Harold Samuels, *The Illustrated Biographical Encyclopedia of Artists of the American West* (Garden City, N.Y., 1976), pp. 252–3.

3. Quotations in Johnson, *The Forty-Niners,* p. 43.

4. Unruh, *The Plains Across,* p. 120.

5. Johnson, *The Forty-Niners,* pp. 32–3.

6. Ibid., p. 32.

7. Unruh, *The Plains Across,* pp. 100–101.

8. Johnson, *The Forty-Niners,* pp. 202–203.

9. Quoted ibid., p. 38.

10. For biographical data on Nahl, see Moreland L. Stevens, *Charles Christian Nahl, Artist of the Gold Rush, 1818–1878* (Sacramento, 1976).

11. On Hahn, see Peggy and Harold Samuels, . . . *Biographical Encyclopedia,* pp. 200–201.

12. See Goetzmann, *Exploration and Empire,* pp. 623–27.

CHAPTER 12.

1. Peggy and Harold Samuels, *Biographical Encyclopedia,* p. 304. Also see Frank Marryat, *Mountains and Molehills* (London, 1855) for colored illustrations.

2. Peter Bacon Hales, *Silver Cities, the Photography of American Urbanization, 1839–1915* (Philadelphia, 1984), pp. 49–50.

3. Details regarding Emperor Norton I can be found in Albert Dressler, *Emperor Norton, Life and Experiences of a Notable Character in San Francisco, 1849–1880* (San Francisco, 1927), passim.

4. Hales, *Silver Cities,* p. 30.

5. Ibid., pp. 79–81.

6. Ibid., p. 48 ff.

7. Ibid., p. 50.

8. Biographical details on Watkins can be found in Peter E. Palmquist, *Carleton E. Watkins, Photographer of the American West* (Albuquerque, 1983).

PART 3.

CHAPTER 13.

1. Clarence King, *Mountaineering in the Sierra Nevadas* (Philadelphia and New York, 1962), p. 133.

2. Ibid., p. 152.

3. Quoted in Gordon Hendricks, *Albert Bierstadt, Painter of the American West* (New York, 1974), p. 63.

4. Ibid., p. 73.

5. Quoted in Barbara Novak, *Nature and Culture, American Landscape Painting 1825–1875* (New York, 1980), p. 154.

6. Hendricks, op. cit., p. 70.

7. Ibid., p. 73.

8. Ibid., p. 155.

9. Quoted in Patricia Trenton and Peter Hassrick, *The Rocky Mountains, A Vision For Artists in the 19th Century* (Norman, Okla., 1983), p. 139.

10. Quoted in Ralf A. Britsch, *Bierstadt and Ludlow, Painter and Writer in the West* (Provo, 1980), p. 31.

11. John Ruskin, *The Art Criticism of John Ruskin* (Gloucester, Ma., 1969), p. 37.

CHAPTER 14.

1. Fitz Hugh Ludlow, "Seven Weeks in the Great Yo-Semite," *Atlantic Monthly* (June 1864), 470.

2. See Weston J. Naef and James N. Wood, *Era of Exploration* (Boston, 1975), for a discussion of the professional and technological rivalries between the two photographers.

3. Quoted in David Robertson, *West of Eden, A History of the Art and Literature of Yosemite* (Yosemite, 1984), p. 23.

4. Quoted in Aubrey L. Haines *The Yellowstone Story* (Yellowstone, Wyo., 1977), p. 348.

CHAPTER 15.

1. For a full discussion of the exploration of the Yellowstone that treats the Hayden Expedition and those that preceded it, see Aubrey L. Haines, *The Yellowstone Story* (Yellowstone, Wyo., 1977).

2. Unless otherwise stated, biographical details about W. H. Jackson are from his autobiography *Time Exposure* (New York, 1940).

3. Unless otherwise stated, biographical details about Thomas Moran are from Thurman Wilkins's biography of the artist, *Thomas Moran, Artist of the Mountains* (Norman, Okla., 1966).

4. Gustave H. Buek, "Thomas Moran, N.A., the Grand Old Man of American Art," reprinted in *Thomas Moran, Explorer in Search of Beauty*, Fritof Fryxell, ed. (East Hampton, N.Y., 1958), 69.

5. Quoted in Thurman Wilkins, p. 61.

6. William H. Jackson, p. 198.

7. Thurman Wilkins, p. 218.

8. Ibid., p. 69.

9. Ibid., p. 65.

10. Aubrey L. Haines, p. 130.

11. Ibid.

12. Quoted in Beaumont Newhall and Diana Edkins, *William H. Jackson* (Fort Worth, 1974), p. 139.

13. William H. Jackson, p. 217.

14. Quoted in Newhall and Edkins, p. 15.

CHAPTER 16.

1. Quoted in William H. Goetzmann, "Limner of Grandeur: William H. Holmes and the Grand Canyon," *The American West* (May/June 1978), Vol. XV, No. 3., p. 17.

2. Thurman Wilkins, p. 87.

3. Thurman Wilkins, p. 93.

4. Ibid.

5. William H. Goetzmann, *Exploration and Empire* (New York, 1966), p. 566.

6. Clarence Dutton, *Tertiary History of the Grand Cañon District* (Washington, D.C., 1882), p. 63.

CHAPTER 17.

1. Thomas Hart Benton, "Benton's Essays on the Road to India" in LeRoy R. Hafen and Ann W. Hafen, eds., *Fremont's Fourth Expedition: A Documentary Account of the Disaster of 1848–9. . . .* (Glendale, Calif., 1960).

2. Keith Wheeler, *The Railroaders* (New York, 1973), p. 28.

3. Ibid., p. 91.

4. Richard Reinhardt, ed. Frank Leslie, *Out West on the Overland Train: Across the Continent Excursion With Leslie's Magazine in 1877 and the Overland Trip in 1867* (Reprint ed., Palo Alto, Calif., 1967), passim.

5. Weston J. Naef and James N. Wood, *The Era of Exploration* (Boston, 1975), p. 43. Also see William H. Jackson, *Time Exposure* (New York, 1950).

6. For biographical details on A. J. Russell see ibid., pp. 201–2.

7. Photo in *American Album*, Oliver Jensen, ed. (New York, 1968), p. 60.

8. Goetzmann, *Exploration and Empire*, p. 433.

9. Quoted in Naef and Wood, *The Era of Exploration*, p. 127.

10. Robert Utley, *The Indian Frontier of the American West, 1846–1860* (Albuquerque, 1984), p. 111.

11. *The Sherman Letters. Correspondence Between General and Senator Sherman*, Rachel Sherman Thorndike, ed. (New York, 1894), p. 320.

12. See especially Frank Leslie's *Illustrated Weekly*, vol. XV, 1883, p. 557.

13. Thorndike, *The Sherman Letters*, p. 321.

CHAPTER 18.

1. David Nevin, *The Soldiers* (New York, 1973), p. 37.

2. Robert M. Utley, *Indian, Soldier, Settler* (St. Louis, 1979), p. 45.

3. Robert M. Utley and Wilcomb E. Washburn, *The American Heritage History of the Indian Wars* (New York, 1977), p. 242.

4. Ibid., pp. 342–3.

5. Ibid., p. 341.

6. For biographical information on Remington, see Peggy and Harold Samuels, *Frederic Remington, A Biography* (Garden City, N.Y., 1982).

7. Calculation based on E. Douglas Allen, "Frederic Remington—Author and Illustrator, A List of His Contributions to American Periodicals," *Bulletin of the New York Public Library*, vol. 49, no. 12 (Dec., 1945): 895–912.

8. For biographical details on Charles Schreyvogel, see James D. Horan, *The Life and Art of Charles Schreyvogel* (New York, 1969).

9. Ibid., p. 5.

10. Ibid., p. 17.

11. Ibid., p. 25.

12. Ibid., pp. 41–2.

13. William Howze, Amon Carter Museum to author.

14. Robert Taft, *Artists and Illustrators of the Old West 1850–1900* (New York, 1953), pp. 137–9.

CHAPTER 19.

1. For a description of the Centennial Fair, see Dee Brown, *The Year of the Century, 1876* (New York, 1966), espec. pp. 123–37.

2. *The Sherman Letters*, Thorndike, ed., p. 289.

3. Donald Jackson, *Custer's Gold* (New Haven, 1966), passim.

4. Goetzmann, *Exploration and Empire*, pp. 630–31.

5. Evan Connell, *Son of the Morning Star, Custer and the Little Big Horn* (San Francisco, 1984), p. 267.

6. Ibid., p. 253.

7. Ibid., p. 266.

8. Don Russell, *Custer's Last* (Fort Worth, 1968), p. 13. Also see Richard Slotkin, *The Fatal Environment* (New York, 1985), p. 9.

9. Leslie Tillett, *Wind on the Buffalo Grass: The Indians' Own Account of the Battle at the Little Big Horn and the Death of Their Life on the Plains* (New York, 1976), p. 71.

10. Ibid., p. 99.

11. Ibid., p. 49.

12. Helen H. Blish, *A Pictographic History of the Oglala Sioux* (Lincoln, Neb., 1967).

13. For a review of Custer paintings see Don Russell, *Custer's Last*. Also see Robert Taft, *Artists and Illustrators of the Old West, 1850–1900* (New York, 1953), pp. 129–48, and Brian Dippie, *Custer's Last Stand: The Anatomy of an American Myth* (Missoula, University of Montana Publications in History, 1976), pp. 34–7, and illustration following p. 50.

14. Taft, *Artists and Illustrators*, pp. 134–41. Whitman quoted in Brian Dippie, see footnote 13.

CHAPTER 20.

1. Florence Curtis Graybill and Victor Boesen, *Edward Sheriff Curtis, Visions of a Vanishing Race* (New York, 1976), p. 13: General biographical details of Curtis's life are also based on this work by his daughter.
2. Ibid., p. 79.
3. Ibid., p. 13.
4. Ibid., p. 7.
5. Ibid., p. 28.
6. Christopher M. Lyman, *The Vanishing Race and Other Illusions: Photographs of Indians by Edward S. Curtis* (New York and Washington, 1982), p. 113, Graybill and Boesen, *Edward Sheriff Curtis*, p. 76.
7. Quoted in Graybill and Boesen, *Edward Sheriff Curtis*, p. 74.
8. Lyman, *The Vanishing Race*, see especially pp. 62–112.
9. Edward S. Curtis, letters to Harriet Leitch, MSS, Seattle Public Library.

PART 4.

CHAPTER 21.

1. Frederic Remington, "A Few Words from Mr. Remington," *Colliers*, XXXIV, March 18, 1905, p. 16.
2. Matthew Baigell, *The Western Art of Frederic Remington* (New York, 1976), p. 10.
3. Frank Norris, "Zola as a Romantic Writer" in *Literary Criticism of Frank Norris*, Donald Pizer, ed. (Austin, Tex., 1964), pp. 71–2.
4. Ibid., p. 72.
5. Unless otherwise stated, biographical details on Remington are based on Peggy and Harold Samuels, *Frederick Remington, A Biography* (Garden City, N.Y., 1982) and Peter Hassrick, *Frederic Remington* (New York, 1973).
6. Samuels, pp. 58–9.
7. See Theodore Roosevelt, *Ranch Life and the Hunting Trail* (New York, 1888).
8. Estelle Jussim, *Frederic Remington, the Camera and the Old West* (Fort Worth, 1983), passim.
9. Quoted in Hassrick, *Frederic Remington*, p. 30.
10. See H. W. Herrick, *Watercolor Painting: Description of Materials With Directions for Their Use in Elementary Practice* (New York, 1882). This work includes 62 pages of MS notes plus annotations by Remington on the leaves. Courtesy William Reese.
11. William Morris Hunt, *On Painting and Drawing*, Dover reprint (New York, 1976), pp. 14–15.
12. Samuels, p. 229.
13. Ibid., p. 228.
14. Ibid., p. 103.
15. See Peter Hassrick, *Frederic Remington, The Late Years* (Denver, 1981).

CHAPTER 22.

1. Frederic G. Renner, *Charles M. Russell* (New York, 1974), frontispiece.
2. Unless otherwise specified, all biographical information about C. M. Russell is from Harold McCracken's definitive biography, *The C. M. Russell Book* (New York, 1957).
3. Quoted in Renner, p. 21.
4. Quoted in McCracken, p. 42.
5. Ibid., p. 51.
6. Quoted in Renner, p. 20.
7. Personal interview with Ned Jacob, August, 1984.
8. Quoted in McCracken, p. 133.
9. Ibid., p. 643.
10. Ibid., p. 106.
11. Ibid., p. 112.
12 Ibid., p. 114.

13. Quoted in ibid., p. 131.

14. Ibid., p. 130.

15. *Paper Talk, Charley Russell's American West*, Brian Dippie, ed. (New York, 1979), p. 152.

16. McCracken, p. 184.

17. Ibid., p. 187.

18. Russell, Austin, C.M.R., *Charles Russell, Cowboy Artist* (New York, 1957), p. 227.

19. Ibid., p. 226.

20. Ibid.

21. Dynamic Dynamism Letter, Collection of the Museum of Western Art, Denver.

22. Dippie, pp. 172–3.

23. Ibid., p. 181.

24. Ibid., p. 121.

25. Charles M. Russell, *Trails Plowed Under* (Garden City, N.Y., 1928), p. xiv.

26. Ibid., p. 1.

27. Ibid., p. xx.

PART 5.

CHAPTER 23.

1. See Don Russell's *The Lives and Legends of Buffalo Bill* (Norman, 1960) for an account of the performance and reviews. Unless otherwise specified, all biographical details about the life of Buffalo Bill are taken from this source.

2. Don Russell, p. 199.

3. Russell Martin, *Cowboy, The Enduring Myth of the Wild West* (New York, 1983), p. 111.

4. "American Beef," *Leslie's Illustrated Weekly*, vol. XII, 1881, p. 619.

5. Louis E. Cooke quoted in Don Russell, p. 291.

CHAPTER 24.

1. Kevin Brownlow, *The War, the West and the Wilderness* (New York, 1973) contains an excellent account of this and other attempts at the early cinematic re-creating of Western history.

2. Brownlow, ibid., p. 229.

3. Ibid., p. 232.

4. Quoted in Don Graham, *Cowboys and Cadillacs, How Hollywood Looks at Texas* (Austin, Tex., 1983), p. 4.

5. Interview with "Bronco" Billy Anderson by William Everson, Killiam Films, 1958.

6. Ibid.

7. Ibid.

8. Kevin Brownlow, pp. 301–302.

9. Ibid., p. 302.

10. Ibid., p. 304.

11. Ibid., p. 296.

12. Ibid., p. 312.

13. Ibid., p. 254 ff.

14. Ibid., p. 257.

15. See Chapter 5, "William Surrey Hart and Realism" in George N. Fenin and William K. Everson, *The Western, From Silents to the Seventies* (New York, 1977).

16. Brownlow, p. 264.

17. MS letter files, William S. Hart Ranch, Newhall, California.

18. Film Clip, William S. Hart, "Farewell Speech" in introduction to sound version of *Tumbleweeds*, 1939.

CHAPTER 25.

1. Frank Luther Mott, *The History of American Magazines* (Cambridge, Mass., 1930), vol. IV, p. 7.
2. Ibid., p. 150.
3. Interview with John Clymer.
4. Author's interview with Hal Shelton, July 1984.
5. Wesley Burnside, *Maynard Dixon, Artist of the West* (Provo, 1974), p. 23.
6. Ibid., p. 29.

CHAPTER 26.

1. Don Dedera, *Visions West, The Story of the Cowboy Artists of America Museum* (Kerrville, 1983), p. 7.
2. Samuels, Peggy and Harold, *The Illustrated Biographical Encyclopedia of Artists of the American West* (Garden City, N.Y., 1976), p. 205.
3. Ibid., p. 148.
4. Dedera, p. 8.
5. Ibid., p. 9.
6. Interview with John Clymer.
7. Ibid.
8. Larry Pointer and Donald Goddard, *Harry Jackson* (New York, 1981), p. 130.
9. Ibid., p. 142.

CHAPTER 27.

1. Interview with A. C. Greene, Historian of Dallas.
2. Joseph McBride and Michael Wilmington, *John Ford* (London, 1974), p. 45n.
3. Quoted in Peter Bogdanovich, *John Ford* (Berkeley and Los Angeles, 1978), p. 22.
4. Ibid.
5. Ibid., pp. 22–3.
6. Ibid., p. 87.
7. Interview with William Howze, media director, Amon Carter Museum.
8. Quoted in McBride and Wilmington, p. 90.
9. Ibid.
10. Ibid., p. 153.
11. John Baxter, *The Cinema of John Ford* (London and New York, 1971), p. 78.
12. Quoted in Garner Simmons, *A Portrait in Montage, Peckinpah* (Austin, Texas, 1982), p. 119.
13. Ibid., p. 110.
14. Ibid., p. 115.
15. Quoted in Paul Seydor, *Peckinpah, The Western Films* (Urbana, Il., 1980), p. 156.

PART 6.

CHAPTER 28.

1. Quoted in Patricia Janis Broder, *Taos, A Painter's Dream* (Boston, 1980), p. 69.
2. Ibid., p. 70.
3. Ibid., p. 9.
4. Ibid., p. 9.
5. Quoted in Lea Rosson DeLong, *Nature's Forms/Nature's Forces, The Art of Alexandre Hogue* (Tulsa, 1984), p. 11.
6. Broder, op. cit., p. 225.
7. Ibid., p. 215.
8. Quoted in Broder, p. 222.
9. Quoted in William C. Foxley, *Frontier Spirit* (Denver, 1983), p. 145.

CHAPTER 29.

1. Quoted in Sharyn Rohlfson Udall, *Modernist Painting in New Mexico 1913–1935* (Albuquerque, 1984), p. 12.

2. Lois Palken Rudnick, *Mabel Dodge Luhan, New Woman, New Worlds* (Albuquerque, 1984), p. 143.

3. *D. H. Lawrence and New Mexico*, Keith Sagar, ed. (Salt Lake City, 1982), p. 5.

4. Ibid., p. 3.

5. Ibid., p. 5.

6. Rudnick, p. 210.

7. Ibid., p. 168.

8. Quoted in Laurie Lysle, *Portrait of An Artist, A Biography of Georgia O'Keeffe* (New York, 1980), p. 222.

CHAPTER 30.

1. Henry Nash Smith, *Virgin Land, The American West as Symbol and Myth*, rev. ed. (Boston, 1970), pp. 123–44, 174–83.

2. For biographical information on Thomas Hart Benton, see Matthew Baigell, *Thomas Hart Benton* (New York, 1973) and Thomas Hart Benton, *An Artist in America* (New York, 1937).

3. Quoted in Peter Hassrick, *The Way West* (New York, 1977), p. 232.

4. Benton, *An Artist in America*, pp. 240–41.

5. Ibid., p. 242.

6. Nancy Edelman, *The Thomas Hart Benton Murals in the Missouri State Capitol: A Social History of the State of Missouri* (Jefferson City, Missouri, 1975), facsimile letter, p. 20.

7. For biographical details on Grant Wood see Wanda M. Corn, *Grant Wood: the Regionalist Vision* (New Haven and London, 1983).

8. This view governs Corn's *Grant Wood* as well.

9. Quoted in Rick Stewart, *Lone Star Regionalism: The Dallas Nine and Their Circle* (Austin, 1985), p. 146.

10. Robert L. Snyder, *Pare Lorenz and the Documentary Film* (Norman, Okla., 1968), see espec. Ch. II.

11. Donald Worster, *Dust Bowl* (New York, 1979), pp. 13, 16, 18, 20–21.

12. Ibid., p. 49.

13. Quoted in Ibid.

14. Interview with William Howze, Media Director, Amon Carter Museum.

15. William Stott, *Documentary Expression and Thirties America* (New York, 1973).

16. Roy Emerson Stryker and Nancy Wood, *In This Proud Land: America, 1935–1943 as Seen in the F.S.A. Photographs* (Boston, 1973), p. 10.

17. Ibid., p. 16.

18. See Arthur Rothstein, *The Depression Years as Photographed by Arthur Rothstein* (New York, 1978), and Stryker and Wood, espec. Stryker's "Shooting Scripts," pp. 187–8. Also see Milton Meltzer, *Dorothea Lange, a Photographer's Life* (New York, 1978).

19. See E. Jack Hurley, *Russell Lee, Photographer* (Dobbs Ferry, N.Y., 1978).

20. For Hogue's work see DeLong, espec. p. 24 for attempt to buy and destroy *Drouth Survivors*. Also see Worster, pp. 32–3.

21. DeLong, p. 7.

22. In addition to Stewart, see Lloyd Goodrich and Jerry Bywaters, *A Retrospective Exhibition, Jerry Bywaters, Feb. 22–March 28, 1976, University Galleries, Southern Methodist University* (Dallas, 1976).

23. Stewart, pp. 20–24.

CHAPTER 31.

1. John Sloan and John LaFarge, *Introduction to American Indian Art* (New York, 1931), p. 7.

2. Ibid.

3. Rudnick, p. 150.

4. Winona Marie Garmhausen, *The Institute of American Indian Arts 1962 to 1978: With Historical Background 1890 to 1962* (PhD. Diss., University of New Mexico, 1982), p. 98.

5. Garmhausen's account treats this and other sociological forces that shaped the experience of the IAIA.

6. ". . . damned if I'll let this get us down . . . dismissed religion . . . ," Aberbach Fine Art, *T. C. Cannon* (New York, 1979), p. 136.

7. Ibid., p. 9.

8. Adelyn D. Breeskin and Rudy H. Turk, *Scholder/Indians,* (n.p., 1972).

CHAPTER 32.

1. Interview with Anastasio Torres, San Antonio, March 1985.

2. Ibid.

3. Dave Hickey, "What Really Happened, I Think" in *Luis Jimenez* exhibition catalogue, Laguna Gloria Art Museum (Austin, 1983), p. 4.

4. For an overview of Jimenez' statuary, see the Laguna Gloria exhibition catalogue of 1983.

CHAPTER 33.

1. Biographical details of Georgia O'Keeffe's life are taken from Laurie Lyle, *Portrait of an Artist, a Biography of Georgia O'Keeffe* (New York, 1980), and from Miss O'Keeffe's own writing in *Georgia O'Keeffe* (New York, 1976).

2. Quoted in Lyle, p. 105.

3. Quoted in ibid., p. 283.

INDEX

Anonymous works, motion pictures, and murals are listed as main headings. All other works are subheadings of the artist.

Italicized page numbers refer to illustrations.